CLASSICAL TALES OF MYTHOLOGY

CLASSICAL TALES OF MYTHOLOGY

Heroes, Gods
and Monsters of
Ancient Rome
and Greece

THOMAS BULFINCH AND
NATHANIEL HAWTHORNE

ARCTURUS

ARCTURUS

This edition published in 2020 by Arcturus Publishing Limited
26/27 Bickels Yard, 151–153 Bermondsey Street,
London SE1 3HA

ISBN: 978-1-83857-423-9
AD007713US

Printed in China

CONTENTS

INTRODUCTION

Thomas Bulfinch and Nathaniel Hawthorne were both born in Massachusetts at around the turn of the nineteenth century, in 1796 and 1804 respectively. Both writers rewrote classical mythology in order to bring it to a wider audience, and the selection contained here is an expansive collection of their popular retellings. Hawthorne specifically rewrote classical Greek myths whereas Bulfinch's writings took their inspiration from the Greek, Norse, and Roman traditions, and also from Arthurian legends. Both hoped to bring mythology to a wider audience, and more particularly to younger readers.

Thomas Bulfinch was one of eleven children born to the famed architect Charles Bulfinch and his wife Hannah. Thomas grew up in Newton, Massachusetts, receiving a classical education at Boston Latin School, Philips Exeter Academy, and later graduating from Harvard University. Following the completion of his studies, he moved with his family to Washington D.C., where his father was partly responsible for designing the US Capitol building, but Thomas later returned to Boston. Books and writing were always his main interests and an undemanding position at the Merchants' Bank of Boston, along with living with his parents for much of his life, allowed him to support himself while pursuing his love of writing. Bulfinch's best-known work is the posthumously assembled *Bulfinch's Mythology* (1867), which brought together his three earlier works from the Greek, Arthurian, and French traditions: *The Age of Fable*, or *Stories of Gods and Heroes* (1855); *The Age of Chivalry*, or *Legends of King Arthur* (1858); and *Legends of Charlemagne*, or *Romance of the Middle Ages* (1863).

The Bulfinch tales presented here all come from his earliest work *The Age of Fable* and in the preface to the original edition he sets out the purpose of his work. Bullfinch felt that the writings and speeches of many authors, poets, and politicians excluded ordinary people by their frequent references to mythology. He decided to present sanitized, prose versions of the tales of Ovid and Virgil, that would be approachable to all. "Our work is not for the learned,

nor for the theologian, nor for the philosopher, but for the reader of English literature, of either sex, who wishes to comprehend the allusions so frequently made by public speakers, lecturers, essayists, and poets, and those which occur in polite conversation."

These simplified versions of the tales, with any sex or unnecessary violence removed, were intended to be accessible sources of entertainment, to sit in the family library and be constantly read and referenced, not as a source of study, but one of enjoyment. Though his main aim was to provide diversion through these traditional tales, there was some semblance of education in his means of presentation. Each of the short retellings is followed by an excerpt or two from the great poets that references the tale or its characters. This was a means of showing the importance of the tales in understanding their many uses as references, as Bulfinch outlines above. The original preface states that these "poetical citations" will "fix in the memory the leading fact of each story, they will help to the attainments of a correct pronunciation of the proper names, and they will enrich the memory with many gems of poetry, some of them such as are most frequently quoted or alluded to in reading and conversation." Bulfinch makes clear these two aims at the close of his preface where he tells us that for young readers he hopes they find amusement and for older readers visiting museums and moving in "cultivated" society that they provide a key to many common allusions.

Nathaniel Hawthorne was born in 1804 to Nathaniel Hathorne Sr and Elizabeth Clark Hathorne in Salem, Massachusetts. Hathorne Sr, a sea captain, died a few years later, leaving his young widow with two daughters and a son and little means to raise them. As a result, she moved the family to the home of her brothers, the Mannings. It is believed Hawthorne added the "w" to his name when he began writing to distance himself from his ancestors. His earliest known American relative, William Hathorne, was a judge with a zealotic belief in the Puritan ideal, of a simple, severe mode of life, who became notorious for his harsh sentencing. Hawthorne even wondered if his family's declining fortunes, as others around them succeeded, were retribution for William's son John's role as a judge during the Salem witch trials. With a childhood spent in Massachusetts and Maine, Nathaniel, supported by his uncles, completed his education at Bowdoin College, before returning to his family in Salem, whom he had missed terribly during his studies.

A painfully shy man, Hawthorne spent the next 12 years living with his family in a state of semi-seclusion. He began writing, finding some success in the publication of short stories, though he worked at the Boston Custom House in order to support himself. He eventually met and married the equally reclusive Sophia Peabody, saving for their marriage by living with other writers of the day such as Ralph Waldo Emerson and Henry David Thoreau at the transcendentalist utopia Brook Farm community—though he would realize transcendentalism was not for him. As his family grew, after some time in Concord, the Hawthornes returned to Salem and this would be where Hawthorne would write his most famous work *The Scarlet Letter* (1850). This book was one of the first mass-produced publications in the United States,

and its themes of dark romanticism were symbolic of much of Hawthorne's writing. This concern with cautionary tales of guilt and sin can be again seen in Hawthorne's approach to mythology in his two works aimed at children, *A Wonder-Book for Girls and Boys* (1851) and *Tanglewood Tales* (1853).

Although Hawthorne also wanted to bring these traditional myths to the attention of young readers he did not intend them just for entertainment, writing: "I shall purge out all the old heathen wickedness, and put in a moral wherever practicable." This can be seen in many of the stories presented here which have been selected from both of his mythology collections. In "The Miraculous Pitcher", for example, we see Philemon and Baucis rewarded for being good and pure when all those around them are punished by the gods with death. Hawthorne, like Bulfinch, wished to bring these tales to a modern audience but he approached them with his romantic sensibility, stating that they would be "taken out of the cold moonshine of classical mythology, and modernized, or perhaps gothicized, so that they may be felt by children of these days." While he may have wished to impart moral teachings with his retellings, subsequent editions used beautiful colour illustrations to visually arrest the imagination as much as the text. One such is the 1921 edition by the Penn Publishing Company in Philadelphia, which used the illustrations of Virginia Frances Sterrett to create spellbinding visions to appeal to both children and adults. A year later, Arthur Rackham illustrated an edition of *A Wonder Book* that also captured hearts and imaginations. Both sets of illustrations retain that appeal almost a century on and some of these have also been reproduced here.

The stories contained within have been abridged, however, they adhere to the original text in every other sense. So Bulfinch's examples of classical poetry are retained as is the gothic morality of Hawthorne's retellings. Each story is accompanied either by illustrations made specifically for the tale in question, such as the Sterrett and Rackham examples mentioned above, or by famous artists' renditions of the myths.

TALES
BY
THOMAS
BULFINCH

ECHO AND NARCISSUS

Echo was a beautiful nymph, fond of the woods and hills, where she devoted herself to woodland sports. She was a favorite of Diana, and attended her in the chase. But Echo had one failing; she was fond of talking, and whether in chat or argument, would have the last word.

One day Juno was seeking her husband, who, she had reason to fear, was amusing himself among the nymphs. Echo by her talk contrived to detain the goddess till the nymphs made their escape. When Juno discovered it, she passed sentence upon Echo in these words: "You shall forfeit the use of that tongue with which you have cheated me, except for that one purpose you are so fond of—*reply*. You shall still have the last word, but no power to speak first."

This nymph saw Narcissus, a beautiful youth, as he pursued the chase upon the mountains. She loved him, and followed his footsteps. Oh, how she longed to address him in the softest accents, and win him to converse, but it was not in her power. She waited with impatience for him to speak first, and had her answer ready.

One day the youth, being separated from his companions, shouted aloud, "Who's here?"

Echo replied, "Here."

Narcissus looked around, but seeing no one, called out, "Come."

Echo answered, "Come."

As no one came, Narcissus called again, "Why do you shun me?"

Echo asked the same question.

"Let us join one another," said the youth.

The maid answered with all her heart in the same words, and hastened to the spot, ready to throw her arms about his neck. He started back, exclaiming, "Hands off! I would rather die than you should have me!"

"Have me," said she; but it was all in vain. He left her, and she went to hide her blushes in the recesses of the woods.

Right: Arthur Rackham's illustration shows a lovelorn Echo banished to caves and mountain cliffs where she still answers all who call out to her.

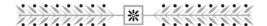

From that time forth she lived in caves and among mountain cliffs. Her form faded with grief, till at last all her flesh shrank away. Her bones were changed into rocks, and there was nothing left of her but her voice. With that she is still ready to reply to anyone who calls her and keeps up her old habit of having the last word.

Narcissus's cruelty in this case was not the only instance. He shunned all the rest of the nymphs, as he had done poor Echo. One day a maiden, who had in vain endeavored to attract him, uttered a prayer that he might some time or other feel what it was to love and meet no return of affection. The avenging goddess heard and granted the prayer.

There was a clear fountain, with water like silver, to which the shepherds never drove their flocks, nor the mountain goats resorted, nor any of the beasts of the forest; neither was it defaced with fallen leaves or branches; but the grass grew fresh around it, and the rocks sheltered it from the sun. Hither came one day the youth fatigued with hunting, heated and thirsty. He stooped down to drink, and saw his own image in the water; he thought it was some beautiful water-spirit living in the fountain.

He stood gazing with admiration at those bright eyes, those locks curled like the locks of Bacchus or Apollo, the rounded cheeks, the ivory neck, the parted lips, and the glow of health and exercise over all. He fell in love with himself. He brought his lips near to take a kiss; he plunged his arms in to embrace the beloved object. It fled at the touch, but returned again after a moment and renewed the fascination. He could not tear himself away; he lost all thought of food or rest, while he hovered over the brink of the fountain gazing upon his own image.

He talked with the supposed spirit: "Why, beautiful being, do you shun me? Surely, my face is not one to repel you. The nymphs love me, and you yourself look not indifferent upon me. When I stretch forth my arms you do the same; and you smile upon me and answer my beckonings with the like." His tears fell into the water and disturbed the image. As he saw it depart, he exclaimed, "Stay, I entreat you! Let me at least gaze upon you, if I may not touch you." With this, and much more of the same kind, he cherished the flame that consumed him, so that by degrees he lost his color, his vigor, and the beauty which formerly had so charmed the nymph Echo. She kept near him, however, and when he exclaimed, "Alas! Alas!" she answered him with the same words.

He pined away and died; and when his shade passed the Stygian river, it leaned over the boat to catch a look of itself in the waters. The nymphs mourned for him, especially the water-nymphs; and when they smote their breasts, Echo smote hers also. They prepared a funeral pile, and would have burned the body, but it was nowhere to be found; but in its place a flower, purple within, and surrounded with white leaves, which bears the name and preserves the memory of Narcissus.

Milton alludes to the story of Echo and Narcissus in the Lady's song in "Comus". She is seeking her brothers in the forest, and sings to attract their attention:

Sweet Echo, sweetest nymph, that liv'st unseen
Within thy aëry shell
By slow Meander's margent green,
And in the violet-embroidered vale,
Where the love-lorn nightingale
Nightly to thee her sad song mourneth well;
Canst thou not tell me of a gentle pair
That likest thy Narcissus are?
Oh, if thou have
Hid them in some flowery cave,
Tell me but where,
Sweet queen of parly, daughter of the sphere,
So may'st thou be translated to the skies,
And give resounding grace to all heaven's harmonies.

Milton has imitated the story of Narcissus in the account which he makes Eve give of the first sight of herself reflected in the fountain:

That day I oft remember when from sleep
I first awaked, and found myself reposed
Under a shade on flowers, much wondering where
And what I was, whence thither brought, and how
Not distant far from thence a murmuring sound
Of waters issued from a cave, and spread
Into a liquid plain, then stood unmoved
Pure as the expanse of heaven; I thither went
With unexperienced thought, and laid me down
On the green bank, to look into the clear
Smooth lake that to me seemed another sky.
As I bent down to look, just opposite
A shape within the watery gleam appeared,
Bending to look on me. I started back;
It started back; but pleased I soon returned,
Pleased it returned as soon with answering looks
Of sympathy and love. There had I fixed
Mine eyes till now, and pined with vain desire,
Had not a voice thus warned me: 'What thou seest,
What there thou seest, fair creature, is thyself.'

Paradise Lost, Book IV

No one of the fables of antiquity has been oftener alluded to by the poets than that of Narcissus. Here are two epigrams which treat it in different ways. The first is by Goldsmith:

On a Beautiful Youth, struck blind by Lightning.

Sure 'twas by Providence designed,
Rather in pity than in hate,
That he should be like Cupid blind,
To save him from Narcissus' fate.

The other is by Cowper:

On an Ugly Fellow.

Beware, my friend, of crystal brook
Or fountain, lest that hideous hook,
Thy nose, thou chance to see;
Narcissus' fate would then be thine,
And self-detested thou would'st pine,
As self-enamoured he.

Left: The youth Narcissus attempts to beguile
his own beloved image in the pond.

HERO AND LEANDER

Leander was a youth of Abydos, a town of the Asian side of the strait which separates Asia and Europe. On the opposite shore in the town of Sestos lived the maiden Hero, a priestess of Venus. Leander loved her, and used to swim the strait nightly to enjoy the company of his mistress.

But one night a tempest arose and the sea was rough; his strength failed, and he was drowned. The waves bore his body to the European shore, where Hero became aware of his death, and in her despair cast herself down from a tower into the sea and perished.

The story of Leander's swimming the Hellespont was looked upon as fabulous, and the feat considered impossible, till Lord Byron proved its possibility by performing it himself. In the "Bride of Abydos" he says, "These limbs that buoyant wave hath borne."

The distance in the narrowest part is almost a mile, and there is a constant current setting out from the Sea of Marmora into the Archipelago. Since Byron's time the feat has

Right: Hero and Leander by Domenico Feti (1588-1623). The drowned Oleander is borne away by sea nymphs as Hero plunges to her death behind them.

been achieved by others; but it yet remains a test of strength and skill in the art of swimming sufficient to give a wide and lasting celebrity to any one of our readers who may dare to make the attempt and succeed in accomplishing it.

In the beginning of the second canto of the same poem, Byron thus alludes to this story:

The winds are high on Helle's wave,
As on that night of stormiest water,
When Love, who sent, forgot to save
The young, the beautiful, the brave,
The lonely hope of Sestos' daughter.
Oh, when alone along the sky
The turret-torch was blazing high,
Though rising gale and breaking foam,
And shrieking sea-birds warned him home
And clouds aloft and tides below,

With signs and sounds forbade to go,
He could not see, he would not hear
Or sound or sight foreboding fear.
His eye but saw that light of love,
The only star it hailed above;
His ear but rang with Hero's song,
'Ye waves, divide not lovers long.'
That tale is old, but love anew
May nerve young hearts to prove as true.

JUNO AND
HER RIVALS

Juno one day perceived it suddenly grow dark, and immediately suspected that her husband had raised a cloud to hide some of his doings that would not bear the light. She brushed away the cloud, and saw her husband, on the banks of a glassy river, with a beautiful heifer standing near him.

J uno suspected the heifer's form concealed some fair nymph of mortal mould—as was, indeed, the case—for it was Io, the daughter of the river god Inachus, whom Jupiter had been flirting with, and, when he became aware of the approach of his wife, had changed into that form.

Juno joined her husband, and noticing the heifer praised its beauty, and asked whose it was, and of what herd. Jupiter, to stop questions, replied that it was a fresh creation from the earth. Juno asked to have it as a gift. What could Jupiter do? He was loath to give his mistress to his wife; yet how refuse so trifling a present as a simple heifer? He could not, without exciting suspicion; so he consented. The goddess was not yet relieved of her suspicions; so she delivered the heifer to Argus, to be strictly watched.

Now Argus had a hundred eyes in his head, and never went to sleep with more than two at a time, so that he kept watch of Io constantly. He suffered her to feed through the day, and at night tied her up with a vile rope round her neck. She would have stretched out her arms to implore freedom of Argus, but she had no arms to stretch out, and her voice was a bellow that frightened even herself. She saw her father and her sisters, went near them, and suffered them to pat her back, and heard them admire her beauty. Her father reached her a tuft of grass, and she licked the outstretched hand. She longed to make herself known to him, and would have uttered her wish; but, alas! words were wanting.

At length she bethought herself of writing, and inscribed her name—it was a short one—with her hoof on the sand. Inachus recognized it, and discovering that his daughter, whom he had

Right: Juno depicted in "Earth under the Protection of Jupiter and Juno" (c. 1520-30), a tapestry of gold, silver, silk and wool. From one of three panels in a series called "The Spheres". These were woven for King John III of Portugal (1502–1557) and his wife, Catherine of Austria (1507–1578).

long sought in vain, was hidden under this disguise, mourned over her, and, embracing her white neck, exclaimed, "Alas ! my daughter, it would have been a less grief to have lost you altogether!"

While he thus lamented, Argus, observing, came and drove her away, and took his seat on a high bank, from whence he could see all round in every direction.

Jupiter was troubled at beholding the sufferings of his mistress, and calling Mercury told him to go and despatch Argus. Mercury made haste, put his winged slippers on his feet, and cap on his head, took his sleep-producing wand, and leaped down from the heavenly towers to the earth. There he laid aside his wings, and kept only his wand, with which he presented himself as a shepherd driving his flock. As he strolled on he blew upon his pipes. These were what are called the Syrinx or Pandean pipes. Argus listened with delight, for he had never seen the instrument before. "Young man," said he, "come and take a seat by me on this stone. There is no better place for your flock to graze in than hereabouts, and here is a pleasant shade such as shepherds love."

Mercury sat down, talked, and told stories till it grew late, and played upon his pipes his most soothing strains, hoping to lull the watchful eyes to sleep, but all in vain; for Argus still contrived to keep some of his eyes open though he shut the rest.

Among other stories, Mercury told him how the instrument on which he played was invented. "There was a certain nymph, whose name was Syrinx, who was much beloved by the satyrs and spirits of the wood; but she would have none of them, but was a faithful worshipper of Diana, and followed the chase. You would have thought it was Diana herself, had you seen her in her hunting dress, only that her bow was of horn and Diana's of silver. One day, as she was returning from the chase, Pan met her, told her just this, and added more of the same sort. She ran away, without stopping to hear his compliments, and he pursued till she came to the bank of the river, where he overtook her, and she had only time to call for help on her friends the water nymphs. They heard and consented. Pan threw his arms around what he supposed to be the form of the nymph, and found he embraced only a tuft of reeds! As he breathed a sigh, the air sounded through the reeds, and produced a plaintive melody. The god, charmed with the novelty, and with the sweetness of the music, said, 'Thus, then, at least, you shall be mine.' And he took some of the reeds, and placing them together, of unequal lengths, side by side, made an instrument which he called Syrinx, in honor of the nymph." Before Mercury had finished his story he saw Argus's eyes all asleep. As his head nodded forward on his breast, Mercury with one stroke cut his neck through, and tumbled his head down the rocks. O, hapless Argus! the light of your hundred eyes is quenched at once! Juno took them and put them as ornaments on the tail of her peacock, where they remain to this day.

But the vengeance of Juno was not yet satiated. She sent a gadfly to torment Io, who fled over the whole world from its pursuit. She swam through the Ionian Sea, which derived its name from her, then roamed over the plains of Illyria, ascended Mount Hæmus, and crossed the Thracian strait, thence named the Bosphorus, (cow-ford,) rambled on through Scythia, and the country of the Cimmerians, and arrived at last on the banks of the Nile.

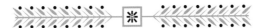

At length Jupiter interceded for her, and upon his promising not to pay her any more attentions Juno consented to restore her to her form. It was curious to see her gradually recover her former self. The coarse hairs fell from her body, her horns shrank up, her eyes grew narrower, her mouth shorter; hands and fingers came instead of hoofs to her fore feet; in fine there was nothing left of the heifer, except her beauty. At first she was afraid to speak for fear she should low, but gradually she recovered her confidence and was restored to her father and sisters.

* * * * *

Callisto was another maiden who excited the jealousy of Juno, and the goddess changed her into a bear.

"I will take away," said she, "that beauty with which you have captivated my husband." Down fell Callisto on her hands and knees; she tried to stretch out her arms in supplication— they were already beginning to be covered with black hair. Her hands grew rounded, became armed with crooked claws, and served for feet; her mouth, which Jove used to praise for its beauty, became a horrid pair of jaws; her voice, which if unchanged would have moved the heart to pity, became a growl, more fit to inspire terror. Yet her former disposition remained, and with continual groaning, she bemoaned her fate, and stood upright as well as she could, lifting up her paws to beg for mercy; and felt that Jove was unkind, though she could not tell him so. Ah, how often, afraid to stay in the woods all night alone, she wandered about the neighborhood of her former haunts; how often, frightened by the dogs, did she, so lately a huntress, fly in terror from the hunters! Often she fled from the wild beasts, forgetting that she was now a wild beast herself; and, bear as she was, was afraid of the bears.

One day a youth espied her as he was hunting. She saw him and recognized him as her own son, now grown a young man. She stopped and felt inclined to embrace him. As she was about to approach, he, alarmed, raised his hunting spear, and was on the point of transfixing her, when Jupiter, beholding, arrested the crime, and snatching away both of them, placed them in the heavens as the Great and Little Bear.

Juno was in a rage to see her rival so set in honor, and hastened to ancient Tethys and Oceanus, the powers of ocean, and in answer to their inquiries, thus told the cause of her coming. "Do you ask why I, the queen of the gods, have left the heavenly plains and sought your depths. Learn that I am supplanted in heaven—my place is given to another. You will hardly believe me; but look when night darkens the world, and you shall see the two of whom I have so much reason to complain exalted to the heavens, in that part where the circle is the smallest, in the neighborhood of the pole. Why should anyone hereafter tremble at the thought of offending Juno, when such rewards are the consequence of my displeasure! See what I have been able to effect! I forbade her to wear the human form—she is placed among the stars! So do my punishments result—such is the extent of my power! Better that she should have resumed her former shape, as I permitted Io to do. Perhaps he means to marry her, and put me away! But you, my foster-parents, if you feel for me, and see with displeasure this unworthy treatment of

me, show it, I beseech you, by forbidding this guilty couple from coming into your waters." The powers of the ocean assented, and consequently the two constellations of the Great and Little Bear move round and round in heaven, but never sink, as the other stars do, beneath the ocean.

Milton alludes to the fact that the constellation of the Bear never sets, when he says:

Let my lamp at midnight hour
Be seen in some high lonely tower,
Where I may oft outwatch the Bear &c.

And Prometheus, in J. R. Lowell's poem, says:

One after one the stars have risen and set,
Sparkling upon the hoar frost of my chain;
The Bear that prowled all night about the fold
Of the North-star, hath shrunk into his den,
Scared by the blithesome footsteps of the Dawn.

The last star in the tail of the Little Bear is the Pole-star, called also the Cynosure. Milton says:

Straight mine eye hath caught new pleasures
While the landscape round it measures.
* * * *
Towers and battlements it sees
Bosomed high in tufted trees,
Where perhaps some beauty lies
The Cynosure of neighbouring eyes.

The reference here is both to the Pole-star as the guide of mariners, and to the magnetic attraction of the North. He calls it also the "Star of Arcady" because Callisto's boy was named Areas, and they lived in Arcadia. In Comus, the brother, benighted in the woods, says:

Some gentle taper!
Though a rush candle, from the wicker hole
Of some clay habitation, visit us
With thy long levelled rule of streaming light,
And thou shalt be our star of Arcady,
Or Tyrian Cynosure.

Right: "Juno Hearing Peacock's Complaint" from a c.1910 postcard displaying a painting attributed to Mme. Jehanne, Paris.

DIANA AND ACTÆON

Thus, in two instances, we have seen Juno's severity to her rivals; now let us learn how a virgin goddess punished an invader of her privacy.

It was midday, and the sun stood equally distant from either goal, when young Actæon, son of King Cadmus, thus addressed the youths who with him were hunting the stag in the mountains: "Friends, our nets and our weapons are wet with the blood of our victims; we have had sport enough for one day, and tomorrow we can renew our labors. Now, while Phœbus parches the earth, let us put by our implements and indulge ourselves with rest."

There was a valley thick enclosed with cypresses and pines, sacred to the huntress queen, Diana. In the extremity of the valley was a cave, not adorned with art, but nature had counterfeited art in its construction, for she had turned the arch of its roof with stones as delicately fitted as if by the hand of man. A fountain burst out from one side, whose open basin was bounded by a grassy rim. Here the goddess of the woods used to come when weary with hunting and lave her virgin limbs in the sparkling water.

One day, having repaired thither with her nymphs, she handed her javelin, her quiver, and her bow to one, her robe to another, while a third unbound the sandals from her feet. Then Crocale, the most skillful of them, arranged her hair, and Nephele, Hyale and the rest drew water in capacious urns. While the goddess was thus employed in the labors of the toilet, behold Actæon, having quitted his companions, and rambling without any especial object, came to the place, led thither by his destiny.

As he presented himself at the entrance of the cave, the nymphs, seeing a man, screamed and rushed towards the goddess to hide her with their bodies. But she was taller than the rest and overtopped them all by a head. Such a color as tinges the clouds at sunset or at dawn, came over the countenance of Diana thus taken by surprise. Surrounded as she was by her nymphs, she yet turned half away, and sought with a sudden impulse for her arrows. As they were not at hand, she dashed the water into the face of the intruder, adding these words

"Now go and tell, if you can, that you have seen Diana unapparelled." Immediately a pair of branching stag's horns grew out of his head, his neck gained in length, his ears grew sharp-

pointed, his hands became feet, his arms long legs, his body was covered with a hairy spotted hide.

Fear took the place of his former boldness, and the hero fled. He could not but admire his own speed; but when he saw his horns in the water, "Ah, wretched me!" he would have said, but no sound followed the effort. He groaned, and tears flowed down the face which had taken the place of his own. Yet his consciousness remained.

What shall he do?—go home to seek the palace, or lie hid in the woods? The latter he was afraid, the former he was ashamed to do. While he hesitated the dogs saw him. First Melampus, a Spartan dog, gave the signal with his bark, then Pamphagus, Dorceus, Lelaps, Theron, Nape, Tigris, and all the rest, rushed after him swifter than the wind. Over rocks and cliffs, through mountain gorges that seemed impracticable, he fled and they followed. Where he had often chased the stag and cheered on his pack, his pack now chased him, cheered on by his huntsmen. He longed to cry out, "I am Actæon; recognize your master!" but the words came not at his will.

The air resounded with the bark of the dogs. Presently one fastened on his back, another seized his shoulder.

While they held their master, the rest of the pack came up and buried their teeth in his flesh. He groaned—not in a human voice, yet certainly not in a stag's—and falling on his knees, raised his eyes, and would have raised his arms in supplication, if he had had them. His friends and fellow-huntsmen cheered on the dogs, and looked everywhere for Actæon, calling on him to join the sport.

At the sound of his name, he turned his head, and heard them regret that he should be away. He earnestly wished he was. He would have been well pleased to see the exploits of his dogs, but to feel them was too much.

They were all around him, rending and tearing; and it was not till they had torn his life out, that the anger of Diana was satisfied.

In Shelley's poem "Adonais" is the following allusion to the story of Actæon:

'Midst others of less note came one frail form,
A phantom among men: companionless
As the last cloud of an expiring storm,
Whose thunder is its knell; he, as I guess,
Had gazed on Nature's naked loveliness,
Actæon-like, and now he fled astray
With feeble steps o'er the world's wilderness;
And his own Thoughts, along that rugged way,
Pursued like raging hounds their father and their prey.

STANZA 31.

The allusion is probably to Shelley himself.

Some thought the goddess in this instance more severe than was just, while others praised her conduct as strictly consistent with her virgin dignity. As usual, the recent event brought older ones to mind, and one of the by-standers told this story. "Some countrymen of Lycia once insulted the goddess Latona, but not with impunity. When I was young, my father, who had grown too old for active labors, sent me to Lycia to drive thence some choice oxen, and there I saw the very pond and marsh where the wonder happened. Near by stood an ancient altar, black with the smoke of sacrifice and almost buried among the reeds. I inquired whose altar it might be, whether of Faunus or the Naiads or some god of the neighboring mountain, and one of the country people replied, 'No mountain or river god possesses this altar, but she whom royal Juno in her jealousy drove from land to land, denying her any spot of earth whereon to rear her twins.' Bearing in her arms the infant deities, Latona reached this land, weary with her burden and parched with thirst. By chance she espied in the bottom of the valley this pond of clear water, where the country people were at work gathering willows and osiers. The goddess approached, and kneeling on the bank would have slaked her thirst in the cool stream, but the rustics forbade her. 'Why do you refuse me water?' said she, 'water is free to all. Nature allows no one to claim as property the sunshine, the air, or the water. I come to take my share of the common blessing. Yet I ask it of you as a favor. I have no intention of washing my limbs in it, weary though they be, but only to quench my thirst. My mouth is so dry that I can hardly speak. A draught of water would be nectar to me; it would revive me, and I would own myself indebted to you for life itself. Let these infants move your pity, who stretch out their little arms as if to plead for me' and the children, as it happened, were stretching out their arms.

"Who would not have been moved with these gentle words of the goddess? But these clowns persisted in their rudeness; they even added jeers and threats of violence if she did not leave the place. Nor was this all. They waded into the pond and stirred up the mud with their feet, so as to make the water unfit to drink. Latona was so angry that she ceased to mind her thirst. She no longer supplicated the clowns, but lifting her hands to heaven exclaimed, 'May they never quit that pool, but pass their lives there!' And it came to pass accordingly.

"They now live in the water, sometimes totally submerged, then raising their heads above the surface or swimming upon it. Sometimes they come out upon the bank, but soon leap back again into the water. They still use their base voices in railing, and though they have the water all to themselves, are not ashamed to croak in the midst of it.

"Their voices are harsh, their throats bloated, their mouths have become stretched by constant railing, their necks have shrunk up and disappeared, and their heads are joined to their bodies. Their backs are green, their disproportioned bellies white, and in short they are now frogs, and dwell in the slimy pool."

Left: Nymphs at a fountain as depicted by Arthur Rackham for *Hawthorne's Wonder Book* by Nathaniel Hawthorne.

This story explains the allusion in one of Milton's sonnets, "On the detraction which followed upon his writing certain treatises":

I did but prompt the age to quit their clogs
By the known laws of ancient liberty,
When straight a barbarous noise environs me
Of owls and cuckoos, asses, apes and dogs.
As when those hinds that were transformed to frogs
Railed at Latona's twin-born progeny,
Which after held the sun and moon in fee.

The persecution which Latona experienced from Juno is alluded to in the story. The tradition was that the future mother of Apollo and Diana, flying from the wrath of Juno, besought all the islands of the Ægean to afford her a place of rest, but all feared too much the potent queen of heaven to assist her rival. Delos alone consented to become the birthplace of the future deities.

Delos was then a floating island; but when Latona arrived there, Jupiter fastened it with adamantine chains to the bottom of the sea, that it might be a secure resting-place for his beloved. Byron alludes to Delos in his "Don Juan":

The isles of Greece! the isles of Greece!
Where burning Sappho loved and sung,
Where grew the arts of war and peace,
Where Delos rose and Phœbus sprung!

Left: Latona, mother of Apollo and Diana, curses peasants who denied her water thereby turning them into frogs. Painting by Italian artist Francesco Tevisani (1656–1746).

GLAUCUS
AND SCYLLA

Glaucus was a fisherman. One day he had drawn his nets to land, and had taken a great many fishes of various kinds. So he emptied his net, and proceeded to sort the fishes on the grass. The place where he stood was a beautiful island in the river, a solitary spot, uninhabited, and not used for pasturage of cattle, nor ever visited by any but himself.

On a sudden, the fishes, which had been laid on the grass, began to revive and move their fins as if they were in the water; and while he looked on astonished, they one and all moved off to the water, plunged in and swam away. He did not know what to make of this, whether some god had done it, or some secret power in the herbage. "What herb has such a power?" he exclaimed; and gathering some of it, he tasted it. Scarce had the juices of the plant reached his palate when he found himself agitated with a longing desire for the water.

He could no longer restrain himself, but bidding farewell to earth, he plunged into the stream. The gods of the water received him graciously, and admitted him to the honor of their society. They obtained the consent of Oceanus and Tethys, the sovereigns of the sea, that all that was mortal in him should be washed away. A hundred rivers poured their waters over him. Then he lost all sense of his former nature and all consciousness.

When he recovered, he found himself changed in form and mind. His hair was sea-green, and trailed behind him on the water; his shoulders grew broad, and what had been thighs and legs assumed the form of a fish's tail.

The sea-gods complimented him on the change of his appearance, and he fancied himself rather a good-looking personage.

One day Glaucus saw the beautiful maiden Scylla, the favorite of the water-nymphs, rambling on the shore, and when she had found a sheltered nook, laving her limbs in the clear water. He fell in love with her, and showing himself on the surface, spoke to her, saying such things as he thought most likely to win her to stay; for she turned to run immediately on the sight of him,

Above: Arthur Rackham's illustration of a slumbering Glaucus after he was transformed by the sovereigns of the sea into a merman.

and ran till she had gained a cliff overlooking the sea. Here she stopped and turned round to see whether it was a god or a sea animal, and observed with wonder his shape and color.

Glaucus partly emerging from the water, and supporting himself against a rock, said, "Maiden, I am no monster, nor a sea animal, but a god; and neither Proteus nor Triton ranks higher than I. Once I was a mortal, and followed the sea for a living; but now I belong wholly to it."

Then he told the story of his metamorphosis, and how he had been promoted to his present dignity, and added, "But what avails all this if it fails to move your heart?"

He was going on in this strain, but Scylla turned and hastened away.

Glaucus was in despair, but it occurred to him to consult the enchantress, Circe. Accordingly he repaired to her island—the same where afterwards Ulysses landed, as we shall see in one of our later stories. After mutual salutations, he said, "Goddess, I entreat your pity; you alone can relieve the pain I suffer. The power of herbs I know as well as any one, for it is to them I owe my change of form. I love Scylla. I am ashamed to tell you how I have sued and promised to her, and how scornfully she has treated me. I beseech you to use your incantations, or potent herbs, if they are more prevailing, not to cure me of my love—for that I do not wish—but to make her share it and yield me a like return."

To which Circe replied, for she was not insensible to the attractions of the sea-green deity, "You had better pursue a willing object; you are worthy to be sought, instead of having to seek in vain. Be not diffident, know your own worth. I protest to you that even I, goddess though I be, and learned in the virtues of plants and spells, should not know how to refuse you. If she scorns you, scorn her; meet one who is ready to meet you half way, and thus make a due return to both at once." To these words Glaucus replied, "Sooner shall trees grow at the bottom of the ocean, and seaweed on the top of the mountains, than I will cease to love Scylla, and her alone."

The goddess was indignant, but she could not punish him, neither did she wish to do so, for she liked him too well; so she turned all her wrath against her rival, poor Scylla. She took plants of poisonous powers and mixed them together, with incantations and charms. Then she passed through the crowd of gambolling beasts, the victims of her art, and proceeded to the coast of Sicily, where Scylla lived. There was a little bay on the shore to which Scylla used to resort, in the heat of the day, to breathe the air of the sea, and to bathe in its waters. Here the goddess poured her poisonous mixture, and muttered over it incantations of mighty power.

Scylla came as usual and plunged into the water up to her waist. What was her horror to perceive a brood of serpents and barking monsters surrounding her! At first she could not imagine they were a part of herself, and tried to run from them, and to drive them away; but as she ran she carried them with her, and when she tried to touch her limbs, she found her hands touch only the yawning jaws of monsters. Scylla remained rooted to the spot. Her temper grew as ugly as her form, and she took pleasure in devouring hapless mariners who came within her grasp.

Thus she destroyed six of the companions of Ulysses, and tried to wreck the ships of Æneas, till at last she was turned into a rock, and as such still continues to be a terror to mariners.

Keats, in his "Endymion", has given a new version of the ending of "Glaucus and Scylla"— Glaucus consents to Circe's blandishments, till he by chance is witness to her transactions with her beasts. Disgusted with her treachery and cruelty, he tries to escape from her, but is taken and brought back, when with reproaches she banishes him, sentencing him to pass a thousand years in decrepitude and pain. He returns to the sea, and there finds the body of Scylla, whom the goddess has not transformed but drowned. Glaucus learns that his destiny is that, if he passes his thousand years in collecting all the bodies of drowned lovers, a youth beloved of the gods will appear and help him. "Endymion" fulfills this prophecy, and aids in restoring Glaucus to youth, and Scylla and all the drowned lovers to life.

The following is Glaucus's account of his feelings after his "sea-change":

I plunged for life or death. To interknit
One's senses with so dense a breathing stuff
Might seem a work of pain; so not enough
Can I admire how crystal-smooth it felt,
And buoyant round my limbs. At first I dwelt
Whole days and days in sheer astonishment;
Forgetful utterly of self-intent,
Moving but with the mighty ebb and flow.
Then like a new-fledged bird that first doth show
His spreaded feathers to the morrow chill,
I tried in fear the pinions of my will.
'Twas freedom! and at once I visited
The ceaseless wonders of this ocean-bed &c.

KEATS

PYGMALION

Pygmalion saw so much wickedness in women that he came at last to abhor the sex, and resolved to live unmarried. He was a sculptor, and had made with wonderful skill a statue of ivory, so beautiful that no living woman came anywhere near it. It was indeed the perfect semblance of a maiden that seemed to be alive, and only prevented from moving by modesty.

His art was so perfect that it concealed itself and its product looked like the workmanship of nature. Pygmalion admired his own work, and at last fell in love with the counterfeit creation.

Oftentimes he laid his hand upon it as if to assure himself whether it were living or not, and could not even then believe that it was only ivory. He caressed it, and gave it presents such as young girls love—bright shells and polished stones, little birds and flowers of various hues, beads and amber. He put raiment on its limbs, and jewels on its fingers, and a necklace about its neck. To the ears he hung earrings, and strings of pearls upon the breast. Her dress became her, and she looked not less charming than when unattired. He laid her on a couch spread with cloths of Tyrian dye, and called her his wife, and put her head upon a pillow of the softest feathers, as if she could enjoy their softness.

The festival of Venus was at hand—a festival celebrated with great pomp at Cyprus. Victims were offered, the altars smoked, and the odor of incense filled the air.

When Pygmalion had performed his part in the solemnities, he stood before the altar and timidly said, "Ye gods, who can do all things, give me, I pray you, for my wife"—he dared not say "my ivory virgin" but said instead—"one like my ivory virgin." Venus, who was present at the festival, heard him and knew the thought he would have uttered; and as an omen of her favor, caused the flame on the altar to shoot up thrice in a fiery point into the air. When he returned home, he went to see his statue, and leaning over the couch, gave a kiss to the mouth. It seemed to be warm. He pressed its lips again, he laid his hand upon the limbs; the ivory felt soft to his touch, and yielded to his fingers like the wax of Hymettus.

Right: The artist Pygmalion and his sculpture that came to life through the blessing of the goddess Venus, as depicted by Jean-Léon Gérôme (1824–1904) in his painting "Pygmalion and Galatea".

While he stands astonished and glad, though doubting, and fears he may be mistaken, again and again with a lover's ardor, he touches the object of his hopes. It was indeed alive! The veins when pressed yielded to the finger and again resumed their roundness. Then at last the votary of Venus found words to thank the goddess, and pressed his lips upon lips as real as his own. The virgin felt the kisses and blushed, and opening her timid eyes to the light, fixed them at the same moment on her lover.

Venus blessed the nuptials she had formed, and from this union Paphos was born, from whom the city, sacred to Venus received its name.

Schiller, in his poem the "Ideals", applies this tale of Pygmalion to the love of nature in a youthful heart. The following translation is furnished by a friend:

As once with prayers in passion flowing,
Pygmalion embraced the stone,
Till from the frozen marble glowing,
The light of feeling o'er him shone,
So did I clasp with young devotion
Bright nature to a poet's heart;
Till breath and warmth and vital motion
Seemed through the statue form to dart.

And then, in all my ardor sharing.
The silent form expression found;
Returned my kiss of youthful daring,
And understood my heart's quick sound.
Then lived for me the bright creation,
The silver rill with song was rife;
The trees, the roses shared sensation,
An echo of my boundless life.

S. G. B.

DRYOPE

Dryope and Iole were sisters. The former was the wife of Andræmon, beloved by her husband, and happy in the birth of her first child. One day the sisters strolled to the bank of a stream that sloped gradually down to the water's edge, while the upland was overgrown with myrtles.

They were intending to gather flowers for forming garlands for the altars of the nymphs, and Dryope carried her child at her bosom, a precious burden, and nursed him as she walked. Near the water grew a lotus plant, full of purple flowers. Dryope gathered some and offered them to the baby, and Iole was about to do the same, when she perceived blood dropping from the places where her sister had broken them off the stem. The plant was no other than the nymph Lotis, who, running from a base pursuer, had been changed into this form. This they learned from the country people when it was too late.

Dryope, horror-struck when she perceived what she had done, would gladly have hastened from the spot, but found her feet rooted to the ground. She tried to pull them away, but moved nothing but her upper limbs. The woodiness crept upward, and by degrees invested her body. In anguish she attempted to tear her hair, but found her hands filled with leaves. The infant felt his mother's bosom begin to harden, and the milk cease to flow. Iole looked on at the sad fate of her sister, and could render no assistance. She embraced the growing trunk, as if she would hold back the advancing wood, and would gladly have been enveloped in the same bark. At this moment, Andraemon, the husband of Dryope, with her father, approached; and when they asked for Dryope, Iole pointed them to the new-formed lotus. They embraced the trunk of the yet warm tree, and showered their kisses on its leaves.

Now there was nothing left of Dryope but her face. Her tears still flowed and fell on her leaves, and while she could she spoke. "I am not guilty. I deserve not this fate. I have injured no one. If I speak falsely, may my foliage perish with drought and my trunk be cut down and burned. Take this infant and give it to a nurse. Let it often be brought and nursed under my branches, and play in my shade; and when he is old enough to talk, let him be taught to call me

mother, and to say with sadness, 'My mother lies hid under this bark.' But bid him be careful of river banks, and beware how he plucks flowers, remembering that every bush he sees may be a goddess in disguise. Farewell, dear husband, and sister, and father. If you retain any love for me, let not the axe wound me, nor the flocks bite and tear my branches.

"Since I cannot stoop to you, climb up hither and kiss me; and while my lips continue to feel, lift up my child that I may kiss him. I can speak no more, for already the bark advances up my neck, and will soon shoot over me. You need not close my eyes, the bark will close them without your aid." Then the lips ceased to move, and life was extinct; but the branches retained for some time longer the vital heat.

Keats, in "Endymion", alludes to Dryope, thus:

She took a lute from which there pulsing came
A lively prelude, fashioning the way
In which her voice should winder. 'Twas a lay
More subtle-cadenced, more forest-wild
Than Dryope's lone lulling of her child &c.

Above: Dryope, wife of Andraemon, is gathering flowers when she unwittingly picks one that is actually the nymph Lotis in disguise, who angrily turns poor Dryope into a tree.

VENUS
AND ADONIS

Venus, playing one day with her boy Cupid, wounded her bosom with one of his arrows. She pushed him away, but the wound was deeper than she thought. Before it healed she beheld Adonis, and was captivated with him.

She no longer took any interest in her favorite resorts—Paphos, and Cnidos, and Amathos, rich in metals. She absented herself even from heaven, for Adonis was dearer to her than heaven. Him she followed and bore him company. She who used to love to recline in the shade, with no care but to cultivate her charms, now rambles through the woods and over the hills, dressed like the huntress Diana; and calls her dogs, and chases hares and stags, or other game that it is safe to hunt, but keeps clear of the wolves and bears, reeking with the slaughter of the herd. She charged Adonis, too, to beware of such dangerous animals. "Be brave towards the timid," said she, "courage against the courageous is not safe. Beware how you expose yourself to danger, and put my happiness to risk. Attack not the beasts that Nature has armed with weapons. I do not value your glory so high as to consent to purchase it by such exposure. Your youth, and the beauty that charms Venus, will not touch the hearts of lions and bristly boars. Think of their terrible claws and prodigious strength! I hate the whole race of them. Do you ask me why?" Then she told him the story of Atalanta and Hippomenes, who were changed into lions for their ingratitude to her.

Having given him this warning, she mounted her chariot drawn by swans, and drove away through the air. But Adonis was too noble to heed such counsels. The dogs had roused a wild boar from his lair, and the youth threw his spear and wounded the animal with a sidelong stroke. The beast drew out the weapon with his jaws, and rushed after Adonis, who turned and ran; but the boar overtook him, and buried his tusks in his side, and stretched him dying upon the plain.

Venus, in her swan-drawn chariot, had not yet reached Cyprus, when she heard coming up through mid air the groans of her beloved, and turned her white-winged coursers back to earth. As she drew near and saw from on high his lifeless body bathed in blood, she alighted, and bending over it beat her breast and tore her hair. Reproaching the Fates, she said, "Yet theirs shall be but a partial triumph; memorials of my grief shall endure, and the spectacle of

Above: Venus and Adonis depicted by Italian painter Paolo Veronese (1528–1588). The goddess became enchanted with the mortal Adonis after she was accidentally wounded by one of her child Cupid's arrows.

your death, my Adonis, and of my lamentation shall be annually renewed. Your blood shall be changed into a flower; that consolation none can envy me." Thus speaking, she sprinkled nectar on the blood; and as they mingled, bubbles rose as in a pool, on which raindrops fall, and in an hour's time there sprang up a flower of bloody hue like that of the pomegranate. But it is short-lived. It is said the wind blows the blossoms open, and afterwards blows the petals away; so it is called Anemone, or Wind Flower, from the cause which assists equally in its production and its decay.

Milton alludes to the story of Venus and Adonis in his "Comus":

Beds of hyacinth and roses
Where young Adonis oft reposes,
Waxing well of his deep wound
In slumber soft, and on the ground
Sadly sits th' Assyrian queen &c.

PHAETON

Phaeton was the son of Apollo and the nymph Clymene. One day a schoolfellow laughed at the idea of his being the son of the god, and Phaeton went in rage and shame and reported it to his mother. "If," said he, "I am indeed of heavenly birth, give me, mother, some proof of it, and establish my claim to the honor."

Clymene stretched forth her hands towards the skies, and said, "I call to witness the Sun which looks down upon us, that I have told you the truth. If I speak falsely, let this be the last time I behold his light. But it needs not much labor to go and inquire for yourself; the land whence the Sun rises lies next to ours. Go and demand of him whether he will own you as a son." Phaeton heard this with delight. He traveled to India, which lies directly in the regions of sunrise, and, full of hope and pride, approached the goal whence his parent begins his course.

The palace of the Sun stood reared aloft on columns, glittering with gold and precious stones, while polished ivory formed the ceilings, and silver the doors. The workmanship surpassed the material; for upon the walls Vulcan had represented earth, sea and skies, with their inhabitants. In the sea were the nymphs, some sporting in the waves, some riding on the backs of fishes, while others sat upon the rocks and dried their sea-green hair.

Their faces were not all alike, nor yet unlike,—but such as sisters' ought to be. The earth had its towns and forests and rivers and rustic divinities. Over all was carved the likeness of the glorious heaven; and on the silver doors the twelve signs of the zodiac, six on each side.

Clymene's son advanced up the steep ascent, and entered the halls of his disputed father. He approached the paternal presence, but stopped at a distance, for the light was more than he could bear. Phœbus, arrayed in a purple vesture, sat on a throne which glittered as with diamonds. On his right hand and his left stood the Day, the Month, and the Year, and, at regular

Right: "The Fall of Phaeton" by Sebastiano Ricci (1659–1734) dramatically shows the hapless youth plunging through the heavens as he loses control of his father's chariot.

intervals, the Hours. Spring stood with her head crowned with flowers, and Summer, with garment cast aside, and a garland formed of spears of ripened grain, and Autumn, with his feet stained with grape-juice, and icy Winter, with his hair stiffened with hoar frost. Surrounded by these attendants, the Sun, with the eye that sees everything, beheld the youth dazzled with the novelty and splendor of the scene, and inquired the purpose of his errand.

The youth replied, "Oh, light of the boundless world, Phœbus, my father,—if you permit me to use that name,—give me some proof, I beseech you, by which I may be known as yours."

He ceased; and his father, laying aside the beams that shone all around his head, bade him approach, and embracing him, said, "My son, you deserve not to be disowned, and I confirm what your mother has told you. To put an end to your doubts, ask what you will, the gift shall be yours. I call to witness that dreadful lake, which I never saw, but which we gods swear by in our most solemn engagements."

Phaeton immediately asked to be permitted for one day to drive the chariot of the sun. The father repented of his promise; thrice and four times he shook his radiant head in warning. "I have spoken rashly," said he; "this only request I would fain deny. I beg you to withdraw it. It is not a safe boon, nor one, my Phaeton, suited to your youth and strength. Your lot is mortal, and you ask what is beyond a mortal's power. In your ignorance you aspire to do that which not even the gods themselves may do. None but myself may drive the flaming car of day. Not even Jupiter, whose terrible right arm hurls the thunderbolts.

"The first part of the way is steep, and such as the horses when fresh in the morning can hardly climb; the middle is high up in the heavens, whence I myself can scarcely, without alarm, look down and behold the earth and sea stretched beneath me. The last part of the road descends rapidly, and requires most careful driving. Tethys, who is waiting to receive me, often trembles for me lest I should fall headlong.

"Add to all this, the heaven is all the time turning around and carrying the stars with it. I have to be perpetually on my guard lest that movement, which sweeps everything else along, should hurry me also away. Suppose I should lend you the chariot, what would you do? Could you keep your course while the sphere was revolving under you?

"Perhaps you think that there are forests and cities, the abodes of gods, and palaces and temples on the way. On the contrary, the road is through the midst of frightful monsters. You pass by the horns of the Bull, in front of the Archer, and near the Lion's jaws, and where the Scorpion stretches its arms in one direction and the Crab in another. Nor will you find it easy to guide those horses, with their breasts full of fire that they breathe forth from their mouths and nostrils. I can scarcely govern them myself, when they are unruly and resist the reins.

"Beware, my son, lest I be the donor of a fatal gift; recall your request while yet you may. Do you ask me for a proof that you are sprung from my blood? I give you a proof in my fears for you. Look at my face—I would that you could look into my breast, you would there see all a father's anxiety.

"Finally," he continued, "look round the world and choose whatever you will of what earth or sea contains most precious—ask it and fear no refusal. This only I pray you not to urge. It

is not honor, but destruction you seek. Why do you hang round my neck and still entreat me? You shall have it if you persist—the oath is sworn and must be kept—but I beg you to choose more wisely."

He ended, but the youth rejected all admonition, and held to his demand. So, having resisted as long as he could, Phœbus at last led the way to where stood the lofty chariot. It was of gold, the gift of Vulcan; the axle was of gold, the pole and wheels of gold, the spokes of silver. Along the seat were rows of chrysolites and diamonds, which reflected all around the brightness of the sun.

While the daring youth gazed in admiration, the early Dawn threw open the purple doors of the east, and showed the pathway strewn with roses. The stars withdrew, marshalled by the Daystar, which last of all retired also.

The father, when he saw the earth beginning to glow, and the Moon preparing to retire, ordered the Hours to harness up the horses. They obeyed, and led forth from the lofty stalls the steeds full fed with ambrosia, and attached the reins. Then the father bathed the face of his son with a powerful unguent, and made him capable of enduring the brightness of the flame. He set the rays on his head, and, with a foreboding sigh, said, "If, my son, you will in this at least heed my advice, spare the whip and hold tight the reins. They go fast enough of their own accord; the labor is to hold them in. You are not to take the straight road directly between the five circles, but turn off to the left. Keep within the limit of the middle zone, and avoid the northern and the southern alike. You will see the marks of the wheels, and they will serve to guide you. And, that the skies and the earth may each receive their due share of heat, go not too high, or you will burn the heavenly dwellings, nor too low, or you will set the earth on fire; the middle course is safest and best.

"And now I leave you to your chance, which I hope will plan better for you than you have done for yourself. Night is passing out of the western gates and we can delay no longer. Take the reins; but if at last your heart fails you, and you will benefit by my advice, stay where you are in safety, and suffer me to light and warm the earth." The agile youth sprang into the chariot, stood erect and grasped the reins with delight, pouring out thanks to his reluctant parent.

Meanwhile the horses fill the air with their snortings and fiery breath, and stamp the ground impatient. Now the bars are let down, and the boundless plain of the universe lies open before them. They dart forward and cleave the opposing clouds, and outrun the morning breezes which started from the same eastern goal. The steeds soon perceived that the load they drew was lighter than usual; and as a ship without ballast is tossed hither and thither on the sea, so the chariot, without its accustomed weight, was dashed about as if empty. They rush headlong and leave the traveled road.

He is alarmed, and knows not how to guide them; nor, if he knew, has he the power. Then, for the first time, the Great and Little Bear were scorched with heat, and would fain, if it were possible, have plunged into the water; and the Serpent which lies coiled up round the north pole, torpid and harmless, grew warm, and with warmth felt its rage revive. Boötes, they say, fled away, though encumbered with his plow, and all unused to rapid motion.

Above: Phaeton speeds past the creatures in the heavenly bodies and fear causes him to lose control of the chariot. Gustave Moreau (1826–1898) shows Phaeton's progression through the constellations of heaven.

When hapless Phaeton looked down upon the earth, now spreading in vast extent beneath him, he grew pale and his knees shook with terror. In spite of the glare all around him, the sight of his eyes grew dim. He wished he had never touched his father's horses, never learned his parentage, never prevailed in his request. He is borne along like a vessel that flies before a tempest, when the pilot can do no more and betakes himself to his prayers. What shall he do?

Much of the heavenly road is left behind, but more remains before. He turns his eyes from one direction to the other; now to the goal whence he began his course, now to the realms of

sunset which he is not destined to reach. He loses his self-command, and knows not what to do, whether to draw tight the reins or throw them loose; he forgets the names of the horses. He sees with terror the monstrous forms scattered over the surface of heaven.

Here the Scorpion extended his two great arms, with his tail and crooked claws stretching over two signs of the zodiac. When the boy beheld him, reeking with poison and menacing with his fangs, his courage failed, and the reins fell from his hands. The horses, when they felt them loose on their backs, dashed headlong, and unrestrained went off into unknown regions of the sky, in among the stars, hurling the chariot over pathless places, now up in high heaven, now down almost to the earth. The moon saw with astonishment her brother's chariot running beneath her own.

The clouds begin to smoke, and the mountain tops take fire; the fields are parched with heat, the plants wither, the trees with their leafy branches burn, the harvest is ablaze! But these are small things. Great cities perished, with their walls and towers; whole nations with their people were consumed to ashes! The forest-clad mountains burned, Athos and Taurus and Tmolus and Œte; Ida, once celebrated for fountains, but now all dry; the Muses' mountain Helicon, and Hæmus; Ætna, with fires within and without, and Parnassus, with his two peaks, and Rhodope, forced at last to part with his snowy crown. Her cold climate was no protection to Scythia, Caucasus burned, and Ossa and Pindus, and, greater than both, Olympus; the Alps high in air, and the Apennines crowned with clouds.

Then Phaeton beheld the world on fire, and felt the heat intolerable. The air he breathed was like the air of a furnace and full of burning ashes, and the smoke was of a pitchy darkness. He dashed forward he knew not whither. Then, it is believed, the people of Æthiopia became black by the blood being forced so suddenly to the surface, and the Libyan desert was dried up to the condition in which it remains to this day. The nymphs of the fountains, with disheveled hair, mourned their waters, nor were the rivers safe beneath their banks; Tanais smoked, and Caicus, Xanthus, and Meander. Babylonian Euphrates and Ganges, Tagus with golden sands, and Cayster where the swans resort. Nile fled away and hid his head in the desert, and there it still remains concealed. Where he used to discharge his waters through seven mouths into the sea, there seven dry channels alone remained.

The earth cracked open, and through the chinks light broke into Tartarus, and frightened the king of shadows and his queen. The sea shrank up. Where before was water, it became a dry plain; and the mountains that lie beneath the waves lifted up their heads and became islands. The fishes sought the lowest depths, and the dolphins no longer ventured as usual to sport on the surface. Even Nereus, and his wife Doris, with the Nereids, their daughters, sought the deepest caves for refuge. Thrice Neptune essayed to raise his head above the surface, and thrice was driven back by the heat. Earth, surrounded as she was by waters, yet with head and shoulders bare, screening her face with her hand, looked up to heaven, and with a husky voice called on Jupiter.

"Oh, ruler of the gods, if I have deserved this treatment, and it is your will that I perish with fire, why withhold your thunderbolts? Let me at least fall by your hand. Is this the reward of

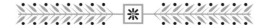

my fertility, of my obedient service? Is it for this that I have supplied herbage for cattle, and fruits for men, and frankincense for your altars?

"But if I am unworthy of regard, what has my brother Ocean done to deserve such a fate? If neither of us can excite your pity, think, I pray you, of your own heaven, and behold how both the poles are smoking which sustain your palace, which must fall if they be destroyed. Atlas faints, and scarce holds up his burden. If sea, earth, and heaven perish, we fall into ancient Chaos. Save what yet remains to us from the devouring flame. Oh, take thought for our deliverance in this awful moment!"

Thus spoke Earth, and overcome with heat and thirst, could say no more. Then Jupiter omnipotent, calling to witness all the gods, including him who had lent the chariot, and showing them that all was lost unless some speedy remedy were applied, mounted the lofty tower from whence he diffuses clouds over the earth, and hurls the forked lightnings. But at that time not a cloud was to be found to interpose for a screen to earth, nor was a shower remaining unexhausted.

He thundered, and brandishing a lightning bolt in his right hand launched it against the charioteer, and struck him at the same moment from his seat and from existence! Phaeton, with his hair on fire, fell headlong, like a shooting star which marks the heavens with its brightness as it falls, and Eridanus, the great river, received him and cooled his burning frame. The Italian Naiads reared a tomb for him, and inscribed these words upon the stone:

Driver of Phœbus' chariot, Phaeton,
Struck by Jove's thunder, rests beneath this stone.
He could not rule his father's car of fire,
Yet was it much so nobly to aspire.

His sisters, the Heliades, as they lamented his fate, were turned into poplar trees, on the banks of the river, and their tears, which continued to flow, became amber as they dropped into the stream.

Milman, in his poem of "Samor", makes the following allusion to Phaeton's story:

As when the palsied universe aghast
Lay... mute and still,
When drove, so poets sing, the Sun-born youth
Devious through Heaven's affrighted signs his sire's
Ill-granted chariot. Him the Thunderer hurled
From th' empyrean headlong to the gulf
Of the half-parched Eridanus, where weep
Even now the sister trees their amber tears
O'er Phaeton untimely dead.

In the beautiful lines of Walter Savage Landor, descriptive of the Sea-shell, there is an allusion to the Sun's palace and chariot. The water-nymph says:

I have sinuous shells of pearly hue
Within, and things that lustre have imbibed
In the sun's palace porch, where when unyoked
His chariot wheel stands midway in the wave.
Shake one and it awakens; then apply
Its polished lip to your attentive ear,
And it remembers its august abodes,
And murmurs as the ocean murmurs there.

GEBIR , BOOK I.

CUPID
AND PSYCHE

A certain king and queen had three daughters. The charms of the two elder were more than common, but the beauty of the youngest was so wonderful that the poverty of language is unable to express its due praise.

The fame of her beauty was so great that strangers from neighboring countries came in crowds to enjoy the sight, and looked on her with amazement, paying her that homage which is due only to Venus herself. In fact, Venus found her altars deserted while men turned their devotion to this young virgin. As she passed along, the people sang her praises, and strewed her way with chaplets and flowers.

This perversion to a mortal of the homage due only to the immortal powers gave great offense to the real Venus. Shaking her ambrosial locks with indignation, she exclaimed, "Am I then to be eclipsed in my honors by a mortal girl? In vain then did that royal shepherd, whose judgment was approved by Jove himself, give me the palm of beauty over my illustrious rivals, Pallas and Juno. But she shall not so quietly usurp my honors. I will give her cause to repent of so unlawful a beauty."

Thereupon she calls her winged son Cupid, mischievous enough in his own nature, and rouses and provokes him yet more by her complaints. She points out Psyche to him and says, "My dear son, punish that contumacious beauty; give thy mother a revenge as sweet as her injuries are great; infuse into the bosom of that haughty girl a passion for some low, mean, unworthy being, so that she may reap a mortification as great as her present exultation and triumph."

Cupid prepared to obey the commands of his mother. There are two fountains in Venus's garden, one of sweet waters, the other of bitter. Cupid filled two amber vases, one from each fountain, and suspending them from the top of his quiver, hastened to the chamber of Psyche, whom he found asleep. He shed a few drops from the bitter fountain over her lips, though the sight of her almost moved him to pity; then touched her side with the point of his arrow. At the touch she awoke, and opened eyes upon Cupid (himself invisible), which so startled him that in his confusion he wounded himself with his own arrow. Heedless of his wound, his whole thought now was to repair the mischief he had done, and he poured the balmy drops of joy over all her silken ringlets.

Above: This painting by Francisco José de Goya y Lucientes (1746–1828) shows Cupid visiting his beloved Pysche.

Psyche, henceforth frowned upon by Venus, derived no benefit from all her charms. True, all eyes were cast eagerly upon her, and every mouth spoke her praises; but neither king, royal youth, nor plebeian presented himself to demand her in marriage. Her two elder sisters of moderate charms had now long been married to two royal princes; but Psyche, in her lonely apartment, deplored her solitude, sick of that beauty which, while it procured abundance of flattery, had failed to awaken love.

Her parents, afraid that they had unwittingly incurred the anger of the gods, consulted the oracle of Apollo, and received this answer: "The virgin is destined for the bride of no mortal lover. Her future husband awaits her on the top of the mountain. He is a monster whom neither gods nor men can resist."

This dreadful decree of the oracle filled all the people with dismay, and her parents abandoned themselves to grief. But Psyche said, "Why, my dear parents, do you now lament me? You should rather have grieved when the people showered upon me undeserved honors, and with one voice called me a Venus. I now perceive that I am a victim to that name. I submit. Lead me to that rock to which my unhappy fate has destined me."

Accordingly, all things being prepared, the royal maid took her place in the procession, which more resembled a funeral than a nuptial pomp, and with her parents, amid the lamentations of the people, ascended the mountain, on the summit of which they left her alone, and with sorrowful hearts returned home.

While Psyche stood on the ridge of the mountain, panting with fear and with eyes full of tears, the gentle Zephyr raised her from the earth and bore her with an easy motion into a flowery dale. By degrees her mind became composed, and she laid herself down on the grassy bank to sleep. When she awoke refreshed with sleep, she looked round and beheld nearby a pleasant grove of tall and stately trees. She entered it, and in the midst discovered a fountain, sending forth clear and crystal waters, and fast by, a magnificent palace whose august front impressed the spectator that it was not the work of mortal hands, but the happy retreat of some god. Drawn by admiration and wonder, she approached the building and ventured to enter. Every object she met filled her with pleasure and amazement. Golden pillars supported the vaulted roof, and the walls were enriched with carvings and paintings representing beasts of the chase and rural scenes, adapted to delight the eye of the beholder. Proceeding onward, she perceived that besides the apartments of state there were others filled with all manner of treasures, and beautiful and precious productions of nature and art.

While her eyes were thus occupied, a voice addressed her, though she saw no one, uttering these words: "Sovereign lady, all that you see is yours. We whose voices you hear are your servants and shall obey all your commands with our utmost care and diligence. Retire, therefore, to your chamber and repose on your bed of down, and when you see fit repair to the bath. Supper awaits you in the adjoining alcove when it pleases you to take your seat there."

Psyche gave ear to the admonitions of her vocal attendants, and after repose and the refreshment of the bath, seated herself in the alcove, where a table immediately presented itself, without any visible aid from waiters or servants, and covered with the greatest delicacies of food and the most nectareous wines. Her ears too were feasted with music from invisible performers; of whom one sang, another played on the lute, and all closed in the wonderful harmony of a full chorus.

She had not yet seen her destined husband. He came only in the hours of darkness and fled before the dawn of morning, but his accents were full of love, and inspired a like passion in her. She often begged him to stay and let her behold him, but he would not consent.

On the contrary he charged her to make no attempt to see him, for it was his pleasure, for the best of reasons, to keep concealed. "Why should you wish to behold me?" he said, "have you any doubt of my love? Have you any wish ungratified? If you saw me, perhaps you would fear me, perhaps adore me, but all I ask of you is to love me. I would rather you would love me as an equal than adore me as a god."

This reasoning somewhat quieted Psyche for a time, and while the novelty lasted she felt quite happy. But at length the thought of her parents, left in ignorance of her fate, and of her sisters, precluded from sharing with her the delights of her situation, preyed on her mind and made her begin to feel her palace as but a splendid prison. When her husband came one night, she told him her distress, and at last drew from him an unwilling consent that her sisters should be brought to see her.

So, calling Zephyr, she acquainted him with her husband's commands, and he, promptly obedient, soon brought them across the mountain down to their sister's valley. They embraced her and she returned their caresses. "Come," said Psyche, "enter with me my house and refresh yourselves with whatever your sister has to offer." Then taking their hands she led them into her golden palace, and committed them to the care of her numerous train of attendant voices, to refresh them in her baths and at her table, and to show them all her treasures. The view of these celestial delights caused envy to enter their bosoms, at seeing their young sister possessed of such state and splendor, so much exceeding their own.

They asked her numberless questions, among others what sort of a person her husband was. Psyche replied that he was a beautiful youth, who generally spent the daytime in hunting upon the mountains. The sisters, not satisfied with this reply, soon made her confess that she had never seen him. Then they proceeded to fill her bosom with dark suspicions. "Call to mind," they said, "the Pythian oracle that declared you destined to marry a direful and tremendous monster. The inhabitants of this valley say that your husband is a terrible and monstrous serpent, who nourishes you for a while with dainties that he may by and by devour you. Take our advice. Provide yourself with a lamp and a sharp knife; put them in concealment that your husband may not discover them, and when he is sound asleep, slip out of bed, bring forth your lamp, and see for yourself whether what they say is true or not. If it is, hesitate not to cut off the monster's head, and thereby recover your liberty."

Psyche resisted these persuasions as well as she could, but they did not fail to have their effect on her mind, and when her sisters were gone, their words and her own curiosity were too strong for her to resist. So she prepared her lamp and a sharp knife, and hid them out of sight of her husband. When he had fallen into his first sleep, she silently rose and uncovering her lamp beheld not a hideous monster, but the most beautiful and charming of the gods, with his golden ringlets wandering over his snowy neck and crimson cheek, with two dewy wings on his shoulders, whiter than snow, and with shining feathers like the tender blossoms of spring. As she leaned the lamp over to have a nearer view of his face a drop of burning oil fell on the shoulder of the god, startled with which he opened his eyes and fixed them full upon her; then, without saying one word, he spread his white wings and flew out of the window.

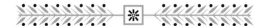

Psyche, in vain endeavoring to follow him, fell from the window to the ground. Cupid, beholding her as she lay in the dust, stopped his flight for an instant and said, "O foolish Psyche, is it thus you repay my love? After having disobeyed my mother's commands and made you my wife, will you think me a monster and cut off my head? But go; return to your sisters, whose advice you seem to think preferable to mine. I inflict no other punishment on you than to leave you forever. Love cannot dwell with suspicion.' So saying, he fled away, leaving poor Psyche prostrate on the ground, filling the place with mournful lamentations.

When she had recovered some degree of composure she looked around her, but the palace and gardens had vanished, and she found herself in the open field not far from the city where her sisters dwelt. She repaired thither and told them the whole story of her misfortunes, at which, pretending to grieve, those spiteful creatures inwardly rejoiced. "For now," said they, "he will perhaps choose one of us." With this idea, without saying a word of her intentions, each of them rose early the next morning and ascended the mountains, and having reached the top, called upon Zephyr to receive her and bear her to his lord; then leaping up, and not being sustained by Zephyr, fell down the precipice and was dashed to pieces.

Psyche meanwhile wandered day and night, without food or repose, in search of her husband. Casting her eyes on a lofty mountain having on its brow a magnificent temple, she sighed and said to herself, "Perhaps my love, my lord, inhabits there," and directed her steps thither.

She had no sooner entered than she saw heaps of corn, some in loose ears and some in sheaves, with mingled ears of barley. Scattered about, lay sickles and rakes, and all the instruments of harvest, without order, as if thrown carelessly out of the weary reapers' hands in the sultry hours of the day.

This unseemly confusion the pious Psyche put an end to, by separating and sorting everything to its proper place and kind, believing that she ought to neglect none of the gods, but endeavor by her piety to engage them all in her behalf. The holy Ceres, whose temple it was, finding her so religiously employed, thus spoke to her: "O Psyche, truly worthy of our pity, though I cannot shield you from the frowns of Venus, yet I can teach you how best to allay her displeasure. Go, then, and voluntarily surrender yourself to your lady and sovereign, and try by modesty and submission to win her forgiveness, and perhaps her favor will restore you the husband you have lost."

Psyche obeyed the commands of Ceres and took her way to the temple of Venus, endeavoring to fortify her mind and ruminating on what she should say and how best propitiate the angry goddess, feeling that the issue was doubtful and perhaps fatal.

Venus received her with angry countenance. "Most undutiful and faithless of servants," said she, "do you at last remember that you really have a mistress? Or have you rather come to see your sick husband, yet laid up of the wound given him by his loving wife? You are so ill-favored and disagreeable that the only way you can merit your lover must be by dint of industry and diligence. I will make trial of your housewifery."

Then she ordered Psyche to be led to the storehouse of her temple, where was laid up a great quantity of wheat, barley, millet, vetches, beans, and lentils prepared for food for her pigeons, and

said, "Take and separate all these grains, putting all of the same kind in a parcel by themselves, and see that you get it done before evening." Then Venus departed and left her to her task.

But Psyche, in a perfect consternation at the enormous work, sat stupid and silent, without moving a finger to the inextricable heap.

While she sat despairing, Cupid stirred up the little ant, a native of the fields, to take compassion on her. The leader of the ant hill, followed by whole hosts of his six-legged subjects, approached the heap, and with the utmost diligence, taking grain by grain, they separated the pile, sorting each kind to its parcel; and when it was all done, they vanished out of sight in a moment.

Venus at the approach of twilight returned from the banquet of the gods, breathing odors and crowned with roses. Seeing the task done, she exclaimed, "This is no work of yours, wicked one, but his, whom to your own and his misfortune you have enticed." So saying, she threw her a piece of black bread for her supper and went away.

Next morning Venus ordered Psyche to be called and said to her, "Behold yonder grove which stretches along the margin of the water. There you will find sheep feeding without a shepherd, with golden-shining fleeces on their backs. Go, fetch me a sample of that precious wool gathered from every one of their fleeces."

Psyche obediently went to the riverside, prepared to do her best to execute the command. But the river god inspired the reeds with harmonious murmurs, which seemed to say, "O maiden, severely tried, tempt not the dangerous flood, nor venture among the formidable rams on the other side, for as long as they are under the influence of the rising sun, they burn with a cruel rage to destroy mortals with their sharp horns or rude teeth. But when the noontide sun has driven the cattle to the shade, and the serene spirit of the flood has lulled them to rest, you may then cross in safety, and you will find the woolly gold sticking to the bushes and the trunks of the trees."

Thus the compassionate river god gave Psyche instructions how to accomplish her task, and by observing his directions she soon returned to Venus with her arms full of the golden fleece; but she received not the approbation of her implacable mistress, who said, "I know very well it is by none of your own doings that you have succeeded in this task, and I am not satisfied yet that you have any capacity to make yourself useful. But I have another task for you. Here, take this box and go your way to the infernal shades, and give this box to Proserpine and say, 'My mistress Venus desires you to send her a little of your beauty, for in tending her sick son she has lost some of her own'. Be not too long on your errand, for I must paint myself with it to appear at the circle of the gods and goddesses this evening."

Psyche was now satisfied that her destruction was at hand, being obliged to go with her own feet directly down to Erebus. Wherefore, to make no delay of what was not to be avoided, she goes to the top of a high tower to precipitate herself headlong, thus to descend the shortest way to the shades below. But a voice from the tower said to her, "Why, poor unlucky girl, dost thou design to put an end to thy days in so dreadful a manner? And what cowardice makes thee sink under this last danger who hast been so miraculously supported in all thy former?" Then the voice told her how by a certain cave she might reach the realms of Pluto, and how to avoid all

the dangers of the road, to pass by Cerberus, the three-headed dog, and prevail on Charon, the ferryman, to take her across the black river and bring her back again. But the voice added, "When Proserpine has given you the box filled with her beauty, of all things this is chiefly to be observed by you, that you never once open or look into the box nor allow your curiosity to pry into the treasure of the beauty of the goddesses."

Psyche, encouraged by this advice, obeyed it in all things, and taking heed to her ways traveled safely to the kingdom of Pluto. She was admitted to the palace of Proserpine, and without accepting the delicate seat or delicious banquet that was offered her, but contented with coarse bread for her food, she delivered her message from Venus. Presently the box was returned to her, shut and filled with the precious commodity. Then she returned the way she came, and glad was she to come out once more into the light of day.

But having got so far successfully through her dangerous task, a longing desire seized her to examine the contents of the box. "What," said she, "shall I, the carrier of this divine beauty, not take the least bit to put on my cheeks to appear to more advantage in the eyes of my beloved husband!" So she carefully opened the box, but found nothing there of any beauty at all, but an infernal and truly Stygian sleep, which being thus set free from its prison, took possession of her, and she fell down in the midst of the road, a sleepy corpse without sense or motion.

But Cupid, being now recovered from his wound, and not able longer to bear the absence of his beloved Psyche, slipping through the smallest crack of the window of his chamber which happened to be left open, flew to the spot where Psyche lay, and gathering up the sleep from her body closed it again in the box, and waked Psyche with a light touch of one of his arrows.

"Again," said he, "hast thou almost perished by the same curiosity. But now perform exactly the task imposed on you by my mother, and I will take care of the rest."

Then Cupid, as swift as lightning penetrating the heights of heaven, presented himself before Jupiter with his supplication. Jupiter lent a favoring ear, and pleaded the cause of the lovers so earnestly with Venus that he won her consent. On this he sent Mercury to bring Psyche up to the heavenly assembly, and when she arrived, handing her a cup of ambrosia, he said, "Drink this, Psyche, and be immortal; nor shall Cupid ever break away from the knot in which he is tied, but these nuptials shall be perpetual."

Thus Psyche became at last united to Cupid, and in due time they had a daughter born to them whose name was Pleasure.

The fable of Cupid and Psyche is usually considered allegorical. The Greek name for a butterfly is Psyche, and the same word means the soul. There is no illustration of the immortality of the soul so striking and beautiful as the butterfly, bursting on brilliant wings from the tomb in which it has lain, after a dull, groveling, caterpillar existence, to flutter in the blaze of day and feed on the most fragrant and delicate productions of the spring. Psyche, then, is the human soul, which is purified by sufferings and misfortunes, and is thus prepared for the enjoyment of true and pure happiness.

In works of art Psyche is represented as a maiden with the wings of a butterfly, along with Cupid, in the different situations described in the allegory.

Milton alludes to the story of Cupid and Psyche in the conclusion of his "Comus":

Celestial Cupid, her famed son, advanced,
Holds his dear Psyche sweet entranced,
After her wandering labours long,
Till free consent the gods among
Make her his eternal bride;
And from her fair unspotted side
Two blissful twins are to be born,
Youth and Joy; so Jove hath sworn.

Left: An illustration from *The Most Pleasant and Delectable Tale of the Marriage of Cupid and Psyche by Apuleius* by Dorothy Mullock (1914) shows the wedding of the two lovers.

TALES
BY
NATHANIEL
HAWTHORNE

THE MIRACULOUS PITCHER

One evening, in times long ago, old Philemon and his old wife Baucis sat at their cottage door, enjoying the calm and beautiful sunset. They had already eaten their frugal supper, and intended now to spend a quiet hour or two before bedtime. So they talked together about their garden, and their cow, and their bees, and their grapevine, which clambered over the cottage wall, and on which the grapes were beginning to turn purple.

But the rude shouts of children and the fierce barking of dogs, in the village near at hand, grew louder and louder, until, at last, it was hardly possible for Baucis and Philemon to hear each other speak.

"Ah, wife," cried Philemon, "I fear some poor traveler is seeking hospitality among our neighbors yonder, and, instead of giving him food and lodging, they have set their dogs at him, as their custom is!"

"Well-a-day!" answered old Baucis, "I do wish our neighbors felt a little more kindness for their fellow-creatures. And only think of bringing up their children in this naughty way, and patting them on the head when they fling stones at strangers!"

"Those children will never come to any good," said Philemon, shaking his white head. "To tell you the truth, wife, I should not wonder if some terrible thing were to happen to all the people in the village unless they mend their manners. But, as for you and me, so long as Providence affords us a crust of bread, let us be ready to give half to any poor, homeless stranger that may come along and need it."

"That's right, husband!" said Baucis. "So we will!"

These old folks, you must know, were quite poor, and had to work pretty hard for a living.

Old Philemon toiled diligently in his garden, while Baucis was always busy with her distaff, or making a little butter and cheese with their cow's milk, or doing one thing and another about the cottage.

Right: The peaceful and kind Philemon and Baucis enjoy a simple and good life despite the unkindness and violence of their neighbouring villagers.

·PHILEMON·&·BAVCIS·

Their food was seldom anything but bread, milk, and vegetables, with sometimes a portion of honey from their beehive, and now and then a bunch of grapes, that had ripened against the cottage wall.

But they were two of the kindest old people in the world, and would cheerfully have gone without their dinners, any day, rather than refuse a slice of their brown loaf, a cup of new milk, and a spoonful of honey, to the weary traveler who might pause before their door. They felt as if such guests had a sort of holiness, and that they ought, therefore, to treat them better and more bountifully than their own selves.

Their cottage stood on a rising ground, at some short distance from a village, which lay in a hollow valley, that was about half a mile in breadth. This valley, in past ages, when the world was new, had probably been the bed of a lake. There, fishes had glided to and fro in the depths, and water-weeds had grown along the margin, and trees and hills had seen their reflected images in the broad and peaceful mirror. But, as the waters subsided, men had cultivated the soil, and built houses on it, so that it was now a fertile spot, and bore no traces of the ancient lake, except a very small brook, which meandered through the midst of the village, and supplied the inhabitants with water. The valley had been dry land so long, that oaks had sprung up, and grown great and high, and perished with old age, and been succeeded by others, as tall and stately as the first.

Never was there a prettier or more fruitful valley.

The very sight of the plenty around them should have made the inhabitants kind and gentle, and ready to show their gratitude to Providence by doing good to their fellow-creatures. But, we are sorry to say, the people of this lovely village were not worthy to dwell in a spot on which Heaven had smiled so beneficently. They were a very selfish and hard-hearted people, and had no pity for the poor, nor sympathy with the homeless. They would only have laughed, had anybody told them that human beings owe a debt of love to one another, because there is no other method of paying the debt of love and care which all of us owe to Providence.

You will hardly believe what I am going to tell you. These naughty people taught their children to be no better than themselves, and used to clap their hands, by way of encouragement, when they saw the little boys and girls run after some poor stranger, shouting at his heels and pelting him with stones. They kept large and fierce dogs, and whenever a traveler ventured to show himself in the village street, this pack of disagreeable curs scampered to meet him, barking, snarling, and showing their teeth. Then they would seize him by his leg, or by his clothes, just as it happened; and if he were ragged when he came, he was generally a pitiable object before he had time to run away. This was a very terrible thing to poor travelers, as you may suppose, especially when they chanced to be sick, or feeble, or lame, or old. Such persons (if they once knew how badly these unkind people, and their unkind children and curs, were in the habit of behaving) would go miles and miles out of their way, rather than try to pass through the village again. What made the matter seem worse, if possible, was that when rich persons came in their chariots, or riding on beautiful horses, with their servants in rich liveries attending on

them, nobody could be more civil and obsequious than the inhabitants of the village. They would take off their hats, and make the humblest bows you ever saw. If the children were rude, they were pretty certain to get their ears boxed; and as for the dogs, if a single cur in the pack presumed to yelp, his master instantly beat him with a club, and tied him up without any supper. This would have been all very well, only it proved that the villagers cared much about the money that a stranger had in his pocket, and nothing whatever for the human soul, which lives equally in the beggar and the prince.

So now you can understand why old Philemon spoke so sorrowfully, when he heard the shouts of the children and the barking of the dogs, at the farther extremity of the village street. There was a confused din, which lasted a good while, and seemed to pass quite through the breadth of the valley.

"I never heard the dogs so loud!" observed the good old man.

"Nor the children so rude!" answered his good old wife.

They sat shaking their heads, one to another, while the noise came nearer and nearer; until, at the foot of the little eminence on which their cottage stood, they saw two travelers approaching on foot. Close behind them came the fierce dogs, snarling at their very heels. A little farther off, ran a crowd of children, who sent up shrill cries, and flung stones at the two strangers, with all their might. Once or twice, the younger of the two men (he was a slender and very active figure) turned about and drove back the dogs with a staff which he carried in his hand. His companion, who was a very tall person, walked calmly along, as if disdaining to notice either the naughty children, or the pack of curs, whose manners the children seemed to imitate.

Both of the travelers were very humbly clad, and looked as if they might not have money enough in their pockets to pay for a night's lodging. And this, I am afraid, was the reason why the villagers had allowed their children and dogs to treat them so rudely.

"Come, wife," said Philemon to Baucis, "let us go and meet these poor people. No doubt, they feel almost too heavy-hearted to climb the hill."

"Go you and meet them," answered Baucis, "while I make haste within doors, and see whether we can get them anything for supper. A comfortable bowl of bread and milk would do wonders towards raising their spirits."

Accordingly, she hastened into the cottage. Philemon, on his part, went forward, and extended his hand with so hospitable an aspect that there was no need of saying what nevertheless he did say, in the heartiest tone imaginable:

"Welcome, strangers! Welcome!"

"Thank you!" replied the younger of the two, in a lively kind of way, notwithstanding his weariness and trouble. "This is quite another greeting than we have met with yonder in the village. Pray, why do you live in such a bad neighborhood?"

"Ah!" observed old Philemon, with a quiet and benign smile, "Providence put me here, I hope, among other reasons, in order that I may make you what amends I can for the inhospitality of my neighbors."

· THE · STRANGERS · IN · THE · VILLAGE

"Well said, old father!" cried the traveler, laughing, "and, if the truth must be told, my companion and myself need some amends. Those children (the little rascals!) have bespattered us finely with their mud-balls; and one of the curs has torn my cloak, which was ragged enough already. But I took him across the muzzle with my staff; and I think you may have heard him yelp, even thus far off."

Philemon was glad to see him in such good spirits; nor, indeed, would you have fancied, by the traveler's look and manner, that he was weary with a long day's journey, besides being disheartened by rough treatment at the end of it. He was dressed in rather an odd way, with a sort of cap on his head, the brim of which stuck out over both ears. Though it was a summer evening, he wore a cloak, which he kept wrapt closely about him, perhaps because his under garments were shabby. Philemon perceived, too, that he had on a singular pair of shoes; but, as it was now growing dusk, and as the old man's eyesight was none the sharpest, he could not precisely tell in what the strangeness consisted. One thing, certainly, seemed queer. The traveler was so wonderfully light and active, that it appeared as if his feet sometimes rose from the ground of their own accord, or could only be kept down by an effort.

"I used to be light-footed, in my youth," said Philemon to the traveler. "But I always found my feet grow heavier towards nightfall."

"There is nothing like a good staff to help one along," answered the stranger, "and I happen to have an excellent one, as you see."

This staff, in fact, was the oddest-looking staff that Philemon had ever beheld. It was made of olive-wood, and had something like a little pair of wings near the top. Two snakes, carved in the wood, were represented as twining themselves about the staff, and were so very skillfully executed that old Philemon (whose eyes, you know, were getting rather dim) almost thought them alive, and that he could see them wriggling and twisting.

"A curious piece of work, sure enough!" said he. "A staff with wings! It would be an excellent kind of stick for a little boy to ride astride of!"

By this time, Philemon and his two guests had reached the cottage door.

"Friends," said the old man, "sit down and rest yourselves here on this bench. My good wife Baucis has gone to see what you can have for supper. We are poor folks, but you shall be welcome to whatever we have in the cupboard."

The younger stranger threw himself carelessly on the bench, letting his staff fall, as he did so.

And here happened something rather marvelous, though trifling enough, too. The staff seemed to get up from the ground of its own accord, and, spreading its little pair of wings, it half hopped, half flew, and leaned itself against the wall of the cottage. There it stood quite still, except that the snakes continued to wriggle. But, in my private opinion, old Philemon's eyesight had been playing him tricks again.

Before he could ask any questions, the elder stranger drew his attention from the wonderful staff, by speaking to him.

Left: Two strangers attacked by children and set upon by dogs as they make their way through the inhospitable village.

"Was there not," asked the stranger, in a remarkably deep tone of voice, "a lake, in very ancient times, covering the spot where now stands yonder village?"

"Not in my day, friend," answered Philemon, "and yet I am an old man, as you see. There were always the fields and meadows, just as they are now, and the old trees, and the little stream murmuring through the midst of the valley. My father, nor his father before him, ever saw it otherwise, so far as I know; and doubtless it will still be the same, when old Philemon shall be gone and forgotten!"

"That is more than can be safely foretold," observed the stranger, and there was something very stern in his deep voice. He shook his head, too, so that his dark and heavy curls were shaken with the movement. "Since the inhabitants of yonder village have forgotten the affections and sympathies of their nature, it were better that the lake should be rippling over their dwellings again!"

The traveler looked so stern that Philemon was really almost frightened; the more so, that, at his frown, the twilight seemed suddenly to grow darker, and that, when he shook his head, there was a roll as of thunder in the air.

But, in a moment afterwards, the stranger's face became so kindly and mild that the old man quite forgot his terror. Nevertheless, he could not help feeling that this elder traveler must be no ordinary personage, although he happened now to be attired so humbly and to be journeying on foot.

Not that Philemon fancied him a prince in disguise, or any character of that sort; but rather some exceedingly wise man, who went about the world in this poor garb, despising wealth and all worldly objects, and seeking everywhere to add a mite to his wisdom. This idea appeared the more probable, because, when Philemon raised his eyes to the stranger's face, he seemed to see more thought there, in one look, than he could have studied out in a lifetime.

While Baucis was getting the supper, the travelers both began to talk very sociably with Philemon. The younger, indeed, was extremely loquacious, and made such shrewd and witty remarks, that the good old man continually burst out a-laughing, and pronounced him the merriest fellow whom he had seen for many a day.

"Pray, my young friend," said he, as they grew familiar together, "what may I call your name?"

"Why, I am very nimble, as you see," answered the traveler. "So, if you call me Quicksilver, the name will fit tolerably well."

"Quicksilver? Quicksilver?" repeated Philemon, looking in the traveler's face, to see if he were making fun of him. "It is a very odd name! And your companion there? Has he as strange a one?"

"You must ask the thunder to tell it you!" replied Quicksilver, putting on a mysterious look. "No other voice is loud enough."

This remark, whether it were serious or in jest, might have caused Philemon to conceive a very great awe of the elder stranger, if, on venturing to gaze at him, he had not beheld so much beneficence in his visage. But, undoubtedly, here was the grandest figure that ever sat so humbly beside a cottage door. When the stranger conversed, it was with gravity, and in

such a way that Philemon felt irresistibly moved to tell him everything which he had most at heart. This is always the feeling that people have, when they meet with any one wise enough to comprehend all their good and evil, and to despise not a tittle of it.

But Philemon, simple and kind-hearted old man that he was, had not many secrets to disclose. He talked, however, quite garrulously, about the events of his past life, in the whole course of which he had never been a score of miles from this very spot. His wife Baucis and himself had dwelt in the cottage from their youth upward, earning their bread by honest labor, always poor, but still contented. He told what excellent butter and cheese Baucis made, and how nice were the vegetables which he raised in his garden. He said, too, that, because they loved one another so very much, it was the wish of both that death might not separate them, but that they should die, as they had lived, together.

As the stranger listened, a smile beamed over his countenance, and made its expression as sweet as it was grand.

"You are a good old man," said he to Philemon, "and you have a good old wife to be your helpmeet. It is fit that your wish be granted."

And it seemed to Philemon, just then, as if the sunset clouds threw up a bright flash from the west, and kindled a sudden light in the sky.

Baucis had now got supper ready, and, coming to the door, began to make apologies for the poor fare which she was forced to set before her guests.

"Had we known you were coming," said she, "my good man and myself would have gone without a morsel, rather than you should lack a better supper. But I took the most part of to-day's milk to make cheese; and our last loaf is already half eaten. Ah me! I never feel the sorrow of being poor, save when a poor traveler knocks at our door."

"All will be very well; do not trouble yourself, my good dame," replied the elder stranger, kindly. "An honest, hearty welcome to a guest works miracles with the fare, and is capable of turning the coarsest food to nectar and ambrosia."

"A welcome you shall have," cried Baucis, "and likewise a little honey that we happen to have left, and a bunch of purple grapes besides."

"Why, Mother Baucis, it is a feast!" exclaimed Quicksilver, laughing, "'n absolute feast! And you shall see how bravely I will play my part at it! I think I never felt hungrier in my life."

"Mercy on us!" whispered Baucis to her husband. "If the young man has such a terrible appetite, I am afraid there will not be half enough supper!"

They all went into the cottage.

Quicksilver's staff, you recollect, had set itself up against the wall of the cottage. Well, when its master entered the door, leaving this wonderful staff behind, what should it do but immediately spread its little wings, and go hopping and fluttering up the doorsteps! Tap, tap, went the staff, on the kitchen floor; nor did it rest until it had stood itself on end with the greatest gravity and decorum, beside Quicksilver's chair. Old Philemon, however, as well as his wife, was so taken up in attending to their guests, that no notice was given to what the staff had been about.

As Baucis had said, there was but a scanty supper for two hungry travelers. In the middle of the table was the remnant of a brown loaf, with a piece of cheese on one side of it, and a dish of honeycomb on the other. There was a pretty good bunch of grapes for each of the guests. A moderately sized earthen pitcher, nearly full of milk, stood at a corner of the board; and when Baucis had filled two bowls, and set them before the strangers, only a little milk remained in the bottom of the pitcher. Alas! it is a very sad business, when a bountiful heart finds itself pinched and squeezed among narrow circumstances.

Poor Baucis kept wishing that she might starve for a week to come, if it were possible, by so doing, to provide these hungry folks a more plentiful supper.

And, since the supper was so exceedingly small, she could not help wishing that their appetites had not been quite so large. Why, at their very first sitting down, the travelers both drank off all the milk in their two bowls, at a draught.

"A little more milk, kind Mother Baucis, if you please," said Quicksilver. "The day has been hot, and I am very much athirst."

"Now, my dear people," answered Baucis, in great confusion, "I am so sorry and ashamed! But the truth is, there is hardly a drop more milk in the pitcher. O husband! husband! why didn't we go without our supper?"

"Why, it appears to me," cried Quicksilver, starting up from table and taking the pitcher by the handle, "it really appears to me that matters are not quite so bad as you represent them. Here is certainly more milk in the pitcher."

So saying, and to the vast astonishment of Baucis, he proceeded to fill, not only his own bowl, but his companion's likewise, from the pitcher, that was supposed to be almost empty.

The good woman could scarcely believe her eyes. She had certainly poured out nearly all the milk, and had peeped in afterwards, and seen the bottom of the pitcher, as she set it down upon the table.

"But I am old," thought Baucis to herself, "and apt to be forgetful. I suppose I must have made a mistake. At all events, the pitcher cannot help being empty now, after filling the bowls twice over."

"What excellent milk!" observed Quicksilver, after quaffing the contents of the second bowl. "Excuse me, my kind hostess, but I must really ask you for a little more."

Now Baucis had seen, as plainly as she could see anything, that Quicksilver had turned the pitcher upside down, and consequently had poured out every drop of milk, in filling the last bowl. Of course, there could not possibly be any left.

However, in order to let him know precisely how the case was, she lifted the pitcher, and made a gesture as if pouring milk into Quicksilver's bowl, but without the remotest idea that any milk would stream forth. What was her surprise, therefore, when such an abundant cascade fell bubbling into the bowl, that it was immediately filled to the brim, and overflowed upon the table! The two snakes that were twisted about Quicksilver's staff (but neither Baucis nor Philemon happened to observe this circumstance) stretched out their heads, and began to lap up the spilt milk.

And then what a delicious fragrance the milk had! It seemed as if Philemon's only cow must have pastured, that day, on the richest herbage that could be found anywhere in the world.

"And now a slice of your brown loaf, Mother Baucis," said Quicksilver, "and a little of that honey!"

Baucis cut him a slice, accordingly; and though the loaf, when she and her husband ate of it, had been rather too dry and crusty to be palatable, it was now as light and moist as if but a few hours out of the oven. Tasting a crumb, which had fallen on the table, she found it more delicious than bread ever was before, and could hardly believe that it was a loaf of her own kneading and baking. Yet, what other loaf could it possibly be?

But, oh the honey! I may just as well let it alone, without trying to describe how exquisitely it smelt and looked. Its color was that of the purest and most transparent gold; and it had the odor of a thousand flowers; but of such flowers as never grew in an earthly garden, and to seek which the bees must have flown high above the clouds. The wonder is, that, after alighting on a flower-bed of so delicious fragrance and immortal bloom, they should have been content to fly down again to their hive in Philemon's garden. Never was such honey tasted, seen, or smelt. The perfume floated around the kitchen, and made it so delightful, that, had you closed your eyes, you would instantly have forgotten the low ceiling and smoky walls, and have fancied yourself in an arbor, with celestial honeysuckles creeping over it.

Although good Mother Baucis was a simple old dame, she could not but think that there was something rather out of the common way, in all that had been going on. So, after helping the guests to bread and honey, and laying a bunch of grapes by each of their plates, she sat down by Philemon, and told him what she had seen, in a whisper.

"Did you ever hear the like?" asked she.

"No, I never did," answered Philemon, with a smile. "And I rather think, my dear old wife, you have been walking about in a sort of a dream. If I had poured out the milk, I should have seen through the business at once. There happened to be a little more in the pitcher than you thought,—that is all.'

"Ah, husband," said Baucis, "say what you will, these are very uncommon people."

"Well, well," replied Philemon, still smiling, "perhaps they are. They certainly do look as if they had seen better days; and I am heartily glad to see them making so comfortable a supper."

Each of the guests had now taken his bunch of grapes upon his plate. Baucis (who rubbed her eyes, in order to see the more clearly) was of opinion that the clusters had grown larger and richer, and that each separate grape seemed to be on the point of bursting with ripe juice. It was entirely a mystery to her how such grapes could ever have been produced from the old stunted vine that climbed against the cottage wall.

"Very admirable grapes these!" observed Quicksilver, as he swallowed one after another, without apparently diminishing his cluster. "Pray, my good host, whence did you gather them?"

"From my own vine," answered Philemon. "You may see one of its branches twisting across the window, yonder. But wife and I never thought the grapes very fine ones."

"I never tasted better," said the guest. "Another cup of this delicious milk, if you please, and I shall then have supped better than a prince."

This time, old Philemon bestirred himself, and took up the pitcher; for he was curious to discover whether there was any reality in the marvels which Baucis had whispered to him. He knew that his good old wife was incapable of falsehood, and that she was seldom mistaken in what she supposed to be true; but this was so very singular a case, that he wanted to see into it with his own eyes. On taking up the pitcher, therefore, he slyly peeped into it, and was fully satisfied that it contained not so much as a single drop. All at once, however, he beheld a little white fountain, which gushed up from the bottom of the pitcher, and speedily filled it to the brim with foaming and deliriously fragrant milk. It was lucky that Philemon, in his surprise, did not drop the miraculous pitcher from his hand.

"Who are ye, wonder-working strangers?" cried he, even more bewildered than his wife had been.

"Your guests, my good Philemon, and your friends," replied the elder traveler, in his mild, deep voice, that had something at once sweet and awe-inspiring in it. "Give me likewise a cup of the milk; and may your pitcher never be empty for kind Baucis and yourself, any more than for the needy wayfarer!"

The supper being now over, the strangers requested to be shown to their place of repose. The old people would gladly have talked with them a little longer, and have expressed the wonder which they felt, and their delight at finding the poor and meager supper prove so much better and more abundant than they hoped. But the elder traveler had inspired them with such reverence, that they dared not ask him any questions.

And when Philemon drew Quicksilver aside, and inquired how under the sun a fountain of milk could have got into an old earthen pitcher, this latter personage pointed to his staff.

"There is the whole mystery of the affair," quoth Quicksilver, "and if you can make it out, I'll thank you to let me know. I can't tell what to make of my staff. It is always playing such odd tricks as this; sometimes getting me a supper, and, quite as often, stealing it away. If I had any faith in such nonsense, I should say the stick was bewitched!"

He said no more, but looked so slyly in their faces, that they rather fancied he was laughing at them. The magic staff went hopping at his heels, as Quicksilver quitted the room. When left alone, the good old couple spent some little time in conversation about the events of the evening, and then lay down on the floor, and fell fast asleep.

They had given up their sleeping-room to the guests, and had no other bed for themselves, save these planks, which I wish had been as soft as their own hearts.

The old man and his wife were stirring, betimes, in the morning, and the strangers likewise arose with the sun, and made their preparations to depart. Philemon hospitably entreated them to remain a little longer, until Baucis could milk the cow, and bake a cake upon the hearth, and, perhaps, find them a few fresh eggs, for breakfast.

Right: The kindly Baucis and Philemon save their guests from the cruel villagers and entertain them with food and drink. Little do the generous couple know that they are entertaining gods.

·THE·STRANGERS·ENTERTAINED·∷·

The guests, however, seemed to think it better to accomplish a good part of their journey before the heat of the day should come on. They, therefore, persisted in setting out immediately, but asked Philemon and Baucis to walk forth with them a short distance, and show them the road which they were to take.

So they all four issued from the cottage, chatting together like old friends. It was very remarkable, indeed, how familiar the old couple insensibly grew with the elder traveler, and how their good and simple spirits melted into his, even as two drops of water would melt into the illimitable ocean. And as for Quicksilver, with his keen, quick, laughing wits, he appeared to discover every little thought that but peeped into their minds, before they suspected it themselves.

They sometimes wished, it is true, that he had not been quite so quick-witted, and also that he would fling away his staff, which looked so mysteriously mischievous, with the snakes always writhing about it. But then, again, Quicksilver showed himself so very good-humored, that they would have been rejoiced to keep him in their cottage, staff, snakes, and all, every day, and the whole day long.

"Ah me! Well-a-day!" exclaimed Philemon, when they had walked a little way from their door. "If our neighbors only knew what a blessed thing it is to show hospitality to strangers, they would tie up all their dogs, and never allow their children to fling another stone."

"It is a sin and shame for them to behave so—that it is!" cried good old Baucis, vehemently. "And I mean to go this very day, and tell some of them what naughty people they are!"

"I fear," remarked Quicksilver, slyly smiling, "that you will find none of them at home."

The elder traveler's brow, just then, assumed such a grave, stern, and awful grandeur, yet serene withal, that neither Baucis nor Philemon dared to speak a word. They gazed reverently into his face, as if they had been gazing at the sky.

"When men do not feel towards the humblest stranger as if he were a brother," said the traveler, in tones so deep that they sounded like those of an organ, "they are unworthy to exist on earth, which was created as the abode of a great human brotherhood!"

"And, by the by, my dear old people," cried Quicksilver, with the liveliest look of fun and mischief in his eyes, "where is this same village that you talk about? On which side of us does it lie? Methinks I do not see it hereabouts."

Philemon and his wife turned towards the valley, where, at sunset, only the day before, they had seen the meadows, the houses, the gardens, the clumps of trees, the wide, green-margined street, with children playing in it, and all the tokens of business, enjoyment, and prosperity. But what was their astonishment! There was no longer any appearance of a village! Even the fertile vale, in the hollow of which it lay, had ceased to have existence. In its stead, they beheld the broad, blue surface of a lake, which filled the great basin of the valley from brim to brim, and reflected the surrounding hills in its bosom with as tranquil an image as if it had been there ever since the creation of the world. For an instant, the lake remained perfectly smooth. Then, a little breeze sprang up, and caused the water to dance, glitter, and sparkle in the early sunbeams, and to dash, with a pleasant rippling murmur, against the hither shore.

The lake seemed so strangely familiar, that the old couple were greatly perplexed, and felt as if they could only have been dreaming about a village having lain there. But, the next moment, they remembered the vanished dwellings, and the faces and characters of the inhabitants, far too distinctly for a dream. The village had been there yesterday, and now was gone!

"Alas!" cried these kind-hearted old people, "what has become of our poor neighbors?"

"They exist no longer as men and women," said the elder traveler, in his grand and deep voice, while a roll of thunder seemed to echo it at a distance. "There was neither use nor beauty in such a life as theirs; for they never softened or sweetened the hard lot of mortality by the exercise of kindly affections between man and man. They retained no image of the better life in their bosoms; therefore, the lake, that was of old, has spread itself forth again, to reflect the sky!"

"And as for those foolish people," said Quicksilver, with his mischievous smile, "they are all transformed to fishes. There needed but little change, for they were already a scaly set of rascals, and the coldest-blooded beings in existence. So, kind Mother Baucis, whenever you or your husband have an appetite for a dish of broiled trout, he can throw in a line, and pull out half a dozen of your old neighbors!"

"Ah," cried Baucis, shuddering, "I would not, for the world, put one of them on the gridiron!"

"No," added Philemon, making a wry face, "we could never relish them!"

"As for you, good Philemon," continued the elder traveler, "and you, kind Baucis, you, with your scanty means, have mingled so much heartfelt hospitality with your entertainment of the homeless stranger, that the milk became an inexhaustible fount of nectar, and the brown loaf and the honey were ambrosia. Thus, the divinities have feasted, at your board, off the same viands that supply their banquets on Olympus. You have done well, my dear old friends. Wherefore, request whatever favor you have most at heart, and it is granted."

Philemon and Baucis looked at one another, and then, I know not which of the two it was who spoke but that one, uttered the desire of both their hearts.

"Let us live together, while we live, and leave the world at the same instant, when we die! For we have always loved one another!"

"Be it so!" replied the stranger, with majestic kindness. "Now, look towards your cottage!"

They did so. But what was their surprise on beholding a tall edifice of white marble, with a wide-open portal, occupying the spot where their humble residence had so lately stood!

"There is your home," said the stranger, beneficently smiling on them both. "Exercise your hospitality in yonder palace as freely as in the poor hovel to which you welcomed us last evening."

The old folks fell on their knees to thank him; but, behold! neither he nor Quicksilver was there.

So Philemon and Baucis took up their residence in the marble palace, and spent their time, with vast satisfaction to themselves, in making everybody jolly and comfortable who happened to pass that way. The milk-pitcher, I must not forget to say, retained its marvelous quality of being never empty, when it was desirable to have it full.

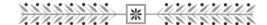

Whenever an honest, good-humored, and free-hearted guest took a draught from this pitcher, he invariably found it the sweetest and most invigorating fluid that ever ran down his throat. But, if a cross and disagreeable curmudgeon happened to sip, he was pretty certain to twist his visage into a hard knot, and pronounce it a pitcher of sour milk!

Thus the old couple lived in their palace a great, great while, and grew older and older, and very old indeed. At length, however, there came a summer morning when Philemon and Baucis failed to make their appearance, as on other mornings, with one hospitable smile overspreading both their pleasant faces, to invite the guests of overnight to breakfast. The guests searched everywhere, from top to bottom of the spacious palace, and all to no purpose. But, after a great deal of perplexity, they espied, in front of the portal, two venerable trees, which nobody could remember to have seen there the day before. Yet there they stood, with their roots fastened deep into the soil, and a huge breadth of foliage overshadowing the whole front of the edifice. One was an oak, and the other a linden-tree. Their boughs—it was strange and beautiful to see—were intertwined together, and embraced one another, so that each tree seemed to live in the other tree's bosom much more than in its own.

While the guests were marveling how these trees, that must have required at least a century to grow, could have come to be so tall and venerable in a single night, a breeze sprang up, and set their intermingled boughs astir. And then there was a deep, broad murmur in the air, as if the two mysterious trees were speaking.

"I am old Philemon!" murmured the oak.

"I am old Baucis!" murmured the linden-tree.

But, as the breeze grew stronger, the trees both spoke at once—"Philemon! Baucis! Baucis! Philemon!—as if one were both and both were one, and talking together in the depths of their mutual heart. It was plain enough to perceive that the good old couple had renewed their age, and were now to spend a quiet and delightful hundred years or so, Philemon as an oak, and Baucis as a linden-tree. And oh, what a hospitable shade did they fling around them. Whenever a wayfarer paused beneath it, he heard a pleasant whisper of the leaves above his head, and wondered how the sound should so much resemble words like these:

"Welcome, welcome, dear traveler, welcome!"

And some kind soul, that knew what would have pleased old Baucis and old Philemon best, built a circular seat around both their trunks, where, for a great while afterwards, the weary, and the hungry, and the thirsty used to repose themselves, and quaff milk abundantly out of the miraculous pitcher.

And I wish, for all our sakes, that we had the pitcher here now!

Above: Philemon and Baucis are transformed into an oak and linden-tree so that they could live together forever entwined and happy.

THE GOLDEN TOUCH

Once upon a time, there lived a very rich man, and a king besides, whose name was Midas; and he had a little daughter, whom nobody but myself ever heard of, and whose name I either never knew, or have entirely forgotten. So, because I love odd names for little girls, I choose to call her Marygold.

This King Midas was fonder of gold than of anything else in the world. He valued his royal crown chiefly because it was composed of that precious metal. If he loved anything better, or half so well, it was the one little maiden who played so merrily around her father's footstool. But the more Midas loved his daughter, the more did he desire and seek for wealth. He thought, foolish man! that the best thing he could possibly do for this dear child would be to bequeath her the immensest pile of yellow, glistening coin, that had ever been heaped together since the world was made. Thus, he gave all his thoughts and all his time to this one purpose. If ever he happened to gaze for an instant at the gold-tinted clouds of sunset, he wished that they were real gold, and that they could be squeezed safely into his strong box. When little Marygold ran to met him, with a bunch of buttercups and dandelions, he used to say, "Poh, poh, child! If these flowers were as golden as they look, they would be worth the plucking!"

And yet, in his earlier days, before he was so entirely possessed of this insane desire for riches. King Midas had shown a great taste for flowers. He had planted a garden, in which grew the biggest and beautifulest and sweetest roses that any mortal ever saw or smelt.

These roses were still growing in the garden, as large, as lovely, and as fragrant, as when Midas used to pass whole hours in gazing at them, and inhaling their perfume. But now, if he looked at them at all, it was only to calculate how much the garden would be worth, if each of the innumerable rose-petals were a thin plate of gold.

And though he once was fond of music (in spite of an idle story about his ears, which were said to resemble those of an

Right: A stranger appears to King Midas in his secret chamber of gold and asks the king what would satisfy his lust for the accumulation of gold.

THE·STRANGER·APPEARING·TO·MIDAS

ass), the only music for poor Midas, now, was the chink of one coin against another.

At length (as people always grow more and more foolish, unless they take care to grow wiser and wiser), Midas had got to be so exceedingly unreasonable, that he could scarcely bear to see or touch any object that was not gold. He made it his custom, therefore, to pass a large portion of every day in a dark and dreary apartment, under ground, at the basement of his palace. It was here that he kept his wealth. To this dismal hole—for it was little better than a dungeon— Midas be-took himself, whenever he wanted to be particularly happy. Here, after carefully locking the door, he would take a bag of gold coin, or a gold cup as big as a wash-bowl, or a heavy golden bar, or a peck-measure of gold-dust, and bring them from the obscure corners of the room into the one bright and narrow sunbeam that fell from the dungeon-like window. He valued the sunbeam for no other reason but that his treasure would not shine without its help. And then would he reckon over the coins in the bag; toss up the bar, and catch it as it came down; sift the gold-dust through his fingers; look at the funny image of his own face, as reflected in the burnished circumference of the cup; and whisper to himself, "O Midas, rich King Midas, what a happy man art thou!" But it was laughable to see how the image of his face kept grinning at him, out of the polished surface of the cup. It seemed to be aware of his foolish behavior, and to have a naughty inclination to make fun of him.

Midas called himself a happy man, but felt that he was not yet quite so happy as he might be. The very tip-top of enjoyment would never be reached, unless the whole world were to become his treasure-room, and be filled with yellow metal which should be all his own.

Now, I need hardly remind such wise little people as you are, that in the old, old time, when King Midas was alive, a great many things came to pass, which we should consider wonderful if they were to happen in our own day and country. And, on the other hand, a great many things take place nowadays, which seem not only wonderful to us, but at which the people of old times would have stared their eyes out. On the whole, I regard our own times as the strangest of the two; but, however that may be, I must go on with my story.

Midas was enjoying himself in his treasure-room, one day, as usual, when he perceived a shadow fall over the heaps of gold; and, looking suddenly up, what should he behold but the figure of a stranger, standing in the bright and narrow sunbeam! It was a young man, with a cheerful and ruddy face. Whether it was that the imagination of King Midas threw a yellow tinge over everything, or whatever the cause might be, he could not help fancying that the smile with which the stranger regarded him had a kind of golden radiance in it. Certainly, although his figure intercepted the sunshine, there was now a brighter gleam upon all the piled-up treasures than before. Even the remotest corners had their share of it, and were lighted up, when the stranger smiled, as with tips of flame and sparkles of fire.

As Midas knew that he had carefully turned the key in the lock, and that no mortal strength could possibly break into his treasure-room, he, of course, concluded that his visitor must be something more than mortal. It is no matter about telling you who he was. In those days, when the earth was comparatively a new affair, it was supposed to be often the resort of beings endowed with supernatural power, and who used to interest themselves

in the joys and sorrows of men, women, and children, half playfully and half seriously. Midas had met such beings before now, and was not sorry to meet one of them again. The stranger's aspect, indeed, was so good-humored and kindly, if not beneficent, that it would have been unreasonable to suspect him of intending any mischief. It was far more probable that he came to do Midas a favor. And what could that favor be, unless to multiply his heaps of treasure?

The stranger gazed about the room; and when his lustrous smile had glistened upon all the golden objects that were there, he turned again to Midas.

"You are a wealthy man, friend Midas!" he observed. "I doubt whether any other four walls, on earth, contain so much gold as you have contrived to pile up in this room."

"I have done pretty well—pretty well," answered Midas, in a discontented tone. "But, after all, it is but a trifle, when you consider that it has taken me my whole life to get it together. If one could live a thousand years, he might have time to grow rich!"

"What!" exclaimed the stranger. "Then you are not satisfied?"

Midas shook his head.

"And pray what would satisfy you?" asked the stranger. "Merely for the curiosity of the thing, I should be glad to know."

Midas paused and meditated. He felt a presentiment that this stranger, with such a golden luster in his good-humored smile, had come hither with both the power and the purpose of gratifying his utmost wishes. Now, therefore, was the fortunate moment, when he had but to speak, and obtain whatever possible, or seemingly impossible thing, it might come into his head to ask.

So he thought, and thought, and thought, and heaped up one golden mountain upon another, in his imagination, without being able to imagine them big enough. At last, a bright idea occurred to King Midas. It seemed really as bright as the glistening metal which he loved so much.

Raising his head, he looked the lustrous stranger in the face.

"Well, Midas," observed his visitor, "I see that you have at length hit upon something that will satisfy you. Tell me your wish."

"It is only this," replied Midas. "I am weary of collecting my treasures with so much trouble, and beholding the heap so diminutive, after I have done my best. I wish everything that I touch to be changed to gold!"

The stranger's smile grew so very broad, that it seemed to fill the room like an outburst of the sun, gleaming into a shadowy dell, where the yellow autumnal leaves—for so looked the lumps and particles of gold—lie strewn in the glow of light.

"The Golden Touch!" exclaimed he. "You certainly deserve credit, friend Midas, for striking out so brilliant a conception. But are you quite sure that this will satisfy you?"

"How could it fail?" said Midas.

"And will you never regret the possession of it?"

"What could induce me?" asked Midas. "I ask nothing else, to render me perfectly happy."

"Be it as you wish, then," replied the stranger, waving his hand in token of farewell. "Tomorrow, at sunrise, you will find yourself gifted with the Golden Touch."

The figure of the stranger then became exceedingly bright, and Midas involuntarily closed his eyes. On opening them again, he beheld only one yellow sunbeam in the room, and, all around him, the glistening of the precious metal which he had spent his life in hoarding up.

Whether Midas slept as usual that night, the story does not say. Asleep or awake, however, his mind was probably in the state of a child's, to whom a beautiful new plaything has been promised in the morning. At any rate, day had hardly peeped over the hills, when King Midas was broad awake, and, stretching his arms out of bed, began to touch the objects that were within reach. He was anxious to prove whether the Golden Touch had really come, according to the stranger's promise. So he laid his finger on a chair by the bedside, and on various other things, but was grievously disappointed to perceive that they remained of exactly the same substance as before. Indeed, he felt very much afraid that he had only dreamed about the lustrous stranger, or else that the latter had been making game of him. And what a miserable affair would it be, if, after all his hopes, Midas must content himself with what little gold he could scrape together by ordinary means, instead of creating it by a touch!

All this while, it was only the gray of the morning, with but a streak of brightness along the edge of the sky, where Midas could not see it. He lay in a very disconsolate mood, regretting the downfall of his hopes, and kept growing sadder and sadder, until the earliest sunbeam shone through the window, and gilded the ceiling over his head. It seemed to Midas that this bright yellow sunbeam was reflected in rather a singular way on the white covering of the bed. Looking more closely, what was his astonishment and delight, when he found that this linen fabric had been transmuted to what seemed a woven texture of the purest and brightest gold! The Golden Touch had come to him, with the first sunbeam!

Midas started up, in a kind of joyful frenzy, and ran about the room, grasping at everything that happened to be in his way. He seized one of the bedposts, and it became immediately a fluted golden pillar. He pulled aside a window-curtain, in order to admit a clear spectacle of the wonders which he was performing; and the tassel grew heavy in his hand—a mass of gold. He took up a book from the table. At his first touch, it assumed the appearance of such a splendidly bound and gilt-edged volume as one often meets with, nowadays; but, on running his fingers through the leaves, behold! it was a bundle of thin golden plates, in which all the wisdom of the book had grown illegible. He hurriedly put on his clothes, and was enraptured to see himself in a magnificent suit of gold cloth, which retained its flexibility and softness, although it burdened him a little with its weight.

He drew out his handkerchief, which little Marygold had hemmed for him. That was likewise gold, with the dear child's neat and pretty stitches running all along the border, in gold thread!

Somehow or other, this last transformation did not quite please King Midas. He would rather that his little daughter's handiwork should have remained just the same as when she climbed his knee and put it into his hand.

But it was not worth while to vex himself about a trifle. Midas now took his spectacles from his pocket, and put them on his nose, in order that he might see more distinctly what he was about. In those days, spectacles for common people had not been invented, but were already worn by kings; else, how could Midas have had any?

To his great perplexity, however, excellent as the glasses were, he discovered that he could not possibly see through them. But this was the most natural thing in the world; for, on taking them off, the transparent crystals turned out to be plates of yellow metal, and, of course, were worthless as spectacles, though valuable as gold. It struck Midas as rather inconvenient, that, with all his wealth, he could never again be rich enough to own a pair of serviceable spectacles.

"It is no great matter, nevertheless," said he to himself, very philosophically. "We cannot expect any great good, without its being accompanied with some small inconvenience. The Golden Touch is worth the sacrifice of a pair of spectacles, at least, if not of one's very eyesight. My own eyes will serve for ordinary purposes, and little Marygold will soon be old enough to read to me."

Wise King Midas was so exalted by his good fortune, that the palace seemed not sufficiently spacious to contain him. He therefore went down stairs, and smiled on observing that the balustrade of the staircase became a bar of burnished gold, as his hand passed over it, in his descent. He lifted the door-latch (it was brass only a moment ago, but golden when his fingers quitted it), and emerged into the garden. Here, as it happened, he found a great number of beautiful roses in full bloom, and others in all the stages of lovely bud and blossom.

Very delicious was their fragrance in the morning breeze.

Their delicate blush was one of the fairest sights in the world; so gentle, so modest, and so full of sweet tranquility, did these roses seem to be.

But Midas knew a way to make them far more precious, according to his way of thinking, than roses had ever been before. So he took great pains in going from bush to bush, and exercised his magic touch most indefatigably; until every individual flower and bud, and even the worms at the heart of some of them, were changed to gold. By the time this good work was completed, King Midas was summoned to breakfast; and, as the morning air had given him an excellent appetite, he made haste back to the palace.

What was usually a king's breakfast in the days of Midas, I really do not know, and cannot stop now to investigate. To the best of my belief, however, on this particular morning, the breakfast consisted of hot cakes, some nice little brook trout, roasted potatoes, fresh boiled eggs, and coffee, for King Midas himself, and a bowl of bread and milk for his daughter Marygold. At all events, this is a breakfast fit to set before a king; and, whether he had it or not, King Midas could not have had a better.

Little Marygold had not yet made her appearance. Her father ordered her to be called, and, seating himself at table, awaited the child's coming, in order to begin his own breakfast. To do Midas justice, he really loved his daughter, and loved her so much the more this morning, on account of the good fortune which had befallen him.

It was not a great while before he heard her coming along the passageway crying bitterly. This circumstance surprised him, because Marygold was one of the cheerfullest little people whom you would see in a summer's day, and hardly shed a thimbleful of tears in a twelvemonth. When Midas heard her sobs, he determined to put little Marygold into better spirits, by an agreeable surprise; so, leaning across the table, he touched his daughter's bowl (which was a China one, with pretty figures all around it), and transmuted it to gleaming gold.

Meanwhile, Marygold slowly and disconsolately opened the door, and showed herself with her apron at her eyes, still sobbing as if her heart would break.

"How now, my little lady!" cried Midas. "Pray what is the matter with you, this bright morning?"

Marygold, without taking the apron from her eyes, held out her hand, in which was one of the roses which Midas had so recently transmuted.

"Beautiful!" exclaimed her father. "And what is there in this magnificent golden rose to make you cry?"

"Ah, dear father!" answered the child, as well as her sobs would let her; "it is not beautiful, but the ugliest flower that ever grew! As soon as I was dressed, I ran into the garden to gather some roses for you; because I know you like them, and like them the better when gathered by your little daughter. But, oh dear, dear me! What do you think has happened? Such a misfortune! All the beautiful roses, that smelled so sweetly and had so many lovely blushes, are blighted and spoilt! They are grown quite yellow, as you see this one, and have no longer any fragrance! What can have been the matter with them?"

"Poh, my dear little girl,—pray don't cry about it!" said Midas, who was ashamed to confess that he himself had wrought the change which so greatly afflicted her. "Sit down and eat your bread and milk! You will find it easy enough to exchange a golden rose like that (which will last hundreds of years) for an ordinary one which would wither in a day."

"I don't care for such roses as this!" cried Marygold, tossing it contemptuously away. "It has no smell, and the hard petals prick my nose!"

The child now sat down to table, but was so occupied with her grief for the blighted roses that she did not even notice the wonderful transmutation of her China bowl.

Perhaps this was all the better; for Marygold was accustomed to take pleasure in looking at the queer figures, and strange trees and houses, that were painted on the circumference of the bowl; and these ornaments were now entirely lost in the yellow hue of the metal.

Midas, meanwhile, had poured out a cup of coffee; and, as a matter of course, the coffee-pot, whatever metal it may have been when he took it up, was gold when he set it down. He thought to himself, that it was rather an extravagant style of splendor, in a king of his simple habits, to breakfast off a service of gold, and began to be puzzled with the difficulty of keeping his treasures safe. The cupboard and the kitchen would no longer be a secure place of deposit for articles so valuable as golden bowls and coffee-pots.

Amid these thoughts, he lifted a spoonful of coffee to his lips, and, sipping it, was astonished to perceive that the instant his lips touched the liquid, it became molten gold, and, the next moment, hardened into a lump!

"Ha!" exclaimed Midas, rather aghast.

"What is the matter, father?" asked little Marygold, gazing at him, with the tears still standing in her eyes.

"Nothing, child, nothing!" said Midas. "Eat your milk, before it gets quite cold."

He took one of the nice little trouts on his plate, and, by way of experiment, touched its tail with his finger. To his horror, it was immediately transmuted from an admirably fried brook trout into a gold fish, though not one of those gold-fishes which people often keep in glass globes, as ornaments for the parlor. No; but it was really a metallic fish, and looked as if it had been very cunningly made by the nicest goldsmith in the world. Its little bones were now golden wires; its fins and tail were thin plates of gold; and there were the marks of the fork in it, and all the delicate, frothy appearance of a nicely fried fish, exactly imitated in metal. A very pretty piece of work, as you may suppose; only King Midas, just at that moment, would much rather have had a real trout in his dish than this elaborate and valuable imitation of one.

"I don't quite see," thought he to himself, "how I am to get any breakfast!"

He took one of the smoking-hot cakes, and had scarcely broken it, when, to his cruel mortification, though, a moment before, it had been of the whitest wheat, it assumed the yellow hue of Indian meal. To say the truth, if it had really been a hot Indian cake, Midas would have prized it a good deal more than he now did, when its solidity and increased weight made him too bitterly sensible that it was gold. Almost in despair, he helped himself to a boiled egg, which immediately underwent a change similar to those of the trout and the cake, The egg, indeed, might have been mistaken for one of those which the famous goose, in the story-book, was in the habit of laying; but King Midas was the only goose that had had anything to do with the matter.

"Well, this is a quandary!" thought he, leaning back in his chair, and looking quite enviously at little Marygold, who was now eating her bread and milk with great satisfaction. "Such a costly breakfast before me, and nothing that can be eaten!"

Hoping that, by dint of great despatch, he might avoid what he now felt to be a considerable inconvenience, King Midas next snatched a hot potato, and attempted to cram it into his mouth, and swallow it in a hurry. But the Golden Touch was too nimble for him. He found his mouth full, not of mealy potato, but of solid metal, which burnt his tongue that he roared aloud, and, jumping up from the table, began to dance and stamp about the room, both with pain and affright.

"Father, dear father!" cried little Marygold, who was a very affectionate child, "pray what is the matter? Have you burnt your mouth?"

"Ah, dear child," groaned Midas, dolefully, "I don't know what is to become of your poor father!"

And, truly, my dear little folks, did you ever hear of such a pitiable case, in all your lives? Here was literally the richest breakfast that could be set before a king, and its very richness made it absolutely good for nothing.

The poorest laborer, sitting down to his crust of bread and cup of water, was far better off than King Midas, whose delicate food was really worth its weight in gold.

And what was to be done? Already, at breakfast, Midas was excessively hungry. Would he be less so by dinnertime? And how ravenous would be his appetite for supper, which must undoubtedly consist of the same sort of indigestible dishes as those now before him! How many days, think you, would he survive a continuance of this rich fare?

These reflections so troubled wise King Midas, that he began to doubt whether, after all, riches are the one desirable thing in the world, or even the most desirable.

But this was only a passing thought. So fascinated was Midas with the glitter of the yellow metal, that he would still have refused to give up the Golden Touch for so paltry a consideration as a breakfast. Just imagine what a price for one meal's victuals! It would have been the same as paying millions and millions of money (and as many millions more as would take forever to reckon up) for some fried trout, an egg, a potato, a hot cake, and a cup of coffee!

"It would be quite too dear," thought Midas.

Nevertheless, so great was his hunger, and the perplexity of his situation, that he again groaned aloud, and very grievously too. Our pretty Marygold could endure it no longer. She sat, a moment gazing at her father, and trying, with all the might of her little wits, to find out what was the matter with him. Then, with a sweet and sorrowful impulse to comfort him, she started from her chair, and, running to Midas, threw her arms affectionately about his knees. He bent down and kissed her. He felt that his little daughter's love was worth a thousand times more than he had gained by the Golden Touch.

"My precious, precious Marygold!" cried he.

But Marygold made no answer.

Alas, what had he done? How fatal was the gift which the stranger bestowed! The moment the lips of Midas touched Marygold's forehead, a change had taken place, her sweet, rosy face, so full of affection as it had been, assumed a glittering yellow color, with yellow tear-drops congealing on her cheeks. Her beautiful brown ringlets took the same tint. Her soft and tender little form grew hard and inflexible within her father's encircling arms. Oh, terrible misfortune! The victim of his insatiable desire for wealth, little Marygold was a human child no longer, but a golden statue!

Yes, there she was, with the questioning look of love, grief, and pity, hardened into her face. It was the prettiest and most woeful sight that ever mortal saw. All the features and tokens of Marygold were there; ever the beloved little dimple remained in her golden chin.

But, the more perfect was the resemblance, the greater was the father's agony at beholding this golden image, which was all that was left him of a daughter. It had been a favorite phrase of Midas, whenever he felt particularly fond of the child, to say that she was worth her weight in gold. And now the phrase had become literally true. And now, at last, when it was too late, he felt how infinitely a warm and tender heart, that loved him, exceeded in value all the wealth that could be piled up betwixt the earth and sky!

It would be too sad a story, if I were to tell you how Midas, in the fulness of all his gratified desires, began to wring his

Right: A distraught Midas realises too late the consequences of his ill-considered wish to turn all that he touches to gold as his beautiful daughter turns to the precious metal in his arms.

·MIDAS' DAUGHTER·TURNED·TO·GOLD·

hands and bemoan himself; and how he could neither bear to look at Marygold, nor yet to look away from her. Except when his eyes were fixed on the image, he could not possibly believe that she was changed to gold. But, stealing another glance, there was the precious little figure, with a yellow tear-drop on its yellow cheek, and a look so piteous and tender, that it seemed as if that very expression must needs soften the gold, and make it flesh again. This, however, could not be. So Midas had only to wring his hands, and to wish that he were the poorest man in the wide world, if the loss of all his wealth might bring back the faintest rose-color to his dear child's face.

While he was in this tumult of despair, he suddenly beheld a stranger, standing near the door. Midas bent down his head, without speaking; for he recognized the same figure which had appeared to him, the day before, in the treasure-room, and had bestowed on him this disastrous faculty of the Golden Touch. The stranger's countenance still wore a smile, which seemed to shed a yellow luster all about the room, and gleamed on little Marygold's image, and on the other objects that had been transmuted by the touch of Midas.

"Well, friend Midas," said the stranger, "pray how do you succeed with the Golden Touch?"

Midas shook his head.

"I am very miserable," said he.

"Very miserable, indeed!" exclaimed the stranger. "And how happens that? Have I not faithfully kept my promise with you? Have you not everything that your heart desired?"

"Gold is not everything," answered Midas. "And I have lost all that my heart really cared for."

"Ah! So you have made a discovery, since yesterday?" observed the stranger. "Let us see, then. Which of these two things do you think is really worth the most—the gift of the Golden Touch, or one cup of clear cold water?"

"O blessed water!" exclaimed Midas. "It will never moisten my parched throat again!"

"The Golden Touch," continued the stranger, "or a crust of bread?"

"A piece of bread," answered Midas, "is worth all the gold on earth!"

"The Golden Touch," asked the stranger, "or your own little Marygold, warm, soft, and loving, as she was an hour ago?"

"O my child, my dear child!" cried poor Midas, wringing his hands. "I would not have given that one small dimple in her chin for the power of changing this whole big earth into a solid lump of gold!"

"You are wiser than you were. King Midas!" said the stranger, looking seriously at him. "Your own heart, I perceive, has not been entirely changed from flesh to gold. Were it so, your case would indeed be desperate. But you appear to be still capable of understanding that the commonest things, such as lie within everybody's grasp, are more valuable than the riches which so many mortals sigh and struggle after. Tell me, now, do you sincerely desire to rid yourself of this Golden Touch?"

"It is hateful to me!" replied Midas.

A fly settled on his nose, but immediately fell to the floor; for it, too, had become gold. Midas shuddered.

"Go, then," said the stranger, "and plunge into the river that glides past the bottom of your garden. Take likewise a vase of the same water, and sprinkle it over any object that you may desire to change back again from gold into its former substance. If you do this in earnestness and sincerity, it may possibly repair the mischief which your avarice has occasioned."

King Midas bowed low; and when he lifted his head, the lustrous stranger had vanished.

You will easily believe that Midas lost no time in snatching up a great earthen pitcher (but, alas me! it was no longer earthen after he touched it), and hastening to the river-side. As he scampered along, and forced his way through the shrubbery, it was positively marvelous to see how the foliage turned yellow behind him, as if the autumn had been there, and nowhere else. On reaching the river's brink, he plunged headlong in, without waiting so much as to pull off his shoes.

"Poof! poof! poof!" snorted King Midas, as his head emerged out of the water. "Well, this is really a refreshing bath, and I think it must have quite washed away the Golden Touch. And now for filling my pitcher!"

As he dipped the pitcher into the water, it gladdened his very heart to see it change from gold into the same good, honest earthen vessel which it had been before he touched it. He was conscious, also, of a change within himself. A cold, hard, and heavy weight seemed to have gone out of his bosom. No doubt, his heart had been gradually losing its human substance, and transmuting itself into insensible metal, but had now softened back again into flesh. Perceiving a violet, that grew on the bank of the river, Midas touched it with his finger, and was overjoyed to find that the delicate flower retained its purple hue, instead of undergoing a yellow blight. The curse of the Golden Touch had, therefore, really been removed from him.

King Midas hastened back to the palace; and, I suppose, the servants knew not what to make of it when they saw their royal master so carefully bringing home an earthen pitcher of water. But that water, which was to undo all the mischief that his folly had wrought, was more precious to Midas than an ocean of molten gold could have been. The first thing he did, as you need hardly be told, was to sprinkle it by handfuls over the golden figure of little Marygold.

No sooner did it fall on her than you would have laughed to see how the rosy color came back to the dear child's cheek!—and how she began to sneeze and sputter!—and how astonished she was to find herself dripping wet, and her father still throwing more water over her!

"Pray do not, dear father!" cried she. "See how you have wet my nice frock, which I put on only this morning!"

For Marygold did not know that she had been a little golden statue; nor could she remember anything that had happened since the moment when she ran with outstretched arms to comfort poor King Midas.

Her father did not think it necessary to tell his beloved child how very foolish he had been, but contented himself with showing how much wiser he had now grown. For this purpose, he led little Marygold into the garden, where he sprinkled all the remainder of the water over the rose-bushes, and with such good effect that above five thousand roses recovered their beautiful bloom.

· MIDAS · WITH · THE · PITCHER ·

There were two circumstances, however, which, as long as he lived, used to put King Midas in mind of the Golden Touch. One was, that the sands of the river sparkled like gold; the other, that little Marygold's hair had now a golden tinge, which he had never observed in it before she had been transmuted by the effect of his kiss. This change of hue was really an improvement, and made Marygold's hair richer than in her babyhood.

When King Midas had grown quite an old man, and used to trot Marygold's children on his knee, he was fond of telling them this marvelous story, pretty much as I have now told it to you. And then would he stroke their glossy ringlets, and tell them that their hair, like-wise, had a rich shade of gold, which they had inherited from their mother.

"And, to tell you the truth, my precious little folks," quoth King Midas, diligently trotting the children all the while, "ever since that morning, I have hated the very sight of all other gold, save this!"

Left: Midas learns the importance of cleansing himself from the lust for gold and redeems himself with blessed water from an earthenware pitcher.

THE GORGON'S HEAD

Perseus was the son of Danaë, who was the daughter of a king. And when Perseus was a very little boy, some wicked people put his mother and himself into a chest, and set them afloat upon the sea. The wind blew freshly, and drove the chest away from the shore, and the uneasy billows, tossed it up and down; while Danaë clasped her child closely to her bosom, and dreaded that some big wave would dash its foamy crest over them both.

The chest sailed on, however, and neither sank nor was upset; until, when night was coming, it floated so near an island that it got entangled in a fisherman's nets, and was drawn out high and dry upon the sand. The island was called Seriphus, and it was reigned over by King Polydectes, who happened to be the fisherman's brother.

This fisherman, I am glad to tell you, was an exceedingly humane and upright man. He showed great kindness to Danaë and her little boy; and continued to befriend them, until Perseus had grown to be a handsome youth, very strong and active, and skillful in the use of arms. Long before this time, King Polydectes had seen the two strangers—the mother and her child—who had come to his dominions in a floating chest. As he was not good and kind, like his brother the fisherman, but extremely wicked, he resolved to send Perseus on a dangerous enterprise, in which he would probably be killed, and then to do some great mischief to Danaë herself. So this bad-hearted king spent a long while in considering what was the most dangerous thing that a young man could possibly undertake to perform. At last, having hit upon an enterprise that promised to turn out as fatally as he desired, he sent for the youthful Perseus.

The young man came to the palace, and found the king sitting upon his throne.

"Perseus," said King Polydectes, smiling craftily upon him, "you are grown up a fine young man. You and your good mother have received a great deal of kindness from myself, as well as from my worthy brother the fisherman, and I suppose you would not be sorry to repay some of it."

Above: Arthur Rackham's illustration of the infant Perseus set adrift on a choppy sea in a chest with his mother Danaë. Eventually they were caught in fishing nets and landed on the island of Seriphus reigned over by the bad-hearted King Polydectes.

"Please your Majesty," answered Perseus, "I would willingly risk my life to do so."

"Well, then," continued the king, still with a cunning smile on his lips, "I have a little adventure to propose to you; and, as you are a brave and enterprising youth, you will doubtless look upon it as a great piece of good luck to have so rare an opportunity of distinguishing yourself. You must know, my good Perseus, I think of getting married to the beautiful Princess Hippodamia; and it is customary, on these occasions, to make the bride a present of some far-fetched and elegant curiosity. I have been a little perplexed, I must honestly confess, where to obtain anything likely to please a princess of her exquisite taste. But, this morning, I flatter myself, I have thought of precisely the article."

"And can I assist your Majesty in obtaining it?" cried Perseus, eagerly.

"You can, if you are as brave a youth as I believe you to be," replied King Polydectes, with the utmost graciousness of manner. "The bridal gift which I have set my heart on presenting to the beautiful Hippodamia is the head of the Gorgon Medusa with the snaky locks; and I depend on you, my dear Perseus, to bring it to me. So, as I am anxious to settle affairs with the princess, the sooner you go in quest of the Gorgon, the better I shall be pleased."

"I will set out tomorrow morning," answered Perseus.

"Pray do so, my gallant youth," rejoined the king. "And, Perseus, in cutting off the Gorgon's head, be careful to make a clean stroke, so as not to injure its appearance. You must bring it home in the very best condition, in order to suit the exquisite taste of the beautiful Princess Hippodamia."

Perseus left the palace, but was scarcely out of hearing before Polydectes burst into a laugh; being greatly amused, wicked king that he was, to find how readily the young man fell into the snare. The news quickly spread abroad that Perseus had undertaken to cut off the head of Medusa with the snaky locks. Everybody was rejoiced; for most of the inhabitants of the island were as wicked as the king himself, and would have liked nothing better than to see some enormous mischief happen to Danaë and her son.

The only good man in this unfortunate island of Seriphus appears to have been the fisherman. As Perseus walked along, therefore, the people pointed after him, and made mouths, and winked to one another, and ridiculed him as loudly as they dared.

"Ho, ho!" cried they; "Medusa's snakes will sting him soundly!"

Now, there were three Gorgons alive at that period; and they were the most strange and terrible monsters that had ever been since the world was made, or that have been seen in after days, or that are likely to be seen in all time to come. I hardly know what sort of creature or hobgoblin to call them. They were three sisters, and seem to have borne some distant resemblance to women, but were really a very frightful and mischievous species of dragon. It is, indeed, difficult to imagine what hideous beings these three sisters were. Why, instead of locks of hair, if you can believe me, they had each of them a hundred enormous snakes growing on their heads, all alive, twisting, wriggling, curling, and thrusting out their venomous tongues, with forked stings at the end! The teeth of the Gorgons were terribly long tusks; their hands were made of brass; and their bodies were all over scales, which, if not iron, were something as

hard and impenetrable. They had wings, too, and exceedingly splendid ones, I can assure you; for every feather in them was pure, bright, glittering, burnished gold, and they looked very dazzlingly, no doubt, when the Gorgons were flying about in the sunshine.

But when people happened to catch a glimpse of their glittering brightness, aloft in the air, they seldom stopped to gaze, but ran and hid themselves as speedily as they could. You will think, perhaps, that they were afraid of being stung by the serpents that served the Gorgons instead of hair or of having their heads bitten off by their ugly tusks or of being torn all to pieces by their brazen claws. Well, to be sure, these were some of the dangers, but by no means the greatest, nor the most difficult to avoid. For the worst thing about these abominable Gorgons was, that, if once a poor mortal fixed his eyes full upon one of their faces, he was certain, that very instant to be changed from warm flesh and blood into cold and lifeless stone!

Thus, as you will easily perceive, it was a very dangerous adventure that the wicked King Polydectes had contrived for this innocent young man. Perseus himself, when he had thought over the matter, could not help seeing that he had very little chance of coming safely through it, and that he was far more likely to become a stone image than to bring back the head of Medusa with the snaky locks. For, not to speak of other difficulties, there was one which it would have puzzled an older man than Perseus to get over. Not only must he fight with and slay this golden-winged, iron-scaled, long-tusked, brazen-clawed, snaky-haired monster, but he must do it with his eyes shut, or, at least, without so much as a glance at the enemy with whom he was contending. Else, while his arm was lifted to strike, he would stiffen into stone, and stand with that uplifted arm for centuries, until time, and the wind and weather, should crumble him quite away. This would be a very sad thing to befall a young man who wanted to perform a great many brave deeds, and to enjoy a great deal of happiness, in this bright and beautiful world.

So disconsolate did these thoughts make him, that Perseus could not bear to tell his mother what he had undertaken to do. He therefore took his shield, girded on his sword, and crossed over from the island to the mainland, where he sat down in a solitary place, and hardly refrained from shedding tears.

But, while he was in this sorrowful mood, he heard a voice close beside him.

"Perseus," said the voice, "why are you sad?"

He lifted his head from his hands, in which he had hidden it, and, behold! all alone as Perseus had supposed himself to be, there was a stranger in the solitary place. It was a brisk, intelligent, and remarkably shrewd-looking young man, with a cloak over his shoulders, an odd sort of cap on his head, a strangely twisted staff in his hand, and a short and very crooked sword hanging by his side. He was exceedingly light and active in his figure, like a person much accustomed to gymnastic exercises, and well able to leap or run.

Above all, the stranger had such a cheerful, knowing, and helpful aspect (though it was certainly a little mischievous, into the bargain), that Perseus could not help feeling his spirits grow livelier as he gazed at him. Besides, being really a courageous youth, he felt greatly

PERSEVS·ARMED·BY·THE·NYMPHS

Above: Perseus with the help of Quicksilver manages to find the favour of the nymphs who arm him for this future quest to bring back the head of Medusa to King Polydectes.

ashamed that anybody should have found him with tears in his eyes, like a timid little school-boy, when, after all, there might be no occasion for despair. So Perseus wiped his eyes, and answered the stranger pretty briskly, putting on as brave a look as he could.

"I am not so very sad," said he, "only thoughtful about an adventure that I have undertaken."

"Oho!" answered the stranger. "Well, tell me all about it, and possibly I may be of service to you. I have helped a good many young men through adventures that looked difficult enough beforehand. Perhaps you may have heard of me. I have more names than one; but the name of Quicksilver suits me as well as any other. Tell me what the trouble is, and we will talk the matter over, and see what can be done."

The stranger's words and manner put Perseus into quite a different mood from his former one. He resolved to tell Quicksilver all his difficulties, since he could not easily be worse off than he already was, and very possibly, his new friend might give him some advice that would turn out well in the end. So he let the stranger know, in few words, precisely what the case was, how that King Polydectes wanted the head of Medusa with the snaky locks as a bridal gift for the beautiful Princess Hippodamia, and how that he had undertaken to get it for him, but was afraid of being turned into stone.

"And that would be a great pity," said Quicksilver, with his mischievous smile. "You would make a very handsome marble statue, it is true, and it would be a considerable number of centuries before you crumbled away; but, on the whole, one would rather be a young man for a few years, than a stone image for a great many."

"Oh, far rather!" exclaimed Perseus, with the tears again standing in his eyes. "And, besides, what would my dear mother do, if her beloved son were turned into a stone?"

"Well, well, let us hope that the affair will not turn out so very badly," replied Quicksilver, in an encouraging tone. "I am the very person to help you, if anybody can. My sister and myself will do our utmost to bring you safe through the adventure, ugly as it now looks."

"Your sister?" repeated Perseus.

"Yes, my sister," said the stranger. "She is very wise, I promise you; and as for myself, I generally have all my wits about me, such as they are. If you show yourself bold and cautious, and follow our advice, you need not fear being a stone image yet awhile. But, first of all, you must polish your shield, till you can see your face in it as distinctly as in a mirror."

This seemed to Perseus rather an odd beginning of the adventure; for he thought it of far more consequence that the shield should be strong enough to defend him from the Gorgon's brazen claws, than that it should be bright enough to show him the reflection of his face. However, concluding that Quicksilver knew better than himself, he immediately set to work, and scrubbed the shield with so much diligence and good-will, that it very quickly shone like the moon at harvest-time. Quicksilver looked at it with a smile, and nodded his approbation. Then, taking off his own short and crooked sword, he girded it about Perseus, instead of the one which he had before worn.

"No sword but mine will answer your purpose," observed he; "the blade has a most excellent temper, and will cut through iron and brass as easily as through the slenderest twig. And now

we will set out. The next thing is to find the Three Gray Women, who will tell us where to find the Nymphs."

"The Three Gray Women!" cried Perseus, to whom this seemed only a new difficulty in the path of his adventure; "pray who may the Three Gray Women be? I never heard of them before."

"They are three very strange old ladies," said Quicksilver, laughing. "They have but one eye among them, and only one tooth. Moreover, you must find them out by starlight, or in the dusk of the evening; for they never show themselves by the light either of the sun or moon."

"But," said Perseus, "why should I waste my time with these Three Gray Women? Would it not be better to set out at once in search of the terrible Gorgons?"

"No, no," answered his friend. "There are other things to be done, before you can find your way to the Gorgons. There is nothing for it but to hunt up these old ladies; and when we meet with them, you may be sure that the Gorgons are not a great way off. Come, let us be stirring!"

Perseus, by this time, felt so much confidence in his companion's sagacity, that he made no more objections, and professed himself ready to begin the adventure immediately. They accordingly set out, and walked at a pretty brisk pace; so brisk, indeed, that Perseus found it rather difficult to keep up with his nimble friend Quicksilver. To say the truth, he had a singular idea that Quicksilver was furnished with a pair of winged shoes, which, of course, helped him along marvelously. And then, too, when Perseus looked sideways at him, out of the corner of his eye, he seemed to see wings on the side of his head; although, if he turned a full gaze, there were no such things to be perceived, but only an odd kind of cap. But, at all events, the twisted staff was evidently a great convenience to Quicksilver, and enabled him to proceed so fast, that Perseus, though a remarkably active young man, began to be out of breath.

"Here!" cried Quicksilver, at last—for he knew well enough, rogue that he was, how hard Perseus found it to keep pace with him—"take you the staff, for you need it a great deal more than I. Are there no better walkers than yourself in the island of Seriphus?"

"I could walk pretty well," said Perseus, glancing slyly at his companion's feet, "If I had only a pair of winged shoes."

"We must see about getting you a pair," answered Quicksilver.

But the staff helped Perseus along so bravely, that he no longer felt the slightest weariness. In fact, the stick seemed to be alive in his hand, and to lend some of its life to Perseus. He and Quicksilver now walked onward at their ease, talking very sociably together; and Quicksilver told so many pleasant stories about his former adventures, and how well his wits had served him on various occasions, that Perseus began to think him a very wonderful person. He evidently knew the world; and nobody is so charming to a young man as a friend who has that kind of knowledge. Perseus listened the more eagerly, in the hope of brightening his own wits by what he heard.

At last, he happened to recollect that Quicksilver had spoken of a sister, who was to lend her assistance in the adventure which they were now bound upon.

"Where is she?" he inquired. "Shall we not meet her soon?"

"All at the proper time," said his companion. "But this sister of mine, you must understand,

is quite a different sort of character from myself. She is very grave and prudent, seldom smiles, never laughs, and makes it a rule not to utter a word unless she has something particularly profound to say. Neither will she listen to any but the wisest conversation."

"Dear me!" ejaculated Perseus; "I shall be afraid to say a syllable."

"She is a very accomplished person, I assure you," continued Quicksilver, "and has all the arts and sciences at her fingers' ends. In short, she is so immoderately wise, that many people call her wisdom personified. But, to tell you the truth, she has hardly vivacity enough for my taste; and I think you would scarcely find her so pleasant a traveling companion as myself. She has her good points, nevertheless; and you will find the benefit of them, in your encounter with the Gorgons."

By this time it had grown quite dusk. They were now come to a very wild and desert place, overgrown with shaggy bushes, and so silent and solitary that nobody seemed ever to have dwelt or journeyed there.

All was waste and desolate, in the gray twilight, which grew every moment more obscure. Perseus looked about him, rather disconsolately, and asked Quicksilver whether they had a great deal farther to go.

"Hist! hist!" whispered his companion. "Make no noise! This is just the time and place to meet the Three Gray Women. Be careful that they do not see you before you see them; for, though they have but a single eye among the three, it is as sharp-sighted as half a dozen common eyes."

"But what must I do," asked Perseus, "when we meet them?"

Quicksilver explained to Perseus how the Three Gray Women managed with their one eye. They were in the habit, it seems, of changing it from one to another, as if it had been a pair of spectacles, or—which would have suited them better—a quizzing-glass. When one of the three had kept the eye a certain time, she took it out of the socket and passed it to one of her sisters, whose turn it might happen to be, and who immediately clapped it into her own head, and enjoyed a peep at the visible world. Thus it will easily be understood that only one of the Three Gray Women could see, while the other two were in utter darkness; and, moreover, at the instant when the eye was passing from hand to hand, neither of the poor old ladies was able to see a wink. I have heard of a great many strange things, in my day, and have witnessed not a few; but none, it seems to me, that can compare with the oddity of these Three Gray Women, all peeping through a single eye.

So thought Perseus, likewise, and was so astonished that he almost fancied his companion was joking with him, and that there were no such old women in the world.

"You will soon find whether I tell the truth or no," observed Quicksilver. "Hark! hush! hist! hist! There they come, now!"

Perseus looked earnestly through the dusk of the evening, and there, sure enough, at no great distance off, he descried the Three Gray Women. The light being so faint, he could not well make out what sort of figures they were; only he discovered that they had long gray hair; and, as they came nearer, he saw that two of them had but the empty socket of an eye,

PERSEVS · & · THE · GRAIÆ

in the middle of their foreheads. But, in the middle of the third sister's forehead, there was a very large, bright, and piercing eye, which sparkled like a great diamond in a ring; and so penetrating did it seem to be, that Perseus could not help thinking it must possess the gift of seeing in the darkest midnight just as perfectly as at noonday. The sight of three persons' eyes was melted and collected into that single one.

Thus the three old dames got along about as comfortably, upon the whole, as if they could all see at once. She who chanced to have the eye in her forehead led the other two by the hands, peeping sharply about her, all the while; insomuch that Perseus dreaded lest she should see right through the thick clump of bushes behind which he and Quicksilver had hidden themselves. My stars! it was positively terrible to be within reach of so very sharp an eye!

But, before they reached the clump of bushes, one of the Three Gray Women spoke.

"Sister! Sister Scarecrow!" cried she, "you have had the eye long enough. It is my turn now!"

"Let me keep it a moment longer, Sister Nightmare," answered Scarecrow. "I thought I had a glimpse of something behind that thick bush."

"Well, and what of that?" retorted Nightmare, peevishly. "Can't I see into a thick bush as easily as yourself? The eye is mine as well as yours; and I know the use of it as well as you, or may be a little better. I insist upon taking a peep immediately!"

But here the third sister, whose name was Shakejoint, began to complain, and said that it was her turn to have the eye, and that Scarecrow and Nightmare wanted to keep it all to themselves. To end the dispute, old Dame Scarecrow took the eye out of her forehead, and held it forth in her hand.

"Take it, one of you," cried she, "and quit this foolish quarrelling. For my part, I shall be glad of a little thick darkness. Take it quickly, however, or I must clap it into my own head again!"

Accordingly, both Nightmare and Shakejoint put out their hands, groping eagerly to snatch the eye out of the hand of Scarecrow. But, being both alike blind, they could not easily find where Scarecrow's hand was; and Scarecrow, being now just as much in the dark as Shakejoint and Nightmare, could not at once meet either of their hands, in order to put the eye into it. Thus (as you will see, with half an eye, my wise little auditors), these good old dames had fallen into a strange perplexity. For, though the eye shone and glistened like a star, as Scarecrow held it out, yet the Gray Women caught not the least glimpse of its light, and were all three in utter darkness, from too impatient a desire to see.

Quicksilver was so much tickled at beholding Shakejoint and Nightmare both groping for the eye, and each finding fault with Scarecrow and one another, that he could scarcely help laughing aloud.

"Now is your time!" he whispered to Perseus.

"Quick, quick! before they can clap the eye into either of their heads. Rush out upon the old ladies, and snatch it from Scarecrow's hand!"

Left: Perseus steals the eye of the Three Gray Women forcing them to reveal where he can find the nymphs who will help him in his quest for Medusa's head.

In an instant, while the Three Gray Women were still scolding each other, Perseus leaped from behind the clump of bushes,

and made himself master of the prize. The marvelous eye, as he held it in his hand, shone very brightly, and seemed to look up into his face with a knowing air, and an expression as if it would have winked, had it been provided with a pair of eyelids for that purpose. But the Gray Women knew nothing of what had happened; and, each supposing that one of her sisters was in possession of the eye, they began their quarrel anew. At last, as Perseus did not wish to put these respectable dames to greater inconvenience than was really necessary, he thought it right to explain the matter.

"My good ladies," said he, "pray do not be angry with one another. If anybody is in fault, it is myself; for I have the honor to hold your very brilliant and excellent eye in my own hand!"

"You! you have our eye! And who are you?" screamed the Three Gray Women, all in a breath; for they were terribly frightened, of course, at hearing a strange voice, and discovering that their eyesight had got into the hands of they could not guess whom. "Oh, what shall we do, sisters? what shall we do? We are all in the dark! Give us our eye! Give us our one, precious, solitary eye! You have two of your own! Give us our eye!"

"Tell them," whispered Quicksilver to Perseus, "that they shall have back the eye as soon as they direct you where to find the Nymphs who have the flying slippers, the magic wallet, and the helmet of darkness."

"My dear, good, admirable old ladies," said Perseus, addressing the Gray Women, "there is no occasion for putting yourselves into such a fright. I am by no means a bad young man. You shall have back your eye, safe and sound, and as bright as ever, the moment you tell me where to find the Nymphs."

"The Nymphs! Goodness me! sisters, what Nymphs does he mean?" screamed Scarecrow. "There are a great many Nymphs, people say; some that go a hunting in the woods, and some that live inside of trees, and some that have a comfortable home in fountains of water. We know nothing at all about them. We are three unfortunate old souls, that go wandering about in the dusk, and never had but one eye amongst us, and that one you have stolen away. Oh, give it back, good stranger!—whoever you are, give it back!"

All this while the Three Gray Women were groping with their outstretched hands, and trying their utmost to get hold of Perseus. But he took good care to keep out of their reach.

"My respectable dames," said he,—for his mother had taught him always to use the greatest civility,—"I hold your eye fast in my hand, and shall keep it safely for you, until you please to tell me where to find these Nymphs. The Nymphs, I mean, who keep the enchanted wallet, the flying slippers, and the—what is it?—the helmet of invisibility."

"Mercy on us, sisters! what is the young man talking about?" exclaimed Scarecrow, Nightmare, and Shakejoint, one to another, with great appearance of astonishment. "A pair of flying slippers, quoth he! His heels would quickly fly higher than his head, if he were silly enough to put them on. And a helmet of invisibility! How could a helmet make him invisible, unless it were big enough for him to hide under it? And an enchanted wallet! What sort of a contrivance may that be, I wonder? No, no, good stranger! we can

tell you nothing of these marvelous things. You have two eyes of your own, and we have but a single one amongst us three. You can find out such wonders better than three blind old creatures, like us."

Perseus, hearing them talk in this way, began really to think that the Gray Women knew nothing of the matter; and, as it grieved him to have put them to so much trouble, he was just on the point of restoring their eye and asking pardon for his rudeness in snatching it away. But Quicksilver caught his hand.

"Don't let them make a fool of you!" said he. "These Three Gray Women are the only persons in the world that can tell you where to find the Nymphs; and, unless you get that information, you will never succeed in cutting off the head of Medusa with the snaky locks. Keep fast hold of the eye, and all will go well."

As it turned out, Quicksilver was in the right. There are but few things that people prize so much as they do their eyesight; and the Gray Women valued their single eye as highly as if it had been half a dozen, which was the number they ought to have had.

Finding that there was no other way of recovering it, they at last told Perseus what he wanted to know. No sooner had they done so, than he immediately, and with the utmost respect, clapped the eye into the vacant socket in one of their foreheads, thanked them for their kindness, and bade them farewell. Before the young man was out of hearing, however, they had got into a new dispute, because he happened to have given the eye to Scarecrow, who had already taken her turn of it when their trouble with Perseus commenced.

It is greatly to be feared that the Three Gray Women were very much in the habit of disturbing their mutual harmony by bickerings of this sort; which was the more pity, as they could not conveniently do without one another, and were evidently intended to be inseparable companions. As a general rule, I would advise all people, whether sisters or brothers, old or young, who chance to have but one eye amongst them, to cultivate forbearance, and not all insist upon peeping through it at once.

Quicksilver and Perseus, in the mean time, were making the best of their way in quest of the Nymphs. The old dames had given them such particular directions, that they were not long in finding them out.

They proved to be very different persons from Nightmare, Shakejoint, and Scarecrow; for, instead of being old, they were young and beautiful; and instead of one eye amongst the sisterhood, each Nymph had two exceedingly bright eyes of her own, with which she looked very kindly at Perseus. They seemed to be acquainted with Quicksilver; and, when he told them the adventure which Perseus had undertaken, they made no difficulty about giving him the valuable articles that were in their custody. In the first place, they brought out what appeared to be a small purse, made of deer skin, and curiously embroidered, and bade him be sure and keep it safe. This was the magic wallet. The Nymphs next produced a pair of shoes, or slippers, or sandals, with a nice little pair of wings at the heel of each.

"Put them on, Perseus," said Quicksilver. "You will find yourself as light-heeled as you can desire for the remainder of our journey."

So Perseus proceeded to put one of the slippers on, while he laid the other on the ground by his side. Unexpectedly, however, this other slipper spread its wings, fluttered up off the ground, and would probably have flown away, if Quicksilver had not made a leap, and luckily caught it in the air.

"Be more careful," said he, as he gave it back to Perseus. "It would frighten the birds, up aloft, if they should see a flying slipper amongst them."

When Perseus had got on both of these wonderful slippers, he was altogether too buoyant to tread on earth. Making a step or two, lo and behold! upward he popped into the air, high above the heads of Quicksilver and the Nymphs, and found it very difficult to clamber down again. Winged slippers, and all such high-flying contrivances, are seldom quite easy to manage until one grows a little accustomed to them.

Quicksilver laughed at his companion's involuntary activity, and told him that he must not be in so desperate a hurry, but must wait for the invisible helmet.

The good-natured Nymphs had the helmet, with its dark tuft of waving plumes, all in readiness to put upon his head. And now there happened about as wonderful an incident as anything that I have yet told you. The instant before the helmet was put on, there stood Perseus, a beautiful young man, with golden ringlets and rosy cheeks, the crooked sword by his side, and the brightly polished shield upon his arm,—a figure that seemed all made up of courage, sprightliness, and glorious light. But when the helmet had descended over his white brow, there was no longer any Perseus to be seen! Nothing but empty air! Even the helmet, that covered him with its invisibility, had vanished!

"Where are you, Perseus?" asked Quicksilver.

"Why, here, to be sure!" answered Perseus, very quietly, although his voice seemed to come out of the transparent atmosphere. "Just where I was a moment ago. Don't you see me?"

"No, indeed!" answered his friend. "You are hidden under the helmet. But, if I cannot see you, neither can the Gorgons. Follow me, therefore, and we will try your dexterity in using the winged slippers."

With these words, Quicksilver's cap spread its wings, as if his head were about to fly away from his shoulders; but his whole figure rose lightly into the air, and Perseus followed. By the time they had ascended a few hundred feet, the young man began to feel what a delightful thing it was to leave the dull earth so far beneath him, and to be able to flit about like a bird.

It was now deep night. Perseus looked upward, and saw the round, bright, silvery moon, and thought that he should desire nothing better than to soar up thither, and spend his life there. Then he looked downward again, and saw the earth, with its seas and lakes, and the silver courses of its rivers, and its snowy mountain-peaks, and the breadth of its fields, and the dark cluster of its woods, and its cities of white marble; and, with the moonshine sleeping over the whole scene, it was as beautiful as the moon or any star could be. And, among other objects, he saw the island of Seriphus, where his dear mother was.

Sometimes he and Quicksilver approached a cloud, that, at a distance, looked as if it were made of fleecy silver; although, when they plunged into it, they found themselves chilled and

moistened with gray mist. So swift was their flight, however, that, in an instant, they emerged from the cloud into the moonlight again. Once, a high-soaring eagle flew right against the invisible Perseus. The bravest sights were the meteors, that gleamed suddenly out, as if a bonfire had been kindled in the sky, and made the moonshine pale for as much as a hundred miles around them.

As the two companions flew onward, Perseus fancied that he could hear the rustle of a garment close by his side; and it was on the side opposite to the one where he beheld Quicksilver, yet only Quicksilver was visible.

"Whose garment is this," inquired Perseus, "that keeps rustling close beside me in the breeze?"

"Oh, it is my sister's!" answered Quicksilver.

"She is coming along with us, as I told you she would. We could do nothing without the help of my sister. You have no idea how wise she is. She has such eyes, too! Why, she can see you, at this moment, just as distinctly as if you were not invisible; and I'll venture to say, she will be the first to discover the Gorgons."

By this time, in their swift voyage through the air, they had come within sight of the great ocean, and were soon flying over it. Far beneath them, the waves tossed themselves tumultuously in mid-sea, or rolled a white surf-line upon the long beaches, or foamed against the rocky cliffs, with a roar that was thunderous, in the lower world; although it became a gentle murmur, like the voice of a baby half asleep, before it reached the ears of Perseus. Just then a voice spoke in the air close by him. It seemed to be a woman's voice, and was melodious, though not exactly what might be called sweet, but grave and mild.

"Perseus," said the voice, "there are the Gorgons."

"Where?" exclaimed Perseus. "I cannot see them."

"On the shore of that island beneath you," replied the voice. "A pebble, dropped from your hand, would strike in the midst of them."

"I told you she would be the first to discover them," said Quicksilver to Perseus. "And— there they are!"

Straight downward, two or three thousand feet below him, Perseus perceived a small island, with the sea breaking into white foam all around its rocky shore, except on one side, where there was a beach of snowy sand. He descended towards it, and, looking earnestly at a cluster or heap of brightness, at the foot of a precipice of black rocks, behold, there were the terrible Gorgons! They lay fast asleep, soothed by the thunder of the sea; for it required a tumult that would have deafened everybody else to lull such fierce creatures into slumber. The moonlight glistened on their steely scales, and on their golden wings, which drooped idly over the sand. Their brazen claws, horrible to look at, were thrust out, and clutched the wave-beaten fragments of rock, while the sleeping Gorgons dreamed of tearing some poor mortal all to pieces. The snakes that served them instead of hair seemed likewise to be asleep; although, now and then, one would writhe, and lift its head, and thrust out its forked tongue, emitting a drowsy hiss, and then let itself subside among its sister snakes.

The Gorgons were more like an awful, gigantic kind of insect,—immense, golden-winged beetles, or dragonflies, or things of that sort,—at once ugly and beautiful,—than like anything else; only that they were a thousand and a million times as big. And, with all this, there was something partly human about them, too. Luckily for Perseus, their faces were completely hidden from him by the posture in which they lay; for, had he but looked one instant at them, he would have fallen heavily out of the air, an image of senseless stone.

"Now," whispered Quicksilver, as he hovered by the side of Perseus,—"now is your time to do the deed! Be quick; for, if one of the Gorgons should awake, you are too late!"

"Which shall I strike at?" asked Perseus, drawing his sword and descending a little lower. "They all three look alike. All three have snaky locks. Which of the three is Medusa?"

It must be understood that Medusa was the only one of these dragon-monsters whose head Perseus could possibly cut off. As for the other two, let him have the sharpest sword that ever was forged, and he might have hacked away by the hour together, without doing them the least harm.

"Be cautious," said the calm voice which had before spoken to him. "One of the Gorgons is stirring in her sleep, and is just about to turn over. That is Medusa. Do not look at her! The sight would turn you to stone! Look at the reflection of her face and figure in the bright mirror of your shield."

Perseus now understood Quicksilver's motive for so earnestly exhorting him to polish his shield. In its surface he could safely look at the reflection of the Gorgon's face. And there it was—that terrible countenance—mirrored in the brightness of the shield, with the moonlight falling over it, and displaying all its horror. The snakes, whose venomous natures could not altogether sleep, kept twisting themselves over the forehead. It was the fiercest and most horrible face that ever was seen or imagined, and yet with a strange, fearful, and savage kind of beauty in it. The eyes were closed, and the Gorgon was still in a deep slumber; but there was an unquiet expression disturbing her features, as if the monster was troubled with an ugly dream. She gnashed her white tusks, and dug into the sand with her brazen claws.

The snakes, too, seemed to feel Medusa's dream, and to be made more restless by it. They twined themselves into tumultuous knots, writhed fiercely, and uplifted a hundred hissing heads, without opening their eyes.

"Now, now!" whispered Quicksilver, who was growing impatient. "Make a dash at the monster!"

"But be calm," said the grave, melodious voice, at the young man's side. "Look in your shield, as you fly downward, and take care that you do not miss your first stroke."

Perseus flew cautiously downward, still keeping his eyes on Medusa's face, as reflected in his shield. The nearer he came, the more terrible did the snaky visage and metallic body of the monster grow. At last, when he found himself hovering over her within arm's length, Perseus uplifted his sword, while, at the same instant, each separate snake upon the Gorgon's head stretched threateningly upward, and Medusa unclosed her eyes.

Right: Perseus cuts off the head of the sleeping gorgon Medusa by looking at her through the reflection in his polished shield.

PERSEVS & THE GORGONS

But she awoke too late. The sword was sharp; the stroke fell like a lightning-flash; and the head of the wicked Medusa tumbled from her body!

"Admirably done!" cried Quicksilver. "Make haste, and clap the head into your magic wallet."

To the astonishment of Perseus, the small, embroidered wallet, which he had hung about his neck, and which had hitherto been no bigger than a purse, grew all at once large enough to contain Medusa's head. As quick as thought, he snatched it up, with the snakes still writhing upon it, and thrust it in.

"Your task is done," said the calm voice. "Now fly; for the other Gorgons will do their utmost to take vengeance for Medusa's death."

It was, indeed, necessary to take flight; for Perseus had not done the deed so quietly but that the clash of his sword, and the hissing of the snakes, and the thump of Medusa's head as it tumbled upon the sea-beaten sand, awoke the other two monsters. There they sat, for an instant, sleepily rubbing their eyes with their brazen fingers, while all the snakes on their heads reared themselves on end with surprise, and with venomous malice against they knew not what. But when the Gorgons saw the scaly carcass of Medusa, headless, and her golden wings all ruffled, and half spread out on the sand, it was really awful to hear what yells and screeches they set up. And then the snakes! They sent forth a hundred-fold hiss, with one consent, and Medusa's snakes answered them out of the magic wallet.

No sooner were the Gorgons broad awake than they hurtled upward into the air, brandishing their brass talons, gnashing their horrible tusks, and flapping their huge wings so wildly, that some of the golden feathers were shaken out, and floated down upon the shore. And there, perhaps, those very feathers lie scattered, till this day. Up rose the Gorgons, as I tell you, staring horribly about, in hopes of turning somebody to stone.

Had Perseus looked them in the face, or had he fallen into their clutches, his poor mother would never have kissed her boy again! But he took good care to turn his eyes another way; and, as he wore the helmet of invisibility, the Gorgon's knew not in what direction to follow him; nor did he fail to make the best use of the winged slippers, by soaring upward a perpendicular mile or so. At that height, when the screams of those abominable creatures sounded faintly beneath him, he made a straight course for the island of Seriphus, in order to carry Medusa's head to King Polydectes.

I have no time to tell you of several marvelous things that befell Perseus, on his way homeward; such as his killing a hideous sea-monster, just as it was on the point of devouring a beautiful maiden; nor how he changed an enormous giant into a mountain of stone, merely by showing him the head of the Gorgon.

If you doubt this latter story, you may make a voyage to Africa, some day or other, and see the very mountain, which is still known by the ancient giant's name.

Finally, our brave Perseus arrived at the island, where he expected to see his dear mother. But, during his absence, the wicked king had treated Danaë so very ill that she was compelled to make her escape, and had taken refuge in a temple, where some good old priests were extremely kind to her. These praise-worthy priests, and the kind-hearted fisherman, who had

first shown hospitality to Danaë and little Perseus when he found them afloat in the chest, seem to have been the only persons on the island who cared about doing right. All the rest of the people, as well as King Polydectes himself, were remarkably ill-behaved, and deserved no better destiny than that which was now to happen.

Not finding his mother at home, Perseus went straight to the palace, and was immediately ushered into the presence of the king. Polydectes was by no means rejoiced to see him; for he had felt almost certain, in his own evil mind, that the Gorgons would have torn the poor young man to pieces, and have eaten him up, out of the way. However, seeing him safely returned, he put the best face he could upon the matter and asked Perseus how he had succeeded.

"Have you performed your promise?" inquired he. "Have you brought me the head of Medusa with the snaky locks? If not, young man, it will cost you dear; for I must have a bridal present for the beautiful Princess Hippodamia, and there is nothing else that she would admire so much."

"Yes, please your Majesty," answered Perseus, in a quiet way, as if it were no very wonderful deed for such a young man as he to perform. "I have brought you the Gorgon's head, snaky locks and all!"

"Indeed! Pray let me see it," quoth King Polydectes. "It must be a very curious spectacle, if all that travelers tell about it be true!"

"Your Majesty is in the right," replied Perseus. "It is really an object that will be pretty certain to fix the regards of all who look at it. And, if your Majesty think fit, I would suggest that a holiday be proclaimed, and that all your Majesty's subjects be summoned to behold this wonderful curiosity. Few of them, I imagine, have seen a Gorgon's head before, and perhaps never may again!"

The king well knew that his subjects were an idle set of reprobates, and very fond of sight-seeing, as idle persons usually are. So he took the young man's advice, and sent out heralds and messengers, in all directions, to blow the trumpet at the street-corners, and in the market-places, and wherever two roads met, and summon everybody to court. Thither, accordingly, came a great multitude of good-for-nothing vagabonds, all of whom, out of pure love of mischief, would have been glad if Perseus had met with some ill-hap in his encounter with the Gorgons. If there were any better people in the island (as I really hope there may have been, although the story tells nothing about any such), they stayed quietly at home, minding their business, and taking care of their little children. Most of the inhabitants, at all events, ran as fast as they could to the palace, and shoved, and pushed, and elbowed one another, in their eagerness to get near a balcony, on which Perseus showed himself, holding the embroidered wallet in his hand.

On a platform, within full view of the balcony, sat the mighty King Polydectes, amid his evil counselors, and with his flattering courtiers in a semicircle round about him. Monarch, counselors, courtiers, and subjects, all gazed eagerly towards Perseus.

"Show us the head! Show us the head!" shouted the people; and there was a fierceness in their cry as if they would tear Perseus to pieces, unless he should satisfy them with what he had to show. "Show us the head of Medusa with the snaky locks!"

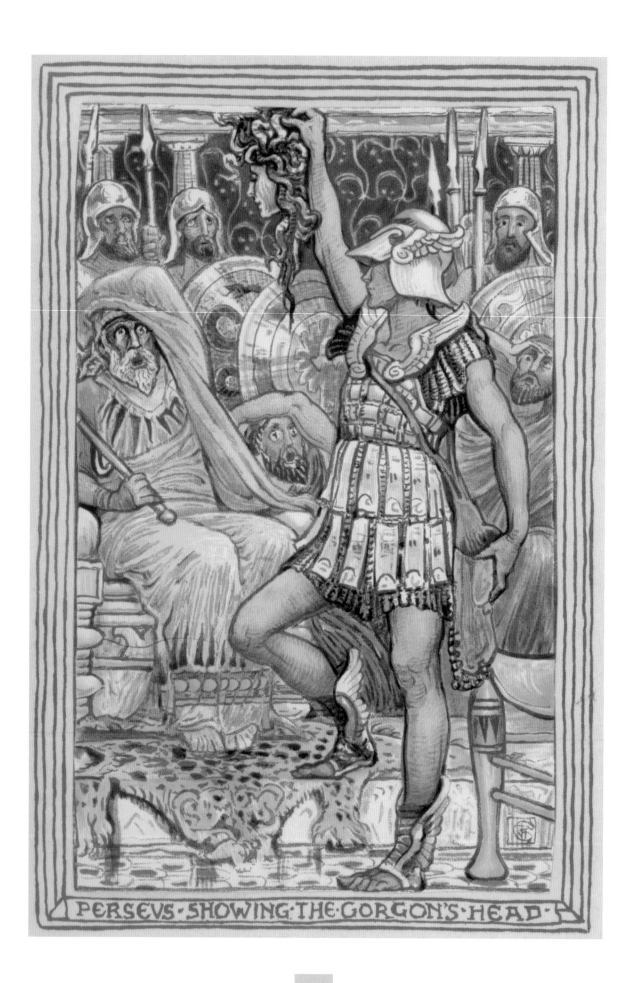

PERSEVS · SHOWING · THE · GORGON'S · HEAD ·

A feeling of sorrow and pity came over the youthful Perseus.

"O King Polydectes," cried he, "and ye many people, I am very loath to show you the Gorgon's head!"

"Ah, the villain and coward!" yelled the people, more fiercely than before. "He is making game of us! He has no Gorgon's head! Show us the head, if you have it, or we will take your own head for a football!"

The evil counselors whispered bad advice in the king's ear; the courtiers murmured, with one consent, that Perseus had shown disrespect to their royal lord and master; and the great King Polydectes himself waved his hand, and ordered him, with the stern, deep voice of authority, on his peril, to produce the head.

"Show me the Gorgon's head, or I will cut off your own!"

And Perseus sighed.

"This instant," repeated Polydectes, "or you die!"

"Behold it, then!" cried Perseus, in a voice like the blast of a trumpet.

And, suddenly holding up the head, not an eyelid had time to wink before the wicked King Polydectes, his evil counselors, and all his fierce subjects were no longer anything but the mere images of a monarch and his people. They were all fixed, forever, in the look and attitude of that moment! At the first glimpse of the terrible head of Medusa, they whitened into marble! And Perseus thrust the head back into his wallet, and went to tell his dear mother that she need no longer be afraid of the wicked King Polydectes.

Left: Perseus shows the head of the gorgon Medusa to the evil King Polydectes turning him and all his wicked counselors to stone.

EPIMETHEUS
AND PANDORA

Long, long ago, when this old world was in its tender infancy, there was a child, named Epimetheus, who never had either father or mother; and that he might not be lonely, another child, fatherless and motherless like himself, was sent from a far country to live with him, and be his playfellow and helpmate. Her name was Pandora.

The first thing that Pandora saw, when she entered the cottage where Epimetheus dwelt, was a great box. And almost the first question which she put to him, after crossing the threshold, was this: "Epimetheus, what have you in that box?"

"My dear little Pandora," answered Epimetheus, "that is a secret, and you must be kind enough not to ask any questions about it. The box was left here to be kept safely, and I do not myself know what it contains."

"But who gave it to you?" asked Pandora. "And where did it come from?"

"That is a secret, too," replied Epimetheus.

"How provoking!" exclaimed Pandora, pouting her lip. "I wish the great ugly box were out of the way!"

"Oh, come, don't think of it any more!" cried Epimetheus. "Let us run out of doors, and have some nice play with the other children."

It is thousands of years since Epimetheus and Pandora were alive; and the world, nowadays, is a very different sort of thing from what it was in their time. Then, everybody was a child. There needed no fathers and mothers to take care of the children, because there was no danger or trouble of any kind, and no clothes to be mended, and there was always plenty to eat and drink. Whenever a child wanted his dinner, he found it growing on a tree; and if he looked at the tree in the morning, he could see the expanding blossom of that night's supper; or, at eventide, he saw the tender bud of tomorrow's breakfast. It was a very pleasant life indeed. No labor to be done, no tasks to be studied; nothing but sports and dances, and sweet voices of children talking, or caroling like birds, or gushing out in merry laughter throughout the livelong day.

Above: Pandora's curiosity about what is contained in the box becomes too much for her and she opens it unleashing all that lies within.

What was most wonderful of all, the children never quarreled among themselves; neither had they any crying fits; nor, since time first began, had a single one of these little mortals ever gone apart into a corner and sulked. Oh, what a good time was that to be alive in? The truth is, those ugly winged little monsters, called Troubles, which are now almost as numerous as mosquitoes, had never yet been seen on the earth. It is probable that the very greatest disquietude which a child had ever experienced was Pandora's vexation at not being able to discover the secret of the mysterious box.

This was at first only the faint shadow of a Trouble; but every day it grew more and more substantial, until before a great while the cottage of Epimetheus and Pandora was less sunshiny than those of the other children.

"Whence can the box have come?" Pandora continually kept saying to herself and to Epimetheus. "And what on earth can be inside of it?"

"Always talking about this box!" said Epimetheus at last; for he had grown extremely tired of the subject. "I wish, dear Pandora, you would try to talk of something else. Come, let us go and gather some ripe figs, and eat them under the trees for our supper. And I know a vine that has the sweetest and juiciest grapes you ever tasted."

"Always talking about grapes and figs!" cried Pandora pettishly.

"Well, then," said Epimetheus, who was a good-tempered child, "let us run out and have a merry time with our playmates."

"I am tired of merry times, and don't care if I never have any more!" answered our pettish little Pandora. "And besides, I never do have any. This ugly box! I am so taken up with thinking about it all the time. I insist upon you telling me what is inside of it."

"As I have already said, fifty times over, I do not know!" replied Epimetheus, getting a little vexed. "How, then, can I tell you what is inside?"

"You might open it," said Pandora, looking sideways at Epimetheus, "and then we could see for ourselves."

"Pandora, what are you thinking of?" exclaimed Epimetheus.

And his face expressed so much horror at the idea of looking into a box which had been confided to him on the condition of his never opening it, that Pandora thought it best not to suggest it any more. Still, she could not help thinking and talking about the box.

"At least," said she, "you can tell me how it came here."

"It was left at the door," replied Epimetheus, "just before you came, by a person who looked very smiling and intelligent, and who could hardly forbear laughing as he put it down. He was dressed in an odd kind of a cloak, and had on a cap that seemed to be made partly of feathers, so that it looked almost as if it had wings."

"What sort of a staff had he?" asked Pandora.

"Oh, the most curious staff you ever saw!" cried Epimetheus. "It was like two serpents twisting around a stick, and was carved so naturally that I, at first, thought the serpents were alive."

"I know him," said Pandora thoughtfully. "Nobody else has such a staff. It was Quicksilver; and he brought me hither, as well as the box. No doubt he intended it for me; and most

probably it contains pretty dresses for me to wear, or toys for you and me to play with, or something very nice for us both to eat!"

"Perhaps so," answered Epimetheus, turning away. "But until Quicksilver comes back and tells us so, we have neither of us any right to lift the lid of the box."

"What a dull boy it is!" muttered Pandora, as Epimetheus left the cottage. "I do wish he had a little more enterprise!"

For the first time since her arrival, Epimetheus had gone out without asking Pandora to accompany him. He was tired to death of hearing about the box, and heartily wished that Quicksilver, or whatever was the messenger's name, had left it at some other child's door, where Pandora would never have set eyes on it. So perseveringly as she did babble about this one thing! The box, the box, and nothing but the box! It seemed as if the box were bewitched, and as if the cottage were not big enough to hold it, without Pandora's continually stumbling over it and making Epimetheus stumble over it likewise, and bruising all four of their shins.

Well, it was really hard that poor Epimetheus should have a box in his ears from morning to night, especially as the little people of the earth were so unaccustomed to vexations, in those happy days, that they knew not how to deal with them. Thus a small vexation made as much disturbance then as a far bigger one would in our own times.

After Epimetheus was gone Pandora stood gazing at the box. She had called it ugly above a hundred times; but in spite of all that she had said against it, it was in truth a very handsome article of furniture. It was made of a beautiful kind of wood, with dark and rich veins spreading over its surface, which was so highly polished that little Pandora could see her face in it. As the child had no other looking-glass, it is odd that she did not value the box, merely on this account.

The edges and corners of the box were carved with wonderful skill. Around the margin there were figures of graceful men and women, and the prettiest children ever seen, reclining or sporting amid a profusion of flowers and foliage; and these various objects were so exquisitely represented, and were wrought together in such harmony, that flowers, foliage, and human beings seemed to combine into a wreath of mingled beauty.

But here and there, peeping forth from behind the carved foliage, Pandora once or twice fancied that she saw a face not so lovely, which stole the beauty out of all the rest. Nevertheless, on looking more closely, she could discover nothing of the kind. Some face, that was really beautiful, had been made to look ugly by her catching a sideway glimpse at it.

The most beautiful face of all was done in what is called high relief, in the center of the lid. There was nothing else save the dark, smooth richness of the polished wood, and this one face in the center, with a garland of flowers about its brow. Pandora had looked at this face a great many times, and imagined that the mouth could smile if it liked, or be grave when it chose, the same as any living mouth. The features, indeed, all wore a very lively and rather mischievous expression, which looked almost as if it needs must burst out of the carved lips and utter itself in words.

Had the mouth spoken, it would probably have been something like this:

· PANDORA · WONDERS · AT · THE · BOX ·

"Do not be afraid, Pandora! What harm can there be in opening the box? Never mind that poor, simple Epimetheus! You are wiser than he, and have ten times as much spirit. Open the box, and see if you do not find something very pretty!"

The box was fastened; not by a lock, nor by any other such contrivance, but by a very intricate knot of gold cord. There appeared to be no end to this knot, and no beginning. Never was a knot so cunningly twisted, nor with so many ins and outs, which roguishly defied the skillfullest fingers to disentangle them. And yet, by the very difficulty that there was in it, Pandora was the more tempted to examine the knot, and just see how it was made. Two or three times already she had stooped over the box, and taken the knot between her thumb and forefinger, but without positively trying to undo it.

"I really believe," said she to herself, "that I begin to see how it was done. Nay, perhaps I could tie it up again after undoing it. There could be no harm in that, surely. Even Epimetheus would not blame me for that. I need not open the box, and should not, of course, without the foolish boy's consent, even if the knot were untied."

First she tried to lift it. It was heavy; much too heavy for the slender strength of a child like Pandora. She raised one end of the box a few inches from the floor, and let it fall again with a pretty loud thump. A moment afterwards she almost fancied that she heard something stir inside of the box. She applied her ear as closely as possible and listened. Positively there did seem to be a kind of stifled murmur within. Or was it merely the singing in Pandora's ears? Or could it be the beating of her heart? The child could not quite satisfy herself whether she had heard anything or no. But, at all events, her curiosity was stronger than ever.

As she drew back her head her eyes fell upon the knot of gold cord.

"It must have been a very ingenious person who tied this knot," said Pandora to herself. "But I think I could untie it, nevertheless. I am resolved, at least, to find the two ends of the cord."

So she took the golden knot in her fingers, and pried into its intricacies as sharply as she could. Almost without intending it, or quite knowing what she was about, she was soon busily engaged in attempting to undo it. Meanwhile the bright sunshine came through the open window, as did likewise the merry voices of the children playing at a distance; and, perhaps, the voice of Epimetheus among them. Pandora stopped to listen. What a beautiful day it was! Would it not be wiser if she were to let the troublesome knot alone, and think no more about the box, but run and join her little playfellows and be happy?

All this time, however, her fingers were half unconsciously busy with the knot; and, happening to glance at the flower-wreathed face on the lid of the enchanted box, she seemed to perceive it slyly grinning at her.

"That face looks very mischievous," thought Pandora. "I wonder whether it smiles because I am doing wrong! I have the greatest mind in the world to run away!"

Left: Illustration by Walter Crane in Hawthorne's 1892 *A Wonder Book For Girls And Boys* shows Pandora and Epimetheus discussing the intriguing chest.

But just then, by the merest accident, she gave the knot a kind of a twist, which produced a wonderful result. The gold cord untwined itself as if by magic, and left the box without a fastening.

"This is the strangest thing I ever knew!" said Pandora. "What will Epimetheus say? And how can I possibly tie it up again?"

She made one or two attempts to restore the knot, but soon found it quite beyond her skill. It had disentangled itself so suddenly that she could not in the least remember how the strings had been doubled into one another; and when she tried to recollect the shape and appearance of the knot, it seemed to have gone entirely out of her mind. Nothing was to be done, therefore, but to let the box remain as it was until Epimetheus should come in.

"But," said Pandora, "when he finds the knot untied, he will know that I have done it. How shall I make him believe that I have not looked into the box?"

And then the thought came into her naughty little heart, that, since she would be suspected of having looked into the box, she might just as well do so at once. Oh, very naughty and very foolish Pandora! You should have thought only of doing what was right, and of leaving undone what was wrong, and not of what your playfellow Epimetheus would have said or believed. And so perhaps she might, if the enchanted face on the lid of the box had not looked so bewitchingly persuasive at her, and if she had not seemed to hear, more distinctly than before, the murmur of small voices within. She could not tell whether it was fancy or no; but there was quite a little tumult of whispers in her ear—or else it was her curiosity that whispered:

"Let us out, dear Pandora; pray let us out! We will be such nice pretty playfellows for you! Only let us out!"

"What can it be?" thought Pandora. "Is there something alive in the box? Well!—yes!—I am resolved to take just one peep! Only one peep; and then the lid shall be shut down as safely as ever! There cannot possibly be any harm in just one little peep!"

But it is now time for us to see what Epimetheus was doing.

This was the first time since his little playmate had come to dwell with him that he had attempted to enjoy any pleasure in which she did not partake. But nothing went right; nor was he nearly so happy as on other days. He could not find a sweet grape or a ripe fig (if Epimetheus had a fault, it was a little too much fondness for figs); or, if ripe at all, they were over-ripe, and so sweet as to be cloying. In short, he grew so uneasy and discontented, that the other children could not imagine what was the matter with Epimetheus. Neither did he himself know what ailed him any better than they did.

At length, discovering that, somehow or other, he put a stop to all the play, Epimetheus judged it best to go back to Pandora, who was in a humor better suited to his own. But, with a hope of giving her pleasure, he gathered some flowers, and made them into a wreath, which he meant to put upon her head. The flowers were very lovely—roses and lilies, and orange-blossoms, and a great many more, which left a trail of fragrance behind as Epimetheus carried them along; and the wreath was put together with as much skill as could reasonably be expected of a boy. The fingers of little girls, it has always appeared to me, are the fittest to twine flower-wreaths; but boys could do it in those days rather better than they can now.

Right: Pandora's obsession with discovering what is within the box consumes her days and attracts her back to the place where it is kept again and again.

PANDORA·DESIRES·TO·OPEN·THE·BOX

Meanwhile a great black cloud had been gathering in the sky for some time past, although it had not yet overspread the sun. But just as Epimetheus reached the cottage door, this cloud began to intercept the sunshine, and thus to make a sudden and sad obscurity.

He entered softly; for he meant, if possible, to steal behind Pandora and fling the wreath of flowers over her head before she should be aware of his approach. But, as it happened, there was no need of his treading so very lightly. He might have trod as heavily as he pleased without much probability of Pandora's hearing his footsteps. She was too intent upon her purpose. At the moment of his entering the cottage the naughty child had put her hand to the lid, and was on the point of opening the mysterious box. Epimetheus beheld her. If he had cried out Pandora would probably have withdrawn her hand, and the fatal mystery of the box might never have been known.

But Epimetheus himself, although he said very little about it, had his own share of curiosity to know what was inside. Perceiving that Pandora was resolved to find out the secret, he determined that his playfellow should not be the only wise person in the cottage. And if there were anything pretty or valuable in the box, he meant to take half of it to himself. Thus, after all his sage speeches to Pandora about restraining her curiosity, Epimetheus turned out to be quite as foolish, and nearly as much in fault, as she. So, whenever we blame Pandora for what happened, we must not forget to shake our heads at Epimetheus likewise.

As Pandora raised the lid the cottage grew very dark and dismal, for the black cloud had now swept quite over the sun, and seemed to have buried it alive. There had, for a little while past, been a low growling and muttering, which all at once broke into a heavy peal of thunder. But Pandora, heeding nothing of all this, lifted the lid nearly upright and looked inside. It seemed as if a sudden swarm of winged creatures brushed past her, taking flight out of the box, while, at the same instant, she heard the voice of Epimetheus, with a lamentable tone, as if he were in pain.

"Oh, I am stung!" cried he. "I am stung! Naughty Pandora! why have you opened this wicked box?"

Pandora let fall the lid, and, starting up, looked about her, to see what had befallen Epimetheus. The thunder-cloud had so darkened the room that she could not very clearly discern what was in it. But she heard a disagreeable buzzing, as if a great many huge flies, or gigantic mosquitoes, were darting about. And, as her eyes grew more accustomed to the imperfect light, she saw a crowd of ugly little shapes, with bats' wings, looking abominably spiteful, and armed with terribly long stings in their tails. It was one of these that had stung Epimetheus. Nor was it a great while before Pandora herself began to scream, in no less pain and affright than her playfellow, and making a vast deal more hubbub about it. An odious little monster had settled on her forehead, and would have stung her I know not how deeply if Epimetheus had not run and brushed it away.

Now, if you wish to know what these ugly things might be which had made their escape out of the box, I must tell you that they were the whole family of earthly Troubles. There were evil Passions; there were a great many species of Cares; there were more than a hundred and fifty Sorrows; there were Diseases, in a vast number of miserable and painful shapes; there were

more kinds of Naughtiness than it would be of any use to talk about. In short, everything that has since afflicted the souls and bodies of mankind had been shut up in the mysterious box, and given to Epimetheus and Pandora to be kept safely, in order that the happy children of the world might never be molested by them. Had they been faithful to their trust, all would have gone well. No grown person would ever have been sad, nor any child have had cause to shed a single tear, from that hour until this moment.

But—and you may see by this how a wrong act of any one mortal is a calamity to the whole world—by Pandora's lifting the lid of that miserable box, and by the fault of Epimetheus, too, in not preventing her, these Troubles have obtained a foothold among us, and do not seem very likely to be driven away in a hurry.

For it was impossible, as you will easily guess, that the two children should keep the ugly swarm in their own little cottage. On the contrary, the first thing they did was to fling open the doors and windows in hope of getting rid of them; and, sure enough, away flew the winged Troubles all abroad, and so pestered and tormented the small people everywhere about that none of them so much as smiled for many days afterwards. And, what was very singular, all the flowers and dewy blossoms on earth, not one of which had hitherto faded, now began to droop and shed their leaves, after a day or two. The children, moreover, who before seemed immortal in their childhood, now grew older, day by day, and came soon to be youths and maidens, and men and women by and by, and aged people, before they dreamed of such a thing.

Meanwhile, the naughty Pandora, and hardly less naughty Epimetheus, remained in their cottage. Both of them had been grievously stung, and were in a good deal of pain, which seemed the more intolerable to them, because it was the very first pain that had ever been felt since the world began. Besides all this, they were in exceedingly bad humor, both with themselves and with one another. In order to indulge it to the utmost, Epimetheus sat down sullenly in a corner with his back towards Pandora; while Pandora flung herself upon the floor and rested her head on the fatal and abominable box. She was crying bitterly, and sobbing as if her heart would break.

Suddenly there was a gentle tap on the inside of the lid.

"What can that be?" cried Pandora, lifting her head.

But either Epimetheus had not heard the tap, or was too much out of humor to notice it. At any rate, he made no answer.

"You are very unkind," said Pandora, sobbing anew, "not to speak to me!"

Again the tap! It sounded like the tiny knuckles of a fairy's hand, knocking lightly and playfully on the inside of the box.

"Who are you?" asked Pandora, with a little of her former curiosity. "Who are you, inside of this naughty box?"

A sweet little voice spoke from within: "Only lift the lid, and you shall see."

"No, no," answered Pandora, again beginning to sob, "I have had enough of lifting the lid! You are inside of the box, naughty creature, and there you shall stay! There are plenty of your ugly brothers and sisters already flying about the world. You need never think that I shall be so foolish as to let you out!"

She looked towards Epimetheus as she spoke, perhaps expecting that he would commend her for her wisdom. But the sullen boy only muttered that she was wise a little too late.

"Ah," said the sweet little voice again, "you had much better let me out. I am not like those naughty creatures that have stings in their tails. They are no brothers and sisters of mine, as you would see at once, if you were only to get a glimpse of me. Come, come, my pretty Pandora! I am sure you will let me out!"

And, indeed, there was a kind of cheerful witchery in the tone, that made it almost impossible to refuse anything which this little voice asked. Pandora's heart had insensibly grown lighter at every word that came from within the box. Epimetheus, too, though still in the corner, had turned half round, and seemed to be in rather better spirits than before.

"My dear Epimetheus," cried Pandora, "have you heard this little voice?"

"Yes, to be sure I have," answered he, but in no very good humor as yet. "And what of it?"

"Shall I lift the lid again?" asked Pandora.

"Just as you please," said Epimetheus. "You have done so much mischief already, that perhaps you may as well do a little more. One other Trouble, in such a swarm as you have set adrift about the world, can make no very great difference."

"You might speak a little more kindly!" murmured Pandora, wiping her eyes.

"Ah, naughty boy!" cried the little voice within the box, in an arch and laughing tone. "He knows he is longing to see me. Come, my dear Pandora, lift up the lid. I am in a great hurry to comfort you. Only let me have some fresh air, and you shall soon see that matters are not quite so dismal as you think them!"

"Epimetheus," exclaimed Pandora, "come what may, I am resolved to open the box!"

"And, as the lid seems very heavy," cried Epimetheus, running across the room, "I will help you!"

So, with one consent, the two children again lifted the lid. Out flew a sunny and smiling little personage, and hovered about the room, throwing a light wherever she went. Have you never made the sunshine dance into dark corners by reflecting it from a bit of looking-glass? Well, so looked the winged cheerfulness of this fairy-like stranger amid the gloom of the cottage. She flew to Epimetheus, and laid the least touch of her finger on the inflamed spot where the Trouble had stung him, and immediately the anguish of it was gone. Then she kissed Pandora on the forehead, and her hurt was cured likewise.

After performing these good offices, the bright stranger fluttered sportively over the children's heads, and looked so sweetly at them that they both began to think it not so very much amiss to have opened the box, since, otherwise, their cheery guest must have been kept a prisoner among those naughty imps with stings in their tails.

"Pray, who are you, beautiful creature?" inquired Pandora.

"I am to be called Hope!" answered the sunshiny figure. "And because I am such a cheery little body, I was packed into the box to make amends to the human race for that swarm of ugly Troubles, which was destined to be let loose among them. Never fear! we shall do pretty well in spite of them all."

Right: Pandora finally opens the box and the troubles within attack Epimetheus on their way out into the world.

·PANDORA·OPENS·THE·BOX·

"Your wings are colored like the rainbow!" exclaimed Pandora. "How very beautiful!"

"Yes, they are like the rainbow," said Hope, "because, glad as my nature is, I am partly made of tears as well as smiles."

"And you will stay with us," asked Epimetheus, "for ever and ever?"

"As long as you need me," said Hope, with her pleasant smile, "and that will be as long as you live in the world—I promise never to desert you. There may be times and seasons, now and then, when you will think that I have utterly vanished. But again, and again, and again, when perhaps you least dream of it, you shall see the glimmer of my wings on the ceiling of your cottage. Yes, my dear children, and I know something very good and beautiful that is to be given you, hereafter!"

"Oh, tell us," they exclaimed; "tell us what it is!"

"Do not ask me," replied Hope, putting her finger on her rosy mouth. "But do not despair, even if it should never happen while you live on this earth. Trust in my promise, for it is true."

"We do trust you!" cried Epimetheus and Pandora, both in one breath.

And so they did; and not only they, but so has everybody trusted Hope, that has since been alive. And, to tell you the truth, I cannot help being glad (though, to be sure, it was an uncommonly naughty thing for her to do)—but I cannot help being glad that our foolish Pandora peeped into the box. No doubt—no doubt—the Troubles are still flying about the world, and have increased in multitude, rather than lessened, and are a very ugly set of imps, and carry most venomous stings in their tails. I have felt them already, and expect to feel them more as I grow older. But then that lovely and lightsome figure of Hope! What in the world could we do without her? Hope spiritualizes the earth; Hope makes it always new; and, even in the earth's best and brightest aspect, Hope shows it to be only the shadow of an infinite bliss hereafter.

Right: Pandora opening the box, depicted in an 1896 painting by John William Waterhouse (1849–1917).

EUROPA AND THE BULL-GOD

Cadmus, Phoenix, and Cilix, the three sons of King Agenor, and their little sister Europa (who was a very beautiful child), were at play together near the seashore in their father's kingdom of Phoenicia. They had rambled to some distance from the palace where their parents dwelt, and were now in a verdant meadow, on one side of which lay the sea, all sparkling and dimpling in the sunshine, and murmuring gently against the beach.

The three boys were very happy gathering flowers and twining them into garlands, with which they adorned the little Europa. Seated on the grass, the child was almost hidden under an abundance of buds and blossoms, whence her rosy face peeped merrily out, and, as Cadmus said, was the prettiest of all the flowers.

Just then there came a splendid butterfly fluttering along the meadow, and Cadmus, Phoenix, and Cilix set off in pursuit of it, crying out that it was a flower with wings. Europa, who was a little wearied with playing all day long, did not chase the butterfly with her brothers, but sat still where they had left her, and closed her eyes. For a while she listened to the pleasant murmur of the sea, which was like a voice saying "Hush!" and bidding her go to sleep. But the pretty child, if she slept at all, could not have slept more than a moment, when she heard something trample on the grass not far from her, and peeping out from the heap of flowers, beheld a snow-white bull.

And whence could this bull have come? Europa and her brothers had been a long time playing in the meadow, and had seen no cattle, nor other living thing, either there or on the neighboring hills.

"Brother Cadmus!" cried Europa, starting up out of the midst of the roses and lilies. "Phoenix! Cilix! Where are you all? Help! Help! Come and drive away this bull!" But her brothers were too far off to hear, especially as the fright took away Europa's voice and hindered her from calling very loudly. So there she stood, with her pretty mouth wide open, as pale as the white lilies that were twisted among the other flowers in her garlands.

Nevertheless, it was the suddenness with which she had perceived the bull, rather than anything frightful in its appearance, that caused Europa so much alarm. On looking at him more attentively, she began to see that he was a beautiful animal, and even fancied a particularly amiable expression in his face. As for his breath—the breath of cattle, you know, is always sweet—it was as fragrant as if he had been grazing on no other food than rosebuds, or, at least, the most delicate of clover blossoms. Never before did a bull have such bright and tender eyes, and such smooth horns of ivory, as this one. And the bull ran little races, and capered sportively around the child; so that she quite forgot how big and strong he was, and, from the gentleness and playfulness of his actions, soon came to consider him as innocent a creature as a pet lamb.

Thus, frightened as she at first was, you might by and by have seen Europa stroking the bull's forehead with her small white hand, and taking the garlands off her own head to hang them on his neck and ivory horns. Then she pulled up some blades of grass, and he ate them out of her hand, not as if he were hungry, but because he wanted to be friends with the child, and took pleasure in eating what she had touched. Well, my stars! was there ever such a gentle, sweet, pretty, and amiable creature as this bull, and ever such a nice playmate for a little girl?

When the animal saw (for the bull had so much intelligence that it is really wonderful to think of), when he saw that Europa was no longer afraid of him, he grew overjoyed, and could hardly contain himself for delight. He frisked about the meadow, now here, now there, making sprightly leaps, with as little effort as a bird expends in hopping from twig to twig. Indeed, his motion was as light as if he were flying through the air, and his hoofs seemed hardly to leave their print in the grassy soil over which he trod. With his spotless hue, he resembled a snowdrift wafted along by the wind. Once he galloped so far away that Europa feared lest she might never see him again; so, setting up her childish voice, she called him back.

"Come back, pretty creature!" she cried. "Here is a nice clover blossom."

And then it was delightful to witness the gratitude of this amiable bull, and how he was so full of joy and thankfulness that he capered higher than ever. He came running and bowed his head before Europa, as if he knew her to be a king's daughter, or else recognized the important truth that a little girl is everybody's queen. And not only did the bull bend his neck, he absolutely knelt down at her feet, and made such intelligent nods, and other inviting gestures, that Europa understood what he meant just as well as if he had put it in so many words.

"Come, dear child," was what he wanted to say, "let me give you a ride on my back."

At the first thought of such a thing Europa drew back. But then she considered in her wise little head that there could be no possible harm in taking just one gallop on the back of this docile and friendly animal, who would certainly set her down the very instant she desired it. And how it would surprise her brothers to see her riding across the green meadow! And what merry times they might have, either taking turns for a gallop, or clambering on the gentle creature, all four children together, and careering round the field with shouts of laughter that would be heard as far off as King Agenor's palace!

"I think I will do it," said the child to herself.

And, indeed, why not? She cast a glance around, and caught a glimpse of Cadmus, Phoenix, and Cilix, who were still in pursuit of the butterfly, almost at the other end of the meadow. It would be the quickest way of rejoining them, to get upon the white bull's back. She came a step nearer to him, therefore; and—sociable creature that he was—he showed so much joy at this mark of her confidence, that the child could not find it in her heart to hesitate any longer. Making one bound (for this little princess was as active as a squirrel), there sat Europa on the beautiful bull, holding an ivory horn in each hand lest she should fall off.

"Softly, pretty bull, softly!" she said, rather frightened at what she had done. "Do not gallop too fast."

Having got the child on his back, the animal gave a leap into the air, and came down so like a feather that Europa did not know when his hoofs touched the ground. He then began to race to that part of the flowery plain where her three brothers were, and where they had just caught their splendid butterfly. Europa screamed with delight; and Phoenix, Cilix, and Cadmus stood gaping at the spectacle of their sister mounted on a white bull, not knowing whether to be frightened, or to wish the same good luck for themselves. The gentle and innocent creature (for who could possibly doubt that he was so?) pranced round among the children as sportively as a kitten. Europa all the while looked down upon her brothers, nodding and laughing, but yet with a sort of stateliness in her rosy little face. As the bull wheeled about to take another gallop across the meadow, the child waved her hand and said "Good-bye," playfully pretending that she was now bound on a distant journey, and might not see her brothers again for nobody could tell how long.

"Good-bye," shouted Cadmus, Phoenix, and Cilix, all in one breath.

But, together with her enjoyment of the sport, there was still a little remnant of fear in the child's heart; so that her last look at the three boys was a troubled one, and made them feel as if their dear sister were really leaving them forever. And what do you think the snowy bull did next? Why, he set off, as swift as the wind, straight down to the seashore, scampered across the sand, took an airy leap, and plunged right in among the foaming billows. The white spray rose in a shower over him and little Europa, and fell spattering down upon the water.

Then what a scream of terror did the poor child send forth! The three brothers screamed manfully, likewise, and ran to the shore as fast as their legs would carry them, with Cadmus at their head. But it was too late. When they reached the margin of the sand, the treacherous animal was already away in the wide blue sea, with only his snowy head and tail emerging, and poor little Europa between them, stretching out one hand towards her dear brothers, while she grasped the bull's ivory horn with the other. And there stood Cadmus, Phoenix, and Cilix, gazing at this sad spectacle through their tears, until they could no longer distinguish the bull's snowy head from the white-capped billows that seemed to boil up out of the sea's depth around him. Nothing more was ever seen of the white bull—nothing more of the beautiful child.

This was a mournful story, as you may well think, for the three boys to carry home to their parents. King Agenor, their father, was the ruler of the whole country; but he loved his little daughter Europa better than his kingdom, or than all his other children, or than anything else

in the world. Therefore, when Cadmus and his two brothers came crying home, and told him how that a white bull had carried off their sister, and swam with her over the sea, the king was quite beside himself with grief and rage. Although it was now twilight, and fast growing dark, he bade them set out instantly in search of her.

"Never shall you see my face again," he cried, "unless you bring me back my little Europa to gladden me with her smiles and her pretty ways. Begone, and enter my presence no more, till you come leading her by the hand."

As King Agenor said this his eyes flashed fire (for he was a very passionate king), and he looked so terribly angry that the poor boys did not even venture to ask for their suppers, but slunk away out of the palace, and only paused on the steps a moment to consult whither they should go first. While they were standing there, all in dismay, their mother, Queen Telephassa (who happened not to be by when they told the story to the king), came hurrying after them, and said that she too would go in quest of her daughter.

"Oh, no, mother!" cried the boys. "The night is dark, and there is no knowing what troubles and perils we may meet with."

"Alas! my dear children," answered poor Queen Telephassa, weeping bitterly, "that is only another reason why I should go with you. If I should lose you too, as well as my little Europa, what would become of me?"

In this manner they went down the palace steps, and began a journey which turned out to be a great deal longer than they dreamed of. The last that they saw of King Agenor, he came to the door, with a servant holding a torch beside him, and called after them into the gathering darkness:

"Remember! Never ascend these steps again without the child!"

"Never!" sobbed Queen Telephassa; and the three brothers answered, "Never! Never! Never! Never!"

And they kept their word. Year after year King Agenor sat in the solitude of his beautiful palace, listening in vain for their returning footsteps, hoping to hear the familiar voice of the queen and the cheerful talk of his sons entering the door together, and the sweet, childish accents of little Europa in the midst of them. But so long a time went by that, at last, if they had really come, the king would not have known that this was the voice of Telephassa, and these the younger voices that used to make such joyful echoes when the children were playing about the palace. We must now leave King Agenor to sit on his throne, and must go along with Queen Telephassa and her three youthful companions.

They went on and on, and traveled a long way, and passed over mountains and rivers and sailed over seas. Here and there, and everywhere, they made continual inquiry if any person could tell them what had become of Europa. The rustic people, of whom they asked this question, paused a little while from their labors in the field, and looked very much surprised. They thought it strange to behold a woman in the garb of a queen (for Telephassa, in her haste, had forgotten to take off her crown and her royal robes) roaming about the country, with three lads around her, on such an errand as this seemed to be. But nobody could give them

any tidings of Europa—nobody had seen a little girl dressed like a princess, and mounted on a snow-white bull, which galloped as swiftly as the wind.

I cannot tell you how long Queen Telephassa, and Cadmus, and Phoenix, and Cilix, her three sons, went wandering along the highways and by-paths, or through the pathless wildernesses of the earth, in this manner. But certain it is that, before they reached any place of rest, their splendid garments were quite worn out. They all looked very much travel-stained, and would have had the dust of many countries on their shoes, if the streams, through which they waded, had not washed it all away. When they had been gone a year, Telephassa threw away her crown, because it chafed her forehead.

"It has given me many a headache," said the poor queen, "and it cannot cure my heartache."

As fast as their princely robes got torn and tattered, they exchanged them for such mean attire as ordinary people wore. By and by they came to have a wild and homeless aspect; so that you would much sooner have taken them for a gipsy family than a queen and three princes, who had once a palace for their home, and a train of servants to do their bidding. The three boys grew up to be tall young men, with sunburnt faces. Each of them girded a sword to defend himself against the perils of the way. When the husbandmen at whose farmhouses they sought hospitality needed their assistance in the harvest-field, they gave it willingly; and Queen Telephassa (who had done no work in her palace, save to braid silk threads with golden ones) came behind them to bind the sheaves. If payment was offered, they shook their heads, and only asked for tidings of Europa.

"There are bulls enough in my pasture," the old farmers would reply; "but I never heard of one like this you tell me of. A snow-white bull with a little princess on his back! Ho! ho! I ask your pardon, good folks; but there never was such a sight seen hereabouts."

At last, when his upper lip began to have the down on it, Phoenix grew weary of rambling hither and thither to no purpose. So one day, when they happened to be passing through a pleasant and solitary tract of country, he sat himself down on a heap of moss.

"I can go no farther," said Phoenix, "it is a mere foolish waste of life to spend it, as we do, in always wandering up and down, and never coming to any home at nightfall. Our sister is lost, and never will be found. She probably perished in the sea, or to whatever shore the white bull may have carried her. It is now so many years ago that there would be neither love nor acquaintance between us, should we meet again. My father has forbidden us to return to his palace, so I shall build me a hut of branches and dwell here."

"Well, son Phoenix," said Telephassa sorrowfully, "you have grown to be a man, and must do as you judge best. But, for my part, I will still go in quest of my poor child."

"And we two will go along with you!" cried Cadmus and Cilix.

But before setting out they all helped Phoenix to build a habitation. When completed it was a sweet rural bower, roofed overhead with an arch of living boughs. Inside there were two pleasant rooms, one of which had a soft heap of moss for a bed, while the other was furnished with a rustic seat or two, curiously

Right: Europa and the Bull drawn by painter and graphic artist Adolf Münzer (1870–1953), first appearing in *Jugend* art magazine on 20th November 1897.

fashioned out of the crooked roots of trees. So comfortable and homelike did it seem, that Telephassa and her two companions could not help sighing to think that they must still roam about the world instead of spending the remainder of their lives in some such cheerful abode as they had there built for Phoenix. But, when they bade him farewell, Phoenix shed tears, and probably regretted that he was no longer to keep them company.

However, he had fixed upon an admirable place to dwell in. And by and by there came other people, who chanced to have no home; and seeing how pleasant a spot it was, they built themselves huts in the neighborhood of Phoenix's habitation. Thus, before many years went by, a city had grown up there, in the center of which was seen a stately palace of marble, wherein dwelt Phoenix, clothed in a purple robe, and wearing a golden crown upon his head. For the inhabitants of the new city, finding that he had royal blood in his veins, had chosen him to be their king. The very first decree of state which King Phoenix issued was, that if a maiden happened to arrive in the kingdom, mounted on a snow-white bull and calling herself Europa, his subjects should treat her with the greatest kindness and respect, and immediately bring her to the palace. You may see by this that Phoenix's conscience never quite ceased to trouble him for giving up the quest of his dear sister, and sitting himself down to be comfortable, while his mother and her companions went onward.

But often and often, at the close of a weary day's journey, did Telephassa, Cadmus, and Cilix remember the pleasant spot in which they had left Phoenix. It was a sorrowful prospect for these wanderers, that on the morrow they must again set forth; and that, after many nightfalls, they would, perhaps, be no nearer the close of their toilsome pilgrimage than now. These thoughts made them all melancholy at times, but appeared to torment Cilix more than the rest of the party. At length, one morning, when they were taking their staffs in hand to set out, he thus addressed them:

"My dear mother, and you, good brother Cadmus, methinks we are like people in a dream. There is no substance in the life which we are leading. It is such a dreary length of time since the white bull carried off my sister Europa, that I have quite forgotten how she looked, and the tones of her voice, and, indeed, almost doubt whether such a little girl ever lived in the world. And whether she once lived or no, I am convinced that she no longer survives, and that therefore it is the merest folly to waste our own lives and happiness in seeking her. Were we to find her, she would now be a woman grown, and would look upon us all as strangers. So, to tell you the truth, I have resolved to take up my abode here; and I entreat you, mother, and you, brother, to follow my example."

"Not I, for one," said Telephassa; although the poor queen, firmly as she spoke, was so travel-worn that she could hardly put her foot to the ground. "Not I, for one! In the depths of my heart little Europa is still the rosy child who ran to gather flowers so many years ago. She has not grown to womanhood, nor forgotten me. At noon, at night, journeying onward, sitting down to rest, her childish voice is always in my ears, calling, 'Mother! mother!' Stop here who may, there is no repose for me."

"Nor for me," said Cadmus, "while my dear mother pleases to go onward."

They remained with Cilix a few days, however, and helped him to build a rustic bower, resembling the one which they had formerly built for Phoenix.

When they were bidding him farewell, Cilix burst into tears, and told his mother that it seemed just as melancholy a dream to stay there in solitude as to go onward. If she really believed that they would ever find Europa, he was willing to continue the search with them even now. But Telephassa bade him remain there, and be happy, if his own heart would let him.

So the pilgrims took their leave of him and departed, and were hardly out of sight before some other wandering people came along that way and saw Cilix's habitation, and were greatly delighted with the appearance of the place. There being abundance of unoccupied ground in the neighborhood, these strangers built huts for themselves, and were soon joined by a multitude of new settlers, who quickly formed a city. In the middle of it was seen a magnificent palace of colored marble, on the balcony of which, every noontide, appeared Cilix, in a long purple robe, and with a jeweled crown upon his head; for the inhabitants, when they found out that he was a king's son, had considered him the fittest of all men to be a king himself.

One of the first acts of King Cilix's government was to send out an expedition, consisting of a grave ambassador and an escort of bold and hardy young men, with orders to visit the principal kingdoms of the earth, and inquire whether a young maiden had passed through those regions, galloping swiftly on a white bull. It is therefore plain to my mind, that Cilix secretly blamed himself for giving up the search for Europa, as long as he was able to put one foot before the other.

Telephassa and Cadmus were now pursuing their weary way, with no companion but each other. The queen leaned heavily upon her son's arm, and could walk only a few miles a day. But for all her weakness and weariness, she would not be persuaded to give up the search. It was enough to bring tears into the eyes of bearded men to hear the melancholy tone with which she inquired of every stranger whether he could tell her any news of the lost child.

"Have you seen a little girl—no, no, I mean a young maiden of full growth— passing by this way, mounted on a snow-white bull, which gallops as swiftly as the wind?"

"We have seen no such wondrous sight," the people would reply; and very often, taking Cadmus aside, they whispered to him, "Is this stately and sad-looking woman your mother? Surely she is not in her right mind; and you ought to take her home, and make her comfortable, and do your best to get this dream out of her fancy."

"It is no dream," said Cadmus. "Everything else is a dream, save that."

But one day Telephassa seemed feebler than usual, and leaned almost her whole weight on the arm of Cadmus, and walked more slowly than ever before. At last they reached a solitary spot, where she told her son that she must needs lie down, and take a good long rest.

"A good long rest!" she repeated, looking Cadmus tenderly in the face. "A good long rest, thou dearest one!"

"As long as you please, dear mother," answered Cadmus.

Telephassa bade him sit down on the turf beside her, and then she took his hand.

"My son," said she, fixing her dim eyes most lovingly upon him, "this rest that I speak of will be very long indeed! You must not wait till it is finished. Dear Cadmus, you do not comprehend me. You must make a grave here, and lay your mother's weary frame into it. My pilgrimage is over."

Cadmus burst into tears, and for a long time refused to believe that his dear mother was now to be taken from him. But Telephassa reasoned with him, and kissed him, and at length made him discern that it was better for her spirit to pass away out of the toil, the weariness, the grief, and disappointment which had burdened her on earth, ever since the child was lost. He therefore repressed his sorrow, and listened to her last words.

"Dearest Cadmus," said she, "thou hast been the truest son that ever mother had, and faithful to the very last. Who else would have borne with my infirmities as thou hast? It is owing to thy care, thou tenderest child, that my grave was not dug long years ago, in some valley or on some hillside, that lies far, far behind us. It is enough. Thou shalt wander no more on this hopeless search. But when thou hast laid thy mother in the earth, then go, my son, to Delphi, and inquire of the oracle what thou shalt do next."

"Oh, mother, mother," cried Cadmus, "couldst thou but have seen my sister before this hour!"

"It matters little now," answered Telephassa, and there was a smile upon her face. "I go now to the better world, and sooner or later, shall find my daughter there."

I will not sadden you with telling how Telephassa died and was buried, but will only say, that her dying smile grew brighter, instead of vanishing from her dead face; so that Cadmus felt convinced that, at her very first step into the better world, she had caught Europa in her arms. He planted some flowers on his mother's grave, and left them to grow there and make the place beautiful when he should be far away.

Left: Europa and a flower-garlanded depiction of the bull, painted in the Baroque style by Guido Reni (1575–1642).

CADMUS AND
THE DRAGON'S TEETH

After performing this last sorrowful duty, he set forth alone, and took the road towards the famous oracle of Delphi, as Telephassa had advised him. On his way thither he still inquired of most people whom he met whether they had seen Europa; for, to say the truth, Cadmus had grown so accustomed to ask the question, that it came to his lips as readily as a remark about the weather. He received various answers.

Some told him one thing, and some another. Among the rest, a mariner affirmed that, many years before, in a distant country, he had heard a rumor about a white bull, which came swimming across the sea with a child on his back, dressed up in flowers that were blighted by the sea water. He did not know what had become of the child or the bull; and Cadmus suspected, indeed, by a queer twinkle in the mariner's eyes, that he was putting a joke upon him, and had never really heard anything about the matter.

Poor Cadmus found it more wearisome to travel alone than to bear all his dear mother's weight, while she had kept him company. His heart, you will understand, was now so heavy that it seemed impossible, sometimes, to carry it any farther. But his limbs were strong and active, and well accustomed to exercise. He walked swiftly along, thinking of King Agenor and Queen Telephassa, and his brothers, all of whom he had left behind him, at one point of his pilgrimage or another, and never expected to see them any more. Full of these remembrances, he came within sight of a lofty mountain, which the people thereabouts told him was called Parnassus. On the slope of Mount Parnassus was the famous Delphi whither Cadmus was going.

This Delphi was supposed to be the very midmost spot of the whole world. The place of the oracle was a certain cavity in the mountain-side, over which, when Cadmus came thither, he found a rude bower of branches. It reminded him of those which he had helped to build for Phoenix and Cilix. In later times, when multitudes of people came from great distances to put questions to the oracle, a spacious temple of marble was erected over the spot. But in the days

of Cadmus, as I have told you, there was only this rustic bower, with its abundance of green foliage and a tuft of shrubbery that ran wild over the mysterious hole in the hillside.

When Cadmus had thrust a passage through the tangled boughs, and made his way into the bower, he did not at first discern the half-hidden cavity. But soon he felt a cold stream of air rushing out of it, with so much force that it shook the ringlets on his cheeks. Pulling away the shrubbery which clustered over the hole, he bent forward and spoke in a distinct but reverential tone, as if addressing some unseen personage inside of the mountain.

"Sacred oracle of Delphi," said he, "whither shall I go next in quest of my dear sister Europa?"

There was at first a deep silence, and then a rushing sound, or a noise like a long sigh, proceeding out of the interior of the earth. This cavity, you must know, was looked upon as a sort of fountain of truth, which sometimes gushed out in audible words; although, for the most part, these words were such a riddle that they might as well have stayed at the bottom of the hole. But Cadmus was more fortunate than many others who went to Delphi in search of truth. By and by the rushing noise began to sound like articulate language. It repeated, over and over again, the following sentence, which, after all, was so like the vague whistle of a blast of air, that Cadmus really did not quite know whether it meant anything or not: "Seek her no more! Seek her no more! Seek her no more!"

"What, then, shall I do?" asked Cadmus.

For ever since he was a child, you know, it had been the great object of his life to find his sister. From the very hour that he left following the butterfly in the meadow, near his father's palace, he had done his best to follow Europa, over land and sea. And now, if he must give up the search, he seemed to have no more business in the world.

But again the sighing gust of air grew into something like a hoarse voice. "Follow the cow!" it said. "Follow the cow! Follow the cow!"

And when these words had been repeated until Cadmus was tired of hearing them (especially as he could not imagine what cow it was, or why he was to follow her), the gusty hole gave vent to another sentence.

"Where the stray cow lies down, there is your home."

These words were pronounced but a single time, and died away into a whisper before Cadmus was fully satisfied that he had caught the meaning. He put other questions but received no answer; only the gust of wind sighed continually out of the cavity, and blew the withered leaves rustling along the ground before it.

"Did there really come any words out of the hole?" thought Cadmus; "or have I been dreaming all this while?"

He turned away from the oracle, and thought himself no wiser than when he came thither. Caring little what might happen to him, he took the first path that offered itself, and went along at a sluggish pace; for, having no object in view, nor any reason to go one way more than another, it would certainly have been foolish to make haste. Whenever he met anybody, the old question was at his tongue's end: "Have you seen a beautiful maiden, dressed like a king's daughter, and mounted on a snow-white bull, that gallops as swiftly as the wind?"

But, remembering what the oracle had said, he only half uttered the words, and then mumbled the rest indistinctly; and from his confusion, people must have imagined that this handsome young man had lost his wits.

I know not how far Cadmus had gone, nor could he himself have told you, when, at no great distance before him, he beheld a brindled cow. She was lying down by the wayside, and quietly chewing her cud; nor did she take any notice of the young man until he had approached pretty nigh. Then getting leisurely upon her feet, and giving her head a gentle toss, she began to move along at a moderate pace, often pausing just long enough to crop a mouthful of grass. Cadmus loitered behind, whistling idly to himself, and scarcely noticing the cow, until the thought occurred to him, whether this could possibly be the animal which, according to the oracle's response, was to serve him for a guide. But he smiled at himself for fancying such a thing. He could not seriously think that this was the cow, because she went along so quietly, behaving just like any other cow. Evidently she neither knew nor cared so much as a wisp of hay about Cadmus, and was only thinking how to get her living along the wayside, where the herbage was green and fresh. Perhaps she was going home to be milked.

"Cow, cow, cow!" cried Cadmus. "Hey, Brindle, hey! Stop, my good cow."

He wanted to come up with the cow, so as to examine her, and see if she would appear to know him, or whether there were any peculiarities to distinguish her from a thousand other cows, whose only business is to fill the milk-pail, and sometimes kick it over. But still the brindled cow trudged on, whisking her tail to keep the flies away, and taking as little notice of Cadmus as she well could. If he walked slowly, so did the cow, and seized the opportunity to graze. If he quickened his pace, the cow went just so much faster; and once, when Cadmus tried to catch her by running, she threw out her heels, stuck her tail straight on end, and set off at a gallop, looking as queerly as cows generally do while putting themselves to their speed.

When Cadmus saw that it was impossible to come up with her, he walked on moderately, as before. The cow, too, went leisurely on, without looking behind. Wherever the grass was greenest, there she nibbled a mouthful or two. Where a brook glistened brightly across the path, there the cow drank, and breathed a comfortable sigh, and drank again, and trudged onward at the pace that best suited herself and Cadmus.

"I do believe," thought Cadmus, "that this may be the cow that was foretold me. If it be the one, I suppose she will lie down somewhere hereabouts."

Whether it was the oracular cow or some other one, it did not seem reasonable that she should travel a great way farther. So, whenever they reached a particularly pleasant spot on a breezy hillside, or in a sheltered vale, or flowery meadow, on the shore of a calm lake, or along the bank of a clear stream, Cadmus looked eagerly around to see if the situation would suit him for a home. But still, whether he liked the place or no, the brindle cow never offered to lie down. On she went at the quiet pace of a cow going homeward to the barn-yard; and every moment Cadmus expected to see a milkmaid approaching with a pail, or a herdsman running to head the stray animal and turn her back towards the pasture. But no

milkmaid came; no herdsman drove her back; and Cadmus followed the stray brindle till he was almost ready to drop down with fatigue.

"Oh, brindled cow," cried he, in a tone of despair, "do you never mean to stop?"

He had now grown too intent on following her to think of lagging behind, however long the way and whatever might be his fatigue. Indeed, it seemed as if there were something about the animal that bewitched people. Several persons who happened to see the brindled cow, and Cadmus following behind, began to trudge after her, precisely as he did. Cadmus was glad of somebody to converse with, and therefore talked very freely to these good people. He told them all his adventures, and how he had left King Agenor in his palace, and Phoenix at one place, and Cilix at another, and his dear mother, Queen Telephassa, under a flowery sod; so that now he was quite alone, both friendless and homeless. He mentioned likewise, that the oracle had bidden him be guided by a cow, and inquired of the strangers whether they supposed that this brindled animal could be the one.

"Why, 'tis a very wonderful affair," answered one of his new companions. "I am pretty well acquainted with the ways of cattle, and I never knew a cow, of her own accord, go so far without stopping. If my legs will let me, I'll never leave following the beast till she lies down."

"Nor I!" said a second.

"Nor I!" cried a third. "If she goes a hundred miles farther, I'm determined to see the end of it."

The secret of it was, you must know, that the cow was an enchanted cow, and that, without their being conscious of it, she threw some of her enchantment over everybody that took so much as half-a-dozen steps behind her. They could not possibly help following her, though all the time they fancied themselves doing it of their own accord. The cow was by no means very nice in choosing her path, so that sometimes they had to scramble over rocks, or wade through mud and mire, and were all in a terribly bedraggled condition, and tired to death, and very hungry, into the bargain. What a weary business it was!

But still they kept trudging stoutly forward, and talking as they went. The strangers grew very fond of Cadmus, and resolved never to leave him, but to help him build a city wherever the cow might lie down. In the center of it there should be a noble palace, in which Cadmus might dwell and be their king, with a throne, a crown and scepter, a purple robe, and everything else that a king ought to have; for in him there were the royal blood, and the royal heart, and the head that knew how to rule.

While they were talking of these schemes, and beguiling the tediousness of the way with laying out the plan of the new city, one of the company happened to look at the cow.

"Joy! joy!" cried he, clapping his hands. "Brindle is going to lie down."

They all looked; and, sure enough, the cow had stopped and was staring leisurely about her, as other cows do when on the point of lying down. And slowly, slowly did she recline herself on the soft grass, first bending her fore-legs, and then crouching her hind ones. When Cadmus and his companions came up with her, there was the brindled cow taking her ease, chewing her cud, and looking them quietly in the face; as if this was just the spot she had been seeking for, and as if it were all a matter of course.

"This, then," said Cadmus, gazing around him, "this is to be my home."

It was a fertile and lovely plain, with great trees flinging their sun-speckled shadows over it, and hills fencing it in from the rough weather. At no great distance they beheld a river gleaming in the sunshine. A home feeling stole into the heart of poor Cadmus. He was very glad to know that here he might awake in the morning without the necessity of putting on his dusty sandals to travel farther and farther. The days and the years would pass over him, and find him still in this pleasant spot. If he could have had his brothers with him, and could have seen his dear mother under a roof of his own, he might here have been happy, after all their disappointments. Some day or other, too, his sister Europa might have come quietly to the door of his home, and smiled round upon the familiar faces. But, indeed, since there was no hope of regaining the friends of his boyhood, or ever seeing his dear sister again, Cadmus resolved to make himself happy with these new companions who had grown so fond of him while following the cow.

"Yes, my friends," said he to them, "this is to be our home. Here we will build our habitations. The brindled cow which has led us hither will supply us with milk. We will cultivate the neighboring soil, and lead an innocent and happy life."

His companions joyfully assented to this plan; and, in the first place, being very hungry and thirsty, they looked about them for the means of providing a comfortable meal. Not far off they saw a tuft of trees, which appeared as if there might be a spring of water beneath them. They went thither to fetch some, leaving Cadmus stretched on the ground along with the brindled cow; for, now that he had found a place of rest, it seemed as if all the weariness of his pilgrimage, ever since he left King Agenor's palace, had fallen upon him at once. But his new friends had not long been gone when he was suddenly startled by cries, shouts, and screams, and the noise of a most terrible struggle, and in the midst of it all a most awful hissing, which went right through his ears like a rough saw.

Running towards the tuft of trees, he beheld the head and fiery eyes of an immense serpent or dragon, with the widest jaws that ever a dragon had, and a vast many rows of horribly sharp teeth. Before Cadmus could reach the spot, this pitiless reptile had killed his poor companions, and was busily devouring them, making but a mouthful of each man.

It appears that the fountain of water was enchanted, and that the dragon had been set to guard it, so that no mortal might ever quench his thirst there. As the neighboring inhabitants carefully avoided the spot, it was now a long time (not less than a hundred years, or thereabouts) since the monster had broken his fast; and, as was natural enough, his appetite had grown to be enormous, and was not half satisfied by the poor people whom he had just eaten up. When he caught sight of Cadmus, therefore, he set up another abominable hiss, and flung back his immense jaws, until his mouth looked like a great red cavern, at the farther end of which were seen the legs of his last victim, whom he had hardly had time to swallow.

Left: Cadmus and the dragon, drawn by Virginia Frances Sterrett, which first appeared in Hawthorne's *Tanglewood Tales.*

But Cadmus was so enraged at the destruction of his friends, that he cared neither for the size of the dragon's jaws nor for his

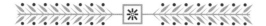

hundreds of sharp teeth. Drawing his sword he rushed at the monster, and flung himself right into his cavernous mouth. This bold method of attacking him took the dragon by surprise; for, in fact, Cadmus had leaped so far down into his throat, that the rows of terrible teeth could not close upon him, nor do him the least harm in the world. Thus, though the struggle was a tremendous one, and though the dragon shattered the tuft of trees into small splinters by the lashing of his tail, yet, as Cadmus was all the while slashing and stabbing at his very vitals, it was not long before the scaly wretch bethought himself of slipping away. He had not gone his length, however, when the brave Cadmus gave him a sword thrust that finished the battle; and, creeping out of the gateway of the creature's jaws, there he beheld him still wriggling his vast bulk, although there was no longer life enough in him to harm a little child.

But do not you suppose that it made Cadmus sorrowful to think of the melancholy fate which had befallen those poor, friendly people, who had followed the cow along with him? It seemed as if he were doomed to lose everybody whom he loved, or to see them perish in one way or another. And here he was, after all his toils and troubles, in a solitary place, with not a single human being to help him build a hut.

"What shall I do?" cried he aloud. "It were better for me to have been devoured by the dragon, as my poor companions were."

"Cadmus," said a voice—but whether it came from above or below him, or whether it spoke within his own breast, the young man could not tell—"Cadmus, pluck out the dragon's teeth, and plant them in the earth."

This was a strange thing to do; nor was it very easy, I should imagine, to dig out all those deep-rooted fangs from the dead dragon's jaws. But Cadmus toiled and tugged, and after pounding the monstrous head almost to pieces with a great stone, he at last collected as many teeth as might have filled a bushel or two. The next thing was to plant them. This, likewise, was a tedious piece of work, especially as Cadmus was already exhausted with killing the dragon and knocking his head to pieces, and had nothing to dig the earth with, that I know of, unless it were his sword-blade. Finally, however, a sufficiently large tract of ground was turned up, and sown with this new kind of seed; although half of the dragon's teeth still remained to be planted some other day.

Cadmus, quite out of breath, stood leaning upon his sword, and wondering what was to happen next. He had waited but a few moments when he began to see a sight which was as great a marvel as the most marvelous thing I ever told you about.

The sun was shining slantwise over the field, and showed all the moist, dark soil, just like any other newly planted piece of ground. All at once, Cadmus fancied he saw something glisten very brightly, first at one spot, then at another, and then at a hundred and a thousand spots together. Soon he perceived them to be the steel heads of spears, sprouting up everywhere like so many stalks of grain, and continually growing taller and taller. Next appeared a vast number of bright sword-blades, thrusting themselves up in the same way. A moment afterwards, the whole surface of the ground was broken by a multitude of polished brass helmets, coming up like a crop of enormous beans. So rapidly did they grow, that Cadmus now discerned the

fierce countenance of a man beneath every one. In short, before he had time to think what a wonderful affair it was, he beheld an abundant harvest of what looked like human beings, armed with helmets and breastplates, shields, swords, and spears; and before they were well out of the earth, they brandished their weapons, and clashed them one against another, seeming to think, little while as they had yet lived, that they had wasted too much of life without battle. Every tooth of the dragon had produced one of these sons of deadly mischief.

Up sprouted, also, a great many trumpeters; and with the first breath that they drew, they put their brazen trumpets to their lips, and sounded a tremendous and ear-shattering blast; so that the whole space, just now so quiet and solitary, reverberated with the clash and clang of arms, the bray of warlike music, and the shouts of angry men. So enraged did they all look, that Cadmus fully expected them to put the whole world to the sword. How fortunate would it be for a great conqueror, if he could get a bushel of the dragon's teeth to sow!

"Cadmus," said the same voice which he had before heard, "throw a stone into the midst of the armed men."

So Cadmus seized a large stone, and, flinging it into the middle of the army, saw it strike the breastplate of a gigantic and fierce-looking warrior. Immediately on feeling the blow, he seemed to take it for granted that somebody had struck him; and, uplifting his weapon, he smote his next neighbor a blow that cleft his helmet asunder and stretched him on the ground. In an instant those nearest the fallen warrior began to strike at one another with their swords, and stab with their spears. The confusion spread wider and wider. Each man smote down his brother, and was himself smitten down before he had time to exult in his victory. The trumpeters, all the while, blew their blasts shriller and shriller; each soldier shouted a battle-cry, and often fell with it on his lips. It was the strangest spectacle of causeless wrath, and of mischief for no good end, that had ever been witnessed; but, after all, it was neither more foolish nor more wicked than a thousand battles that have since been fought, in which men have slain their brothers with just as little reason as these children of the dragon's teeth. It ought to be considered, too, that the dragon people were made for nothing else; whereas other mortals were born to love and help one another.

Well, this memorable battle continued to rage until the ground was strewn with helmeted heads that had been cut off. Of all the thousands that began the fight, there were only five left standing. These now rushed from different parts of the field, and, meeting in the middle of it, clashed their swords and struck at each other's hearts as fiercely as ever.

"Cadmus," said the voice again, "bid those five warriors sheathe their swords. They will help you to build the city."

Without hesitating an instant, Cadmus stepped forward, with the aspect of a king and a leader, and extending his drawn sword amongst them, spoke to the warriors in a stern and commanding voice.

"Sheathe your weapons!" said he.

And forthwith, feeling themselves bound to obey him, the five remaining sons of the dragon's teeth made him a military salute with their swords, returned them to the scabbards,

and stood before Cadmus in a rank, eying him as soldiers eye their captain while awaiting the word of command.

These five men had probably sprung from the biggest of the dragon's teeth, and were the boldest and strongest of the whole army. They were almost giants, indeed, and had good need to be so, else they never could have lived through so terrible a fight. They still had a very furious look, and, if Cadmus happened to glance aside, would glare at one another with fire flashing out of their eyes. It was strange, too, to observe how the earth, out of which they had so lately grown, was incrusted here and there on their bright breastplates, and even begrimed their faces; just as you may have seen it clinging to beets and carrots when pulled out of their native soil. Cadmus hardly knew whether to consider them as men, or some odd kind of vegetable; although, on the whole, he concluded that there was human nature in them, because they were so fond of trumpets and weapons, and so ready to shed blood.

They looked him earnestly in the face, waiting for his next order, and evidently desiring no other employment than to follow him from one battlefield to another, all over the wide world. But Cadmus was wiser than these earthborn creatures, with the dragon's fierceness in them, and knew better how to use their strength and hardihood.

"Come!" said he. "You are sturdy fellows. Make yourselves useful! Quarry some stones with those great swords of yours, and help me to build a city."

The five soldiers grumbled a little, and muttered that it was their business to overthrow cities, not to build them up. But Cadmus looked at them with a stern eye, and spoke to them in a tone of authority, so that they knew him for their master, and never again thought of disobeying his commands. They set to work in good earnest, and toiled so diligently, that, in a very short time, a city began to make its appearance. At first, to be sure, the workmen showed a quarrelsome disposition. Like savage beasts, they would doubtless have done one another mischief, if Cadmus had not kept watch over them and quelled the fierce old serpent that lurked in their hearts when he saw it gleaming out of their wild eyes. But, in course of time, they got accustomed to honest labor, and had sense enough to feel that there was more true enjoyment in living at peace, and doing good to one's neighbor, than in striking at him with a two-edged sword. It may not be too much to hope that the rest of mankind will by and by grow as wise and peaceable as these five earth-begrimed warriors who sprang from the dragon's teeth.

And now the city was built, and there was a home in it for each of the workmen. But the palace of Cadmus was not yet erected, because they had left it till the last, meaning to introduce all the new improvements of architecture, and make it very commodious, as well as stately and beautiful. After finishing the rest of their labors, they all went to bed betimes, in order to rise in the gray of the morning, and to get at least the foundation of the edifice laid before nightfall. But, when Cadmus arose and took his way towards the site where the palace was to be built, followed by his five sturdy workmen marching all in a row, what do you think he saw?

What should it be but the most magnificent palace that had ever been seen in the world? It was built of marble and other beautiful kinds of stone, and rose high into the air, with a splendid dome and a portico along the front, and carved pillars, and everything else that

befitted the habitation of a mighty king. It had grown up out of the earth in almost as short a time as it had taken the armed host to spring from the dragon's teeth; and what made the matter more strange, no seed of the stately edifice had ever been planted.

When the five workmen beheld the dome, with the morning sunshine making it look golden and glorious, they gave a great shout.

"Long live King Cadmus," they cried, "in his beautiful palace!"

And the new king, with his five faithful followers at his heels, shouldering their pickaxes and marching in a rank (for they still had a soldier-like sort of behavior, as their nature was), ascended the palace steps. Halting at the entrance, they gazed through a long vista of lofty pillars that were ranged from end to end of a great hall. At the farther extremity of this hall, approaching slowly towards him, Cadmus beheld a female figure, wonderfully beautiful, and adorned with a royal robe, and a crown of diamonds over her golden ringlets, and the richest necklace that ever a queen wore. His heart thrilled with delight. He fancied it his long-lost sister Europa, now grown to womanhood, coming to make him happy, and to repay him, with her sweet sisterly affection, for all those weary wanderings in quest of her since he left King Agenor's palace—for the tears that he had shed, on parting with Phoenix and Cilix—for the heartbreakings that had made the whole world seem dismal to him over his dear mother's grave.

But, as Cadmus advanced to meet the beautiful stranger, he saw that her features were unknown to him, although, in the little time that it required to tread along the hall, he had already felt a sympathy betwixt himself and her.

"No, Cadmus," said the same voice that had spoken to him in the field of the armed men, "this is not that dear sister Europa whom you have sought so faithfully all over the wide world. This is Harmonia, a daughter of the sky, who is given you instead of sister, and brothers, and mother. You will find all those dear ones in her alone."

So King Cadmus dwelt in the palace, with his new friend Harmonia, and found a great deal of comfort in his magnificent abode, but would doubtless have found as much, if not more, in the humblest cottage by the wayside. Before many years went by, there was a group of rosy little children (but how they came thither has always been a mystery to me) sporting in the great hall, and on the marble steps of the palace, and running joyfully to meet King Cadmus when affairs of state left him at leisure to play with them. They called him father, and Queen Harmonia mother. The five old soldiers of the dragon's teeth grew very fond of these small urchins, and were never weary of showing them how to shoulder sticks, flourish wooden swords, and march in military order, blowing a penny trumpet, or beating an abominable rub-a-dub upon a little drum.

But King Cadmus, lest there should be too much of the dragon's tooth in his children's disposition, used to find time from his kingly duties to teach them their A B Cs—which he invented for their benefit, and for which many little people, I am afraid, are not half so grateful to him as they ought to be.

HERCULES AND THE GOLDEN APPLES

Did you ever hear of the golden apples that grew in the garden of the Hesperides? Ah, those were such apples as would bring a great price by the bushel, if any of them could be found growing in the orchards of nowadays! But there is not, I suppose, a graft of that wonderful fruit on a single tree in the wide world. Not so much as a seed of those apples exists any longer.

And even in the old, old, half-forgotten times, before the garden of the Hesperides was overrun with weeds, many doubted whether there could be real trees that bore apples of solid gold upon their branches. All had heard of them, but nobody remembered to have seen any. Children, nevertheless, used to listen, open-mouthed, to stories of the golden apple tree, and resolved to discover it when they should be big enough. Adventurous young men, who desired to do a braver thing than any of their fellows, set out in quest of this fruit. Many of them returned no more; none of them brought back the apples. No wonder that they found it impossible to gather them! It is said that there was a dragon beneath the tree, with a hundred terrible heads, fifty of which were always on the watch while the other fifty slept.

But it was quite a common thing with youths, when tired of too much peace and rest, to go in search of the garden of the Hesperides. And once the adventure was undertaken by a hero who had enjoyed very little peace or rest since he came into the world. At the time of which I am going to speak, he was wandering through the pleasant land of Italy, with a mighty club in his hand and a bow and quiver slung across his shoulders. He was wrapped in the skin of the biggest and fiercest lion that ever had been seen, and which he himself had killed; and though, on the whole, he was kind and generous and noble, there was a good deal of the lion's fierceness in his heart. As he went on his way, he continually inquired whether that were the right road to the famous garden. But none of the country people knew anything about the matter, and many looked as if they would have laughed at the question, if the stranger had not carried so big a club.

Right: Illustration by Walter Crane (1845–1915) of Hercules meeting the nymphs and asking the way to the garden of Hesperides.

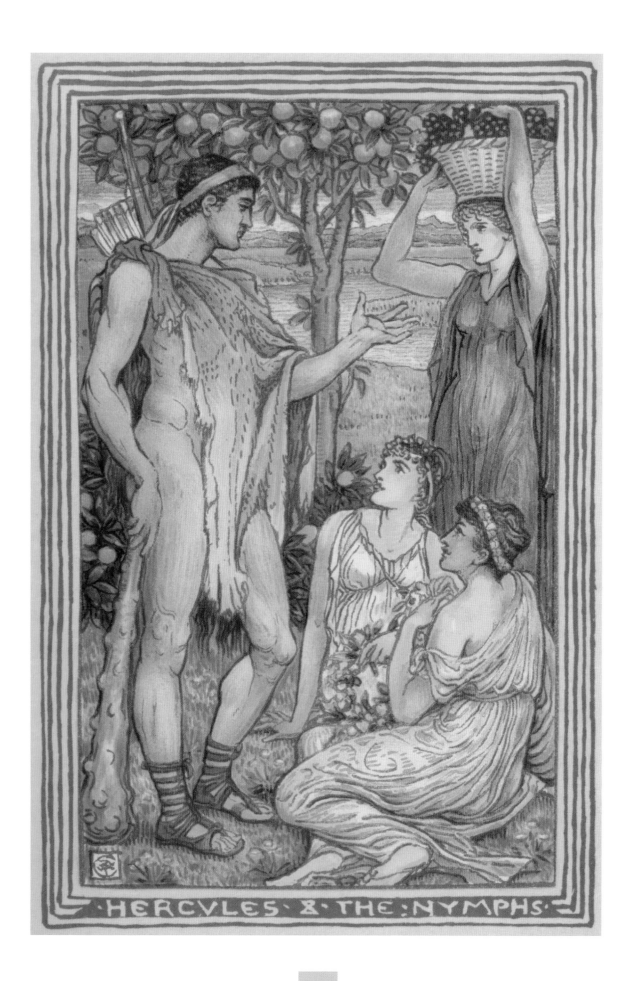

HERCVLES & THE NYMPHS

145

So he journeyed on, still making the same inquiry, until at last he came to the brink of a river, where some beautiful girls sat twining wreaths of flowers.

"Can you tell me, pretty maidens," asked the stranger, "whether this is the right way to the garden of the Hesperides?"

The girls had been having a fine time together, weaving the flowers into wreaths, and crowning one another's heads. But, on hearing the stranger's question, they dropped all their flowers on the grass and gazed at him with astonishment.

"The garden of the Hesperides!" cried one. "We thought mortals had been weary of seeking it, after so many disappointments. And pray, bold stranger, what do you want there?"

"A certain king, who is my cousin," replied he, "has ordered me to get him three of the golden apples."

"Most of the young men who go in quest of these apples," observed another of the damsels, "desire to obtain them for themselves, or to present to some fair maiden whom they love. Do you, then, love this king, your cousin, so very much?"

"Perhaps not," replied the stranger, sighing. "He has often been severe and cruel to me. But it is my destiny to obey him."

"And do you know," asked the damsel who had first spoken, "that a terrible dragon, with a hundred heads, keeps watch under the golden apple tree?"

"I know it well," answered the stranger calmly. "But from my cradle upwards, it has been my business, and almost my pastime, to deal with serpents and dragons."

The maidens looked at his massive club, and at the shaggy lion's skin which he wore, and likewise at his heroic limbs and figure; and they whispered to each other that the stranger appeared to be one who might reasonably expect to perform deeds far beyond the might of other men. But then, the dragon with a hundred heads! What mortal, even if he possessed a hundred lives, could hope to escape the fangs of such a monster? So kind-hearted were the maidens, that they could not bear to see this brave and handsome traveler attempt what was so very dangerous, and devote himself, most probably, to become a meal for the dragon's hundred ravenous mouths.

"Go back," cried they all; "go back to your own home! Your mother, beholding you safe and sound, will shed tears of joy; and what can she do more, should you win ever so great a victory? No matter for the golden apples! No matter for the king, your cruel cousin! We do not wish the dragon with the hundred heads to eat you up!"

The stranger seemed to grow impatient at these remonstrances. He carelessly lifted his mighty club, and let it fall upon a rock that lay half buried in the earth near by. With the force of that idle blow, the great rock was shattered all to pieces. It cost the stranger no more effort to achieve this feat of strength than for one of the young maidens to touch her sister's rosy cheek with a flower.

"Do you not believe," said he, looking at the damsels with a smile, "that such a blow would have crushed one of the dragon's hundred heads?"

Then he sat down on the grass and told them the story of his life, or as much of it as he could remember, from the day when he was first cradled in a warrior's brazen shield.

When the stranger had finished the story of his adventures, he looked around at the attentive faces of the maidens.

"Perhaps you may have heard of me before," said he, modestly. "My name is Hercules."

"We had already guessed it," replied the maidens; "for your wonderful deeds are known all over the world. We do not think it strange any longer that you should set out in quest of the golden apples of the Hesperides. Come, sisters, let us crown the hero with flowers!"

Then they flung beautiful wreaths over his stately head and mighty shoulders, so that the lion's skin was almost entirely covered with roses. They took possession of his ponderous club, and so entwined it about with the brightest, softest, and most fragrant blossoms that not a finger's breadth of its oaken substance could be seen. It looked all like a huge bunch of flowers. Lastly, they joined hands, and danced around him, chanting words which became poetry of their own accord, and grew into a choral song in honor of the illustrious Hercules.

And Hercules was rejoiced, as any other hero would have been, to know that these fair young girls had heard of the valiant deeds which it had cost him so much toil and danger to achieve. But still he was not satisfied. He could not think that what he had already done was worthy of so much honor, while there remained any bold adventure to be undertaken.

"Dear maidens," said he, when they paused to take breath, "now that you know my name, will you not tell me how I am to reach the garden of the Hesperides?"

"Ah! must you go so soon?" they exclaimed. "You that have performed so many wonders, and spent such a toilsome life—cannot you content yourself to repose a little while on the margin of this peaceful river?"

Hercules shook his head. "I must depart now," said he.

"We will then give you the best directions we can," replied the damsels. "You must go to the seashore, and find out the Old One, and compel him to inform you where the golden apples are to be found."

"The Old One!" repeated Hercules, laughing at this odd name. "And pray who may the Old One be?"

"Why, the Old Man of the Sea, to be sure!" answered one of the damsels. "He has fifty daughters, whom some people call very beautiful; but we do not think it proper to be acquainted with them, because they have sea-green hair, and taper away like fishes. You must talk to this Old Man of the Sea. He is a seafaring person, and knows all about the garden of the Hesperides, for it is situated in an island which he is often in the habit of visiting."

Hercules then asked whereabouts the Old One was most likely to be met with. When the damsels had informed him, he thanked them for all their kindness; most of all for telling him the right way; and immediately set forth upon his journey.

But, before he was out of hearing, one of the maidens called after him.

"Keep fast hold of the Old One when you catch him!" cried she, smiling, and lifting her finger to make the caution more impressive. "Do not be astonished at anything that may happen. Only hold him fast, and he will tell you what you wish to know."

Hercules again thanked her, and pursued his way, while the maidens resumed their pleasant labor of making flower-wreaths. They talked about the hero long after he was gone.

"We will crown him with the loveliest of our garlands," said they, "when he returns hither with the three golden apples, after slaying the dragon with a hundred heads."

Meanwhile Hercules traveled constantly onward, over hill and dale, and through the solitary woods.

Hastening forward, without ever pausing or looking behind, he by and by heard the sea roaring at a distance. At this sound he increased his speed, and soon came to a beach, where the great surf-waves tumbled themselves upon the hard sand, in a long line of snowy foam. At one end of the beach, however, there was a pleasant spot, where some green shrubbery clambered up a cliff, making its rocky face look soft and beautiful. A carpet of verdant grass, largely intermixed with sweet-smelling clover, covered the narrow space between the bottom of the cliff and the sea. And what should Hercules espy there but an old man, fast asleep!

But was it really and truly an old man? Certainly, at first sight, it looked very like one; but on closer inspection it rather seemed to be some kind of a creature that lived in the sea. For on his legs and arms there were scales such as fishes have; he was web-footed and web-fingered, after the fashion of a duck; and his long beard, being of a greenish tinge, had more the appearance of a tuft of seaweed than of an ordinary beard. Have you never seen a stick of timber that has long been tossed about by the waves, and has got all overgrown with barnacles, and at last, drifting ashore, seems to have been thrown up from the very deepest bottom of the sea? Well, the old man would have put you in mind of just such a wave-tossed spar! But Hercules, the instant he set his eyes on this strange figure, was convinced that it could be no other than the Old One, who was to direct him on his way.

Yes; it was the self-same Old Man of the Sea whom the hospitable maidens had talked to him about. Thanking his stars for the lucky accident of finding the old fellow asleep, Hercules stole on tiptoe towards him and caught him by the arm and leg.

"Tell me," cried he, before the Old One was well awake, "which is the way to the garden of the Hesperides?"

As you may imagine, the Old Man of the Sea awoke in a fright. But his astonishment could hardly have been greater than was that of Hercules the next moment. For, all of a sudden, the Old One seemed to disappear out of his grasp, and he found himself holding a stag by the fore and hind leg! But still he kept fast hold. Then the stag disappeared, and in its stead there was a sea-bird, fluttering and screaming, while Hercules clutched it by the wing and claw! But the bird could not get away. Immediately afterwards, there was an ugly three-headed dog, which growled and barked at Hercules, and snapped fiercely at the hands by which he held him! But Hercules would not let him go. In another minute, instead of the three-headed dog, what should appear but Geryon, the six-legged man-monster, kicking at Hercules with five of his legs in order to get the remaining one at liberty! But Hercules held on. By and by no Geryon was there, but a huge snake, like one of those which Hercules had strangled in his babyhood, only a hundred times as big; and it twisted and twined about the hero's neck and body, and

threw its tail high in the air, and opened its deadly jaws as if to devour him outright; but Hercules was no whit disheartened, and squeezed the great snake so tightly that he soon began to hiss with pain.

But, as Hercules held on so stubbornly and only squeezed the Old One so much the tighter at every change of shape, and really put him to no small torture, he finally thought it best to reappear in his own figure. So there he was again, a fishy, scaly, web-footed sort of personage, with something like a tuft of seaweed at his chin.

"Pray, what do you want with me?" cried the Old One, as soon as he could take his breath; for it was quite a tiresome affair to go through so many false shapes. "Why do you squeeze me so hard? Let me go this moment, or I shall begin to consider you an extremely uncivil person!"

"My name is Hercules!" roared the mighty stranger. "And you will never get out of my clutch until you tell me the nearest way to the garden of the Hesperides!"

When the old fellow heard who it was that had caught him, he saw with half an eye that it would be necessary to tell him everything that he wanted to know. He had often heard of the fame of Hercules, and of the wonderful things that he was constantly performing in various parts of the earth, and how determined he always was to accomplish whatever he undertook. He therefore made no more attempts to escape, but told the hero how to find the garden of the Hesperides, and likewise warned him of many difficulties which must be overcome before he could arrive thither.

"You must go on, thus and thus," said the Old Man of the Sea, after taking the points of the compass, "till you come in sight of a very tall giant, who holds the sky on his shoulders. And the giant, if he happens to be in the humor, will tell you exactly where the garden of the Hesperides lies."

"And if the giant happens not to be in the humor," remarked Hercules, balancing his club on the tip of his finger, "perhaps I shall find means to persuade him!"

Thanking the Old Man of the Sea, and begging his pardon for having squeezed him so roughly, the hero resumed his journey. Nothing was before him save the foaming, dashing, measureless ocean. But suddenly, as he looked towards the horizon, he saw something, a great way off, which he had not seen the moment before. It gleamed very brightly, almost as you may have beheld the round, golden disk of the sun when it rises or sets over the edge of the world. It evidently drew nearer; for at every instant this wonderful object became larger and more lustrous. At length it had come so nigh that Hercules discovered it to be an immense cup or bowl, made either of gold or burnished brass. How it had got afloat upon the sea is more than I can tell you. There it was, at all events, rolling on the tumultuous billows, which tossed it up and down and heaved their foamy tops against its sides, but without ever throwing their spray over the brim.

"I have seen many giants in my time," thought Hercules, "but never one that would need to drink his wine out of a cup like this!"

And, true enough, what a cup it must have been! It was as large—as large— but, in short, I am afraid to say how immeasurably large it was. To speak within bounds, it was ten times

larger than a great mill-wheel; and, all of metal as it was, it floated over the heaving surges more lightly than an acorn-cup adown the brook. The waves tumbled it onward until it grazed against the shore within a short distance of the spot where Hercules was standing.

As soon as this happened, he knew what was to be done; for he had not gone through so many remarkable adventures without learning pretty well how to conduct himself whenever anything came to pass a little out of the common rule. It was just as clear as daylight that this marvelous cup had been set adrift by some unseen power, and guided hitherward, in order to carry Hercules across the sea on his way to the garden of the Hesperides. Accordingly, without a moment's delay, he clambered over the brim and slid down on the inside, where, spreading out his lion's skin, he proceeded to take a little repose. He had scarcely rested until now, since he bade farewell to the damsels on the margin of the river. The waves dashed there with a pleasant and ringing sound against the sides of the hollow cup; it rocked lightly to and fro, and the motion was so soothing that it speedily rocked Hercules into an agreeable slumber.

His nap had probably lasted a good while, when the cup chanced to graze against a rock, and resounded and reverberated through its metal substance a hundred times as loudly as ever you heard a church-bell. The noise awoke Hercules, who instantly started up and gazed around him, wondering whereabouts he was. He was not long in discovering that the cup had floated across a great part of the sea, and was approaching the shore of what seemed to be an island. And on that island, what do you think he saw? It was a giant!

But such an intolerably big giant! A giant as tall as a mountain; so vast a giant, that the clouds rested about his midst like a girdle, and hung like a hoary beard from his chin, and flitted before his huge eyes, so that he could neither see Hercules nor the golden cup in which he was voyaging. And, most wonderful of all, the giant held up his great hands and appeared to support the sky, which, so far as Hercules could discern through the clouds, was resting upon his head!

Meanwhile the bright cup continued to float onward, and finally touched the strand. Just then a breeze wafted away the clouds from before the giant's visage, and Hercules beheld it, with all its enormous features: eyes, each of them as big as yonder lake, a nose a mile long, and a mouth of the same width.

Poor fellow! He had evidently stood there a long while. An ancient forest had been growing and decaying round his feet; and oak trees, of six or seven centuries old, had sprung from the acorn, and forced themselves between his toes.

The giant now looked down from the far height of his great eyes, and perceiving Hercules, roared out in a voice that resembled thunder proceeding out of the cloud that had just flitted away from his face:

"Who are you down at my feet there? And whence do you come in that little cup?"

"I am Hercules!" thundered back the hero, in a voice pretty nearly or quite as loud as the giant's own. "And I am seeking the garden of the Hesperides!"

"Ho! ho! ho!" roared the giant, in a fit of immense laughter. "That is a wise adventure, truly!"

"And why not?" cried Hercules, getting a little angry at the giant's mirth. "Do you think I am afraid of the dragon with a hundred heads!"

Just at this time, while they talking together, some black clouds gathered about the giant's middle and burst into a tremendous storm of thunder and lightning, causing such a pother that Hercules found it impossible to distinguish a word. Only the giant's immeasurable legs were to be seen, standing up into the obscurity of the tempest; and now and then a momentary glimpse of his whole figure mantled in a volume of mist. He seemed to be speaking most of the time; but his big, deep, rough voice chimed in with the reverberations of the thunder-claps, and rolled away over the hills, like them.

At last the storm swept over as suddenly as it had come. And there again was the clear sky, and the weary giant holding it up, and the pleasant sunshine beaming over his vast height, and illuminating it against the background of the sullen thunder-clouds. So far above the shower had been his head, that not a hair of it was moistened by the raindrops!

When the giant could see Hercules still standing on the seashore, he roared out to him anew.

"I am Atlas, the mightiest giant in the world! And I hold up the sky upon my head!"

"So I see," answered Hercules. "But can you show me the way to the garden of the Hesperides?"

"What do you want there?" asked the giant.

"I want three of the golden apples," shouted Hercules, "for my cousin, the king."

"There is nobody but myself," quoth the giant, "that can go to the garden of the Hesperides and gather the golden apples. If it were not for this little business of holding up the sky, I would make half a dozen steps across the sea and get them for you."

"You are very kind," replied Hercules. "And cannot you rest the sky upon a mountain?"

"None of them are quite high enough," said Atlas, shaking his head, "But if you were to take your stand on the summit of that nearest me, your head would be pretty nearly on a level with mine. You seem to be a fellow of some strength. What if you should take my burden on your shoulders while I do your errand for you?"

Hercules, as you must be careful to remember, was a remarkably strong man; and though it certainly requires a great deal of muscular power to uphold the sky, yet, if any mortal could be supposed capable of such an exploit, he was the one. Nevertheless, it seemed so difficult an undertaking that, for the first time in his life, he hesitated.

"Is the sky very heavy?" he inquired.

"Why, not particularly so, at first," answered the giant, shrugging his shoulders. "But it gets to be a little burthensome after a thousand years!"

"And how long a time," asked the hero, "will it take you to get the golden apples?"

"Oh, that will be done in a few moments," cried Atlas. "I shall take ten or fifteen miles at a stride, and be at the garden and back again before your shoulders begin to ache."

"Well, then," answered Hercules, "I will climb the mountain behind you there and relieve you of your burden."

The truth is, Hercules had a kind heart of his own, and considered that he should be doing the giant a favor by allowing him this opportunity for a ramble. And besides, he thought that it

HERCVLES & THE·OLD·MAN·OF·THE·SEA

would be still more for his own glory, if he could boast of upholding the sky, than merely to do so ordinary a thing as to conquer a dragon with a hundred heads. Accordingly, without more words, the sky was shifted from the shoulders of Atlas and placed upon those of Hercules.

When this was safely accomplished, the first thing that the giant did was to stretch himself; and you may imagine what a prodigious spectacle he was then. Next, he slowly lifted one of his feet out of the forest that had grown up around it; then the other. Then, all at once he began to caper, and leap, and dance for joy at his freedom; flinging himself nobody knows how high into the air, and floundering down again with a shock that made the earth tremble. Then he laughed—Ho! ho! ho!—with a thunderous roar that was echoed from the mountains, far and near, as if they and the giant had been so many rejoicing brothers. When his joy had a little subsided, he stepped into the sea; ten miles at the first stride, which brought him mid-leg deep; and ten miles at the second, when the water came just above his knees; and ten miles more at the third, by which he was immersed nearly to his waist. This was the greatest depth of the sea.

Hercules watched the giant, as he still went onward; for it was really a wonderful sight, this immense human form, more than thirty miles off, half hidden in the ocean, but with his upper half as tall, and misty, and blue, as a distant mountain. At last the gigantic shape faded entirely out of view. And now Hercules began to consider what he should do, in case Atlas should be drowned in the sea, or if he were to be stung to death by the dragon with the hundred heads which guarded the golden apples of the Hesperides. If any such misfortune were to happen, how could he ever get rid of the sky? And, by the by, its weight began already to be a little irksome to his head and shoulders.

"I really pity the poor giant," thought Hercules. "If it wearies me so much in ten minutes, how must it have wearied him in a thousand years?"

I know not how long it was before, to his unspeakable joy, he beheld the huge shape of the giant, like a cloud, on the far-off edge of the sea. At his nearer approach, Atlas held up his hand, in which Hercules could perceive three magnificent golden apples, as big as pumpkins, all hanging from one branch.

"I am glad to see you again," shouted Hercules, when the giant was within hearing. "So you have got the golden apples?"

"Certainly, certainly," answered Atlas; "and very fair apples they are. I took the finest that grew on the tree, I assure you. Ah! it is a beautiful spot, that garden of the Hesperides. Yes; and the dragon with a hundred heads is a sight worth any man's seeing. After all, you had better have gone for the apples yourself."

"No matter," replied Hercules. "You have had a pleasant ramble, and have done the business as well as I could. I heartily thank you for your trouble. And now, as I have a long way to go and am rather in haste—and as the king, my cousin, is anxious to receive the golden apples—will you be kind enough to take the sky off my shoulders again?"

Left: Hercules wrestles with the Old Man of the Sea so that he will reveal the way to the garden of Hesperides where the golden apples can be obtained.

"Why, as to that," said the giant, chucking the golden apples into the air twenty miles high, or thereabouts, and catching

153

them as they came down—"as to that, my good friend, I consider you a little unreasonable. Cannot I carry the golden apples to the king, your cousin, much quicker than you could? As his majesty is in such a hurry to get them, I promise you to take my longest strides. And besides, I have no fancy for burdening myself with the sky just now."

Here Hercules grew impatient, and gave a great shrug of his shoulders. It being now twilight, you might have seen two or three stars tumble out of their places. Everybody on earth looked upward in affright, thinking that the sky might be going to fall next.

"Oh, that will never do!" cried Giant Atlas, with a great roar of laughter. "I have not let fall so many stars within the last five centuries. By the time you have stood there as long as I did, you will begin to learn patience!"

"What!" shouted Hercules very wrathfully, "do you intend to make me bear this burden forever?"

"We will see about that, one of these days," answered the giant. "At all events, you ought not to complain, if you have to bear it the next hundred years, or perhaps the next thousand. I bore it a good while longer, in spite of the back-ache. Well, then, after a thousand years, if I happen to feel in the mood, we may possibly shift about again. You are certainly a very strong man, and can never have a better opportunity to prove it. Posterity will talk of you, I warrant it!"

"Pish! a fig for its talk!" cried Hercules, with another hitch of his shoulders. "Just take the sky upon your head one instant, will you? I want to make a cushion of my lion's skin for the weight to rest upon. It really chafes me, and will cause unnecessary inconvenience in so many centuries as I am to stand here."

"That's no more than fair, and I'll do it!" quoth the giant; for he had no unkind feeling toward Hercules, and was merely acting with a too selfish consideration of his own ease. "For just five minutes, then, I'll take back the sky. Only for five minutes, recollect! I have no idea of spending another thousand years as I spent the last. Variety is the spice of life, say I."

Ah, the thick-witted old rogue of a giant! He threw down the golden apples, and received back the sky from the head and shoulders of Hercules upon his own, where it rightly belonged. And Hercules picked up the three golden apples, that were as big or bigger than pumpkins, and straightway set out on his journey homeward, without paying the slightest heed to the thundering tones of the giant, who bellowed after him to come back. Another forest sprang up around his feet, and grew ancient there; and again might be seen oak trees of six or seven centuries old, that had waxed thus aged betwixt his enormous toes.

And there stands the giant to this day; or, at any rate, there stands a mountain as tall as he, and which bears his name; and when the thunder rumbles about its summit, we may imagine it to be the voice of Giant Atlas bellowing after Hercules!

Right: Hercules meets the giant Atlas and strikes a deal to hold up the heavy sky for a spell while Atlas obtains the golden apples for the hero.

·HERCVLES·AND·ATLAS·

HOW THESEUS
FOUND HIS FATHER

In the old city of Troezene, at the foot of a lofty mountain, there lived, a very long time ago, a little boy named Theseus. His grandfather, King Pittheus, was the sovereign of that country, and was reckoned a very wise man; so that Theseus, being brought up in the royal palace, and being naturally a bright lad, could hardly fail of profiting by the old king's instructions.

His mother's name was Æthra. As for his father, the boy had never seen him. But, from his earliest remembrance, Æthra used to go with little Theseus into a wood, and sit down upon a moss-grown rock, which was deeply sunken into the earth. Here she often talked with her son about his father, and said that he was called Ægeus, and that he was a great king, and ruled over Attica, and dwelt at Athens, which was as famous a city as any in the world. Theseus was very fond of hearing about King Ægeus, and often asked his good mother Æthra why he did not come and live with them at Troezene.

"Ah, my dear son," answered Æthra, with a sigh, "a monarch has his people to take care of. The men and women over whom he rules are in the place of children to him; and he can seldom spare time to love his own children as other parents do. Your father will never be able to leave his kingdom for the sake of seeing his little boy."

"Well, but, dear mother," asked the boy, "why cannot I go to this famous city of Athens, and tell King Ægeus that I am his son?"

"That may happen by and by," said Æthra. "Be patient, and we shall see. You are not yet big and strong enough to set out on such an errand."

"And how soon shall I be strong enough?" Theseus persisted in inquiring. "You are but a tiny boy as yet," replied his mother. "See if you can lift this rock on which we are sitting."

The little fellow had a great opinion of his own strength. So, grasping the rough protuberances of the rock, he tugged and toiled amain, and got himself quite out of breath, without being able to stir the heavy stone. It seemed to be rooted into the ground. No wonder he could not move it; for it would have taken all the force of a very strong man to lift it out of its earthy bed.

His mother stood looking on, with a sad kind of a smile on her lips and in her eyes, to see the zealous and yet puny efforts of her little boy. She could not help being sorrowful at finding him already so impatient to begin his adventures in the world.

"You see how it is, my dear Theseus," said she. "You must possess far more strength than now before I can trust you to go to Athens, and tell King Ægeus that you are his son. But when you can lift this rock, and show me what is hidden beneath it, I promise you my permission to depart."

Often and often, after this, did Theseus ask his mother whether it was yet time for him to go to Athens; and still his mother pointed to the rock, and told him that, for years to come, he could not be strong enough to move it. And again and again the rosy-cheeked and curly-headed boy would tug and strain at the huge mass of stone, striving, child as he was, to do what a giant could hardly have done without taking both of his great hands to the task. Meanwhile the rock seemed to be sinking farther and farther into the ground. The moss grew over it thicker and thicker, until at last it looked almost like a soft green seat, with only a few gray knobs of granite peeping out. The overhanging trees, also, shed their brown leaves upon it, as often as the autumn came; and at its base grew ferns and wild flowers, some of which crept quite over its surface. To all appearance the rock was as firmly fastened as any other portion of the earth's substance.

But difficult as the matter looked, Theseus was now growing up to be such a vigorous youth that, in his own opinion, the time would quickly come when he might hope to get the upper hand of this ponderous lump of stone.

"Mother, I do believe it has started!" cried he, after one of his attempts. "The earth around it is certainly a little cracked!"

"No, no, child!" his mother hastily answered. "It is not possible that you can have moved it, such a boy as you still are!"

Nor would she be convinced, although Theseus showed her the place where he fancied that the stem of a flower had been partly uprooted by the movement of the rock. But Æthra sighed and looked disquieted; for, no doubt, she began to be conscious that her son was no longer a child, and that, in a little while hence, she must send him forth among the perils and troubles of the world.

It was not more than a year afterwards when they were again sitting on the moss-covered stone. Æthra had once more told him the oft-repeated story of his father, and how gladly he would receive Theseus at his stately palace, and how he would present him to his courtiers and the people, and tell them that here was the heir of his dominions. The eyes of Theseus glowed with enthusiasm, and he would hardly sit still to hear his mother speak.

"Dear mother Æthra," he exclaimed, "I never felt half so strong as now! I am no longer a child, nor a boy, nor a mere youth! I feel myself a man! It is now time to make one earnest trial to remove the stone."

"Ah, my dearest Theseus," replied his mother, "not yet! not yet!"

"Yes, mother," he said resolutely, "the time has come!"

Then Theseus bent himself in good earnest to the task, and strained every sinew, with manly strength and resolution. He put his whole brave heart into the effort. He wrestled with the big and sluggish stone, as if it had been a living enemy. He heaved, he lifted, he resolved now to succeed, or else to perish there and let the rock be his monument forever! Æthra stood gazing at him, and clasped her hands, partly with a mother's pride and partly with a mother's sorrow. The great rock stirred! Yes; it was raised slowly from the bedded moss and earth, uprooting the shrubs and flowers along with it, and was turned upon its side. Theseus had conquered!

While taking breath he looked joyfully at his mother, and she smiled upon him through her tears.

"Yes, Theseus," she said, "the time has come, and you must stay no longer at my side! See what King Ægeus, your royal father, left for you, beneath the stone, when he lifted it in his mighty arms and laid it on the spot whence you have now removed it."

Theseus looked, and saw that the rock had been placed over another slab of stone, containing a cavity within it; so that it somewhat resembled a roughly made chest or coffer, of which the upper mass had served as the lid. Within the cavity lay a sword, with a golden hilt, and a pair of sandals.

"That was your father's sword," said Æthra, "and those were his sandals. When he went to be King of Athens, he bade me treat you as a child until you should prove yourself a man by lifting this heavy stone. That task being accomplished, you are to put on his sandals, in order to follow in your father's footsteps, and to gird on his sword, so that you may fight giants and dragons, as King Ægeus did in his youth."

"I will set out for Athens this very day!" cried Theseus.

But his mother persuaded him to stay a day or two longer, while she got ready some necessary articles for his journey. When his grandfather, the wise King Pittheus, heard that Theseus intended to present himself at his father's palace, he earnestly advised him to get on board of a vessel, and go by sea; because he might thus arrive within fifteen miles of Athens, without either fatigue or danger.

"The roads are very bad by land," quoth the venerable king; "and they are terribly infested with robbers and monsters. A mere lad like Theseus is not fit to be trusted on such a perilous journey all by himself. No, no; let him go by sea!"

But when Theseus heard of robbers and monsters, he pricked up his ears and was so much the more eager to take the road along which they were to be met with. On the third day, therefore, he bade a respectful farewell to his grandfather, thanking him for all his kindness; and, after affectionately embracing his mother, he set forth, with a good many of her tears glistening on his cheeks, and some, if the truth must be told, that had gushed out of his own eyes. But he let the sun and wind dry them, and walked stoutly on, playing with the golden hilt of his sword and taking very manly strides in his father's sandals.

I cannot stop to tell you hardly any of the adventures that befell Theseus on the road to Athens. It is enough to say that he

Right: The wicked enchantress Medea atop her fiery serpent. An illustration by Virginia Frances Sterrett (1900–1931) that first appeared in Nathaniel Hawthorne's *Tanglewood Tales*.

quite cleared that part of the country of the robbers about whom King Pittheus had been so much alarmed. One of these bad people was named Procrustes, and he was indeed a terrible fellow, and had an ugly way of making fun of the poor travelers who happened to fall into his clutches. In his cavern he had a bed, on which, with great pretense of hospitality, he invited his guests to lie down; but if they happened to be shorter than the bed, this wicked villain stretched them out by main force; or, if they were too tall, he lopped off their heads or feet, and laughed at what he had done as an excellent joke. Thus, however weary a man might be, he never liked to lie in the bed of Procrustes. Another of these robbers, named Scinis, must likewise have been a very great scoundrel. He was in the habit of flinging his victims off a high cliff into the sea; and in order to give him exactly his deserts, Theseus tossed him off the very same place. But if you will believe me, the sea would not pollute itself by receiving such a bad person into its bosom, neither would the earth, having once got rid of him, consent to take him back; so that, between the cliff and the sea, Scinis stuck fast in the air, which was forced to bear the burden of his naughtiness.

Thus, by the time he reached his journey's end, Theseus had done many valiant feats with his father's golden-hilted sword, and had gained the renown of being one of the bravest young men of the day. His fame traveled faster than he did, and reached Athens before him. As he entered the city, he heard the inhabitants talking at the street corners and saying that Hercules was brave, and Jason too, and Castor and Pollux likewise, but that Theseus, the son of their own king, would turn out as great a hero as the best of them. Theseus took longer strides on hearing this, and fancied himself sure of a magnificent reception at his father's court, since he came thither with Fame to blow her trumpet before him, and cry to King Ægeus, "Behold your son!"

Theseus little suspected, innocent youth that he was, that here in this very Athens, where his father reigned, a greater danger awaited him than any which he had encountered on the road. Yet this was the truth. You must understand that the father of Theseus, though not very old in years, was almost worn out with the cares of government, and had thus grown aged before his time. His nephews, not expecting him to live a very great while, intended to get all the power of the kingdom into their own hands. But when they heard that Theseus had arrived in Athens, and learned what a gallant young man he was, they saw that he would not be at all the kind of person to let them steal away his father's crown and scepter, which ought to be his own by right of inheritance. Thus these bad-hearted nephews of King Ægeus, who were the own cousins of Theseus, at once became his enemies. A still more dangerous enemy was Medea, the wicked enchantress; for she was now the king's wife, and wanted to give the kingdom to her son Medus, instead of letting it be given to the son of Æthra, whom she hated.

It so happened that the king's nephews met Theseus, and found out who he was, just as he reached the entrance of the royal palace. With all their evil designs against him, they pretended to be their cousin's best friends, and expressed great joy at making his acquaintance. They proposed to him that he should come into the king's presence as a stranger, in order to try whether Ægeus would discover in the young man's features any likeness either to himself or his

mother Æthra, and thus recognize him for a son. Theseus consented, for he fancied that his father would know him in a moment, by the love that was in his heart. But while he waited at the door, the nephews ran and told King Ægeus that a young man had arrived in Athens, who, to their certain knowledge, intended to put him to death and get possession of his royal crown.

"And he is now waiting for admission to your Majesty's presence," added they.

"Aha!" cried the old king, on hearing this. "Why, he must be a very wicked young fellow, indeed! Pray, what would you advise me to do with him?"

In reply to this question, the wicked Medea put in her word. You have heard already of this enchantress, and the wicked arts that she practiced upon men. Amongst a thousand other bad things, she knew how to prepare a poison, that was instantly fatal to whomsoever might so much as touch it with his lips.

So when the king asked what he should do with Theseus, this naughty woman had an answer ready at her tongue's end.

"Leave that to me, please your Majesty," she replied. "Only admit this evil-minded young man to your presence, treat him civilly, and invite him to drink a goblet of wine. Your Majesty is well aware that I sometimes amuse myself with distilling very powerful medicines. Here is one of them in this small phial. As to what it is made of, that is one of my secrets of state. Do but let me put a single drop into the goblet, and let the young man taste it, and I will answer for it, he shall quite lay aside the bad designs with which he comes hither."

As she said this, Medea smiled; but, for all her smiling face, she meant nothing less than to poison the poor innocent Theseus before his father's eyes. And King Ægeus, like most other kings, thought any punishment mild enough for a person who was accused of plotting against his life. He therefore made little or no objection to Medea's scheme, and as soon as the poisonous wine was ready, gave orders that the young stranger should be admitted into his presence. The goblet was set on a table beside the king's throne, and a fly, meaning just to sip a little from the brim, immediately tumbled into it, dead. Observing this, Medea looked round at the nephews and smiled again.

When Theseus was ushered into the royal apartment, the only object that he seemed to behold was the white-bearded old king. There he sat on his magnificent throne, a dazzling crown on his head, and a scepter in his hand. His aspect was stately and majestic, although his years and infirmities weighed heavily upon him, as if each year were a lump of lead and each infirmity a ponderous stone, and all were bundled up together and laid upon his weary shoulders. The tears, both of joy and sorrow, sprang into the young man's eyes; for he thought how sad it was to see his dear father so infirm, and how sweet it would be to support him with his own youthful strength, and to cheer him up with the alacrity of his loving spirit. When a son takes his father into his warm heart, it renews the old man's youth in a better way than by the heat of Medea's magic cauldron. And this was what Theseus resolved to do. He could scarcely wait to see whether King Ægeus would recognize him, so eager was he to throw himself into his arms.

Advancing to the foot of the throne, he attempted to make a little speech, which he had been thinking about as he came up the stairs. But he was almost choked by a great many

tender feelings that gushed out of his heart and swelled into his throat, all struggling to find utterance together. And therefore, unless he could have laid his full, over-brimming heart into the king's hand, poor Theseus knew not what to do or say. The cunning Medea observed what was passing in the young man's mind. She was more wicked at that moment than ever she had been before; for (and it makes me tremble to tell you of it) she did her worst to turn all this unspeakable love with which Theseus was agitated to his own ruin and destruction.

"Does your Majesty see his confusion?" she whispered in the king's ear. "He is so conscious of guilt that he trembles and cannot speak. The wretch lives too long! Quick; Offer him the wine!"

Now King Ægeus had been gazing earnestly at the young stranger as he drew near the throne. There was something, he knew not what, either in his white brow, or in the fine expression of his mouth, or in his beautiful and tender eyes, that made him indistinctly feel as if he had seen this youth before; as if, indeed, he had trotted him on his knee when a baby, and had beheld him growing to be a stalwart man, while he himself grew old. But Medea guessed how the king felt, and would not suffer him to yield to these natural sensibilities, although they were the voice of his deepest heart, telling him, as plainly as it could speak, that here was his dear son, and Æthra's son, coming to claim him for a father. The enchantress again whispered in the king's ear, and compelled him, by her witchcraft, to see everything under a false aspect.

He made up his mind therefore to let Theseus drink of the poisoned wine.

"Young man," said he, "you are welcome! I am proud to show hospitality to so heroic a youth. Do me the favor to drink the contents of this goblet. It is brimming over, as you see, with delicious wine, such as I bestow only on those who are worthy of it! None is more worthy to quaff it than yourself!"

So saying, King Ægeus took the golden goblet from the table and was about to offer it to Theseus. But, partly through his infirmities and partly because it seemed so sad a thing to take away this young man's life, however wicked he might be, and partly, no doubt, because his heart was wiser than his head, and quaked within him at the thought of what he was going to do—for all these reasons the king's hand trembled so much that a great deal of the wine slopped over.

In order to strengthen his purpose, and fearing lest the whole of the precious poison should be wasted, one of his nephews now whispered to him: "Has your Majesty any doubt of this stranger's guilt? There is the very sword with which he meant to slay you. How sharp, and bright, and terrible it is! Quick!—let him taste the wine, or perhaps he may do the deed even yet."

At these words Ægeus drove every thought and feeling out of his breast, except the one idea of how justly the young man deserved to be put to death. He sat erect on his throne, and held out the goblet of wine with a steady hand, and bent on Theseus a frown of kingly severity; for, after all, he had too noble a spirit to murder even a treacherous enemy with a deceitful smile upon his face. "Drink!" said he, in the stern tone with which he was wont to condemn a criminal to be beheaded. "You have well deserved of me such wine as this!" Theseus held out his hand to take the wine. But before he touched it, King Ægeus trembled again. His eyes had fallen on the gold-hilted sword that hung at the young man's side. He drew back the goblet.

"That sword!" he cried. "How came you by it?"

"It was my father's sword," replied Theseus, with a tremulous voice. "These were his sandals. My dear mother (her name is Æthra) told me his story while I was yet a little child. But it is only a month since I grew strong enough to lift the heavy stone and take the sword and sandals from beneath it and come to Athens to seek my father."

"My son! my son!" cried King Ægeus, flinging away the fatal goblet and tottering down from the throne, to fall into the arms of Theseus. "Yes, these are Æthra's eyes; it is my son."

I have quite forgotten what became of the king's nephews. But when the wicked Medea saw this new turn of affairs she hurried out of the room, and going to her private chamber, lost no time in setting her enchantments at work. In a few moments she heard a great noise of hissing snakes outside of the chamber window; and behold! there was her fiery chariot and four huge winged serpents, wriggling and twisting in the air, flourishing their tails higher than the top of the palace, and all ready to set off on an aerial journey. Medea stayed only long enough to take her son with her, and to steal the crown jewels, together with the king's best robes and whatever other valuable things she could lay hands on; and getting into the chariot, she whipped up the snakes and ascended high over the city.

The king, hearing the hiss of the serpents, scrambled as fast as he could to the window and bawled out to the abominable enchantress never to come back. The whole people of Athens too, who had run out of doors to see this wonderful spectacle, set up a shout of joy at the prospect of getting rid of her. Medea, almost bursting with rage, uttered precisely such a hiss as one of her own snakes, only ten times more venomous and spiteful; and glaring fiercely out of the blaze of the chariot, she shook her hands over the multitude below, as if she were scattering a million of curses among them. In so doing, however, she unintentionally let fall about five hundred diamonds of the first water, together with a thousand great pearls and two thousand emeralds, rubies, sapphires, opals, and topazes, to which she had helped herself out of the king's strong-box. All these came pelting down, like a shower of many-colored hailstones, upon the heads of grown people and children, who forthwith gathered them up and carried them back to the palace. But King Ægeus told them that they were welcome to the whole, and to twice as many more, if he had them, for the sake of his delight at finding his son and losing the wicked Medea. And, indeed, if you had seen how hateful was her last look, as the flaming chariot flew upward, you would not have wondered that both king and people should think her departure a good riddance.

THESEUS GOES TO SLAY THE MINOTAUR

And now Prince Theseus was taken into great favor by his royal father. The old king was never weary of having him sit beside him on his throne (which was quite wide enough for two), and of hearing him tell about his dear mother, and his childhood, and his many boyish efforts to lift the ponderous stone.

Theseus, however, was much too brave and active a young man to be willing to spend all his time in relating things which had already happened. His ambition was to perform other and more heroic deeds, which should be better worth telling in prose and verse. Nor had he been long in Athens before he caught and chained a terrible mad bull, and made a public show of him, greatly to the wonder and admiration of good King Ægeus and his subjects. But pretty soon he undertook an affair that made all his foregone adventures seem like mere boy's play. The occasion of it was as follows:

One morning, when Prince Theseus awoke, he fancied that he must have had a very sorrowful dream, and that it was still running in his mind, even now that his eyes were open. For it appeared as if the air was full of a melancholy wail; and when he listened more attentively, he could hear sobs, and groans, and screams of woe, mingled with deep, quiet sighs, which came from the king's palace, and from the streets, and from the temples, and from every habitation in the city.

And all these mournful noises, issuing out of thousands of separate hearts, united themselves into the one great sound of affliction which had startled Theseus from slumber. He put on his clothes as quickly as he could (not forgetting his sandals and gold-hilted sword), and hastening to the king, inquired what it all meant.

"Alas! my son," quoth King Ægeus, heaving a long sigh, "here is a very lamentable matter in hand! This is the woefulest anniversary in the whole year. It is the day when we annually draw lots to see which of the youths and maidens of Athens shall go to be devoured by the horrible Minotaur!"

Above: Theseus meets with Ariadne, daughter of Minos, king of Crete, and obtains her help in attempting to defeat the Minotaur. Illustration by Virginia Frances Sterrett (1900–1931), originally appearing in Hawthorne's *Tanglewood Tales*.

"The Minotaur!" exclaimed Prince Theseus; and, like a brave young prince as he was, he put his hand to the hilt of his sword. "What kind of a monster may that be? Is it not possible, at the risk of one's life, to slay him?"

But King Ægeus shook his venerable head, and to convince Theseus that it was quite a hopeless case, he gave him an explanation of the whole affair. It seems that in the island of Crete there lived a certain dreadful monster, called a Minotaur, which was shaped partly like a man and partly like a bull, and was altogether such a hideous sort of a creature that it is really disagreeable to think of him. If he were suffered to exist at all, it should have been on some desert island, or in the duskiness of some deep cavern, where nobody would ever be tormented by his abominable aspect. But King Minos, who reigned over Crete, laid out a vast deal of money in building a habitation for the Minotaur, and took great care of his health and comfort, merely for mischief's sake. A few years before this time there had been a war between the city of Athens and the island of Crete, in which the Athenians were beaten, and compelled to beg for peace. No peace could they obtain, however, except on condition that they should send seven young men and seven maidens, every year, to be devoured by the pet monster of the cruel King Minos. For three years past this grievous calamity had been borne. And the sobs, and groans, and shrieks with which the city was now filled were caused by the people's woe, because the fatal day had come again when the fourteen victims were to be chosen by lot; and the old people feared lest their sons or daughters might be taken, and the youths and damsels dreaded lest they themselves might be destined to glut the ravenous maw of that detestable man-brute.

But when Theseus heard the story, he straightened himself up, so that he seemed taller than ever before; and as for his face, it was indignant, despiteful, bold, tender, and compassionate, all in one look.

"Let the people of Athens this year draw lots for only six young men, instead of seven," said he. "I will myself be the seventh; and let the Minotaur devour me if he can!"

"Oh, my dear son!" cried King Ægeus, "why should you expose yourself to this horrible fate? You are a royal prince, and have a right to hold yourself above the destinies of common men."

"It is because I am a prince, your son, and the rightful heir to your kingdom, that I freely take upon me the calamity of your subjects," answered Theseus. "And you, my father, being king over this people, and answerable to Heaven for their welfare, are bound to sacrifice what is dearest to you, rather than that the son or daughter of the poorest citizen should come to any harm."

The old king shed tears, and besought Theseus not to leave him desolate in his old age, more especially as he had but just begun to know the happiness of possessing a good and valiant son. Theseus, however, felt that he was in the right, and therefore would not give up his resolution. But he assured his father that he did not intend to be eaten up unresistingly, like a sheep, and that, if the Minotaur devoured him, it should not be without a battle for his dinner. And finally, since he could not help it, King Ægeus consented to let him go. So a vessel was got ready, and rigged with black sails; and Theseus, with six other young men and seven

tender and beautiful damsels, came down to the harbor to embark. A sorrowful multitude accompanied them to the shore. There was the poor old king, too, leaning on his son's arm, and looking as if his single heart held all the grief of Athens.

Just as Prince Theseus was going on board his father bethought himself of one last word to say.

"My beloved son," said he, grasping the prince's hand, "you observe that the sails of this vessel are black, as indeed they ought to be, since it goes upon a voyage of sorrow and despair. Now, being weighed down with infirmities, I know not whether I can survive till the vessel shall return. But as long as I do live, I shall creep daily to the top of yonder cliff, to watch if there be a sail upon the sea. And, dearest Theseus, if by some happy chance you should escape the jaws of the Minotaur, then tear down those dismal sails, and hoist others that shall be bright as the sunshine. Beholding them on the horizon, myself and all the people will know that you are coming back victorious, and will welcome you with such a festal uproar as Athens never heard before."

Theseus promised that he would do so. Then, going on board, the mariners trimmed the vessel's black sails to the wind, which blew faintly off the shore, being pretty much made up of the sighs that everybody kept pouring forth on this melancholy occasion. But by and by, when they got fairly out to sea, there came a stiff breeze from the north-west, and drove them along as merrily over the white-capped waves as if they had been going on the most delightful errand imaginable. And though it was a sad business enough, I rather question whether fourteen young people, without any old persons to keep them in order, could continue to spend the whole time of the voyage in being miserable. There had been some few dances upon the undulating deck, I suspect, and some hearty bursts of laughter, and other such unseasonable merriment among the victims, before the high, blue mountains of Crete began to show themselves among the far-off clouds. That sight, to be sure, made them all very grave again.

No sooner had they entered the harbor than a party of the guards of King Minos came down to the waterside and took charge of the fourteen young men and damsels. Surrounded by these armed warriors, Prince Theseus and his companions were led to the king's palace and ushered into his presence. Now Minos was a stern and pitiless king. He bent his shaggy brows upon the poor Athenian victims. Any other mortal, beholding their fresh and tender beauty and their innocent looks, would have felt himself sitting on thorns until he had made every soul of them happy by bidding them go free as the summer wind. But this immitigable Minos cared only to examine whether they were plump enough to satisfy the Minotaur's appetite. For my part, I wish he himself had been the only victim; and the monster would have found him a pretty tough one.

One after another, King Minos called these pale, frightened youths and sobbing maidens to his footstool, gave them each a poke in the ribs with his scepter (to try whether they were in good flesh or no), and dismissed them with a nod to his guards. But when his eyes rested on Theseus, the king looked at him more attentively, because his face was calm and grave.

"Young man," asked he, with his stern voice, "are you not appalled at the certainty of being devoured by this terrible Minotaur?"

"I have offered my life in a good cause," answered Theseus, "and therefore I give it freely and gladly. But thou, King Minos, art thou not thyself appalled, who, year after year, hast perpetrated this dreadful wrong, by giving seven innocent youths and as many maidens to be devoured by a monster? Dost thou not tremble, wicked king, to turn thine eyes inward on thine own heart? Sitting there on thy golden throne and in thy robes of majesty, I tell thee to thy face, King Minos, thou art a more hideous monster than the Minotaur himself!"

"Aha! do you think me so?" cried the king, laughing in his cruel way. "Tomorrow, at breakfast time, you shall have an opportunity of judging which is the greater monster, the Minotaur or the king! Take them away, guards; and let this free-spoken youth be the Minotaur's first morsel!"

Near the king's throne stood his daughter Ariadne. She was a beautiful and tender-hearted maiden, and looked at these poor doomed captives with very different feelings from those of the iron-breasted King Minos. She really wept, indeed, at the idea of how much human happiness would be needlessly thrown away by giving so many young people, in the first bloom and rose-blossom of their lives, to be eaten up by a creature who, no doubt, would have preferred a fat ox, or even a large pig, to the plumpest of them. And when she beheld the brave-spirited figure of Prince Theseus bearing himself so calmly in his terrible peril, she grew a hundred times more pitiful than before. As the guards were taking him away, she flung herself at the king's feet and besought him to set all the captives free, and especially this one young man.

"Peace, foolish girl!" answered King Minos. "What hast thou to do with an affair like this? It is a matter of state policy, and therefore quite beyond thy weak comprehension. Go water thy flowers, and think no more of these Athenian caitiffs, whom the Minotaur shall as certainly eat up for breakfast as I will eat a partridge for my supper."

So saying, the king looked cruel enough to devour Theseus and all the rest of the captives himself, had there been no Minotaur to save him the trouble. As he would not hear another word in their favor, the prisoners were now led away and clapped into a dungeon, where the jailer advised them to go to sleep as soon as possible, because the Minotaur was in the habit of calling for breakfast early. The seven maidens and six young men soon sobbed themselves to slumber. But Theseus was not like them. He felt conscious that he was wiser and braver and stronger than his companions, and that therefore he had the responsibility of all their lives upon him, and must consider whether there was no way to save them, even in this last extremity. So he kept himself awake, and paced to and fro across the gloomy dungeon in which they were shut up.

Just before midnight the door was softly unbarred, and the gentle Ariadne showed herself, with a torch in her hand.

"Are you awake, Prince Theseus?" she whispered.

"Yes," answered Theseus. "With so little time to live, I do not choose to waste any of it in sleep."

"Then follow me," said Ariadne, "and tread softly."

What had become of the jailer and the guards Theseus never knew. But however that might be, Ariadne opened all the doors and led him forth from the darksome prison into the pleasant moonlight.

"Theseus," said the maiden, "you can now get on board your vessel and sail away for Athens."

"No," answered the young man; "I will never leave Crete unless I can first slay the Minotaur, and save my poor companions, and deliver Athens from this cruel tribute."

"I knew that this would be your resolution," said Ariadne. "Come, then, with me, brave Theseus. Here is your own sword which the guards deprived you of. You will need it; and pray Heaven you may use it well."

Then she led Theseus along by the hand until they came to a dark, shadowy grove, where the moonlight wasted itself on the tops of the trees, without shedding hardly so much as a glimmering beam upon their pathway. After going a good way through this obscurity, they reached a high marble wall, which was overgrown with creeping plants, that made it shaggy with their verdure. The wall seemed to have no door, nor any windows, but rose up, lofty and massive and mysterious, and was neither to be clambered over nor, so far as Theseus could perceive, to be passed through. Nevertheless, Ariadne did but press one of her soft little fingers against a particular block of marble and, though it looked as solid as any other part of the wall, it yielded to her touch, disclosing an entrance just wide enough to admit them. They crept through, and the marble stone swung back into its place.

"We are now," said Ariadne, "in the famous labyrinth which Dædalus built before he made himself a pair of wings and flew away from our island like a bird. That Dædalus was a very cunning workman, but of all his artful contrivances this labyrinth is the most wondrous. Were we to take but a few steps from the doorway, we might wander about all our lifetime and never find it again. Yet in the very center of this labyrinth is the Minotaur, and, Theseus, you must go thither to seek him."

"But how shall I ever find him?" asked Theseus, "if the labyrinth so bewilders me, as you say it will?"

Just as he spoke they heard a rough and very disagreeable roar, which greatly resembled the lowing of a fierce bull, but yet had some sort of sound like the human voice. Theseus even fancied a rude articulation in it, as if the creature that uttered it were trying to shape his hoarse breath into words. It was at some distance, however, and he really could not tell whether it sounded most like a bull's roar or a man's harsh voice.

"That is the Minotaur's noise," whispered Ariadne, closely grasping the hand of Theseus, and pressing one of her own hands to her heart, which was all in a tremble. "You must follow that sound through the windings of the labyrinth, and, by and by, you will find him. Stay! take the end of this silken string; I will hold the other end; and then, if you win the victory, it will lead you again to this spot. Farewell, brave Theseus."

So the young man took the end of the silken string in his left hand, and his gold-hilted sword, ready drawn from its scabbard, in the other, and trod boldly into the inscrutable labyrinth. How this labyrinth was built is more than I can tell you, but so cunningly contrived a mizmaze was never seen in the world before nor since. Theseus had not taken five steps before he lost sight of Ariadne; and in five more his head was growing dizzy. But he still went on, now creeping through a low arch, now ascending a flight of steps, now in one crooked passage, and now in another, with here a door opening before him, and there one banging behind, until it

really seemed as if the walls spun round and whirled him along with them. And all the while, through these hollow avenues, now nearer, now farther off again, resounded the cry of the Minotaur; and the sound was so fierce, so cruel, so ugly, so like a bull's roar, and withal so like a human voice, and yet like neither of them, that the brave heart of Theseus grew sterner and angrier at every step; for he felt it an insult to the moon and sky, and to our affectionate and simple Mother Earth, that such a monster should have the audacity to exist.

As he passed onward, the clouds gathered over the moon, and the labyrinth grew so dusky that Theseus could no longer discern the bewilderment through which he was passing. He would have felt quite lost, and utterly hopeless of ever again walking in a straight path, if every little while he had not been conscious of a gentle twitch at the silken cord. Then he knew that the tender-hearted Ariadne was still holding the other end, and that she was fearing for him, and hoping for him, and giving him just as much of her sympathy as if she were close by his side. But still he followed the dreadful roar of the Minotaur, which now grew louder and louder, and finally so very loud that Theseus fully expected to come close upon him, at every new zigzag and wriggle of the path. And at last, in an open space, in the very center of the labyrinth, he did discern the hideous creature.

Sure enough, what an ugly monster it was! Only his horned head belonged to a bull; and yet, somehow or other, he looked like a bull all over, preposterously waddling on his hind legs; or, if you happened to view him in another way, he seemed wholly a man, and all the more monstrous for being so. And there he was, the wretched thing, with no society, no companion, no kind of a mate, living only to do mischief, and incapable of knowing what affection means. Theseus hated him, and shuddered at him, and yet could not but be sensible of some sort of pity; and all the more, the uglier and more detestable the creature was. For he kept striding to and fro in a solitary frenzy of rage, continually emitting a hoarse roar, which was oddly mixed up with half-shaped words; and, after listening awhile, Theseus understood that the Minotaur was saying to himself how miserable he was, and how hungry, and how he hated everybody, and how he longed to eat up the human race alive.

Was Theseus afraid? By no means, my dear auditors. What! a hero like Theseus afraid! Not had the Minotaur had twenty bull heads instead of one. Bold as he was, however, I fancy that it strengthened his valiant heart, just at this crisis, to feel a tremulous twitch at the silken cord, which he was still holding in his left hand. It was as if Ariadne were giving him all her might and courage; and, much as he already had, and little as she had to give, it made his own seem twice as much. And to confess the honest truth, he needed the whole; for now the Minotaur, turning suddenly about, caught sight of Theseus, and instantly lowered his horribly sharp horns, exactly as a mad bull does when he means to rush against an enemy. At the same time he belched forth a tremendous roar, in which there was something like the words of human language, but all disjointed and shaken to pieces by passing through the gullet of a miserably enraged brute.

Theseus could only guess what the creature intended to say, and that rather by his gestures than his words; for the Minotaur's horns were sharper than his wits, and of a great deal more service to him than his tongue. But probably this was the sense of what he uttered:

"Ah, wretch of a human being! I'll stick my horns through you, and toss you fifty feet high, and eat you up the moment you come down."

"Come on, then, and try it!" was all that Theseus deigned to reply; for he was far too magnanimous to assault his enemy with insolent language.

Without more words on either side, there ensued the most awful fight between Theseus and the Minotaur that ever happened beneath the sun or moon. I really know not how it might have turned out, if the monster, in his first headlong rush against Theseus, had not missed him, by a hair's-breadth, and broken one of his horns short off against the stone wall. On this mishap he bellowed so intolerably that a part of the labyrinth tumbled down, and all the inhabitants of Crete mistook the noise for an uncommonly heavy thunder-storm. Smarting with the pain, he galloped around the open space in so ridiculous a way that Theseus laughed at it long afterwards, though not precisely at the moment. After this the two antagonists stood valiantly up to one another, and fought sword to horn, for a long while. At last, the Minotaur made a run at Theseus, grazed his left side with his horn, and flung him down; and thinking that he had stabbed him to the heart, he cut a great caper in the air, opened his bull mouth from ear to ear, and prepared to snap his head off. But Theseus by this time had leaped up, and caught the monster off his guard. Fetching a sword-stroke at him with all his force, he hit him fair upon the neck, and made his bull head skip six yards from his human body, which fell down flat upon the ground.

So now the battle was ended. Immediately the moon shone out as brightly as if all the troubles of the world, and all the wickedness and the ugliness that infest human life, were past and gone forever. And Theseus, as he leaned on his sword, taking breath, felt another twitch of the silken cord; for all through the terrible encounter he had held it fast in his left hand. Eager to let Ariadne know of his success, he followed the guidance of the thread, and soon found himself at the entrance of the labyrinth.

"Thou hast slain the monster," cried Ariadne, clasping her hands.

"Thanks to thee, dear Ariadne," answered Theseus, "I return victorious."

"Then," said Ariadne, "we must quickly summon thy friends, and get them and thyself on board the vessel before dawn. If morning finds thee here, my father will avenge the Minotaur."

To make my story short, the poor captives were awakened, and hardly knowing whether it was not a joyful dream, were told of what Theseus had done, and that they must set sail for Athens before daybreak. Hastening down to the vessel, they all clambered on board, except Prince Theseus, who lingered behind them, on the strand, holding Ariadne's hand clasped in his own.

"Dear maiden," said he, "thou wilt surely go with us. Thou art too gentle and sweet a child for such an iron-hearted father as King Minos. He cares no more for thee than a granite rock cares for the little flower that grows in one of its crevices. But my father, King Ægeus, and my dear mother, Æthra, and all the fathers and mothers in Athens, and all the sons and daughters too, will love and honor thee as their benefactress. Come with us, then; for King Minos will be very angry when he knows what thou hast done."

Now, some low-minded people, who pretend to tell the story of Theseus and Ariadne, have the face to say that this royal and honorable maiden did really flee away, under cover of the

Above: Theseus slays the mighty minotaur in an illustration by Henry Matthew Brock (1875–1960).

night, with the young stranger whose life she had preserved. They say, too, that Prince Theseus (who would have died sooner than wrong the meanest creature in the world) ungratefully deserted Ariadne on a solitary island, where the vessel touched on its voyage to Athens. But had the noble Theseus heard these falsehoods, he would have served their slanderous authors as he served the Minotaur! Here is what Ariadne answered, when the brave Prince of Athens besought her to accompany him: "No, Theseus," the maiden said, pressing his hand and then drawing back a step or two, "I cannot go with you. My father is old, and has nobody but myself to love him. Hard as you think his heart is, it would break to lose me. At first King Minos will be angry; but he will soon forgive his only child; and, by and by, he will rejoice, I know, that no more youths and maidens must come from Athens to be devoured by the Minotaur. I have saved you, Theseus, as much for my father's sake as for your own. Farewell! Heaven bless you!"

All this was so true, and so maiden-like, and was spoken with so sweet a dignity, that Theseus would have blushed to urge her any longer. Nothing remained for him, therefore, but to bid Ariadne an affectionate farewell, and go on board the vessel and set sail.

In a few moments the white foam was boiling up before their prow, as Prince Theseus and his companions sailed out of the harbor, with a whistling breeze behind them.

On the homeward voyage the fourteen youths and damsels were in excellent spirits, as you will easily suppose. They spent most of their time in dancing, unless when the sidelong breeze made the deck slope too much. In due season they came within sight of the coast of Attica, which was their native country. But here, I am grieved to tell you, happened a sad misfortune.

You will remember (what Theseus unfortunately forgot) that his father, King Ægeus, had enjoined it upon him to hoist sunshiny sails, instead of black ones, in case he should overcome the Minotaur, and return victorious. In the joy of their success, however, and amidst the sports, dancing, and other merriment with which these young folks wore away the time, they never once thought whether their sails were black, white, or rainbow colored, and, indeed, left it entirely to the mariners whether they had any sails at all. Thus the vessel returned, like a raven, with the same sable wings that had wafted her away. But poor King Ægeus, day after day, infirm as he was, had clambered to the summit of a cliff that overhung the sea, and there sat watching for Prince Theseus, homeward bound; and no sooner did he behold the fatal blackness of the sails, than he concluded that his dear son, whom he loved so much, and felt so proud of, had been eaten by the Minotaur. He could not bear the thought of living any longer; so, first flinging his crown and scepter into the sea (useless baubles that they were to him now!) King Ægeus merely stooped forward, and fell headlong over the cliff, and was drowned, poor soul, in the waves that foamed at its base!

This was melancholy news for Prince Theseus, who, when he stepped ashore, found himself king of all the country, whether he would or no; and such a turn of fortune was enough to make any young man feel very much out of spirits. However, he sent for his dear mother to Athens, and, by taking her advice in matters of state, became a very excellent monarch, and was greatly beloved by his people.

CIRCE'S PALACE

After escaping from the Cyclopes, and enduring many other perils by land and sea in the course of his weary voyage to Ithaca, Ulysses arrived at a green island, the name of which was unknown to him, and was glad to moor his tempest-beaten bark in a quiet cove. But he had encountered so many dangers from giants, and one-eyed Cyclopes, and monsters of the sea and land, that he could not help dreading some mischief, even in this pleasant and seemingly solitary spot.

For two days, therefore, the poor weather-worn voyagers kept quiet, and either stayed on board of their vessel, or merely crept along under the cliffs that bordered the shore; and to keep themselves alive, they dug shellfish out of the sand, and sought for any little rill of fresh water that might be running towards the sea.

Before the two days were spent, they grew very weary of this kind of life; for the followers of King Ulysses were terrible gormandizers, and pretty sure to grumble if they missed their regular meals, and their irregular ones besides. Their stock of provisions was quite exhausted, and even the shellfish began to get scarce, so that they had now to choose between starving to death or venturing into the interior of the island, where perhaps some huge three-headed dragon, or other horrible monster, had his den.

But King Ulysses was a bold man as well as a prudent one; and on the third morning he determined to discover what sort of a place the island was, and whether it were possible to obtain a supply of food for the hungry mouths of his companions. So, taking a spear in his hand, he clambered to the summit of a cliff and gazed round about him. At a distance, towards the center of the island, he beheld the stately towers of what seemed to be a palace, built of snow-white marble, and rising in the midst of a grove of lofty trees. The thick branches of these trees stretched across the front of the edifice, and more than half concealed it, although, from

Right: The voyagers see themselves in the cloth that Circe and her women have been weaving. Illustration by Virginia Frances Sterrett (1900–1931).

the portion which he saw, Ulysses judged it to be spacious and exceedingly beautiful, and probably the residence of some great nobleman or prince. A blue smoke went curling up from the chimney, and was almost the pleasantest part of the spectacle to Ulysses. For, from the abundance of this smoke, it was reasonable to conclude that there was a good fire in the kitchen, and that, at dinnertime, a plentiful banquet would be served up to the inhabitants of the palace, and to whatever guests might happen to drop in.

With so agreeable a prospect before him, Ulysses fancied that he could not do better than to go straight to the palace gate, and tell the master of it that there was a crew of poor shipwrecked mariners, not far off, who had eaten nothing for a day or two save a few clams and oysters, and would therefore be thankful for a little food. And the prince or nobleman must be a very stingy curmudgeon, to be sure, if, at least, when his own dinner was over, he would not bid them welcome to the broken victuals from the table.

Pleasing himself with this idea, King Ulysses had made a few steps in the direction of the palace, when there was a great twittering and chirping from the branch of a neighboring tree. A moment afterwards a bird came flying towards him, and hovered in the air, so as almost to brush his face with its wings. It was a very pretty little bird, with purple wings and body, and yellow legs, and a circle of golden feathers round its neck, and on its head a golden tuft, which looked like a king's crown in miniature. Ulysses tried to catch the bird. But it fluttered nimbly out of his reach, still chirping in a piteous tone, as if it could have told a lamentable story, had it only been gifted with human language. And when he attempted to drive it away, the bird flew no farther than the bough of the next tree, and again came fluttering about his head, with its doleful chirp, as soon as he showed a purpose of going forward.

"Have you anything to tell me, little bird?" asked Ulysses.

"Peep!" said the bird, "peep, peep, pe—weep!" And nothing else would it say, but only, "Peep, peep, pe—weep!" in a melancholy cadence, and over and over and over again. As often as Ulysses moved forward, however, the bird showed the greatest alarm, and did its best to drive him back with the anxious flutter of its purple wings. Its unaccountable behavior made him conclude, at last, that the bird knew of some danger that awaited him, and which must needs be very terrible, beyond all question, since it moved even a little fowl to feel compassion for a human being. So he resolved, for the present, to return to the vessel, and tell his companions what he had seen.

This appeared to satisfy the bird. As soon as Ulysses turned back, it ran up the trunk of a tree, and began to pick insects out of the bark with its long, sharp bill; for it was a kind of woodpecker, you must know, and had to get its living in the same manner as other birds of that species. But every little while, as it pecked at the bark of the tree, the purple bird bethought itself of some secret sorrow, and repeated its plaintive note of "Peep, peep, pe—weep!"

On his way to the shore, Ulysses had the good luck to kill a large stag. Taking it on his shoulders he lugged it along with him, and flung it down before his hungry companions.

But the next morning their appetites were as sharp as ever. They looked at Ulysses, as if they expected him to clamber up the cliff again and come back with another fat deer upon his

shoulders. Instead of setting out, however, he summoned the whole crew together, and told them it was in vain to hope that he could kill a stag every day for their dinner, and therefore it was advisable to think of some other mode of satisfying their hunger.

"Now," said he, "when I was on the cliff yesterday, I discovered that this island is inhabited. At a considerable distance from the shore stood a marble palace, which appeared to be very spacious, and had a great deal of smoke curling out of one of its chimneys."

"Aha!" muttered some of his companions, smacking their lips. "That smoke must have come from the kitchen fire. There was a good dinner on the spit; and no doubt there will be as good a one today."

"But," continued the wise Ulysses, "you must remember, my good friends, our misadventure in the cavern of one-eyed Polyphemus, the Cyclops! To tell you the truth, if we go to yonder palace, there can be no question that we shall make our appearance at the dinner-table; but whether seated as guests, or served up as food, is a point to be seriously considered."

"Either way," murmured some of the hungriest of the crew, "it will be better than starvation; particularly if one could be sure of being well fattened beforehand, and daintily cooked afterwards."

"That is a matter of taste," said King Ulysses, "and, for my own part, neither the most careful fattening nor the daintiest of cookery would reconcile me to being dished at last. My proposal is, therefore, that we divide ourselves into two equal parties, and ascertain, by drawing lots, which of the two shall go to the palace and beg for food and assistance. If these can be obtained, all is well. If not, and if the inhabitants prove as inhospitable as Polyphemus, or the Læstrygons, then there will but half of us perish, and the remainder may set sail and escape."

As nobody objected to this scheme, Ulysses proceeded to count the whole band, and found that there were forty-six men including himself. He then numbered off twenty-two of them, and put Eurylochus (who was one of his chief officers, and second only to himself in sagacity) at their head. Ulysses took command of the remaining twenty-two men in person. Then, taking off his helmet, he put two shells into it, on one of which was written, "Go," and on the other, "Stay." Another person now held the helmet, while Ulysses and Eurylochus drew out each a shell; and the word "Go" was found written on that which Eurylochus had drawn. In this manner it was decided that Ulysses and his twenty-two men were to remain at the seaside until the other party should have found out what sort of treatment they might expect at the mysterious palace. As there was no help for it, Eurylochus immediately set forth at the head of his twenty-two followers, who went off in a very melancholy state of mind, leaving their friends in hardly better spirits than themselves.

No sooner had they clambered up the cliff than they discerned the tall marble towers of the palace, ascending, as white as snow, out of the lovely green shadow of the trees which surrounded it. A gush of smoke came from a chimney in the rear of the edifice. The vapor rose high in the air, and, meeting with a breeze, was wafted seaward, and made to pass over the heads of the hungry mariners. When people's appetites are keen, they have a very quick scent for anything savory in the wind.

"That smoke comes from the kitchen!" cried one of them, turning up his nose as high as he could, and snuffing eagerly. "And, as sure as I'm a half-starved vagabond, I smell roast meat in it."

"Pig, roast pig!" said another. "Ah, the dainty little porker! My mouth waters for him."

"Let us make haste," cried the others, "or we shall be too late for the good cheer!"

But scarcely had they made half a dozen steps from the edge of the cliff, when a bird came fluttering to meet them. It was the same pretty little bird, with the purple wings and body, the yellow legs, the golden collar round its neck, and the crown-like tuft upon its head, whose behavior had so much surprised Ulysses. It hovered about Eurylochus, and almost brushed his face with its wings.

"Peep, peep, pe—weep!" chirped the bird.

So plaintively intelligent was the sound, that it seemed as if the little creature were going to break its heart with some mighty secret that it had to tell, and only this one poor note to tell it with.

"My pretty bird," said Eurylochus—for he was a wary person, and let no token of harm escape his notice—"my pretty bird, who sent you hither? And what is the message which you bring?"

"Peep, peep, pe—weep!" replied the bird, very sorrowfully.

Then it flew towards the edge of the cliff, and looked round at them, as if exceedingly anxious that they should return whence they came. Eurylochus and a few others were inclined to turn back. They could not help suspecting that the purple bird must be aware of something mischievous that would befall them at the palace, and the knowledge of which affected its airy spirit with a human sympathy and sorrow. But the rest of the voyagers, snuffing up the smoke from the palace kitchen, ridiculed the idea of returning to the vessel. One of them (more brutal than his fellows, and the most notorious gormandizer in the whole crew) said such a cruel and wicked thing, that I wonder the mere thought did not turn him into a wild beast, in shape, as he already was in his nature.

"This troublesome and impertinent little fowl," said he, "would make a delicate titbit to begin dinner with. Just one plump morsel, melting away between the teeth. If he comes within my reach, I'll catch him, and give him to the palace cook to be roasted on a skewer."

The words were hardly out of his mouth, before the purple bird flew away, crying, "Peep, peep, pe—weep!" more dolorously than ever.

"That bird," remarked Eurylochus, "knows more than we do about what awaits us at the palace."

"Come on, then," cried his comrades, "and we'll soon know as much as he does."

The party, accordingly, went onward through the green and pleasant wood. Every little while they caught new glimpses of the marble palace, which looked more and more beautiful the nearer they approached it.

At one place they came to a crystal spring, and paused to drink at it for want of liquor which they liked better. Looking into its bosom, they beheld their own faces dimly reflected, but so extravagantly distorted by the gush and motion of the water, that each one of them appeared to be laughing at himself and all his companions. So ridiculous were these images of

themselves, indeed, that they did really laugh aloud, and could hardly be grave again as soon as they wished. And after they had drank, they grew still merrier than before.

"It has a twang of the wine-cask in it," said one, smacking his lips.

"Make haste!" cried his fellows; "we'll find the wine-cask itself at the palace; and that will be better than a hundred crystal fountains."

Then they quickened their pace, and capered for joy at the thought of the savory banquet at which they hoped to be guests. But Eurylochus told them that he felt as if he were walking in a dream.

"If I am really awake," continued he, "then, in my opinion, we are on the point of meeting with some stranger adventure than any that befell us in the cave of Polyphemus, or among the gigantic man-eating Læstrygons, or in the windy palace of King Æolus, which stands on a brazen-walled island. This kind of dreamy feeling always comes over me before any wonderful occurrence. If you take my advice, you will turn back."

"No, no," answered his comrades, snuffing the air, in which the scent from the palace kitchen was now very perceptible. "We would not turn back, though we were certain that the king of the Læstrygons, as big as a mountain, would sit at the head of the table, and huge Polyphemus, the one-eyed Cyclops, at its foot."

At length they came within full sight of the palace, which proved to be very large and lofty, with a great number of airy pinnacles upon its roof. Though it was now midday, and the sun shone brightly over the marble front, yet its snowy whiteness, and its fantastic style of architecture, made it look unreal, like the frostwork on a window pane, or like the shapes of castles which one sees among the clouds by moonlight. But, just then, a puff of wind brought down the smoke of the kitchen chimney among them, and caused each man to smell the odor of the dish that he liked best and, after scenting it, they thought everything else moonshine, and nothing real save this palace, and save the banquet that was evidently ready to be served up in it.

So they hastened their steps towards the portal, but had not got halfway across the wide lawn, when a pack of lions, tigers, and wolves came bounding to meet them. The terrified mariners started back, expecting no better fate than to be torn to pieces and devoured. To their surprise and joy, however, these wild beasts merely capered around them, wagging their tails, offering their heads to be stroked and patted, and behaving just like so many well-bred house-dogs, when they wish to express their delight at meeting their master or their master's friends. The biggest lion licked the feet of Eurylochus; and every other lion, and every wolf and tiger, singled out one of his two-and-twenty followers, whom the beast fondled as if he loved him better than a beef-bone.

But, for all that, Eurylochus imagined that he saw something fierce and savage in their eyes; nor would he have been surprised, at any moment, to feel the big lion's terrible claws, or to see each of the tigers make a deadly spring, or each wolf leap at the throat of the man whom he had fondled. Their mildness seemed unreal, and a mere freak; but their savage nature was as true as their teeth and claws.

Nevertheless, the men went safely across the lawn with the wild beasts frisking about them, and doing no manner of harm; although, as they mounted the steps of the palace, you might possibly have heard a low growl, particularly from the wolves, as if they thought it a pity, after all, to let the strangers pass without so much as tasting what they were made of.

Eurylochus and his followers now passed under a lofty portal, and looked through the open doorway into the interior of the palace. The first thing that they saw was a spacious hall, and a fountain in the middle of it, gushing up towards the ceiling out of a marble basin, and falling back into it with a continual plash. The water of this fountain, as it spouted upward, was constantly taking new shapes, not very distinctly, but plainly enough for a nimble fancy to recognize what they were. Now it was the shape of a man in a long robe, the fleecy whiteness of which was made out of the fountain's spray; now it was a lion, or a tiger, or a wolf, or an ass, or, as often as anything else, a hog, wallowing in the marble basin as if it were his sty. But, before the strangers had time to look closely at this wonderful sight, their attention was drawn off by a very sweet and agreeable sound. A woman's voice was singing melodiously in another room of the palace, and with her voice was mingled the noise of a loom, at which she was probably seated, weaving a rich texture of cloth, and intertwining the high and low sweetness of her voice into a rich tissue of harmony.

By and by the song came to an end; and then, all at once, there were several feminine voices, talking airily and cheerfully, with now and then a merry burst of laughter, such as you may always hear when three or four young women sit at work together.

"What a sweet song that was!" exclaimed one of the voyagers.

"Too sweet, indeed," answered Eurylochus, shaking his head. "Yet it was not so sweet as the song of the Sirens, those bird-like damsels who wanted to tempt us on the rocks so that our vessel might be wrecked, and our bones left whitening along the shore."

"But just listen to the pleasant voices of those maidens, and that buzz of the loom as the shuttle passes to and fro," said another comrade. "What a domestic, household, homelike sound it is! Ah, before that weary siege of Troy, I used to hear the buzzing loom and the women's voices under my own roof. Shall I never hear them again? nor taste those nice little savory dishes which my dearest wife knew how to serve up?"

"Tush! we shall fare better here," said another. "But how innocently those women are babbling together, without guessing that we overhear them! And mark that richest voice of all, so pleasant and familiar, but which yet seems to have the authority of a mistress among them. Let us show ourselves at once. What harm can the lady of the palace and her maidens do to mariners and warriors like us?"

"Remember," said Eurylochus, "that it was a young maiden who beguiled three of our friends into the palace of the king of the Læstrygons, who ate up one of them in the twinkling of an eye."

No warning or persuasion, however, had any effect on his companions. They went up to a pair of folding doors at the

Right: The beautiful Circe delights in her wicked power to turn men into animals, each according to their nature. Illustration by Virginia Frances Sterrett.

farther end of the hall, and throwing them wide open, passed into the next room. Eurylochus, meanwhile, had stepped behind a pillar. In the short moment, while the folding doors opened and closed again, he caught a glimpse of a very beautiful woman rising from the loom, and coming to meet the poor weather-beaten wanderers, with a hospitable smile, and her hand stretched out in welcome. There were four other young women, who joined their hands and danced merrily forward, making gestures of obeisance to the strangers. They were only less beautiful than the lady who seemed to be their mistress. Yet Eurylochus fancied that one of them had sea-green hair, and that the close-fitting bodice of a second looked like the bark of a tree, and that both the others had something odd in their aspect, although he could not quite determine what it was, in the little while that he had to examine them.

The folding doors swung quickly back, and left him standing behind the pillar, in the solitude of the outer hall. There Eurylochus waited until he was quite weary, and listened eagerly to every sound, but without hearing anything that could help him to guess what had become of his friends. Footsteps, it is true, seemed to be passing and repassing in other parts of the palace. Then there was a clatter of silver dishes, or golden ones, which made him imagine a rich feast in a splendid banqueting hall. But by and by he heard a tremendous grunting and squealing, and then a sudden scampering, like that of small, hard hoofs over a marble floor, while the voices of the mistress and her four handmaidens were screaming all together, in tones of anger and derision. Eurylochus could not conceive what had happened, unless a drove of swine had broken into the palace, attracted by the smell of the feast. Chancing to cast his eyes at the fountain, he saw that it did not shift its shape as formerly, nor looked either like a long-robed man, or a lion, a tiger, a wolf, or an ass. It looked like nothing but a hog, which lay wallowing in the marble basin, and filled it from brim to brim.

But we must leave the prudent Eurylochus waiting in the outer hall, and follow his friends into the inner secrecy of the palace. As soon as the beautiful woman saw them, she arose from the loom, as I have told you, and came forward smiling, and stretching out her hand. She took the hand of the foremost among them, and bade him and the whole party welcome.

"You have been long expected, my good friends," said she. "I and my maidens are well acquainted with you, although you do not appear to recognize us. Look at this piece of tapestry, and judge if your faces must not have been familiar to us."

So the voyagers examined the web of cloth which the beautiful woman had been weaving in her loom; and, to their vast astonishment, they saw their own figures perfectly represented in different colored threads. It was a life-like picture of their recent adventures, showing them in the cave of Polyphemus, and how they had put out his one great moony eye; while in another part of the tapestry they were untying the leathern bags, puffed out with contrary winds; and farther on they beheld themselves scampering away from the gigantic king of the Læstrygons, who had caught one of them by the leg. Lastly, there they were, sitting on the desolate shore of this very island, hungry and downcast, and looking ruefully at the bare bones of the stag which they devoured yesterday. This was as far as the work had yet proceeded; but when the beautiful woman should again sit down at her loom, she would

probably make a picture of what had since happened to the strangers, and of what was now going to happen.

"You see," she said, "that I know all about your troubles; and you cannot doubt that I desire to make you happy for as long a time as you may remain with me. For this purpose, my honored guests, I have ordered a banquet to be prepared. Fish, fowl, and flesh, roasted and in luscious stews, and seasoned, I trust, to all your tastes, are ready to be served up. If your appetites tell you it is dinnertime, then come with me to the festal saloon."

At this kind invitation the hungry mariners were quite overjoyed; and one of them, taking upon himself to be spokesman, assured their hospitable hostess that any hour of the day was dinnertime with them, whenever they could get flesh to put in the pot, and fire to boil it with. So the beautiful woman led the way; and the four maidens (one of them had sea-green hair, another a bodice of oak bark, a third sprinkled a shower of water drops from her fingers' ends, and the fourth had some other oddity, which I have forgotten), all these followed behind, and hurried the guests along until they entered a magnificent saloon. It was built in a perfect oval, and lighted from a crystal dome above. Around the walls were ranged two-and-twenty thrones, overhung by canopies of crimson and gold, and provided with the softest of cushions, which were tasseled and fringed with gold cord. Each of the strangers was invited to sit down; and there they were, two-and-twenty storm-beaten mariners, in worn and tattered garb, sitting on two-and-twenty cushioned and canopied thrones, so rich and gorgeous that the proudest monarch had nothing more splendid in his stateliest hall.

Then you might have seen the guests nodding, winking with one eye, and leaning from one throne to another, to communicate their satisfaction in hoarse whispers.

"Our good hostess has made kings of us all," said one. "Ha! do you smell the feast? I'll engage it will be fit to set before two-and-twenty kings."

But the beautiful woman now clapped her hands; and immediately there entered a train of two-and-twenty serving-men, bringing dishes of the richest food, all hot from the kitchen fire, and sending up such a steam that it hung like a cloud below the crystal dome of the saloon. An equal number of attendants brought great flagons of wine of various kinds, some of which sparkled as it was poured out, and went bubbling down the throat; while of other sorts, the purple liquor was so clear that you could see the wrought figures at the bottom of the goblet. While the servants supplied the two-and-twenty guests with food and drink, the hostess and her four maidens went from one throne to another, exhorting them to eat their fill, and to quaff wine abundantly, and thus to recompense themselves at this one banquet for the many days when they had gone without a dinner. But, whenever the mariners were not looking at them (which was pretty often, as they looked chiefly into the basins and platters), the beautiful woman and her damsels turned aside and laughed. Even the servants, as they knelt down to present the dishes, might be seen to grin and sneer while the guests were helping themselves to the offered dainties.

And once in a while the strangers seemed to taste something that they did not like.

"Here is an odd kind of a spice in this dish," said one. "I can't say it quite suits my palate. Down it goes, however."

"Send a good draught of wine down your throat," said his comrade on the next throne; "that is the stuff to make this sort of cookery relish well. Though I must needs say, the wine has a queer taste, too. But the more I drink of it the better I like the flavor."

Whatever little fault they might find with the dishes, they sat at dinner a prodigiously long while. They forgot all about their homes, and their wives and children, and all about Ulysses, and everything else, except this banquet, at which they wanted to keep feasting forever. But at length they began to give over, from mere incapacity to hold any more.

"That last bit of fat is too much for me," said one.

"And I have not room for another morsel," said his next neighbor, heaving a sigh. "What a pity! My appetite is as sharp as ever."

In short, they all left off eating, and leaned back on their thrones, with such a stupid and helpless aspect as made them ridiculous to behold. When their hostess saw this, she laughed aloud; so did her four damsels; so did the two-and-twenty serving-men that bore the dishes, and their two-and-twenty fellows that poured out the wine. And the louder they all laughed, the more stupid and helpless did the two-and-twenty gormandizers look. Then the beautiful woman took her stand in the middle of the saloon, and stretching out a slender rod (it had been all the while in her hand, although they never noticed it till this moment), she turned it from one guest to another, until each had felt it pointed at himself. Beautiful as her face was, and though there was a smile on it, it looked just as wicked and mischievous as the ugliest serpent that ever was seen; and fat-witted as the voyagers had made themselves, they began to suspect that they had fallen into the power of an evil-minded enchantress.

"Wretches," cried she, "you have abused a lady's hospitality; and in this princely saloon your behavior has been suited to a hog-pen. You are already swine in everything but the human form, which you disgrace, and which I myself should be ashamed to keep a moment longer, were you to share it with me. But it will require only the slightest exercise of magic to make the exterior conform to the hoggish disposition. Assume your proper shapes, gormandizers, and begone to the sty!"

Uttering these last words, she waved her wand; and stamping her foot imperiously, each of the guests was struck aghast at beholding, instead of his comrades in human shape, one-and-twenty hogs sitting on the same number of golden thrones. Each man (as he still supposed himself to be) essayed to give a cry of surprise, but found that he could merely grunt, and that, in a word, he was just such another beast as his companions. It looked so intolerably absurd to see hogs on cushioned thrones, that they made haste to wallow down upon all fours, like other swine. They tried to groan and beg for mercy, but forthwith emitted the most awful grunting and squealing that ever came out of swinish throats. They would have wrung their hands in despair, but, attempting to do so, grew all the more desperate for seeing themselves squatted on their hams, and pawing the air with their fore-trotters. Dear me! what pendulous ears they had! what little red eyes, half buried in fat! and what long snouts, instead of Grecian noses!

"Begone to your sty!" cried the enchantress, giving them some smart strokes with her wand; and then she turned to the serving-men—"Drive out these swine, and throw down some acorns for them to eat."

Meantime Eurylochus had waited, and waited, and waited in the entrance hall of the palace, without being able to comprehend what had befallen his friends. At last, when the swinish uproar sounded through the palace, and when he saw the image of a hog in the marble basin, he thought it best to hasten back to the vessel and inform the wise Ulysses of these marvelous occurrences. So he ran as fast as he could down the steps, and never stopped to draw breath till he reached the shore.

"Why do you come alone?" asked King Ulysses, as soon as he saw him. "Where are your two-and-twenty comrades?"

At these questions Eurylochus burst into tears.

"Alas!" cried he, "I greatly fear we shall never see one of their faces again." Then he told Ulysses all that had happened, as far as he knew it; and added that he suspected the beautiful woman to be a vile enchantress, and the marble palace, magnificent as it looked, to be only a dismal cavern in reality. As for his companions, he could not imagine what had become of them, unless they had been given to the swine to be devoured alive. At this intelligence all the voyagers were greatly affrighted. But Ulysses lost no time in girding on his sword, and hanging his bow and quiver over his shoulders, and taking a spear in his right hand. When his followers saw their wise leader making these preparations, they inquired whither he was going, and earnestly besought him not to leave them.

"You are our king," cried they; "and what is more, you are the wisest man in the whole world, and nothing but your wisdom and courage can get us out of this danger. If you desert us, and go to the enchanted palace, you will suffer the same fate as our poor companions, and not a soul of us will ever see our dear Ithaca again."

"As I am your king," answered Ulysses, "and wiser than any of you, it is therefore the more my duty to see what has befallen our comrades, and whether anything can yet be done to rescue them. Wait for me here until tomorrow. If I do not then return, you must hoist sail and endeavor to find your way to our native land. For my part, I am answerable for the fate of these poor mariners, who have stood by my side in battle, and been so often drenched to the skin, along with me, by the same tempestuous surges. I will either bring them back with me or perish."

Had his followers dared, they would have detained him by force. But King Ulysses frowned sternly on them, and shook his spear, and bade them stop him at their peril. Seeing him so determined they let him go, and sat down on the sand, as disconsolate a set of people as could be, waiting and praying for his return.

It happened to Ulysses, just as before, that, when he had gone a few steps from the edge of the cliff, the purple bird came fluttering towards him, crying, "Peep, peep, pe—weep!" and using all the art it could to persuade him to go no farther.

"What mean you, little bird?" cried Ulysses. "You are arrayed like a king in purple and gold, and wear a golden crown upon your head. Is it because I too am a king, that you desire so earnestly to speak with me? If you can talk in human language, say what you would have me do."

"Peep!" answered the purple bird, very dolorously. "Peep, peep, pe—we—ep!"

Certainly there lay some heavy anguish at the little bird's heart; and it was a sorrowful predicament that he could not at least have the consolation of telling what it was. But Ulysses had no time to waste in trying to get at the mystery. He therefore quickened his pace, and had gone a good way along the pleasant wood-path, when there met him a young man of very brisk and intelligent aspect, and clad in a rather singular garb. He wore a short cloak, and a sort of cap that seemed to be furnished with a pair of wings; and from the lightness of his step, you would have supposed that there might likewise be wings on his feet. To enable him to walk still better (for he was always on one journey or another), he carried a winged staff, around which two serpents were wriggling and twisting. In short, I have said enough to make you guess that it was Quicksilver (the Romans called him Mercury, and the Greeks Hermes); and Ulysses (who knew him of old, and had learned a great deal of his wisdom from him) recognized him in a moment.

"Whither are you going in such a hurry, wise Ulysses?" asked Quicksilver. "Do you not know that this island is enchanted? The wicked enchantress (whose name is Circe, the sister of King Æetes) dwells in the marble palace which you see yonder among the trees. By her magic arts she changes every human being into the brute beast or fowl whom he happens most to resemble."

"That little bird, which met me at the edge of the cliff," exclaimed Ulysses; "was he a human being once?"

"Yes," answered Quicksilver. "He was once a king, named Picus, and a pretty good sort of a king too, only rather too proud of his purple robe, and his crown, and the golden chain about his neck; so he was forced to take the shape of a gaudy-feathered bird. The lions, and wolves, and tigers, who will come running to meet you, in front of the palace, were formerly fierce and cruel men, resembling in their dispositions the wild beasts whose forms they now rightfully wear."

"And my poor companions," said Ulysses, "have they undergone a similar change through the arts of this wicked Circe?"

"You well know what gormandizers they were," replied Quicksilver; and, rogue that he was, he could not help laughing at the joke. "So you will not be surprised to hear that they have all taken the shapes of swine! If Circe had never done anything worse, I really should not think her so very much to blame."

"But can I do nothing to help them?" inquired Ulysses.

"It will require all your wisdom," said Quicksilver, "and a little of my own into the bargain, to keep your royal and sagacious self from being transformed into a fox. But do as I bid you, and the matter may end better than it has begun."

While he was speaking, Quicksilver seemed to be in search of something; he went stooping along the ground, and soon laid his hand on a little plant with a snow-white flower, which he plucked and smelt. Ulysses had been looking at that very spot only just before; and it appeared to him that the plant had burst into full flower the instant when Quicksilver touched it with his fingers.

"Take this flower, King Ulysses," said he. "Guard it as you do your eyesight; for I can assure you it is exceedingly rare and precious, and you might seek the whole earth over without ever finding another like it. Keep it in your hand, and smell of it frequently after you enter the palace, and while you are talking with the enchantress. Especially when she offers you food or a draught of wine out of her goblet, be careful to fill your nostrils with the flower's fragrance. Follow these directions, and you may defy her magic arts to change you into a fox."

When Ulysses reached the lawn in front of the palace, the lions and other savage animals came bounding to meet him, and would have fawned upon him and licked his feet. But the wise king struck at them with his long spear, and sternly bade them begone out of his path; for he knew that they had once been bloodthirsty men, and would now tear him limb from limb, instead of fawning upon him, could they do the mischief that was in their hearts. The wild beasts yelped and glared at him, and stood at a distance while he ascended the palace steps.

On entering the hall, Ulysses saw the magic fountain in the center of it. The up-gushing water had now again taken the shape of a man in a long, white, fleecy robe, who appeared to be making gestures of welcome. The king likewise heard the noise of the shuttle in the loom, and the sweet melody of the beautiful woman's song, and then the pleasant voices of herself and the four maidens talking together, with peals of merry laughter intermixed. But Ulysses did not waste much time in listening to the laughter or the song. He leaned his spear against one of the pillars of the hall, and then, after loosening his sword in the scabbard, stepped boldly forward and threw the folding doors wide open. The moment she beheld his stately figure standing in the doorway, the beautiful woman rose from the loom and ran to meet him, with a glad smile throwing its sunshine over her face and both her hands extended.

"Welcome, brave stranger!" cried she. "We were expecting you. Your companions have already been received into my palace, and have enjoyed the hospitable treatment to which the propriety of their behavior so well entitles them. If such be your pleasure, you shall first take some refreshment, and then join them in the elegant apartments which they now occupy. See, I and my maidens have been weaving their figures into this piece of tapestry."

She pointed to the web of beautifully woven cloth in the loom. Circe and the four nymphs must have been very diligently at work since the arrival of the mariners; for a great many yards of tapestry had now been wrought, in addition to what I before described. In this new part Ulysses saw his two-and-twenty friends represented as sitting on cushioned and canopied thrones, greedily devouring dainties and quaffing deep draughts of wine. The work had not yet gone any farther. Oh, no, indeed. The enchantress was far too cunning to let Ulysses see the mischief which her magic arts had since brought upon the gormandizers.

"As for yourself, valiant sir," said Circe, "judging by the dignity of your aspect, I take you to be nothing less than a king. Deign to follow me, and you shall be treated as befits your rank."

So Ulysses followed her into the oval saloon where his two-and-twenty comrades had devoured the banquet which ended so disastrously for themselves, but all this while he had held the snow-white flower in his hand, and had constantly smelt of it while Circe was speaking; and as he crossed the threshold of the saloon, he took good care to inhale several long and

deep snuffs of its fragrance. Instead of two-and-twenty thrones, which had before been ranged around the wall, there was now only a single throne in the center of the apartment. But this was surely the most magnificent seat that ever a king or an emperor reposed himself upon, all made of chased gold, studded with precious stones, with a cushion that looked like a soft heap of living roses, and overhung by a canopy of sunlight which Circe knew how to weave into drapery. The enchantress took Ulysses by the hand, and made him sit down upon this dazzling throne. Then, clapping her hands, she summoned the chief butler.

"Bring hither," said she, "the goblet that is set apart for kings to drink out of. And fill it with the same delicious wine which my royal brother, King Æetes, praised so highly when he last visited me with my fair daughter Medea. That good and amiable child! Were she now here, it would delight her to see me offering this wine to my honored guest."

But Ulysses, while the butler was gone for the wine, held the snow-white flower to his nose. "Is it a wholesome wine?" he asked.

At this the four maidens tittered; whereupon the enchantress looked round at them with an aspect of severity.

"It is the wholesomest juice that ever was squeezed out of the grape," said she; "for, instead of disguising a man, as other liquor is apt to do, it brings him to his true self and shows him as he ought to be."

The chief butler liked nothing better than to see people turned into swine, or making any kind of beast of themselves; so he made haste to bring the royal goblet, filled with a liquid as bright as gold, and which kept sparkling upward and throwing a sunny spray over the brim. But, delightful as the wine looked, it was mingled with the most potent enchantments that Circe knew how to concoct. For every drop of the pure grape juice there were two drops of the pure mischief; and the danger of the thing was, that the mischief made it taste all the better. The mere smell of the bubbles, which effervesced at the brim, was enough to turn a man's beard into pig's bristles, or make a lion's claws grow out of his fingers, or a fox's brush behind him.

"Drink, my noble guest," said Circe, smiling as she presented him with the goblet. "You will find in this draught a solace for all your troubles."

King Ulysses took the goblet with his right hand, while with his left he held the snow-white flower to his nostrils, and drew in so long a breath that his lungs were quite filled with its pure and simple fragrance. Then, drinking off all the wine, he looked the enchantress calmly in the face.

"Wretch," cried Circe, giving him a smart stroke with her wand, "how dare you keep your human shape a moment longer? Take the form of the brute whom you most resemble. If a hog, go join your fellow-swine in the sty; if a lion, a wolf, a tiger, go howl with the wild beasts on the lawn; if a fox, go exercise your craft in stealing poultry. Thou hast quaffed off my wine, and canst be man no longer."

But such was the virtue of the snow-white flower, instead of wallowing down from his throne in swinish shape, or taking any other brutal form, Ulysses looked even more manly and

king-like than before. He gave the magic goblet a toss, and sent it clashing over the marble floor to the farthest end of the saloon. Then, drawing his sword, he seized the enchantress by her beautiful ringlets, and made a gesture as if he meant to strike off her head at one blow.

"Wicked Circe," cried he, in a terrible voice, "this sword shall put an end to thy enchantments. Thou shalt die, vile wretch, and do no more mischief in the world by tempting human beings into the vices which make beasts of them."

The tone and countenance of Ulysses were so awful, and his sword gleamed so brightly and seemed to have so intolerably keen an edge, that Circe was almost killed by the mere fright, without waiting for a blow. The chief butler scrambled out of the saloon, picking up the golden goblet as he went; and the enchantress and the four maidens fell on their knees, wringing their hands, and screaming for mercy.

"Spare me!" cried Circe. "Spare me, royal and wise Ulysses. For now I know that thou art he of whom Quicksilver forewarned me, the most prudent of mortals, against whom no enchantments can prevail. Thou only couldst have conquered Circe. Spare me, wisest of men. I will show thee true hospitality, and even give myself to be thy slave, and this magnificent palace to be henceforth thy home."

The four nymphs, meanwhile, were making a most piteous ado; and especially the ocean nymph, with the sea-green hair, wept a great deal of salt water, and the fountain nymph, besides scattering dewdrops from her fingers' ends, nearly melted away into tears. But Ulysses would not be pacified until Circe had taken a solemn oath to change back his companions, and as many others as he should direct, from their present forms of beast or bird into their former shapes of men.

"On these conditions," said he, "I consent to spare your life. Otherwise you must die upon the spot."

With a drawn sword hanging over her, the enchantress would readily have consented to do as much good as she had hitherto done mischief, however little she might like such employment. She therefore led Ulysses out of the back entrance of the palace, and showed him the swine in their sty. There were about fifty of these unclean beasts in the whole herd; and though the greater part were hogs by birth and education, there was wonderfully little difference to be seen betwixt them and their new brethren who had so recently worn the human shape.

The comrades of Ulysses, however, had not quite lost the remembrance of having formerly stood erect. When he approached the sty, two-and-twenty enormous swine separated themselves from the herd and scampered towards him with such a chorus of horrible squealing as made him clap both hands to his ears. And yet they did not seem to know what they wanted, nor whether they were merely hungry, or miserable from some other cause. It was curious, in the midst of their distress, to observe them thrusting their noses into the mire in quest of something to eat. The nymph with the bodice of oaken bark (she was the hamadryad of an oak) threw a handful of acorns among them; and the two-and- twenty hogs scrambled and fought for the prize, as if they had tasted not so much as a noggin of sour milk for a twelvemonth.

"These must certainly be my comrades," said Ulysses. "I recognize their dispositions. They are hardly worth the trouble of changing them into the human form again. Nevertheless, we will have it done, lest their bad example should corrupt the other hogs. Let them take their original shapes, therefore, Dame Circe, if your skill is equal to the task. It will require greater magic, I trow, than it did to make swine of them."

So Circe waved her wand again, and repeated a few magic words, at the sound of which the two-and-twenty hogs pricked up their pendulous ears. It was a wonder to behold how their snouts grew shorter and shorter, and their mouths (which they seemed to be sorry for, because they could not gobble so expeditiously) smaller and smaller, and how one and another began to stand upon his hind-legs, and scratch his nose with his fore-trotters. At first the spectators hardly knew whether to call them hogs or men, but by and by they came to the conclusion that they rather resembled the latter. Finally, there stood the twenty-two comrades of Ulysses, looking pretty much the same as when they left the vessel.

You must not imagine, however, that the swinish quality had entirely gone out of them. When once it fastens itself into a person's character, it is very difficult getting rid of it. This was proved by the hamadryad, who, being exceedingly fond of mischief, threw another handful of acorns before the twenty-two newly restored people; whereupon down they wallowed, in a moment, and gobbled them up in a very shameful way. Then recollecting themselves, they scrambled to their feet, and looked more than commonly foolish.

"Thanks, noble Ulysses!" they cried. "From brute beasts you have restored us to the condition of men again."

"Do not put yourselves to the trouble of thanking me," said the wise king. "I fear I have done but little for you."

To say the truth, there was a suspicious kind of a grunt in their voices, and for a long time afterwards they spoke gruffly, and were apt to set up a squeal.

"It must depend upon your own future behavior," added Ulysses, "whether you do not find your way back to the sty."

At this moment the note of a bird sounded from the branch of a neighboring tree. "Peep, peep, pe—weep—ep!"

It was the purple bird who, all this while, had been sitting over their heads, watching what was going forward, and hoping that Ulysses would remember how he had done his utmost to keep him and his followers out of harm's way. Ulysses ordered Circe instantly to make a king of this good little fowl, and leave him exactly as she found him. Hardly were the words spoken, and before the bird had time to utter another "Pe—weep," King Picus leaped down from the bough of the tree, as majestic a sovereign as any in the world, dressed in a long purple robe and gorgeous yellow stockings, with a splendidly wrought collar about his neck and a golden crown upon his head. He and King Ulysses exchanged with one another the courtesies which belong to their elevated rank. But from that time forth, King Picus was no longer proud of his crown and his trappings of royalty, nor of the fact of his being a king; he felt himself merely the upper servant of his people, and that it must be his lifelong labor to make them better and happier.

As for the lions, tigers, and wolves (though Circe would have restored them to their former shapes at his slightest word), Ulysses thought it advisable that they should remain as they now were, and thus give warning of their cruel dispositions, instead of going about under the guise of men and pretending to human sympathies, while their hearts had the blood-thirstiness of wild beasts. So he let them howl as much as they liked, but never troubled his head about them. And when everything was settled according to his pleasure, he sent to summon the remainder of his comrades, whom he had left at the seashore. These being arrived, with the prudent Eurylochus at their head, they all made themselves comfortable in Circe's enchanted palace until quite rested and refreshed from the toils and hardships of their voyage.

THE POMEGRANATE SEEDS

Mother Ceres was exceedingly fond of her daughter Proserpina, and seldom let her go alone into the fields. But, just at the time when my story begins, the good lady was very busy, because she had the care of the wheat, and the Indian corn, and the rye and barley, and, in short, of the crops of every kind, all over the earth; and as the season had thus far been uncommonly backward, it was necessary to make the harvest ripen more speedily than usual.

So she put on her turban, made of poppies, (a kind of flower which she was always noted for wearing,) and got into her car drawn by a pair of winged dragons, and was just ready to set off.

"Dear mother," said Proserpina, "I shall be very lonely while you are away. May I not run down to the shore, and ask some of the sea nymphs to come up out of the waves and play with me?"

"Yes, child," answered Mother Ceres. "The sea nymphs are good creatures, and will never lead you into any harm. But you must take care not to stray away from them, nor go wandering about the fields by yourself. Young girls, without their mothers to take care of them, are very apt to get into mischief."

The child promised to be as prudent as if she were a grown-up woman; and, by the time the winged dragons had whirled the car out of sight, she was already on the shore, calling to the sea nymphs to come and play with her. They knew Proserpina's voice, and were not long in showing their glistening faces and sea-green hair above the water, at the bottom of which was their home. They brought along with them a great many beautiful shells; and sitting down on the moist sand, where the surf wave broke over them, they busied themselves in making a necklace, which they hung round Proserpina's neck. By way of showing her gratitude, the child besought them to go with her a little way into the fields, so that they might gather abundance of flowers, with which she would make each of her kind playmates a wreath.

Right: The delightful sea nymphs with whom Prosperina cultivates a friendship. Illustration by Virginia Frances Sterrett for Hawthorne's *Tanglewood Tales*.

"Oh, no, dear Proserpina," cried the sea nymphs; "we dare not go with you upon the dry land. We are apt to grow faint, unless at every breath we can snuff up the salt breeze of the ocean. And don't you see how careful we are to let the surf wave break over us every moment or two, so as to keep ourselves comfortably moist? If it were not for that, we should soon look like bunches of uprooted seaweed dried in the sun."

"It is a great pity," said Proserpina. "But do you wait for me here, and I will run and gather my apron full of flowers, and be back again before the surf wave has broken ten times over you. I long to make you some wreaths that shall be as lovely as this necklace of many-colored shells."

"We will wait, then," answered the sea nymphs. "But, while you are gone, we may as well lie down on a bank of soft sponge, under the water. The air today is a little too dry for our comfort. But we will pop up our heads every few minutes to see if you are coming."

The young Proserpina ran quickly to a spot, where, only the day before, she had seen a great many flowers. These, however, were now a little past their bloom; and wishing to give her friends the freshest and loveliest blossoms, she strayed farther into the fields, and found some that made her scream with delight. Never had she met with such exquisite flowers before violets so large and fragrant roses, with so rich and delicate a blush such superb hyacinths and such aromatic pinks and many others, some of which seemed to be of new shapes and colors. Two or three times, moreover, she could not help thinking that a tuft of most splendid flowers had suddenly sprouted out of the earth before her very eyes, as if on purpose to tempt her a few steps farther.

Proserpina's apron was soon filled and brimming over with delightful blossoms. She was on the point of turning back in order to rejoin the sea nymphs, and sit with them on the moist sands, all twining wreaths together. But, a little farther on, what should she behold? It was a large shrub, completely covered with the most magnificent flowers in the world.

"The darlings!" cried Proserpina; and then she thought to herself, "I was looking at that spot only a moment ago. How strange it is that I did not see the flowers!"

The nearer she approached the shrub, the more attractive it looked, until she came quite close to it; and then, although its beauty was richer than words can tell, she hardly knew whether to like it or not. It bore above a hundred flowers of the most brilliant hues, and each different from the others, but all having a kind of resemblance among themselves, which showed them to be sister blossoms. But there was a deep, glossy luster on the leaves of the shrub, and on the petals of the flowers, that made Proserpina doubt whether they might not be poisonous. To tell you the truth, foolish as it may seem, she was half inclined to turn round and run away.

"What a silly child I am!" thought she, taking courage. "It is really the most beautiful shrub that ever sprang out of the earth. I will pull it up by the roots, and carry it home, and plant it in my mother's garden."

Holding up her apron full of flowers with her left hand, Proserpina seized the large shrub with the other, and pulled, and pulled, but was hardly able to loosen the soil about its roots. What a deep-rooted plant it was! Again, the girl pulled with all her might, and observed

that the earth began to stir and crack to some distance around the stem. She gave another pull, but relaxed her hold, fancying that there was a rumbling sound right beneath her feet. Did the roots extend down into some enchanted cavern? Then, laughing at herself for so childish a notion, she made another effort: up came the shrub, and Proserpina staggered back, holding the stem triumphantly in her hand, and gazing at the deep hole which its roots had left in the soil.

Much to her astonishment, this hole kept spreading wider and wider, and growing deeper and deeper, until it really seemed to have no bottom; and all the while, there came a rumbling noise out of its depths, louder and louder, and nearer and nearer, and sounding like the tramp of horses' hoofs and the rattling of wheels. Too much frightened to run away, she stood straining her eyes into this wonderful cavity, and soon saw a team of four sable horses, snorting smoke out of their nostrils, and tearing their way out of the earth with a splendid golden chariot whirling at their heels. They leaped out of the bottomless hole, chariot and all; and there they were, tossing their black manes, flourishing their black tails, and curveting with every one of their hoofs off the ground at once, close by the spot where Proserpina stood. In the chariot sat the figure of a man, richly dressed, with a crown on his head, all flaming with diamonds. He was of a noble aspect, and rather handsome, but looked sullen and discontented; and he kept rubbing his eyes and shading them with his hand, as if he did not live enough in the sunshine to be very fond of its light.

As soon as this personage saw the affrighted Proserpina, he beckoned her to come a little nearer.

"Do not be afraid," said he, with as cheerful a smile as he knew how to put on. "Come! Will not you like to ride a little way with me, in my beautiful chariot?"

But Proserpina was so alarmed, that she wished for nothing but to get out of his reach. And no wonder. The stranger did not look remarkably good natured, in spite of his smile; and as for his voice, its tones were deep and stern, and sounded as much like the rumbling of an earthquake underground as anything else. As is always the case with children in trouble, Proserpina's first thought was to call for her mother.

"Mother, Mother Ceres!" cried she, all in a tremble. "Come quickly and save me."

But her voice was too faint for her mother to hear. Indeed, it is most probable that Ceres was then a thousand miles off, making the corn grow in some far distant country. Nor could it have availed her poor daughter, even had she been within hearing; for no sooner did Proserpina begin to cry out than the stranger leaped to the ground, caught the child in his arms, and again mounting the chariot, shook the reins, and shouted to the four black horses to set off. They immediately broke into so swift a gallop, that it seemed rather like flying through the air than running along the earth. In a moment, Proserpina lost sight of the pleasant vale of Enna, in which she had always dwelt. Another instant, and even the summit of Mount Etna had become so blue in the distance, that she could scarcely distinguish it from the smoke that gushed out of its crater. But still the poor child screamed, and scattered her apron full of flowers along the way, and left a long cry trailing behind the chariot; and many mothers, to whose ears it came, ran quickly to see if any mischief had befallen their children. But Mother Ceres was a great way off, and could not hear the cry.

As they rode on, the stranger did his best to soothe her.

"Why should you be so frightened, my pretty child?" said he, trying to soften his rough voice. "I promise not to do you any harm. What! You have been gathering flowers? Wait till we come to my palace, and I will give you a garden full of prettier flowers than those, all made of pearls, and diamonds, and rubies. Can you guess who I am? They call my name Pluto; and I am the king of diamonds and all other precious stones. Every atom of the gold and silver that lies under the earth belongs to me, to say nothing of the copper and iron, and of the coal mines, which supply me with abundance of fuel. Do you see this splendid crown upon my head? You may have it for a plaything. O, we shall be very good friends, and you will find me more agreeable than you expect, when once we get out of this troublesome sunshine."

"Let me go home!" cried Proserpina. "Let me go home!"

"My home is better than your mother's," answered King Pluto. "It is a palace, all made of gold, with crystal windows; and because there is little or no sunshine thereabouts, the apartments are illuminated with diamond lamps. You never saw anything half so magnificent as my throne. If you like, you may sit down on it, and be my little queen, and I will sit on the footstool."

"I don't care for golden palaces and thrones," sobbed Proserpina. "O my mother, my mother! Carry me back to my mother!"

But King Pluto, as he called himself, only shouted to his steeds to go faster.

"Pray do not be foolish, Proserpina," said he, in rather a sullen tone. "I offer you my palace and my crown, and all the riches that are under the earth; and you treat me as if I were doing you an injury. The one thing which my palace needs is a merry little maid, to run up stairs and down, and cheer up the rooms with her smile. And this is what you must do for King Pluto."

"Never!" answered Proserpina, looking as miserable as she could. "I shall never smile again till you set me down at my mother's door."

But she might just as well have talked to the wind that whistled past them; for Pluto urged on his horses, and went faster than ever. Proserpina continued to cry out, and screamed so long and so loudly, that her poor little voice was almost screamed away; and when it was nothing but a whisper, she happened to cast her eyes over a great, broad field of waving grain and whom do you think she saw? Who, but Mother Ceres, making the corn grow, and too busy to notice the golden chariot as it went rattling along. The child mustered all her strength, and gave one more scream, but was out of sight before Ceres had time to turn her head.

King Pluto had taken a road which now began to grow excessively gloomy. It was bordered on each side with rocks and precipices, between which the rumbling of the chariot wheels was reverberated with a noise like rolling thunder. The trees and bushes that grew in the crevices of the rocks had very dismal foliage; and by and by, although it was hardly noon, the air became obscured with a gray twilight. The black horses had rushed along so swiftly, that they were already beyond the limits of the sunshine.

But the duskier it grew, the more did Pluto's visage assume an air of satisfaction. After all, he was not an ill-looking person, especially when he left off twisting his features into a smile that

Above: Sea nymphs wait for their friend Prosperina to return from flower-collecting. Illustration by Arthur Rackham (1867–1939).

did not belong to them. Proserpina peeped at his face through the gathering dusk, and hoped that he might not be so very wicked as she at first thought him.

"Ah, this twilight is truly refreshing," said King Pluto, "after being so tormented with that ugly and impertinent glare of the sun. How much more agreeable is lamplight or torchlight, more particularly when reflected from diamonds! It will be a magnificent sight, when we get to my palace."

"Is it much farther?" asked Proserpina. "And will you carry me back when I have seen it?"

"We will talk of that by and by," answered Pluto. "We are just entering my dominions. Do you see that tall gateway before us? When we pass those gates, we are at home. And there lies my faithful mastiff at the threshold. Cerberus! Cerberus! Come hither, my good dog!"

So saying, Pluto pulled at the reins, and stopped the chariot right between the tall, massive pillars of the gateway. The mastiff of which he had spoken got up from the threshold, and stood on his hinder legs, so as to put his fore paws on the chariot wheel. But, my stars, what a strange dog it was! Why, he was a big, rough, ugly-looking monster, with three separate heads, and each of them fiercer than the two others; but fierce as they were, King Pluto patted them all. He seemed as fond of his three-headed dog as if it had been a sweet little spaniel, with silken ears and curly hair. Cerberus, on the other hand, was evidently rejoiced to see his master, and expressed his attachment, as other dogs do, by wagging his tail at a great rate. Proserpina's eyes being drawn to it by its brisk motion, she saw that this tail was neither more nor less than a live dragon, with fiery eyes, and fangs that had a very poisonous aspect. And while the three-headed Cerberus was fawning so lovingly on King Pluto, there was the dragon tail wagging against its will, and looking as cross and ill-natured as you can imagine, on its own separate account.

"Will the dog bite me?" asked Proserpina, shrinking closer to Pluto. "What an ugly creature he is!"

"Oh, never fear," answered her companion. "He never harms people, unless they try to enter my dominions without being sent for, or to get away when I wish to keep them here. Down, Cerberus! Now, my pretty Proserpina, we will drive on."

On went the chariot, and King Pluto seemed greatly pleased to find himself once more in his own kingdom. He drew Proserpina's attention to the rich veins of gold that were to be seen among the rocks, and pointed to several places where one stroke of a pickaxe would loosen a bushel of diamonds. All along the road, indeed, there were sparkling gems, which would have been of inestimable value above ground, but which here were reckoned of the meaner sort, and hardly worth a beggar's stooping for.

Not far from the gateway, they came to a bridge, which seemed to be built of iron. Pluto stopped the chariot, and bade Proserpina look at the stream which was gliding so lazily beneath it. Never in her life had she beheld so torpid, so black, so muddy-looking a stream: its waters reflected no images of anything that was on the banks, and it moved as sluggishly as if it had quite forgotten which way it ought to flow, and had rather stagnate than flow either one way or the other.

"This is the River Lethe," observed King Pluto. "Is it not a very pleasant stream?"

"I think it a very dismal one," said Proserpina.

"It suits my taste, however," answered Pluto, who was apt to be sullen when anybody disagreed with him. "At all events, its water has one very excellent quality; for a single draught of it makes people forget every care and sorrow that has hitherto tormented them. Only sip a little of it, my dear Proserpina, and you will instantly cease to grieve for your mother, and will have nothing in your memory that can prevent your being perfectly happy in my palace. I will send for some, in a golden goblet, the moment we arrive."

"O, no, no, no!" cried Proserpina, weeping afresh. "I had a thousand times rather be miserable with remembering my mother, than be happy in forgetting her. That dear, dear mother! I never, never will forget her."

"We shall see," said King Pluto. "You do not know what fine times we will have in my palace. Here we are just at the portal. These pillars are solid gold, I assure you."

He alighted from the chariot, and taking Proserpina in his arms, carried her up a lofty flight of steps into the great hall of the palace. It was splendidly illuminated by means of large precious stones, of various hues, which seemed to burn like so many lamps, and glowed with a hundred-fold radiance all through the vast apartment.

And yet there was a kind of gloom in the midst of this enchanted light; nor was there a single object in the hall that was really agreeable to behold, except the little Proserpina herself, a lovely child, with one earthly flower which she had not let fall from her hand. It is my opinion that even King Pluto had never been happy in his palace, and that this was the true reason why he had stolen away Proserpina, in order that he might have something to love, instead of cheating his heart any longer with this tiresome magnificence. And, though he pretended to dislike the sunshine of the upper world, yet the effect of the child's presence, bedimmed as she was by her tears, was as if a faint and watery sunbeam had somehow or other found its way into the enchanted hall.

Pluto now summoned his domestics, and bade them lose no time in preparing a most sumptuous banquet, and above all things, not to fail of setting a golden beaker of the water of Lethe by Proserpina's plate.

"I will neither drink that nor anything else," said Proserpina. "Nor will I taste a morsel of food, even if you keep me forever in your palace."

"I should be sorry for that," replied King Pluto, patting her cheek; for he really wished to be kind, if he had only known how. "You are a spoiled child, I perceive, my little Proserpina; but when you see the nice things which my cook will make for you, your appetite will quickly come again."

Then, sending for the head cook, he gave strict orders that all sorts of delicacies, such as young people are usually fond of, should be set before Proserpina. He had a secret motive in this; for, you are to understand, it is a fixed law, that, when persons are carried off to the land of magic, if they once taste any food there, they can never get back to their friends. Now, if King Pluto had been cunning enough to offer Proserpina some fruit, or bread and milk, (which was the simple fare to which the child had always been accustomed,) it is very probable that she

would soon have been tempted to eat it. But he left the matter entirely to his cook, who, like all other cooks, considered nothing fit to eat unless it were rich pastry, or highly-seasoned meat, or spiced sweet cakes things which Proserpina's mother had never given her, and the smell of which quite took away her appetite, instead of sharpening it.

But my story must now clamber out of King Pluto's dominions, and see what Mother Ceres has been about, since she was bereft of her daughter. We had a glimpse of her, as you remember, half hidden among the waving grain, while the four black steeds were swiftly whirling along the chariot, in which her beloved Proserpina was so unwillingly borne away. You recollect, too, the loud scream which Proserpina gave, just when the chariot was out of sight.

Of all the child's outcries, this last shriek was the only one that reached the ears of Mother Ceres. She had mistaken the rumbling of the chariot wheels for a peal of thunder, and imagined that a shower was coming up, and that it would assist her in making the corn grow. But, at the sound of Proserpina's shriek, she started, and looked about in every direction, not knowing whence it came, but feeling almost certain that it was her daughter's voice. It seemed so unaccountable, however, that the girl should have strayed over so many lands and seas (which she herself could not have traversed without the aid of her winged dragons) that the good Ceres tried to believe that it must be the child of some other parent, and not her own darling Proserpina, who had uttered this lamentable cry. Nevertheless, it troubled her with a vast many tender fears, such as are ready to bestir themselves in every mother's heart, when she finds it necessary to go away from her dear children without leaving them under the care of some maiden aunt, or other such faithful guardian. So she quickly left the field in which she had been so busy; and, as her work was not half done, the grain looked, next day, as if it needed both sun and rain, and as if it were blighted in the ear, and had something the matter with its roots.

The pair of dragons must have had very nimble wings; for, in less than an hour, Mother Ceres had alighted at the door of her home, and found it empty. Knowing, however, that the child was fond of sporting on the seashore, she hastened thither as fast as she could, and there beheld the wet faces of the poor sea nymphs peeping over a wave. All this while, the good creatures had been waiting on the bank of sponge, and, once every half minute or so, had popped up their four heads above water, to see if their playmate were yet coming back. When they saw Mother Ceres, they sat down on the crest of the surf wave, and let it toss them ashore at her feet.

"Where is Proserpina?" cried Ceres. "Where is my child? Tell me, you naughty sea nymphs, have you enticed her under the sea?"

"Oh, no, good Mother Ceres," said the innocent sea nymphs, tossing back their green ringlets, and looking her in the face. "We never should dream of such a thing. Proserpina has been at play with us, it is true; but she left us a long while ago, meaning only to run a little way upon the dry land, and gather some flowers for a wreath. This was early in the day, and we have seen nothing of her since."

Ceres scarcely waited to hear what the nymphs had to say, before she hurried off to make inquiries all through the neighborhood. But nobody told her anything that could enable the

poor mother to guess what had become of Proserpina. A fisherman, it is true, had noticed her little footprints in the sand, as he went homeward along the beach with a basket of fish; a rustic had seen the child stooping to gather flowers; several persons had heard either the rattling of chariot wheels, or the rumbling of distant thunder; and one old woman, while plucking vervain and catnip, had heard a scream, but supposed it to be some childish nonsense, and therefore did not take the trouble to look up. The stupid people! It took them such a tedious while to tell the nothing that they knew, that it was dark night before Mother Ceres found out that she must seek her daughter elsewhere. So she lighted a torch, and set forth, resolving never to come back until Proserpina was discovered.

In her haste and trouble of mind, she quite forgot her car and the winged dragons; or, it may be, she thought that she could follow up the search more thoroughly on foot. At all events, this was the way in which she began her sorrowful journey, holding her torch before her, and looking carefully at every object along the path. And as it happened, she had not gone far before she found one of the magnificent flowers which grew on the shrub that Proserpina had pulled up.

"Ha!" thought Mother Ceres, examining it by torchlight. "There is mischief in this flower! The earth did not produce it by any help of mine, nor of its own accord. It is the work of enchantment, and is therefore poisonous; and perhaps it has poisoned my poor child."

But she put the poisonous flower in her bosom, not knowing whether she might ever find any other memorial of Proserpina.

All night long, at the door of every cottage and farm house, Ceres knocked, and called up the weary laborers to inquire if they had seen her child; and they stood, gaping and half asleep, at the threshold, and answered her pityingly, and besought her to come in and rest. At the portal of every palace, too, she made so loud a summons that the menials hurried to throw open the gate, thinking that it must be some great king or queen, who would demand a banquet for supper and a stately chamber to repose in. And when they saw only a sad and anxious woman, with a torch in her hand and a wreath of withered poppies on her head, they spoke rudely, and sometimes threatened to set the dogs upon her. But nobody had seen Proserpina, nor could give Mother Ceres the least hint which way to seek her. Thus passed the night; and still she continued her search without sitting down to rest or stopping to take food, or even remembering to put out the torch; although first the rosy dawn, and then the glad light of the morning sun, made its red flame look thin and pale. But I wonder what sort of stuff this torch was made of; for it burned dimly through the day, and, at night, was as bright as ever, and never was extinguished by the rain or wind, in all the weary days and nights while Ceres was seeking for Proserpina.

It was not merely of human beings that she asked tidings of her daughter. In the woods and by the streams, she met creatures of another nature, who used, in those old times, to haunt the pleasant and solitary places, and were very sociable with persons who understood their language and customs, as Mother Ceres did. Sometimes, for instance, she tapped with her finger against the knotted trunk of a majestic oak; and immediately its rude bark would

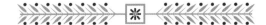

cleave asunder, and forth would step a beautiful maiden, who was the hamadryad of the oak, dwelling inside of it, and sharing its long life, and rejoicing when its green leaves sported with the breeze. But not one of these leafy damsels had seen Proserpina.

Then, going a little farther, Ceres would, perhaps, come to a fountain, gushing out of a pebbly hollow in the earth, and would dabble with her hand in the water. Behold, up through its sandy and pebbly bed, along with the fountain's gush, a young woman with dripping hair would arise, and stand gazing at Mother Ceres, half out of the water, and undulating up and down with its ever-restless motion. But when the mother asked whether her poor lost child had stopped to drink out of the fountain, the naiad, with weeping eyes, (for these water nymphs had tears to spare for everybody's grief,) would answer "No!" in a murmuring voice, which was just like the murmur of the stream.

Often, likewise, she encountered fauns, who looked like sunburnt country people, except that they had hairy ears, and little horns upon their foreheads, and the hinder legs of goats, on which they gamboled merrily about the woods and fields. They were a frolicsome kind of creature, but grew as sad as their cheerful dispositions would allow, when Ceres inquired for her daughter, and they had no good news to tell. But sometimes she came suddenly upon a rude gang of satyrs, who had faces like monkeys, and horses' tails behind them, and who were generally dancing in a very boisterous manner, with shouts of noisy laughter. When she stopped to question them, they would only laugh the louder, and make new merriment out of the lone woman's distress. How unkind of those ugly satyrs! And once, while crossing a solitary sheep pasture, she saw a personage named Pan, seated at the foot of a tall rock, and making music on a shepherd's flute. He, too, had horns, and hairy ears, and goat's feet; but, being acquainted with Mother Ceres, he answered her question as civilly as he knew how, and invited her to taste some milk and honey out of a wooden bowl. But neither could Pan tell her what had become of Proserpina, any better than the rest of these wild people.

And thus Mother Ceres went wandering about for nine long days and nights, finding no trace of Proserpina, unless it were now and then a withered flower; and these she picked up and put in her bosom, because she fancied that they might have fallen from her poor child's hand. All day she traveled onward through the hot sun, and at night, again, the flame of the torch would redden and gleam along the pathway, and she continued her search by its light, without ever sitting down to rest.

On the tenth day, she chanced to espy the mouth of a cavern, within which (though it was bright noon everywhere else) there would have been only a dusky twilight; but it so happened that a torch was burning there. It flickered, and struggled with the duskiness, but could not half light up the gloomy cavern with all its melancholy glimmer. Ceres was resolved to leave no spot without a search; so she peeped into the entrance of the cave, and lighted it up a little more, by holding her own torch before her.

In so doing, she caught a glimpse of what seemed to be a woman, sitting on the brown leaves of the last autumn, a great heap of which had been swept into the cave by the wind.

This woman (if woman it were) was by no means so beautiful as many of her sex; for her head, they tell me, was shaped very much like a dog's, and, by way of ornament, she wore a wreath of snakes around it. But Mother Ceres, the moment she saw her, knew that this was an odd kind of a person, who put all her enjoyment in being miserable, and never would have a word to say to other people, unless they were as melancholy and wretched as she herself delighted to be.

"I am wretched enough now," thought poor Ceres, "to talk with this melancholy Hecate, were she ten times sadder than ever she was yet."

So she stepped into the cave, and sat down on the withered leaves by the dog-headed woman's side. In all the world, since her daughter's loss, she had found no other companion.

"O Hecate," said she, "if ever you lose a daughter, you will know what sorrow is. Tell me, for pity's sake, have you seen my poor child Proserpina pass by the mouth of your cavern?"

"No," answered Hecate, in a cracked voice, and sighing betwixt every word or two; "no, Mother Ceres, I have seen nothing of your daughter. But my ears, you must know, are made in such a way, that all cries of distress and affright, all over the world, are pretty sure to find their way to them; and nine days ago, as I sat in my cave, making myself very miserable, I heard the voice of a young girl, shrieking as if in great distress. Something terrible has happened to the child, you may rest assured. As well as I could judge, a dragon or some other cruel monster, was carrying her away."

"You kill me by saying so," cried Ceres, almost ready to faint. "Where was the sound, and which way did it seem to go?"

"It passed very swiftly along," said Hecate, "and, at the same time, there was a heavy rumbling of wheels towards the eastward. I can tell you nothing more, except that, in my honest opinion, you will never see your daughter again. The best advice I can give you is, to take up your abode in this cavern, where we will be the two most wretched women in the world."

"Not yet, dark Hecate," replied Ceres. "But do you first come with your torch, and help me to seek for my lost child. And when there shall be no more hope of finding her, if that black day is ordained to come, then, if you will give me room to fling myself down, either on these withered leaves or on the naked rock, I will show you what it is to be miserable. But, until I know that she has perished from the face of the earth, I will not allow myself space even to grieve."

The dismal Hecate did not much like the idea of going abroad into the sunny world. But then she reflected that the sorrow of the disconsolate Ceres would be like a gloomy twilight round about them both, let the sun shine ever so brightly, and that therefore she might enjoy her bad spirits quite as well as she if she were to stay in the cave. So she finally consented to go, and they set out together, both carrying torches, although it was broad daylight and clear sunshine. The torchlight seemed to make a gloom; so that the people whom they met, along the road, could not very distinctly see their figures; and, indeed, if they once caught a glimpse of Hecate, with the wreath of snakes round her forehead, they generally thought it prudent to run away, without waiting for a second glance.

As the pair traveled along in this woe-begone manner, a thought struck Ceres.

"There is one person," she exclaimed, "who must have seen my poor child, and can doubtless tell what has become of her. Why did not I think of him before? It is Phœbus."

"What," said Hecate, "the young man that always sits in the sunshine? Oh, pray do not think of going near him. He is a gay, light, frivolous young fellow, and will only smile in your face. And besides, there is such a glare of the sun about him, that he will quite blind my poor eyes, which I have almost wept away already."

"You have promised to be my companion," answered Ceres. "Come, let us make haste, or the sunshine will be gone, and Phœbus along with it."

Accordingly, they went along in quest of Phœbus, both of them sighing grievously, and Hecate, to say the truth, making a great deal worse lamentation than Ceres; for all the pleasure she had, you know, lay in being miserable, and therefore she made the most of it. By and by, after a pretty long journey, they arrived at the sunniest spot in the whole world. There they beheld a beautiful young man, with long, curling ringlets, which seemed to be made of golden sunbeams; his garments were like light summer clouds; and the expression of his face was so exceedingly vivid, that Hecate held her hands before her eyes, muttering that he ought to wear a black veil. Phœbus (for this was the very person whom they were seeking) had a lyre in his hands, and was making its chords tremble with sweet music; at the same time singing a most exquisite song, which he had recently composed. For, besides a great many other accomplishments, this young man was renowned for his admirable poetry.

As Ceres and her dismal companion approached him, Phœbus smiled on them so cheerfully that Hecate's wreath of snakes gave a spiteful hiss, and Hecate heartily wished herself back in her cave. But as for Ceres, she was too earnest in her grief either to know or care whether Phœbus smiled or frowned.

"Phœbus!" exclaimed she, "I am in great trouble, and have come to you for assistance. Can you tell me what has become of my dear child Proserpina?"

"Proserpina! Proserpina, did you call her name?" answered Phœbus, endeavoring to recollect; for there was such a continual flow of pleasant ideas in his mind, that he was apt to forget what had happened no longer ago than yesterday. "Ah, yes, I remember her now. A very lovely child, indeed. I am happy to tell you, my dear madam, that I did see the little Proserpina not many days ago. You may make yourself perfectly easy about her. She is safe, and in excellent hands."

"Oh, where is my dear child?" cried Ceres, clasping her hands and flinging herself at his feet.

"Why," said Phœbus, and as he spoke, he kept touching his lyre so as to make a thread of music run in and out among his words, "as the little damsel was gathering flowers, (and she has really a very exquisite taste for flowers) she was suddenly snatched up by King Pluto, and carried off to his dominions. I have never been in that part of the universe; but the royal palace, I am told, is built in a very noble style of architecture, and of the most splendid and costly materials. Gold, diamonds, pearls, and all manner of precious stones, will be your daughter's ordinary playthings. I recommend to you, my dear lady, to give yourself no uneasiness. Proserpina's sense of beauty will be duly gratified, and, even in spite of the lack of sunshine, she will lead a very enviable life."

"Hush! Say not such a word!" answered Ceres, indignantly. "What is there to gratify her heart? What are all the splendors you speak of, without affection? I must have her back again. Will you go with me, Phœbus, to demand my daughter of this wicked Pluto?"

"Pray excuse me," replied Phœbus, with an elegant obeisance. "I certainly wish you success, and regret that my own affairs are so immediately pressing that I cannot have the pleasure of attending you. Besides, I am not upon the best of terms with King Pluto. To tell you the truth, his three-headed mastiff would never let me pass the gateway; for I should be compelled to take a sheaf of sunbeams along with me, and those, you know, are forbidden things in Pluto's kingdom."

"Ah, Phœbus," said Ceres, with bitter meaning in her words, "you have a harp instead of a heart. Farewell."

"Will not you stay a moment," asked Phœbus, "and hear me turn the pretty and touching story of Proserpina into extemporary verses?"

But Ceres shook her head, and hastened away, along with Hecate. Phœbus (who, as I have told you, was an exquisite poet) forthwith began to make an ode about the poor mother's grief; and, if we were to judge of his sensibility by this beautiful production, he must have been endowed with a very tender heart. But when a poet gets into the habit of using his heartstrings to make chords for his lyre, he may thrum upon them as much as he will, without any great pain to himself. Accordingly, though Phœbus sang a very sad song, he was as merry all the while as were the sunbeams amid which he dwelt.

Poor Mother Ceres had now found out what had become of her daughter, but was not a whit happier than before. Her case, on the contrary, looked more desperate than ever. As long as Proserpina was above ground, there might have been hopes of regaining her. But now that the poor child was shut up within the iron gates of the king of the mines, at the threshold of which lay the three-headed Cerberus, there seemed no possibility of her ever making her escape. The dismal Hecate, who loved to take the darkest view of things, told Ceres that she had better come with her to the cavern, and spend the rest of her life in being miserable. Ceres answered that Hecate was welcome to go back thither herself, but that, for her part, she would wander about the earth in quest of the entrance to King Pluto's dominions. And Hecate took her at her word, and hurried back to her beloved cave, frightening a great many little children with a glimpse of her dog's face, as she went.

Poor Mother Ceres! It is melancholy to think of her, pursuing her toilsome way, all alone, and holding up that never-dying torch, the flame of which seemed an emblem of the grief and hope that burned together in her heart. So much did she suffer, that, though her aspect had been quite youthful when her troubles began, she grew to look like an elderly person in a very brief time.

She cared not how she was dressed, nor had she ever thought of flinging away the wreath of withered poppies, which she put on the very morning of Proserpina's disappearance. She roamed about in so wild a way, and with her hair so disheveled, that people took her for some distracted creature, and never dreamed that this was Mother Ceres, who had the oversight of every seed which the husbandman planted. Nowadays, however, she gave herself no trouble about seed time nor harvest, but left the farmers to take care of their own affairs, and the crops to fade or flourish, as the case might be. There was nothing, now, in which Ceres seemed to feel an interest, unless when she saw children at play, or gathering flowers along the wayside.

Then, indeed, she would stand and gaze at them with tears in her eyes. The children, too, appeared to have a sympathy with her grief, and would cluster themselves in a little group about her knees, and look up wistfully in her face; and Ceres, after giving them a kiss all round, would lead them to their homes, and advise their mothers never to let them stray out of sight.

"For if they do," said she, "it may happen to you, as it has to me, that the iron-hearted King Pluto will take a liking to your darlings, and snatch them up in his chariot, and carry them away."

One day, during her pilgrimage in quest of the entrance to Pluto's kingdom, she came to the palace of King Celeus, who reigned at Eleusis. Ascending a lofty flight of steps, she entered the portal, and found the royal household in very great alarm about the queen's baby.

The infant, it seems, was sickly, (being troubled with its teeth, I suppose,) and would take no food, and was all the time moaning with pain.

The queen her name was Metanira was desirous of finding a nurse; and when she beheld a woman of matronly aspect coming up the palace steps, she thought, in her own mind, that here was the very person whom she needed. So Queen Metanira ran to the door, with the poor wailing baby in her arms, and besought Ceres to take charge of it, or, at least, to tell her what would do it good.

"Will you trust the child entirely to me?" asked Ceres.

"Yes, and gladly too," answered the queen, "if you will devote all your time to him. For I can see that you have been a mother."

"You are right," said Ceres. "I once had a child of my own. Well, I will be the nurse of this poor, sickly boy. But beware, I warn you, that you do not interfere with any kind of treatment which I may judge proper for him. If you do so, the poor infant must suffer for his mother's folly."

Then she kissed the child, and it seemed to do him good; for he smiled and nestled closely into her bosom.

So Mother Ceres set her torch in a corner, (where it kept burning all the while,) and took up her abode in the palace of King Celeus, as nurse to the little Prince Demophoön. She treated him as if he were her own child, and allowed neither the king nor the queen to say whether he should be bathed in warm or cold water, or what he should eat, or how often he should take the air, or when he should be put to bed. You would hardly believe me, if I were to tell how quickly the baby prince got rid of his ailments, and grew fat, and rosy, and strong, and how he had two rows of ivory teeth in less time than any other little fellow, before or since. Instead of the palest, and wretchedest, and puniest imp in the world, (as his own mother confessed him to be, when Ceres first took him in charge,) he was now a strapping baby, crowing, laughing, kicking up his heels, and rolling from one end of the room to the other. All the good women of the neighborhood crowded to the palace, and held up their hands, in unutterable amazement, at the beauty and wholesomeness of this darling little prince. Their wonder was the greater, because he was never seen to taste any food; not even so much as a cup of milk.

"Pray, nurse," the queen kept saying, "how is it that you make the child thrive so?"

"I was a mother once," Ceres always replied, "and having nursed my own child, I know what other children need."

But Queen Metanira, as was very natural, had a great curiosity to know precisely what the nurse did to her child. One night, therefore, she hid herself in the chamber where Ceres and the little prince were accustomed to sleep. There was a fire in the chimney, and it had now crumbled into great coals and embers, which lay glowing on the hearth, with a blaze flickering up now and then, and flinging a warm and ruddy light upon the walls. Ceres sat before the hearth with the child in her lap, and the fire light making her shadow dance upon the ceiling overhead. She undressed the little prince, and bathed him all over with some fragrant liquid out of a vase. The next thing she did was to rake back the red embers, and make a hollow place among them, just where the backlog had been. At last, while the baby was crowing, and clapping its fat little hands, and laughing in the nurse's face, (just as you may have seen your little brother or sister do before going into its warm bath,) Ceres suddenly laid him, all naked as he was, in the hollow among the red-hot embers. She then raked the ashes over him, and turned quietly away.

You may imagine, if you can, how Queen Metanira shrieked, thinking nothing less than that her dear child would be burned to a cinder. She burst forth from her hiding place, and running to the hearth, raked open the fire, and snatched up poor little Prince Demophoön out of his bed of live coals, one of which he was griping in each of his fists. He immediately set up a grievous cry, as babies are apt to do, when rudely startled out of a sound sleep. To the queen's astonishment and joy, she could perceive no token of the child's being injured by the hot fire in which he had lain. She now turned to Mother Ceres, and asked her to explain the mystery.

"Foolish woman," answered Ceres, "did you not promise to entrust this poor infant entirely to me? You little know the mischief you have done him. Had you left him to my care, he would have grown up like a child of celestial birth, endowed with superhuman strength and intelligence, and would have lived forever. Do you imagine that earthly children are to become immortal without being tempered to it in the fiercest heat of the fire? But you have ruined your own son. For though he will be a strong man and a hero in his day, yet, on account of your folly, he will grow old, and finally die, like the sons of other women. The weak tenderness of his mother has cost the poor boy an immortality. Farewell."

Saying these words, she kissed the little Prince Demophoön, and sighed to think what he had lost, and took her departure without heeding Queen Metanira, who entreated her to remain, and cover up the child among the hot embers as often as she pleased. Poor baby! He never slept so warmly again.

While she dwelt in the king's palace, Mother Ceres had been so continually occupied with taking care of the young prince, that her heart was a little lightened of its grief for Proserpina. But now, having nothing else to busy herself about, she became just as wretched as before.

At length, in her despair, she came to the dreadful resolution that not a stalk of grain, nor a blade of grass, not a potato, nor a turnip, nor any other vegetable that was good for man or beast to eat, should be suffered to grow until her daughter were restored. She even forbade the flowers to bloom, lest somebody's heart should be cheered by their beauty.

Now, as not so much as a head of asparagus ever presumed to poke itself out of the ground, without the especial permission of Ceres, you may conceive what a terrible calamity had here fallen upon the earth. The husbandmen plowed and planted as usual; but there lay the rich black furrows, all as barren as a desert of sand. The pastures looked as brown in the sweet month of June as ever they did in chill November. The rich man's broad acres and the cottager's small garden patch were equally blighted. Every little girl's flower bed showed nothing but dry stalks. The old people shook their white heads, and said that the earth had grown aged like themselves, and was no longer capable of wearing the warm smile of summer on its face. It was really piteous to see the poor, starving cattle and sheep, how they followed behind Ceres, lowing and bleating, as if their instinct taught them to expect help from her; and everybody that was acquainted with her power besought her to have mercy on the human race, and, at all events, to let the grass grow. But Mother Ceres, though naturally of an affectionate disposition, was now inexorable.

"Never," said she. "If the earth is ever again to see any verdure, it must first grow along the path which my daughter will tread in coming back to me."

Finally, as there seemed to be no other remedy, our old friend Quicksilver was sent post haste to King Pluto, in hopes that he might be persuaded to undo the mischief he had done, and to set everything right again, by giving up Proserpina. Quicksilver accordingly made the best of his way to the great gate, took a flying leap right over the three-headed mastiff, and stood at the door of the palace in an inconceivably short time. The servants knew him both by his face and garb; for his short cloak, and his winged cap and shoes, and his snaky staff had often been seen thereabouts in times gone by.

He requested to be shown immediately into the king's presence; and Pluto, who heard his voice from the top of the stairs, and who loved to recreate himself with Quicksilver's merry talk, called out to him to come up. And while they settle their business together, we must inquire what Proserpina has been doing ever since we saw her last.

The child had declared, as you may remember, that she would not taste a mouthful of food as long as she should be compelled to remain in King Pluto's palace. How she contrived to maintain her resolution, and at the same time to keep herself tolerably plump and rosy, is more than I can explain; but some young ladies, I am given to understand, possess the faculty of living on air, and Proserpina seems to have possessed it too. At any rate, it was now six months since she left the outside of the earth; and not a morsel, so far as the attendants were able to testify, had yet passed between her teeth. This was the more creditable to Proserpina, inasmuch as King Pluto had caused her to be tempted day after day, with all manner of sweetmeats, and richly-preserved fruits, and delicacies of every sort, such as young people are generally most fond of. But her good mother had often told her of the hurtfulness of these things; and for that reason alone, if there had been no other, she would have resolutely refused to taste them.

All this time, being of a cheerful and active disposition, the little damsel was not quite so unhappy as you may have supposed. The immense palace had a thousand rooms, and was full of beautiful and wonderful objects. There was a never-ceasing gloom, it is true, which

half hid itself among the innumerable pillars, gliding before the child as she wandered among them, and treading stealthily behind her in the echo of her footsteps. Neither was all the dazzle of the precious stones, which flamed with their own light, worth one gleam of natural sunshine; nor could the most brilliant of the many-colored gems, which Proserpina had for playthings, vie with the simple beauty of the flowers she used to gather. But still, wherever the girl went, among those gilded halls and chambers, it seemed as if she carried nature and sunshine along with her, and as if she scattered dewy blossoms on her right hand and on her left. After Proserpina came, the palace was no longer the same abode of stately artifice and dismal magnificence that it had before been. The inhabitants all felt this, and King Pluto more than any of them.

"My own little Proserpina," he used to say, "I wish you could like me a little better. We gloomy and cloudy-natured persons have often as warm hearts, at bottom, as those of a more cheerful character. If you would only stay with me of your own accord, it would make me happier than the possession of a hundred such palaces as this."

"Ah," said Proserpina, "you should have tried to make me like you before carrying me off. And the best thing you can now do is, to let me go again. Then I might remember you some times, and think that you were as kind as you knew how to be. Perhaps, too, one day or other, I might come back, and pay you a visit."

"No, no," answered Pluto, with his gloomy smile, "I will not trust you for that. You are too fond of living in the broad daylight, and gathering flowers. What an idle and childish taste that is! Are not these gems, which I have ordered to be dug for you, and which are richer than any in my crown are they not prettier than a violet?"

"Not half so pretty," said Proserpina, snatching the gems from Pluto's hand, and flinging them to the other end of the hall. "Oh, my sweet violets, shall I never see you again?"

And then she burst into tears. But young people's tears have very little saltness or acidity in them, and do not inflame the eyes so much as those of grown persons; so that it is not to be wondered at, if, a few moments afterwards, Proserpina was sporting through the hall almost as merrily as she and the four sea nymphs had sported along the edge of the surf wave. King Pluto gazed after her, and wished that he, too, was a child. And little Proserpina, when she turned about, and beheld this great king standing in his splendid hall, and looking so grand, and so melancholy, and so lonesome, was smitten with a kind of pity. She ran back to him, and, for the first time in all her life, put her small, soft hand in his.

"I love you a little," whispered she, looking up in his face.

"Do you, indeed, my dear child?" cried Pluto, bending his dark face down to kiss her; but Proserpina shrank away from the kiss, for, though his features were noble, they were very dusky and grim. "Well, I have not deserved it of you, after keeping you a prisoner for so many months, and starving you, besides. Are you not terribly hungry? Is there nothing which I can get you to eat?"

In asking this question, the king of the mines had a very cunning purpose; for, you will recollect, if Proserpina tasted a morsel of food in his dominions, she would never afterwards be at liberty to quit them.

"No, indeed," said Proserpina. "Your head cook is always baking, and stewing, and roasting, and rolling out paste, and contriving one dish or another, which he imagines may be to my liking. But he might just as well save himself the trouble, poor, fat little man that he is. I have no appetite for anything in the world, unless it were a slice of bread, of my mother's own baking, or a little fruit out of her garden."

When Pluto heard this, he began to see that he had mistaken the best method of tempting Proserpina to eat. The cook's made dishes and artificial dainties were not half so delicious, in the good child's opinion, as the simple fare to which Mother Ceres had accustomed her. Wondering that he had never thought of it before, the king now sent one of his trusty attendants, with a large basket, to get some of the finest and juiciest pears, peaches, and plums which could anywhere be found in the upper world. Unfortunately, however, this was during the time when Ceres had forbidden any fruits or vegetables to grow; and, after seeking all over the earth, King Pluto's servant found only a single pomegranate, and that so dried up as to be not worth eating. Nevertheless, since there was no better to be had, he brought this dry, old, withered pomegranate home to the palace, put it on a magnificent golden salver, and carried it up to Proserpina. Now, it happened, curiously enough, that, just as the servant was bringing the pomegranate into the back door of the palace, our friend Quicksilver had gone up the front steps, on his errand to get Proserpina away from King Pluto.

As soon as Proserpina saw the pomegranate on the golden salver, she told the servant he had better take it away again.

"I shall not touch it, I assure you," said she. "If I were ever so hungry, I should never think of eating such a miserable, dry pomegranate as that."

"It is the only one in the world," said the servant.

He set down the golden salver, with the wizened pomegranate upon it, and left the room. When he was gone, Proserpina could not help coming close to the table, and looking at this poor specimen of dried fruit with a great deal of eagerness; for, to say the truth, on seeing something that suited her taste, she felt all the six months' appetite taking possession of her at once. To be sure, it was a very wretched-looking pomegranate, and seemed to have no more juice in it than an oyster shell. But there was no choice of such things in King Pluto's palace. This was the first fruit she had seen there, and the last she was ever likely to see; and unless she ate it up immediately, it would grow drier than it already was, and be wholly unfit to eat.

"At least, I may smell it," thought Proserpina.

So she took up the pomegranate, and applied it to her nose; and, somehow or other, being in such close neighborhood to her mouth, the fruit found its way into that little red cave. Dear me! what an everlasting pity! Before Proserpina knew what she was about, her teeth had actually bitten it, of their own accord. Just as this fatal deed was done, the door of the apartment opened, and in came King Pluto, followed by Quicksilver, who had been urging him to let his little prisoner go. At the first noise of their entrance, Proserpina withdrew the pomegranate

Right: Proserina refuses to eat, but is tempted when a single pomegranate is sent in to her by her cunning captor Pluto. Illustration by Virginia Frances Sterrett.

from her mouth. But Quicksilver (whose eyes were very keen, and his wits the sharpest that ever anybody had) perceived that the child was a little confused; and seeing the empty salver, he suspected that she had been taking a sly nibble of something or other. As for honest Pluto, he never guessed at the secret.

"My little Proserpina," said the king, sitting down, and affectionately drawing her between his knees, "here is Quicksilver, who tells me that a great many misfortunes have befallen innocent people on account of my detaining you in my dominions. To confess the truth, I myself had already reflected that it was an unjustifiable act to take you away from your good mother. But, then, you must consider, my dear child, that this vast palace is apt to be gloomy, (although the precious stones certainly shine very bright,) and that I am not of the most cheerful disposition, and that therefore it was a natural thing enough to seek for the society of some merrier creature than myself. I hoped you would take my crown for a plaything, and me, ah, you laugh, naughty Proserpina me, grim as I am, for a playmate. It was a silly expectation."

"Not so extremely silly," whispered Proserpina. "You have really amused me very much, sometimes."

"Thank you," said King Pluto, rather dryly. "But I can see, plainly enough, that you think my palace a dusky prison, and me the iron-hearted keeper of it. And an iron heart I should surely have, if I could detain you here any longer, my poor child, when it is now six months since you tasted food. I give you your liberty. Go with Quicksilver. Hasten home to your dear mother."

Now, although you may not have supposed it, Proserpina found it impossible to take leave of poor King Pluto without some regrets, and a good deal of compunction for not telling him about the pomegranate. She even shed a tear or two, thinking how lonely and cheerless the great palace would seem to him, with all its ugly glare of artificial light, after she herself his one little ray of natural sunshine, whom he had stolen, to be sure, but only because he valued her so much after she should have departed. I know not how many kind things she might have said to the disconsolate king of the mines, had not Quicksilver hurried her away.

"Come along quickly," whispered he in her ear, "or his majesty may change his royal mind. And take care, above all things, that you say nothing of what was brought you on the golden salver."

In a very short time, they had passed the great gateway, (leaving the three-headed Cerberus, barking, and yelping, and growling, with three-fold din, behind them,) and emerged upon the surface of the earth. It was delightful to behold, as Proserpina hastened along, how the path grew verdant behind and on either side of her. Wherever she set her blessed foot, there was at once a dewy flower. The violets gushed up along the wayside. The grass and the grain began to sprout with tenfold vigor and luxuriance, to make up for the dreary months that had been wasted in barrenness. The starved cattle immediately set to work grazing, after their long fast, and ate enormously, all day, and got up at midnight to eat more. But I can assure you it was a busy time of year with the farmers, when they found the summer coming upon them with such a rush. Nor must I forget to say, that all the birds in the whole world hopped about upon the newly-blossoming trees, and sang together, in a prodigious ecstasy of joy.

Mother Ceres had returned to her deserted home, and was sitting disconsolately on the doorstep, with her torch burning in her hand. She had been idly watching the flame for some moments past, when, all at once, it flickered and went out.

"What does this mean?" thought she. "It was an enchanted torch, and should have kept burning till my child came back."

Lifting her eyes, she was surprised to see a sudden verdure flashing over the brown and barren fields, exactly as you may have observed a golden hue gleaming far and wide across the landscape, from the just risen sun.

"Does the earth disobey me?" exclaimed Mother Ceres, indignantly. "Does it presume to be green, when I have bidden it be barren, until my daughter shall be restored to my arms?"

"Then open your arms, dear mother," cried a well-known voice, "and take your little daughter into them."

And Proserpina came running, and flung herself upon her mother's bosom. Their mutual transport is not to be described. The grief of their separation had caused both of them to shed a great many tears; and now they shed a great many more, because their joy could not so well express itself in any other way.

When their hearts had grown a little more quiet, Mother Ceres looked anxiously at Proserpina.

"My child," said she, "did you taste any food while you were in King Pluto's palace?"

"Dearest mother," answered Proserpina, "I will tell you the whole truth. Until this very morning, not a morsel of food had passed my lips. But today, they brought me a pomegranate, (a very dry one it was, and all shriveled up, till there was little left of it but seeds and skin,) and having seen no fruit for so long a time, and being faint with hunger, I was tempted just to bite it. The instant I tasted it, King Pluto and Quicksilver came into the room. I had not swallowed a morsel; but dear mother, I hope it was no harm but six of the pomegranate seeds, I am afraid, remained in my mouth."

"Ah, unfortunate child, and miserable me!" exclaimed Ceres. "For each of those six pomegranate seeds, you must spend one month of every year in King Pluto's palace. You are but half restored to your mother. Only six months with me, and six with that good-for-nothing King of Darkness!"

"Do not speak so harshly of poor King Pluto," said Proserpina, kissing her mother. "He has some very good qualities; and I really think I can bear to spend six months in his palace, if he will only let me spend the other six with you. He certainly did very wrong to carry me off; but then, as he says, it was but a dismal sort of life for him, to live in that great gloomy place, all alone; and it has made a wonderful change in his spirits to have a little girl to run up stairs and down. There is some comfort in making him so happy; and so, upon the whole, dearest mother, let us be thankful that he is not to keep me the whole year round."

THE CHIMERA

Once, in the old, old times (for all the strange things which I tell you about happened long before anybody can remember), a fountain gushed out of a hillside, in the marvelous land of Greece. And, for aught I know, after so many thousand years, it is still gushing out of the very self-same spot.

At any rate, there was the pleasant fountain, welling freshly forth and sparkling adown the hillside, in the golden sunset, when a handsome young man named Bellerophon drew near its margin. In his hand he held a bridle, studded with brilliant gems, and adorned with a golden bit. Seeing an old man, and another of middle age, and a little boy, near the fountain, and likewise a maiden, who was dipping up some of the water in a pitcher, he paused, and begged that he might refresh himself with a draught.

"This is very delicious water," he said to the maiden as he rinsed and filled her pitcher, after drinking out of it. "Will you be kind enough to tell me whether the fountain has any name?"

"Yes; it is called the Fountain of Pirene," answered the maiden; and then she added, "My grandmother has told me that this clear fountain was once a beautiful woman; and when her son was killed by the arrows of the huntress Diana, she melted all away into tears. And so the water, which you find so cool and sweet, is the sorrow of that poor mother's heart!"

"I should not have dreamed," observed the young stranger, "that so clear a well-spring, with its gush and gurgle, and its cheery dance out of the shade into the sunlight, had so much as one tear-drop in its bosom! And this, then, is Pirene? I thank you, pretty maiden, for telling me its name. I have come from a faraway country to find this very spot."

A middle-aged country fellow (he had driven his cow to drink out of the spring) stared hard at young Bellerophon, and at the handsome bridle which he carried in his hand.

"The water-courses must be getting low, friend, in your part of the world," remarked he, "if you come so far only to find the Fountain of Pirene. But, pray, have you lost a horse? I see you carry the bridle in your hand; and a very pretty one it is with that double row of bright stones upon it. If the horse was as fine as the bridle, you are much to be pitied for losing him."

"I have lost no horse," said Bellerophon, with a smile.

"But I happen to be seeking a very famous one, which, as wise people have informed me, must be found hereabouts, if anywhere. Do you know whether the winged horse Pegasus still haunts the Fountain of Pirene as he used to do, in your forefathers' days?"

But then the country fellow laughed. Some of you, my little friends, have probably heard, that this Pegasus was a snow-white steed, with beautiful silvery wings, who spent most of his time on the summit of Mount Helicon. He was as wild, and as swift, and as buoyant, in his flight through the air, as any eagle that ever soared into the clouds. There was nothing else like him in the world. He had no mate; he never had been backed or bridled by a master; and, for many a long year, he led a solitary and a happy life.

Oh, how fine a thing it is to be a winged horse! Sleeping at night, as he did, on a lofty mountaintop, and passing the greater part of the day in the air, Pegasus seemed hardly to be a creature of the earth. Whenever he was seen, up very high above people's heads, with the sunshine on his silvery wings, you would have thought that he belonged to the sky, and that, skimming a little too low, he had got astray among our mists and vapors, and was seeking his way back again. It was very pretty to behold him plunge into the fleecy bosom of a bright cloud, and be lost in it, for a moment or two, and then break forth from the other side. Or, in a sullen rainstorm, when there was a gray pavement of clouds over the whole sky, it would sometimes happen that the winged horse descended right through it, and the glad light of the upper region would gleam after him. In another instant, it is true, both Pegasus and the pleasant light would be gone away together. But any one that was fortunate enough to see this wondrous spectacle felt cheerful the whole day afterwards, and as much longer as the storm lasted.

In the summertime, and in the beautifulest of weather, Pegasus often alighted on the solid earth, and, closing his silvery wings, would gallop over hill and dale for pastime, as fleetly as the wind. Oftener than in any other place, he had been seen near the fountain of Pirene, drinking the delicious water, or rolling himself upon the soft grass of the margin. Sometimes, too (but Pegasus was very dainty in his food), he would crop a few of the clover-blossoms that happened to be sweetest.

To the fountain of Pirene, therefore, people's great-grandfathers had been in the habit of going (as long as they were youthful, and retained their faith in winged horses), in hopes of getting a glimpse at the beautiful Pegasus. But, of late years, he had been very seldom seen. Indeed, there were many of the country folks, dwelling within half an hour's walk of the fountain, who had never beheld Pegasus, and did not believe that there was any such creature in existence. The country fellow to whom Bellerophon was speaking chanced to be one of those incredulous persons. And that was the reason why he laughed.

"Pegasus, indeed!" cried he, turning up his nose as high as such a flat nose could be turned up,—"Pegasus, indeed! A winged horse, truly! Why, friend, are you in your senses? Of what use would wings be to a horse? Could he drag the plow so well, think you? To be sure, there might be a little saving in the expense of shoes; but then, how would a man like to see his horse flying out of the stable window?—yes; or whisking him up above the clouds, when he only

wanted to ride to mill? No, no! I don't believe in Pegasus. There never was such a ridiculous kind of a horse-fowl made!"

"I have some reason to think otherwise," said Bellerophon, quietly.

And then he turned to an old, gray man, who was leaning on a staff, and listening very attentively, with his head stretched forward, and one hand at his ear, because, for the last twenty years, he had been getting rather deaf.

"And what say you, venerable sir?" inquired he. "In your younger days, I should imagine, you must frequently have seen the winged steed!"

"Ah, young stranger, my memory is very poor!" said the aged man. "When I was a lad, if I remember rightly, I used to believe there was such a horse, and so did everybody else. But, nowadays, I hardly know what to think, and very seldom think about the winged horse at all. If I ever saw the creature, it was a long, long while ago; and, to tell you the truth, I doubt whether I ever did see him. One day, to be sure, when I was quite a youth, I remember seeing some hoof-tramps round about the brink of the fountain. Pegasus might have made those hoof-marks; and so might some other horse."

"And have you never seen him, my fair maiden?" asked Bellerophon of the girl, who stood with the pitcher on her head, while this talk went on. "You certainly could see Pegasus, if anybody can, for your eyes are very bright."

"Once I thought I saw him," replied the maiden, with a smile and a blush. "It was either Pegasus, or a large white bird, a very great way up in the air. And one other time, as I was coming to the fountain with my pitcher, I heard a neigh. Oh, such a brisk and melodious neigh as that was! My very heart leaped with delight at the sound. But it startled me, nevertheless; so that I ran home without filling my pitcher."

"That was truly a pity!" said Bellerophon.

And he turned to the child, whom I mentioned at the beginning of the story, and who was gazing at him, as children are apt to gaze at strangers, with his rosy mouth wide open.

"Well, my little fellow," cried Bellerophon, playfully pulling one of his curls, "I suppose you have often seen the winged horse."

"That I have," answered the child, very readily. "I saw him yesterday, and many times before."

"You are a fine little man!" said Bellerophon, drawing the child closer to him. "Come, tell me all about it."

"Why," replied the child, "I often come here to sail little boats in the fountain, and to gather pretty pebbles out of its basin. And sometimes, when I look down into the water, I see the image of the winged horse, in the picture of the sky that is there. I wish he would come down, and take me on his back, and let me ride him up to the moon! But, if I so much as stir to look at him, he flies far away out of sight."

And Bellerophon put his faith in the child, who had seen the image of Pegasus in the water, and in the maiden, who had heard him neigh so melodiously, rather than in the middle-aged

Right: Bellerophon visits the fountain in the hopes of catching a glimpse of the fabled Pegasus, the Horse of the Muses. Illustration Walter Crane originally for Hawthorne's *A Wonder Book For Girls And Boys*.

· BELLEROPHON · AT · THE · FOVNTAIN ·

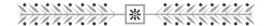

clown, who believed only in cart horses, or in the old man who had forgotten the beautiful things of his youth.

Therefore, he haunted about the Fountain of Pirene for a great many days afterwards. He kept continually on the watch, looking upward at the sky, or else down into the water, hoping forever that he should see either the reflected image of the winged horse, or the marvelous reality. He held the bridle, with its bright gems and golden bit, always ready in his hand. The rustic people, who dwelt in the neighborhood, and drove their cattle to the fountain to drink, would often laugh at poor Bellerophon, and sometimes take him pretty severely to task. They told him that an able-bodied young man, like himself, ought to have better business than to be wasting his time in such an idle pursuit. They offered to sell him a horse, if he wanted one; and when Bellerophon declined the purchase, they tried to drive a bargain with him for his fine bridle.

Even the country boys thought him so very foolish, that they used to have a great deal of sport about him, and were rude enough not to care a fig, although Bellerophon saw and heard it. One little urchin, for example, would play Pegasus, and cut the oddest imaginable capers, by way of flying, while one of his schoolfellows would scamper after him, holding forth a twist of bulrushes, which was intended to represent Bellerophon's ornamental bridle. But the gentle child, who had seen the picture of Pegasus in the water, comforted the young stranger more than all the naughty boys could torment him. The dear little fellow, in his play-hours, often sat down beside him, and, without speaking a word, would look down into the fountain and up towards the sky, with so innocent a faith, that Bellerophon could not help feeling encouraged.

Now you will, perhaps, wish to be told why it was that Bellerophon had undertaken to catch the winged horse. And we shall find no better opportunity to speak about this matter than while he is waiting for Pegasus to appear.

If I were to relate the whole of Bellerophon's previous adventures, they might easily grow into a very long story. It will be quite enough to say, that, in a certain country of Asia, a terrible monster, called a Chimera, had made its appearance, and was doing more mischief than could be talked about between now and sunset.

According to the best accounts which I have been able to obtain, this Chimera was nearly, if not quite, the ugliest and most poisonous creature, and the strangest and unaccountablest, and the hardest to fight with, and the most difficult to run away from, that ever came out of the earth's inside. It had a tail like a boa-constrictor; its body was like I do not care what; and it had three separate heads, one of which was a lion's, the second a goat's, and the third an abominably great snake's. And a hot blast of fire came flaming out of each of its three mouths! Being an earthly monster, I doubt whether it had any wings; but, wings or no, it ran like a goat and a lion, and wriggled along like a serpent, and thus contrived to make about as much speed as all the three together.

Oh, the mischief, and mischief, and mischief that this naughty creature did! With its flaming breath, it could set a forest on fire, or burn up a field of grain, or, for that matter, a village, with all its fences and houses. It laid waste the whole country round about, and

used to eat up people and animals alive, and cook them afterwards in the burning oven of its stomach. Mercy on us, little children, I hope neither you nor I will ever happen to meet a Chimera!

While the hateful beast (if a beast we can anywise call it) was doing all these horrible things, it so chanced that Bellerophon came to that part of the world, on a visit to the king. The king's name was Iobates, and Lycia was the country which he ruled over. Bellerophon was one of the bravest youths in the world, and desired nothing so much as to do some valiant and beneficent deed, such as would make all mankind admire and love him. In those days, the only way for a young man to distinguish himself was by fighting battles, either with the enemies of his country, or with wicked giants, or with troublesome dragons, or with wild beasts, when he could find nothing more dangerous to encounter. King Iobates, perceiving the courage of his youthful visitor, proposed to him to go and fight the Chimera, which everybody else was afraid of, and which, unless it should be soon killed, was likely to convert Lycia into a desert. Bellerophon hesitated not a moment, but assured the king that he would either slay this dreaded Chimera, or perish in the attempt.

But, in the first place, as the monster was so prodigiously swift, he bethought himself that he should never win the victory by fighting on foot. The wisest thing he could do, therefore, was to get the very best and fleetest horse that could anywhere be found. And what other horse, in all the world, was half so fleet as the marvelous horse Pegasus, who had wings, as well as legs, and was even more active in the air than on the earth? To be sure, a great many people denied that there was any such horse with wings, and said that the stories about him were all poetry and nonsense. But, wonderful as it appeared, Bellerophon believed that Pegasus was a real steed, and hoped that he himself might be fortunate enough to find him; and, once fairly mounted on his back, he would be able to fight the Chimera at better advantage.

And this was the purpose with which he had traveled from Lycia to Greece, and had brought the beautifully ornamented bridle in his hand. It was an enchanted bridle. If he could only succeed in putting the golden bit into the mouth of Pegasus, the winged horse would be submissive, and would own Bellerophon for his master, and fly whithersoever he might choose to turn the rein.

But, indeed, it was a weary and anxious time, while Bellerophon waited and waited for Pegasus, in hopes that he would come and drink at the Fountain of Pirene. He was afraid lest King Iobates should imagine that he had fled from the Chimera. It pained him, too, to think how much mischief the monster was doing, while he himself, instead of fighting with it, was compelled to sit idly poring over the bright waters of Pirene, as they gushed out of the sparkling sand. And as Pegasus came thither so seldom, in these latter years, and scarcely alighted there more than once in a lifetime, Bellerophon feared that he might grow an old man, and have no strength left in his arms nor courage in his heart, before the winged horse would appear. Oh, how heavily passes the time, while an adventurous youth is yearning to do his part in life, and to gather in the harvest of his renown! How hard a lesson it is to wait! Our life is brief, and how much of it is spent in teaching us only this!

Well was it for Bellerophon that the gentle child had grown so fond of him, and was never weary of keeping him company. Every morning, the child gave him a new hope to put in his bosom, instead of yesterday's withered one.

"Dear Bellerophon," he would cry, looking up hopefully into his face, "I think we shall see Pegasus today!"

And, at length, if it had not been for the little boy's unwavering faith, Bellerophon would have given up all hope, and would have gone back to Lycia, and have done his best to slay the Chimera without the help of the winged horse. And in that case poor Bellerophon would at least have been terribly scorched by the creature's breath, and would most probably have been killed and devoured. Nobody should ever try to fight an earthborn Chimera, unless he can first get upon the back of an aerial steed.

One morning the child spoke to Bellerophon even more hopefully than usual.

"Dear, dear Bellerophon," cried he, "I know not why it is, but I feel as if we should certainly see Pegasus today!"

And all that day he would not stir a step from Bellerophon's side; so they ate a crust of bread together, and drank some of the water of the fountain. In the afternoon, there they sat, and Bellerophon had thrown his arm around the child, who likewise had put one of his little hands into Bellerophon's. The latter was lost in his own thoughts, and was fixing his eyes vacantly on the trunks of the trees that overshadowed the fountain and on the grapevines that clambered up among their branches. But the gentle child was gazing down into the water; he was grieved, for Bellerophon's sake, that the hope of another day should be deceived, like so many before it; and two or three quiet teardrops fell from his eyes, and mingled with what were said to be the many tears of Pirene, when she wept for her slain children.

But, when he least thought of it, Bellerophon felt the pressure of the child's little hand, and heard a soft, almost breathless whisper.

"See there, dear Bellerophon! There is an image in the water!"

The young man looked down into the dimpling mirror of the fountain, and saw what he took to be the reflection of a bird which seemed to be flying at a great height in the air, with a gleam of sunshine on its snowy or silvery wings.

"What a splendid bird it must be!" said he. "And how very large it looks, though it must really be flying higher than the clouds!"

"It makes me tremble!" whispered the child. "I am afraid to look up into the air! It is very beautiful, and yet I dare only look at its image in the water. Dear Bellerophon, do you not see that it is no bird! It is the winged horse Pegasus!"

Bellerophon's heart began to throb! He gazed keenly upward, but could not see the winged creature, whether bird or horse; because, just then, it had plunged into the fleecy depths of a summer cloud. It was but a moment, however, before the object reappeared, sinking lightly down out of the cloud, although still at a vast distance from the earth. Bellerophon caught the

Right: Pegasus attempts to throw Bellerophon off his back, outraged at his capture and the hero's desire to tame him. Illustration by Walter Crane, originally for Hawthorne's *A Wonder Book for Girls and Boys.*

·BELLEROPHON·ON·PEGASVS·

child in his arms, and shrank back with him, so that they were both hidden among the thick shrubbery which grew all around the fountain. Not that he was afraid of any harm, but he dreaded lest, if Pegasus caught a glimpse of them, he would fly far away, and alight in some inaccessible mountaintop. For it was really the winged horse. After they had expected him so long, he was coming to quench his thirst with the water of Pirene.

Nearer and nearer came the aerial wonder, flying in great circles, as you may have seen a dove when about to alight. Downward came Pegasus, in those wide, sweeping circles, which grew narrower, and narrower still, as he gradually approached the earth. The nigher the view of him, the more beautiful he was, and the more marvelous the sweep of his silvery wings. At last, with so light a pressure as hardly to bend the grass about the fountain, or imprint a hoof-tramp in the sand of its margin, he alighted, and, stooping his wild head, began to drink. He drew in the water, with long and pleasant sighs, and tranquil pauses of enjoyment; and then another draught, and another, and another. For, nowhere in the world, or up among the clouds, did Pegasus love any water as he loved this of Pirene. And when his thirst was slaked, he cropt a few of the honey-blossoms of the clover, delicately tasting them, but not caring to make a hearty meal, because the herbage, just beneath the clouds, on the lofty sides of Mount Helicon, suited his palate better than this ordinary grass.

After thus drinking to his heart's content, and, in his dainty fashion, condescending to take a little food, the winged horse began to caper to and fro, and dance, as it were, out of mere idleness and sport. There never was a more playful creature made than this very Pegasus.

So there he frisked, in a way that it delights me to think about, fluttering his great wings as lightly as ever did a linnet, and running little races, half on earth and half in air, and which I know not whether to call a flight or a gallop. When a creature is perfectly able to fly, he sometimes chooses to run, just for the pastime of the thing; and so did Pegasus, although it cost him some little trouble to keep his hoofs so near the ground.

Bellerophon, meanwhile, holding the child's hand, peeped forth from the shrubbery, and thought that never was any sight so beautiful as this, nor ever a horse's eyes so wild and spirited as those of Pegasus. It seemed a sin to think of bridling him and riding on his back.

Once or twice, Pegasus stopped, and snuffed the air, pricking up his ears, tossing his head, and turning it on all sides, as if he partly suspected some mischief or other. Seeing nothing, however, and hearing no sound, he soon began his antics again.

At length—not that he was weary, but only idle and luxurious—Pegasus folded his wings, and lay down on the soft green turf. But, being too full of aerial life to remain quiet for many moments together, he soon rolled over on his back, with his four slender legs in the air. It was beautiful to see him, this one solitary creature, whose mate had never been created, but who needed no companion, and, living a great many hundred years, was as happy as the centuries were long. The more he did such things as mortal horses are accustomed to do, the less earthly and the more wonderful he seemed. Bellerophon and the child almost held their breath, partly from a delightful awe, but still more because they dreaded lest the slightest stir or murmur should send him up, with the speed of an arrow-flight, into the farthest blue of the sky.

Finally, when he had had enough of rolling over and over, Pegasus turned himself about, and, indolently, like any other horse, put out his fore legs, in order to rise from the ground; and Bellerophon, who had guessed that he would do so, darted suddenly from the thicket, and leaped astride of his back.

Yes, there he sat, on the back of the winged horse!

But what a bound did Pegasus make, when, for the first time, he felt the weight of a mortal man upon his loins! A bound, indeed! Before he had time to draw a breath, Bellerophon found himself above hundred feet aloft, and still shooting upward, while the winged horse snorted and trembled with terror and anger. Upward he went, up, up, up, until he plunged into the cold, misty bosom of a cloud, at which, only a little while before, Bellerophon had been gazing, and fancying it a very pleasant spot. Then again, out of the heart of the cloud, Pegasus shot down like a thunderbolt, as if he meant to dash both himself and his rider headlong against a rock. Then he went through about a thousand of the wildest caprioles that had ever been performed either by a bird or a horse.

I cannot tell you half that he did. He skimmed straight forward, and sideways, and backward. He reared himself erect, with his fore legs on a wreath of mist, and his hind legs on nothing at all. He flung out his heels behind, and put down his head between his legs, with his wings pointing right upward. At about two miles' height above the earth, he turned a somerset, so that Bellerophon's heels were where his head should have been, and he seemed to look down into the sky, instead of up. He twisted his head about, and, looking Bellerophon in the face, with fire flashing from his eyes, made a terrible attempt to bite him. He fluttered his pinions so wildly that one of the silver feathers was shaken out, and floating earthward, was picked up by the child, who kept it as long as he lived, in memory of Pegasus and Bellerophon.

But the latter (who, as you may judge, was as good a horseman as ever galloped) had been watching his opportunity, and at last clapped the golden bit of the enchanted bridle between the winged steed's jaws. No sooner was this done, than Pegasus became as manageable as if he had taken food all his life out of Bellerophon's hand. To speak what I really feel, it was almost a sadness to see so wild a creature grow suddenly so tame. And Pegasus seemed to feel it so, likewise. He looked round to Bellerophon, with the tears in his beautiful eyes, instead of the fire that so recently flashed from them. But when Bellerophon patted his head, and spoke a few authoritative, yet kind and soothing words, another look came into the eyes of Pegasus; for he was glad at heart, after so many lonely centuries, to have found a companion and a master.

Thus it always is with winged horses, and with all such wild and solitary creatures. If you can catch and overcome them, it is the surest way to win their love.

While Pegasus had been doing his utmost to shake Bellerophon off his back, he had flown a very long distance; and they had come within sight of a lofty mountain by the time the bit was in his mouth. Bellerophon had seen this mountain before, and knew it to be Helicon, on the summit of which was the winged horse's abode. Thither (after looking gently into his rider's face, as if to ask leave) Pegasus now flew, and, alighting, waited patiently until Bellerophon should please to dismount. The young man, accordingly, leaped from his steed's back, but still

held him fast by the bridle. Meeting his eyes, however, he was so affected by the gentleness of his aspect, and by his beauty, and by the thought of the free life which Pegasus had heretofore lived, that he could not bear to keep him a prisoner, if he really desired his liberty.

Obeying this generous impulse, he slipped the enchanted bridle off the head of Pegasus, and took the bit from his mouth.

"Leave me, Pegasus!" said he. "Either leave me, or love me."

In an instant, the winged horse shot almost out of sight, soaring straight upward from the summit of Mount Helicon. Being long after sunset, it was now twilight on the mountaintop, and dusky evening over all the country round about. But Pegasus flew so high that he overtook the departed day, and was bathed in the upper radiance of the sun. Ascending higher and higher, he looked like a bright speck, and, at last, could no longer be seen in the hollow waste of the sky. And Bellerophon was afraid that he should never behold him more. But, while he was lamenting his own folly, the bright speck reappeared, and drew nearer and nearer, until it descended lower than the sunshine; and behold, Pegasus had come back! After this trial there was no more fear of the winged horse's making his escape. He and Bellerophon were friends, and put loving faith in one another.

That night they lay down and slept together, with Bellerophon's arm about the neck of Pegasus, not as a caution, but for kindness. And they awoke at peep of day, and bade one another good morning, each in his own language.

In this manner, Bellerophon and the wondrous steed spent several days, and grew better acquainted and fonder of each other, all the time. They went on long aerial journeys, and sometimes ascended so high that the earth looked hardly bigger than—the moon. They visited distant countries, and amazed the inhabitants, who thought that the beautiful young man, on the back of the winged horse, must have come down out of the sky. A thousand miles a day was no more than an easy space for the fleet Pegasus to pass over. Bellerophon was delighted with this kind of life, and would have liked nothing better than to live always in the same way, aloft in the clear atmosphere; for it was always sunny weather up there, however cheerless and rainy it might be in the lower region. But he could not forget the horrible Chimera, which he had promised King Iobates to slay. So, at last, when he had become well accustomed to feats of horsemanship in the air, and could manage Pegasus with the least motion of his hand, and had taught him to obey his voice, he determined to attempt the performance of this perilous adventure.

At daybreak, therefore, as soon as he unclosed his eyes, he gently pinched the winged horse's ear, in order to arouse him. Pegasus immediately started from the ground, and pranced about a quarter of a mile aloft, and made a grand sweep around the mountaintop, by way of showing that he was wide awake, and ready for any kind of an excursion. During the whole of this little flight, he uttered a loud, brisk, and melodious neigh, and finally come down at Bellerophon's side, as lightly as ever you saw a sparrow hop upon a twig.

Left: Bellerophon astride the powerful Pegasus battles and slays the horrible Chimera. Illustration by Arthur Rackham.

"Well done, dear Pegasus! well done, my sky-skimmer!" cried Bellerophon, fondly stroking the horse's neck. "And now, my fleet and beautiful friend, we must break our fast. Today we are to fight the terrible Chimera."

As soon as they had eaten their morning meal, and drank some sparkling water from a spring called Hippocrene, Pegasus held out his head, of his own accord, so that his master might put on the bridle. Then, with a great many playful leaps and airy caperings, he showed his impatience to be gone; while Bellerophon was girding on his sword, and hanging his shield about his neck, and preparing himself for battle. When everything was ready, the rider mounted, and (as was his custom, when going a long distance) ascended five miles perpendicularly, so as the better to see whither he was directing his course. He then turned the head of Pegasus towards the east, and set out for Lycia. In their flight they overtook an eagle, and came so nigh him, before he could get out of their way, that Bellerophon might easily have caught him by the leg. Hastening onward at this rate, it was still early in the forenoon when they beheld the lofty mountains of Lycia, with their deep and shaggy valleys. If Bellerophon had been told truly, it was in one of those dismal valleys that the hideous Chimera had taken up its abode.

Being now so near their journey's end, the winged horse gradually descended with his rider; and they took advantage of some clouds that were floating over the mountaintops, in order to conceal themselves. Hovering on the upper surface of a cloud, and peeping over its edge, Bellerophon had a pretty distinct view of the mountainous part of Lycia, and could look into all its shadowy vales at once. At first there appeared to be nothing remarkable. It was a wild, savage, and rocky tract of high and precipitous hills. In the more level part of the country, there were the ruins of houses that had been burnt, and, here and there, the carcasses of dead cattle, strewn about the pastures where they had been feeding.

"The Chimera must have done this mischief," thought Bellerophon. "But where can the monster be?"

As I have already said, there was nothing remarkable to be detected, at first sight, in any of the valleys and dells that lay among the precipitous heights of the mountains. Nothing at all; unless, indeed, it were three spires of black smoke, which issued from what seemed to be the mouth of a cavern, and clambered sullenly into the atmosphere. Before reaching the mountaintop, these three black smoke-wreaths mingled themselves into one. The cavern was almost directly beneath the winged horse and his rider, at the distance of about a thousand feet. The smoke, as it crept heavily upward, had an ugly, sulphurous, stifling scent, which caused Pegasus to snort and Bellerophon to sneeze. So disagreeable was it to the marvelous steed (who was accustomed to breathe only the purest air), that he waved his wings, and shot half a mile out of the range of this offensive vapor.

But, on looking behind him, Bellerophon saw something that induced him first to draw the bridle, and then to turn Pegasus about. He made a sign, which the winged horse understood, and sunk slowly through the air, until his hoofs were scarcely more than a man's height above the rocky bottom of the valley. In front, as far off as you could throw a stone, was the cavern's mouth, with the three smoke-wreaths oozing out of it. And what else did Bellerophon behold there?

There seemed to be a heap of strange and terrible creatures curled up within the cavern. Their bodies lay so close together, that Bellerophon could not distinguish them apart; but, judging by their heads, one of these creatures was a huge snake, the second a fierce lion, and the third an ugly goat. The lion and the goat were asleep; the snake was broad awake, and kept staring around him with a great pair of fiery eyes. But—and this was the most wonderful part of the matter—the three spires of smoke evidently issued from the nostrils of these three heads! So strange was the spectacle, that, though Bellerophon had been all along expecting it, the truth did not immediately occur to him, that here was the terrible three-headed Chimera. He had found out the Chimera's cavern. The snake, the lion, and the goat, as he supposed them to be, were not three separate creatures, but one monster!

The wicked, hateful thing! Slumbering as two thirds of it were, it still held, in its abominable claws, the remnant of an unfortunate lamb—or possibly (but I hate to think so) it was a dear little boy—which its three mouths had been gnawing, before two of them fell asleep!

All at once, Bellerophon started as from a dream, and knew it to be the Chimera. Pegasus seemed to know it, at the same instant, and sent forth a neigh, that sounded like the call of a trumpet to battle. At the sound the three heads reared themselves erect, and belched out great flashes of flame. Before Bellerophon had time to consider what to do next, the monster flung itself out of the cavern and sprung straight towards him, with its immense claws extended, and its snaky tail twisting itself venomously behind. If Pegasus had not been as nimble as a bird, both he and his rider would have been overthrown by the Chimera's headlong rush, and thus the battle have been ended before it was well begun. But the winged horse was not to be caught so. In the twinkling of an eye he was up aloft, halfway to the clouds, snorting with anger. He shuddered, too, not with affright, but with utter disgust at the loathsomeness of this poisonous thing with three heads.

The Chimera, on the other hand, raised itself up so as to stand absolutely on the tip-end of its tail, with its talons pawing fiercely in the air, and its three heads spluttering fire at Pegasus and his rider. My stars, how it roared, and hissed, and bellowed! Bellerophon, meanwhile, was fitting his shield on his arm, and drawing his sword.

"Now, my beloved Pegasus," he whispered in the winged horse's ear, "thou must help me to slay this insufferable monster; or else thou shalt fly back to thy solitary mountain-peak without thy friend Bellerophon. For either the Chimsera dies, or its three mouths shall gnaw this head of mine, which has slumbered upon your neck!"

Pegasus whinnied, and, turning back his head, rubbed his nose tenderly against his rider's cheek. It was his way of telling him that, though he had wings and was an immortal horse, yet he would perish, if it were possible for immortality to perish, rather than leave Bellerophon behind.

"I thank you, Pegasus," answered Bellerophon. "Now, then, let us make a dash at the monster!"

Uttering these words, he shook the bridle; and Pegasus darted down aslant, as swift as the flight of an arrow, right towards the Chimera's threefold head, which, all this time, was poking itself as high as it could into the air. As he came within arm's length, Bellerophon made a cut at the monster, but was carried onward by his steed, before he could see whether

· BELLEROPHON · SLAYS · THE · CHIMÆRA ·

the blow had been successful. Pegasus continued his course, but soon wheeled round, at about the same distance from the Chimera as before. Bellerophon then perceived that he had cut the goat's head of the monster almost off, so that it dangled downward by the skin, and seemed quite dead.

But, to make amends, the snake's head and the lion's head had taken all the fierceness of the dead one into themselves, and spit flame, and hissed, and roared, with a vast deal more fiery than before.

"Never mind, my brave Pegasus!" cried Bellerophon. "With another stroke like that, we will stop either its hissing or its roaring."

And again he shook the bridle. Dashing aslantwise, as before, the winged horse made another arrow-flight towards the Chimera, and Bellerophon aimed another downright stroke at one of the two remaining heads, as he shot by. But, this time, neither he nor Pegasus escaped so well as at first. With one of its claws, the Chimera had given the young man a deep scratch in his shoulder, and had slightly damaged the left wing of the flying steed with the other. On his part, Bellerophon had mortally wounded the lion's head of the monster, insomuch that it now hung downward, with its fire almost extinguished, and sending out gasps of thick black smoke. The snake's head, however (which was the only one now left), was twice as fierce and venomous as ever before. It belched forth shoots of fire five hundred yards long, and emitted hisses so loud, so harsh, and so ear-piercing, that King Iobates heard them, fifty miles off, and trembled till the throne shook under him.

"Well-a-day!" thought the poor king; "the Chimera is certainly coming to devour me!"

Meanwhile Pegasus had again paused in the air, and neighed angrily, while sparkles of a pure, crystal flame darted out of his eyes. How unlike the lurid fire of the Chimera! The aerial steed's spirit was all aroused, and so was that of Bellerophon.

"Dost thou bleed, my immortal horse?" cried the young man, caring less for his own hurt than for the anguish of this glorious creature, that ought never to have tasted pain. "The execrable Chimera shall pay for this mischief, with his last head!"

Then he shook the bridle, shouted loudly, and guided Pegasus, not aslantwise as before, but straight at the monster's hideous front. So rapid was the onset, that it seemed but a dazzle and a flash before Bellerophon was at close gripes with his enemy.

The Chimera, by this time, after losing its second head, had got into a red-hot passion of pain and rampant rage. It so flounced about, half on earth and partly in the air, that it was impossible to say which element it rested upon. It opened its snake-jaws to such an abominable width, that Pegasus might almost, I was going to say, have flown right down its throat, wings outspread, rider and all! At their approach it shot out a tremendous blast of its fiery breath, and enveloped Bellerophon and his steed in a perfect atmosphere of flame, singeing the wings of Pegasus, scorching off one whole side of the young man's golden ringlets, and making them both far hotter than was comfortable, from head to foot.

Left: Walter Crane's depiction of Bellerophon slaying the Chimera for Hawthorne's *A Wonder Book for Girls and Boys*.

But this was nothing to what followed.

When the airy rush of the winged horse had brought him within the distance of a hundred yards, the Chimera gave a spring, and flung its huge, awkward, venomous, and utterly detestable carcass right upon poor Pegasus, clung round him with might and main, and tied up its snaky tail into a knot! Up flew the aerial steed, higher, higher, higher, above the mountain-peaks, above the clouds, and almost out of sight of the solid earth. But still the earthborn monster kept its hold, and was borne upward, along with the creature of light and air. Bellerophon, meanwhile, turning about, found himself face to face with the ugly grimness of the Chimera's visage, and could only avoid being scorched to death, or bitten right in twain, by holding up his shield. Over the upper edge of the shield, he looked sternly into the savage eyes of the monster.

But the Chimera was so mad and wild with pain, that it did not guard itself so well as might else have been the case. Perhaps, after all, the best way to fight a Chimera is by getting as close to it as you can. In its efforts to stick its horrible iron claws into its enemy, the creature left its own breast quite exposed; and perceiving this, Bellerophon thrust his sword up to the hilt into its cruel heart. Immediately the snaky tail untied its knot. The monster let go its hold of Pegasus, and fell from that vast height, downward; while the fire within its bosom, instead of being put out, burned fiercer than ever, and quickly began to consume the dead carcass. Thus it fell out of the sky, all aflame, and (it being nightfall before it reached the earth) was mistaken for a shooting star or a comet. But, at early sunrise, some cottagers were going to their day's labor, and saw, to their astonishment, that several acres of ground were strewn with black ashes. In the middle of a field, there was a heap of whitened bones, a great deal higher than a haystack. Nothing else was ever seen of the dreadful Chimera!

And when Bellerophon had won the victory, he bent forward and kissed Pegasus, while the tears stood in his eyes.

"Back now, my beloved steed!" said he. "Back to the Fountain of Pirene!"

Pegasus skimmed through the air, quicker than ever be did before, and reached the fountain in a very short time. And there he found the old man leaning on his staff, and the country fellow watering his cow, and the pretty maiden filling her pitcher.

"I remember now," quoth the old man, "I saw this winged horse once before, when I was quite a lad. But he was ten times handsomer in those days."

"I own a cart horse, worth three of him!" said the country fellow. "If this pony were mine, the first thing I should do would be to clip his wings!"

But the poor maiden said nothing, for she had always the luck to be afraid at the wrong time. So she ran away, and let her pitcher tumble down, and broke it.

"Where is the gentle child," asked Bellerophon, "who used to keep me company, and never lost his faith, and never was weary of gazing into the fountain?"

"Here am I, dear Bellerophon!" said the child, softly.

For the little boy had spent day after day, on the margin of Pirene, waiting for his friend to come back, but when he perceived Bellerophon descending through the clouds, mounted on

the winged horse, he had shrunk back into the shrubbery. He was a delicate and tender child, and dreaded lest the old man and the country fellow should see the tears gushing from his eyes.

"Thou hast won the victory," said he, joyfully, running to the knee of Bellerophon, who still sat on the back of Pegasus. "I knew thou wouldst."

"Yes, dear child!" replied Bellerophon, alighting from the winged horse. "But if thy faith had not helped me, I should never have waited for Pegasus, and never have gone up above the clouds, and never have conquered the terrible Chimera. Thou, my beloved little friend, hast done it all. And now let us give Pegasus his liberty."

So he slipped off the enchanted bridle from the head of the marvelous steed.

"Be free, forevermore, my Pegasus!" cried he, with a shade of sadness in his tone. "Be as free as thou art fleet!"

But Pegasus rested his head on Bellerophon's shoulder, and would not be persuaded to take flight.

"Well then," said Bellerophon, caressing the airy horse, "thou shalt be with me, as long as thou wilt; and we will go together, forthwith, and tell King Iobates that the Chimera is destroyed."

Then Bellerophon embraced the gentle child, and promised to come to him again, and departed. But, in after years, that child took higher flights upon the aerial steed than ever did Bellerophon, and achieved more honorable deeds than his friend's victory over the Chimera.

For, gentle and tender as he was, he grew to be a mighty poet!

THE GOLDEN FLEECE

When Jason, the son of the dethroned King of Iolchos, was a little boy, he was sent away from his parents, and placed under the queerest schoolmaster that ever you heard of. This learned person was one of the people, or quadrupeds, called Centaurs. He lived in a cavern, and had the body and legs of a white horse, with the head and shoulders of a man.

His name was Chiron; and, in spite of his odd appearance, he was a very excellent teacher, and had several scholars, who afterwards did him credit by making a great figure in the world. The famous Hercules was one, and so was Achilles, and Philoctetes, likewise, and Æsculapius, who acquired immense repute as a doctor. The good Chiron taught his pupils how to play upon the harp, and how to cure diseases, and how to use the sword and shield, together with various other branches of education, in which the lads of those days used to be instructed, instead of writing and arithmetic.

I have sometimes suspected that Master Chiron was not really very different from other people, but that, being a kindhearted and merry old fellow, he was in the habit of making believe that he was a horse, and scrambling about the school room on all fours, and letting the little boys ride upon his back. And so, when his scholars had grown up, and grown old, and were trotting their grandchildren on their knees, they told them about the sports of their school days; and these young folks took the idea that their grandfathers had been taught their letters by a Centaur, half man and half horse. Little children, not quite understanding what is said to them, often get such absurd notions into their heads, you know.

Be that as it may, it has always been told for a fact, (and always will be told, as long as the world lasts,) that Chiron, with the head of a schoolmaster, had the body and legs of a horse. Just imagine the grave old gentleman clattering and stamping into the school room on his four hoofs, perhaps treading on some little fellow's toes, flourishing his switch tail instead of a rod, and, now and then, trotting out of doors to eat a mouthful of grass! I wonder what the blacksmith charged him for a set of iron shoes.

So Jason dwelt in the cave, with this four-footed Chiron, from the time that he was an infant, only a few months old, until he had grown to the full height of a man. He became a very good harper, I suppose, and skillful in the use of weapons, and tolerably acquainted with herbs and other doctor's stuff, and, above all, an admirable horseman; for, in teaching young people to ride, the good Chiron must have been without a rival among schoolmasters. At length, being now a tall and athletic youth, Jason resolved to seek his fortune in the world, without asking Chiron's advice, or telling him anything about the matter. This was very unwise, to be sure; and I hope none of you, my little hearers, will ever follow Jason's example. But, you are to understand, he had heard how that he himself was a prince royal, and how his father, King Æson, had been deprived of the kingdom of Iolchos by a certain Pelias, who would also have killed Jason, had he not been hidden in the Centaur's cave. And, being come to the strength of a man, Jason determined to set all this business to rights, and to punish the wicked Pelias for wronging his dear father, and to cast him down from the throne, and seat himself there instead.

With this intention, he took a spear in each hand, and threw a leopard's skin over his shoulders, to keep off the rain, and set forth on his travels, with his long yellow ringlets waving in the wind.

The part of his dress on which he most prided himself was a pair of sandals, that had been his father's. They were handsomely embroidered, and were tied upon his feet with strings of gold. But his whole attire was such as people did not very often see; and as he passed along, the women and children ran to the doors and windows, wondering whither this beautiful youth was journeying, with his leopard's skin and his golden-tied sandals, and what heroic deeds he meant to perform, with a spear in his right hand and another in his left.

I know not how far Jason had traveled when he came to a turbulent river, which rushed right across his pathway, with specks of white foam among its black eddies, hurrying tumultuously onward, and roaring angrily as it went. Though not a very broad river in the dry seasons of the year, it was now swollen by heavy rains and by the melting of the snow on the sides of Mount Olympus; and it thundered so loudly, and looked so wild and dangerous, that Jason, bold as he was, thought it prudent to pause upon the brink. The bed of the stream seemed to be strewn with sharp and rugged rocks, some of which thrust themselves above the water. By and by, an uprooted tree, with shattered branches, came drifting along the current, and got entangled among the rocks. Now and then, a drowned sheep, and once the carcass of a cow, floated past.

In short the swollen river had already done a great deal of mischief. It was evidently too deep for Jason to wade, and too boisterous for him to swim; he could see no bridge; and as for a boat, had there been any, the rocks would have broken it to pieces in an instant.

"See the poor lad," said a cracked voice close to his side. "He must have had but a poor education, since he does not know how to cross a little stream like this. Or is he afraid of wetting his fine golden-stringed sandals? It is a pity his four-footed schoolmaster is not here to carry him safely across on his back!"

Jason looked round greatly surprised, for he did not know that anybody was near. But beside him stood an old woman, with a ragged mantle over her head, leaning on a staff, the top of which was carved into the shape of a cuckoo. She looked very aged, and wrinkled, and infirm; and yet her eyes, which were as brown as those of an ox, were so extremely large and beautiful, that, when they were fixed on Jason's eyes, he could see nothing else but them. The old woman had a pomegranate in her hand, although the fruit was then quite out of season.

"Whither are you going, Jason?" she now asked.

She seemed to know his name, you will observe; and indeed, those great brown eyes looked as if they had a knowledge of everything, whether past or to come. While Jason was gazing at her, a peacock strutted forward, and took his stand at the old woman's side.

"I am going to Iolchos," answered the young man, "to bid the wicked King Pelias come down from my father's throne, and let me reign in his stead."

"Ah, well, then," said the old woman, still with the same cracked voice, "if that is all your business, you need not be in a very great hurry. Just take me on your back, there's a good youth, and carry me across the river. I and my peacock have something to do on the other side, as well as yourself."

"Good mother," replied Jason, "your business can hardly be so important as the pulling down a king from his throne. Besides, as you may see for yourself, the river is very boisterous; and if I should chance to stumble, it would sweep both of us away more easily than it has carried off yonder uprooted tree. I would gladly help you if I could; but I doubt whether I am strong enough to carry you across."

"Then," said she, very scornfully, "neither are you strong enough to pull King Pelias off his throne. And, Jason, unless you will help an old woman at her need, you ought not to be a king. What are kings made for, save to succor the feeble and distressed? But do as you please. Either take me on your back, or with my poor old limbs I shall try my best to struggle across the stream."

Saying this, the old woman poked with her staff in the river, as if to find the safest place in its rocky bed where she might make the first step. But Jason, by this time, had grown ashamed of his reluctance to help her. He felt that he could never forgive himself, if this poor feeble creature should come to any harm in attempting to wrestle against the headlong current. The good Chiron, whether half horse or no, had taught him that the noblest use of his strength was to assist the weak; and also that he must treat every young woman as if she were his sister, and every old one like a mother. Remembering these maxims, the vigorous and beautiful young man knelt down, and requested the good dame to mount upon his back.

"The passage seems to me not very safe," he remarked. "But as your business is so urgent, I will try to carry you across. If the river sweeps you away, it shall take me too."

"That, no doubt, will be a great comfort to both of us," quoth the old woman. "But never fear. We shall get safely across."

So she threw her arms around Jason's neck; and lifting her from the ground, he stepped boldly into the raging and foamy

Right: On his epic travels Jason is destined to meet Princess Medea who will help him to obtain the golden fleece. Illustration by Virginia Frances Sterrett.

current, and began to stagger away from the shore. As for the peacock, it alighted on the old dame's shoulder. Jason's two spears, one in each hand, kept him from stumbling, and enabled him to feel his way among the hidden rocks; although, every instant, he expected that his companion and himself would go down the stream, together with the driftwood of shattered trees, and the carcasses of the sheep and cow. Down came the cold, snowy torrent from the steep side of Olympus, raging and thundering as if it had a real spite against Jason, or, at all events, were determined to snatch off his living burden from his shoulders. When he was half way across, the uprooted tree (which I have already told you about) broke loose from among the rocks, and bore down upon him, with all its splintered branches sticking out like the hundred arms of the giant Briareus. It rushed past, however, without touching him. But the next moment, his foot was caught in a crevice between two rocks, and stuck there so fast, that, in the effort to get free he lost one of his golden-stringed sandals.

At this accident Jason could not help uttering a cry of vexation.

"What is the matter, Jason?" asked the old woman.

"Matter enough," said the young man. "I have lost a sandal here among the rocks. And what sort of a figure shall I cut, at the court of King Pelias, with a golden-stringed sandal on one foot, and the other foot bare!"

"Do not take it to heart," answered his companion cheerily. "You never met with better fortune than in losing that sandal. It satisfies me that you are the very person whom the Speaking Oak has been talking about."

There was no time, just then, to inquire what the Speaking Oak had said. But the briskness of her tone encouraged the young man; and besides, he had never in his life felt so vigorous and mighty as since taking this old woman on his back. Instead of being exhausted, he gathered strength as he went on; and, struggling up against the torrent, he at last gained the opposite shore, clambered up the bank, and set down the old dame and her peacock safely on the grass. As soon as this was done, however, he could not help looking rather despondently at his bare foot, with only a remnant of the golden string of the sandal clinging round his ankle.

"You will get a handsomer pair of sandals by and by," said the old woman, with a kindly look out of her beautiful brown eyes. "Only let King Pelias get a glimpse of that bare foot, and you shall see him turn as pale as ashes, I promise you. There is your path. Go along, my good Jason, and my blessing go with you. And when you sit on your throne, remember the old woman whom you helped over the river."

With these words, she hobbled away, giving him a smile over her shoulders as she departed. Whether the light of her beautiful brown eyes threw a glory round about her, or whatever the cause might be, Jason fancied that there was something very noble and majestic in her figure, after all, and that, though her gait seemed to be a rheumatic hobble, yet she moved with as much grace and dignity as any queen on earth. Her peacock, which had now fluttered down from her shoulder, strutted behind her in prodigious pomp, and spread out its magnificent tail on purpose for Jason to admire it.

When the old dame and her peacock were out of sight, Jason set forward on his journey. After traveling a pretty long distance, he came to a town situated at the foot of a mountain, and not a great way from the shore of the sea. On the outside of the town there was an immense crowd of people, not only men and women, but children too, all in their best clothes, and evidently enjoying a holiday. The crowd was thickest towards the seashore; and in that direction, over the people's heads, Jason saw a wreath of smoke curling upward to the blue sky. He inquired of one of the multitude what town it was nearby, and why so many persons were here assembled together.

"This is the kingdom of Iolchos," answered the man, "and we are the subjects of King Pelias. Our monarch has summoned us together, that we may see him sacrifice a black bull to Neptune, who, they say, is his majesty's father. Yonder is the king, where you see the smoke going up from the altar."

While the man spoke he eyed Jason with great curiosity; for his garb was quite unlike that of the Iolchians, and it looked very odd to see a youth with a leopard's skin over his shoulders, and each hand grasping a spear. Jason perceived, too, that the man stared particularly at his feet, one of which, you remember, was bare, while the other was decorated with his father's golden-stringed sandal.

"Look at him! only look at him!" said the man to his next neighbor. "Do you see? He wears but one sandal!"

Upon this, first one person, and then another, began to stare at Jason, and everybody seemed to be greatly struck with something in his aspect; though they turned their eyes much oftener towards his feet than to any other part of his figure. Besides, he could hear them whispering to one another.

"One sandal! One sandal!" they kept saying. "The man with one sandal! Here he is at last! Whence has he come? What does he mean to do? What will the king say to the one-sandaled man?"

Poor Jason was greatly abashed, and made up his mind that the people of Iolchos were exceedingly ill-bred, to take such public notice of an accidental deficiency in his dress. Meanwhile, whether it were that they hustled him forward, or that Jason, of his own accord, thrust a passage through the crowd, it so happened that he soon found himself close to the smoking altar where King Pelias was sacrificing the black bull. The murmur and hum of the multitude, in their surprise at the spectacle of Jason with his one bare foot, grew so loud that it disturbed the ceremonies; and the king, holding the great knife with which he was just going to cut the bull's throat, turned angrily about, and fixed his eyes on Jason. The people had now withdrawn from around him, so that the youth stood in an open space, near the smoking altar, front to front with the angry King Pelias.

"Who are you?" cried the king, with a terrible frown. "And how dare you make this disturbance, while I am sacrificing a black bull to my father Neptune?"

"It is no fault of mine," answered Jason. "Your majesty must blame the rudeness of your subjects, who have raised all this tumult because one of my feet happens to be bare."

When Jason said this, the king gave a quick, startled glance down at his feet.

"Ha!" muttered he, "here is the one-sandaled fellow, sure enough! What can I do with him?"

And he clutched more closely the great knife in his hand, as if he were half a mind to slay Jason, instead of the black bull. The people round about caught up the king's words, indistinctly as they were uttered; and first there was a murmur among them, and then a loud shout.

"The one-sandaled man has come! The prophecy must be fulfilled!"

For you are to know, that, many years before, King Pelias had been told by the Speaking Oak of Dodona, that a man with one sandal should cast him down from his throne. On this account, he had given strict orders that nobody should ever come into his presence, unless both sandals were securely tied upon his feet; and he kept an officer in his palace, whose sole business it was to examine people's sandals, and to supply them with a new pair, at the expense of the royal treasury, as soon as the old ones began to wear out. In the whole course of the king's reign, he had never been thrown into such a fright and agitation as by the spectacle of poor Jason's bare foot. But, as he was naturally a bold and hard-hearted man, he soon took courage, and began to consider in what way he might rid himself of this terrible one-sandaled stranger.

"My good young man," said King Pelias, taking the softest tone imaginable, in order to throw Jason off his guard, "you are excessively welcome to my kingdom. Judging by your dress, you must have traveled a long distance; for it is not the fashion to wear leopard skins in this part of the world. Pray what may I call your name, and where did you receive your education?"

"My name is Jason," answered the young stranger. "Ever since my infancy, I have dwelt in the cave of Chiron the Centaur. He was my instructor, and taught me music, and horsemanship, and how to cure wounds, and likewise how to inflict wounds with my weapons."

"I have heard of Chiron the schoolmaster," replied King Pelias, "and how that there is an immense deal of learning and wisdom in his head, although it happens to be set on a horse's body. It gives me great delight to see one of his scholars at my court. But, to test how much you have profited under so excellent a teacher, will you allow me to ask you a single question?"

"I do not pretend to be very wise," said Jason. "But ask me what you please, and I will answer to the best of my ability."

Now King Pelias meant cunningly to entrap the young man, and to make him say something that should be the cause of mischief and destruction to himself. So, with a crafty and evil smile upon his face, he spoke as follows:

"What would you do, brave Jason," asked he, "if there were a man in the world, by whom, as you had reason to believe, you were doomed to be ruined and slain—what would you do, I say, if that man stood before you, and in your power?"

When Jason saw the malice and wickedness which King Pelias could not prevent from gleaming out of his eyes, he probably guessed that the king had discovered what he came for, and that he intended to turn his own words against himself. Still he scorned to tell a falsehood. Like an upright and honorable prince, as he was, he determined to speak out the real truth. Since the king had chosen to ask him the question, and since Jason had promised him an answer, there was no right way, save to tell him precisely what would be the most prudent thing to do, if he had his worst enemy in his power.

Therefore, after a moment's consideration, he spoke up, with a firm and manly voice.

"I would send such a man," said he, "in quest of the Golden Fleece!"

This enterprise, you will understand, was, of all others, the most difficult and dangerous in the world. In the first place, it would be necessary to make a long voyage through unknown seas. There was hardly a hope, or a possibility, that any young man who should undertake this voyage would either succeed in obtaining the Golden Fleece, or would survive to return home, and tell of the perils he had run. The eyes of King Pelias sparkled with joy, therefore, when he heard Jason's reply.

"Well said, wise man with the one sandal!" cried he. "Go, then, and at the peril of your life, bring me back the Golden Fleece."

"I go," answered Jason, composedly. "If I fail, you need not fear that I will ever come back to trouble you again. But if I return to Iolchos with the prize, then, King Pelias, you must hasten down from your lofty throne, and give me your crown and scepter."

"That I will," said the king, with a sneer. "Meantime, I will keep them very safely for you."

The first thing that Jason thought of doing, after he left the king's presence, was to go to Dodona, and inquire of the Talking Oak what course it was best to pursue. This wonderful tree stood in the center of an ancient wood. Its stately trunk rose up a hundred feet into the air, and threw a broad and dense shadow over more than an acre of ground. Standing beneath it, Jason looked up among the knotted branches and green leaves, and into the mysterious heart of the old tree, and spoke aloud, as if he were addressing some person who was hidden in the depths of the foliage.

"What shall I do," said he, "in order to win the Golden Fleece?"

At first there was a deep silence, not only within the shadow of the Talking Oak, but all through the solitary wood. In a moment or two, however, the leaves of the oak began to stir and rustle, as if a gentle breeze were wandering amongst them, although the other trees of the wood were perfectly still. The sound grew louder, and became like the roar of a high wind. By and by, Jason imagined that he could distinguish words, but very confusedly, because each separate leaf of the tree seemed to be a tongue, and the whole myriad of tongues were babbling at once. But the noise waxed broader and deeper, until it resembled a tornado sweeping through the oak, and making one great utterance out of the thousand and thousand of little murmurs which each leafy tongue had caused by its rustling. And now, though it still had the tone of a mighty wind roaring among the branches, it was also like a deep bass voice, speaking, as distinctly as a tree could be expected to speak, the following words:

"Go to Argus, the ship builder, and bid him build a galley with fifty oars."

Then the voice melted again into the indistinct murmur of the rustling leaves, and died gradually away. When it was quite gone, Jason felt inclined to doubt whether he had actually heard the words, or whether his fancy had not shaped them out of the ordinary sound made by a breeze, while passing through the thick foliage of the tree.

But on inquiry among the people of Iolchos, he found that there was really a man in the city, by the name of Argus, who was a very skillful builder of vessels. This showed some intelligence in the oak; else how should it have known that any such person existed? At Jason's request, Argus readily consented to build him a galley so big that it should require fifty strong men to row it; although no vessel of such a size and burden had heretofore been seen in the world. So the head carpenter, and all his journeymen and apprentices, began their work and for a good while afterwards, there they were, busily employed, hewing out the timbers, and making a great clatter with their hammers; until the new ship, which was called the *Argo*, seemed to be quite ready for the sea. And, as the Talking Oak had already given him such good advice, Jason thought that it would not be amiss to ask for a little more. He visited it again, therefore, and standing beside its huge, rough trunk, inquired what he should do next.

This time, there was no such universal quivering of the leaves, throughout the whole tree, as there had been before. But after a while, Jason observed that the foliage of a great branch which stretched above his head had begun to rustle, as if the wind were stirring that one bough, while all the other boughs of the oak were at rest.

"Cut me off!" said the branch, as soon as it could speak distinctly; "cut me off! cut me off! and carve me into a figure head for your galley."

Accordingly, Jason took the branch at its word, and lopped it off the tree. A carver in the neighborhood engaged to make the figure head. He was a tolerably good workman, and had already carved several figure heads, in what he intended for feminine shapes, and looking pretty much like those which we see nowadays stuck up under a vessel's bowsprit, with great staring eyes, that never wink at the dash of the spray. But (what was very strange) the carver found that his hand was guided by some unseen power, and by a skill beyond his own, and that his tools shaped out an image which he had never dreamed of. When the work was finished, it turned out to be the figure of a beautiful woman, with a helmet on her head, from beneath which the long ringlets fell down upon her shoulders. On the left arm was a shield, and in its center appeared a lifelike representation of the head of Medusa with the snaky locks. The right arm was extended, as if pointing onward. The face of this wonderful statue, though not angry or forbidding, was so grave and majestic, that perhaps you might call it severe; and as for the mouth, it seemed just ready to unclose its lips, and utter words of the deepest wisdom.

Jason was delighted with the oaken image, and gave the carver no rest until it was completed, and set up where a figure head has always stood, from that time to this, in the vessel's prow.

"And now," cried he, as he stood gazing at the calm, majestic face of the statue, "I must go to the Talking Oak, and inquire what next to do."

"There is no need of that, Jason," said a voice which, though it was far lower, reminded him of the mighty tones of the great oak. "When you desire good advice, you can seek it of me."

Jason had been looking straight into the face of the image when these words were spoken. But he could hardly believe either his ears or his eyes. The truth was, however, that the oaken lips had moved, and, to all appearance, the voice had proceeded from the statue's mouth.

Recovering a little from his surprise, Jason bethought himself that the image had been carved out of the wood of the Talking Oak, and that, therefore, it was really no great wonder, but, on the contrary, the most natural thing in the world, that it should possess the faculty of

speech. It would have been very odd, indeed, if it had not. But certainly it was a great piece of good fortune that he should be able to carry so wise a block of wood along with him in his perilous voyage.

"Tell me, wonderous image," exclaimed Jason, "since you inherit the wisdom of the Speaking Oak of Dodona, whose daughter you are, tell me, where shall I find fifty bold youths, who will take each of them an oar of my galley? They must have sturdy arms to row, and brave hearts to encounter perils, or we shall never win the Golden Fleece."

"Go," replied the oaken image, "go, summon all the heroes of Greece."

And, in fact, considering what a great deed was to be done, could any advice be wiser than this which Jason received from the figure head of his vessel? He lost no time in sending messages to all the cities, and making known to the whole people of Greece, that Prince Jason, the son of King Æson, was going in quest of the Fleece of Gold, and that he desired the help of forty-nine of the bravest and strongest young men alive, to row his vessel and share his dangers. And Jason himself would be the fiftieth.

At this news, the adventurous youths, all over the country, began to bestir themselves. Some of them had already fought with giants, and slain dragons; and the younger ones, who had not yet met with such good fortune, thought it a shame to have lived so long without getting astride of a flying serpent, or sticking their spears into a Chimera, or, at least, thrusting their right arms down a monstrous lion's throat. There was a fair prospect that they would meet with plenty of such adventures before finding the Golden Fleece. As soon as they could furbish up their helmets and shields, therefore, and gird on their trusty swords, they came thronging to Iolchos, and clambered on board the new galley. Shaking hands with Jason, they assured him that they did not care a pin for their lives, but would help row the vessel to the remotest edge of the world, and as much farther as he might think it best to go.

Many of these brave fellows had been educated by Chiron, the four-footed pedagogue, and were therefore old schoolmates of Jason, and knew him to be a lad of spirit. The mighty Hercules, whose shoulders afterwards held up the sky, was one of them. And there were Castor and Pollux, the twin brothers, who were never accused of being chicken-hearted, although they had been hatched out of an egg; and Theseus, who was so renowned for killing the Minotaur; and Lynceus, with his wonderfully sharp eyes, which could see through a millstone, or look right down into the depths of the earth, and discover the treasures that were there; and Orpheus, the very best of harpers, who sang and played upon his lyre so sweetly, that the brute beasts stood upon their hind legs, and capered merrily to the music. Yes, and at some of his more moving tunes, the rocks bestirred their moss-grown bulk out of the ground, and a grove of forest trees uprooted themselves, and, nodding their tops to one another, performed a country dance.

One of the rowers was a beautiful young woman, named Atalanta, who had been nursed among the mountains by a bear. So light of foot was this fair damsel, that she could step from one foamy crest of a wave to the foamy crest of another, without wetting more than the sole of her sandal. She had grown up in a very wild way, and talked much about the rights of

women, and loved hunting and war far better than her needle. But, in my opinion, the most remarkable of this famous company were two sons of the North Wind, (airy youngsters, and of rather a blustering disposition,) who had wings on their shoulders, and, in case of a calm, could puff out their cheeks, and blow almost as fresh a breeze as their father. I ought not to forget the prophets and conjurers, of whom there were several in the crew, and who could foretell what would happen tomorrow, or the next day, or a hundred years hence, but were generally quite unconscious of what was passing at the moment.

Jason appointed Tiphys to be helmsman, because he was a stargazer, and knew the points of the compass. Lynceus, on account of his sharp sight, was stationed as a lookout in the prow, where he saw a whole day's sail ahead, but was rather apt to overlook things that lay directly under his nose. If the sea only happened to be deep enough, however, Lynceus could tell you exactly what kind of rocks or sand were at the bottom of it; and he often cried out to his companions, that they were sailing over heaps of sunken treasure, which he was none the richer for beholding. To confess the truth, few people believed him when he said it.

Well! But when the Argonauts, as these fifty brave adventurers were called, had prepared everything for the voyage, an unforeseen difficulty threatened to end it before it was begun. The vessel, you must understand, was so long, and broad, and ponderous, that the united force of all the fifty was insufficient to shove her into the water.

Hercules, I suppose, had not grown to his full strength, else he might have set her afloat as easily as a little boy launches his boat upon a puddle. But here were these fifty heroes, pushing, and straining, and growing red in the face, without making the *Argo* start an inch.

At last, quite wearied out, they sat themselves down on the shore, exceedingly disconsolate, and thinking that the vessel must be left to rot and fall in pieces, and that they must either swim across the sea or lose the Golden Fleece.

All at once, Jason bethought himself of the galley's miraculous figure head.

"O, daughter of the Talking Oak," cried he, "how shall we set to work to get our vessel into the water?"

"Seat yourselves," answered the image, (for it had known what had ought to be done from the very first, and was only waiting for the question to be put,) "seat yourselves, and handle your oars, and let Orpheus play upon his harp."

Immediately the fifty heroes got on board, and seizing their oars, held them perpendicularly in the air, while Orpheus (who liked such a task far better than rowing) swept his fingers across the harp. At the first ringing note of the music, they felt the vessel stir. Orpheus thrummed away briskly, and the galley slid at once into the sea, dipping her prow so deeply that the figure head drank the wave with its marvelous lips, and rising again as buoyant as a swan. The rowers plied their fifty oars; the white foam boiled up before the prow; the water gurgled and bubbled in their wake; while Orpheus continued to play so lively a strain of music, that the vessel seemed to dance over the billows by way of keeping time to it. Thus triumphantly did the *Argo* sail out of the harbor, amidst the huzzahs and good wishes of everybody except the wicked old Pelias, who stood on a promontory, scowling at her, and wishing that he could blow out of

his lungs the tempest of wrath that was in his heart, and so sink the galley with all on board. When they had sailed above fifty miles over the sea, Lynceus happened to cast his sharp eyes behind, and said that there was this bad-hearted king, still perched upon the promontory, and scowling so gloomily that it looked like a black thunder cloud in that quarter of the horizon.

In order to make the time pass away more pleasantly during the voyage, the heroes talked about the Golden Fleece. It originally belonged, it appears, to a Bœotian ram, who had taken on his back two children, when in danger of their lives, and fled with them over land and sea, as far as Colchis. One of the children, whose name was Helle, fell into the sea and was drowned. But the other, (a little boy, named Phrixus) was brought safe ashore by the faithful ram, who, however, was so exhausted that he immediately lay down and died. In memory of this good deed, and as a token of his true heart, the fleece of the poor dead ram was miraculously changed to gold, and became one of the most beautiful objects ever seen on earth. It was hung upon a tree in a sacred grove, where it had now been kept I know not how many years, and was the envy of mighty kings, who had nothing so magnificent in any of their palaces.

If I were to tell you all the adventures of the Argonauts, it would take me till nightfall, and perhaps a great deal longer. There was no lack of wonderful events, as you may judge from what you have already heard. At a certain island they were hospitably received by King Cyzicus, its sovereign, who made a feast for them, and treated them like brothers. But the Argonauts saw that this good king looked downcast and very much troubled, and they therefore inquired of him what was the matter. King Cyzicus hereupon informed them that he and his subjects were greatly abused and incommoded by the inhabitants of a neighboring mountain, who made war upon them, and killed many people, and ravaged the country. And while they were talking about it, Cyzicus pointed to the mountain, and asked Jason and his companions what they saw there.

"I see some very tall objects," answered Jason; "but they are at such a distance that I cannot distinctly make out what they are. To tell your majesty the truth, they look so very strangely that I am inclined to think them clouds, which have chanced to take something like human shapes."

"I see them very plainly," remarked Lynceus, whose eyes, you know, were as far sighted as a telescope. "They are a band of enormous giants, all of whom have six arms apiece, and a club, a sword, or some other weapon in each of their hands."

"You have excellent eyes," said King Cyzicus. "Yes, they are six armed giants, as you say, and these are the enemies whom I and my subjects have to contend with."

The next day, when the Argonauts were about setting sail, down came these terrible giants, stepping a hundred yards at a stride, brandishing their six arms apiece and looking very formidable, so far aloft in the air. Each of these monsters was able to carry on a whole war by himself, for with one of his arms he could fling immense stones, and wield a club with another, and a sword with a third, while the fourth was poking a long spear at the enemy, and the fifth and sixth were shooting him with a bow and arrow. But, luckily, though the giants were so huge, and had so many arms, they had each but one heart, and that no bigger nor braver than the heart of an ordinary man. Besides, if they had been like the hundred-armed Briareus, the brave

Argonauts would have given them their hands full of fight. Jason and his friends went boldly to meet them, slew a great many, and made the rest take to their heels, so that, if the giants had had six legs apiece instead of six arms, it would have served them better to run away with.

Another strange adventure happened when the voyagers came to Thrace, where they found a poor blind king, named Phineus, deserted by his subjects, and living in a very sorrowful way, all by himself.

On Jason's inquiring whether they could do him any service, the king answered that he was terribly tormented by three great winged creatures, called Harpies, which had the faces of women, and the wings, bodies, and claws of vultures. These ugly wretches were in the habit of snatching away his dinner, and allowed him no peace of his life. Upon hearing this, the Argonauts spread a plentiful feast on the seashore, well knowing, from what the blind king said of their greediness, that the Harpies would snuff up the scent of the victuals, and quickly come to steal them away. And so it turned out; for, hardly was the table set, before the three hideous vulture women came flapping their wings, seized the food in their talons, and flew off as fast as they could.

But the two sons of the North Wind drew their swords, spread their pinions, and set off through the air in pursuit of the thieves, whom they at last overtook among some islands, after a chase of hundreds of miles. The two winged youths blustered terribly at the Harpies, (for they had the rough temper of their father,) and so frightened them with their drawn swords, that they solemnly promised never to trouble King Phineus again.

Then the Argonauts sailed onward, and met with many other marvelous incidents, any one of which would make a story by itself. At one time, they landed on an island, and were reposing on the grass, when they suddenly found themselves assailed by what seemed a shower of steel-headed arrows. Some of them stuck in the ground, while others hit against their shields, and several penetrated their flesh. The fifty heroes started up, and looked about them for the hidden enemy, but could find none, nor see any spot, on the whole island, where even a single archer could lie concealed. Still, however, the steel-headed arrows came whizzing among them, and, at last, happening to look upward, they beheld a large flock of birds, hovering and wheeling aloft, and shooting their feathers down upon the Argonauts. These feathers were the steel-headed arrows that had so tormented them.

There was no possibility of making any resistance; and the fifty heroic Argonauts might all have been killed or wounded by a flock of troublesome birds, without ever setting eyes on the Golden Fleece, if Jason had not thought of asking the advice of the oaken image.

So he ran to the galley as fast as his legs would carry him.

"O, daughter of the Speaking Oak," cried he, all out of breath, "we need your wisdom more than ever before! We are in great peril from a flock of birds, who are shooting us with their steel-pointed feathers. What can we do to drive them away?"

"Make a clatter on your shields," said the image.

On receiving this excellent counsel, Jason hurried back to his companions, (who were far more dismayed than when they fought with the six-armed giants,) and bade them strike with

their swords upon their brazen shields. Forthwith the fifty heroes set heartily to work, banging with might and main, and raised such a terrible clatter, that the birds made what haste they could to get away; and though they had shot half the feathers out of their wings, they were soon seen skimming among the clouds, a long distance off, and looking like a flock of wild geese. Orpheus celebrated this victory by playing a triumphant anthem on his harp, and sang so melodiously that Jason begged him to desist, lest, as the steel-feathered birds had been driven away by an ugly sound, they might be enticed back again by a sweet one.

While the Argonauts remained on this island, they saw a small vessel approaching the shore, in which were two young men of princely demeanor, and exceedingly handsome, as young princes generally were, in those days. Now, who do you imagine these two voyagers turned out to be? Why, if you will believe me, they were the sons of that very Phrixus, who, in his childhood, had been carried to Colchis on the back of the golden-fleeced ram. Since that time, Phrixus had married the king's daughter; and the two young princes had been born and brought up at Colchis, and had spent their play days in the outskirts of the grove, in the center of which the Golden Fleece was hanging upon a tree. They were now on their way to Greece, in hopes of getting back a kingdom that had been wrongfully taken from their father.

When the princes understood whither the Argonauts were going, they offered to turn back, and guide them to Colchis. At the same time, however, they spoke as if it were very doubtful whether Jason would succeed in getting the Golden Fleece. According to their account, the tree on which it hung was guarded by a terrible dragon, who never failed to devour, at one mouthful, every person who might venture within his reach.

"There are other difficulties in the way," continued the young princes. "But is not this enough? Ah, brave Jason, turn back before it is too late. It would grieve us to the heart, if you and your nine and forty brave companions should be eaten up, at fifty mouthfuls, by this execrable dragon."

"My young friends," quietly replied Jason, "I do not wonder that you think the dragon very terrible. You have grown up from infancy in the fear of this monster, and therefore still regard him with the awe that children feel for the bugbears and hobgoblins which their nurses have talked to them about. But, in my view of the matter, the dragon is merely a pretty large serpent, who is not half so likely to snap me up at one mouthful as I am to cut off his ugly head, and strip the skin from his body. At all events, turn back who may, I will never see Greece again, unless I carry with me the Golden Fleece."

"We will none of us turn back!" cried his nine and forty brave comrades. "Let us get on board the galley this instant; and if the dragon is to make a breakfast of us, much good may it do him."

And Orpheus (whose custom it was to set everything to music) began to harp and sing most gloriously, and made every mother's son of them feel as if nothing in this world were so delectable as to fight dragons, and nothing so truly honorable as to be eaten up at one mouthful, in case of the worst.

After this, (being now under the guidance of the two princes, who were well acquainted with the way,) they quickly sailed to Colchis. When the king of the country, whose name

was Æetes, heard of their arrival, he instantly summoned Jason to court. The king was a stern and cruel-looking potentate; and though he put on as polite and hospitable an expression as he could, Jason did not like his face a whit better than that of the wicked King Pelias, who dethroned his father.

"You are welcome, brave Jason," said King Æetes. "Pray, are you on a pleasure voyage? Or do you meditate the discovery of unknown islands? Or what other cause has procured me the happiness of seeing you at my court?"

"Great sir," replied Jason, with an obeisance, for Chiron had taught him how to behave with propriety, whether to kings or beggars, "I have come hither with a purpose which I now beg your majesty's permission to execute. King Pelias, who sits on my father's throne, (to which he has no more right than to the one on which your excellent majesty is now seated,) has engaged to come down from it, and give me his crown and scepter, provided I bring him the Golden Fleece. This, as your majesty is aware, is now hanging on a tree here at Colchis; and I humbly solicit your gracious leave to take it away."

In spite of himself, the king's face twisted itself into an angry frown; for, above all things else in the world, he prized the Golden Fleece and was even suspected of having done a very wicked act, in order to get it into his own possession. It put him into the worst possible humor, therefore, to hear that the gallant Prince Jason, and forty-nine of the bravest young warriors of Greece, had come to Colchis with the sole purpose of taking away his chief treasure.

"Do you know," asked King Æetes, eyeing Jason very sternly, "what are the conditions which you must fulfill before getting possession of the Golden Fleece?"

"I have heard," rejoined the youth, "that a dragon lies beneath the tree on which the prize hangs, and that whoever approaches him runs the risk of being devoured at a mouthful."

"True," said the king, with a smile that did not look particularly good-natured. "Very true, young man. But there are other things as hard, or perhaps a little harder, to be done, before you can even have the privilege of being devoured by the dragon. For example, you must first tame my two brazen-footed and brazen-lunged bulls, which Vulcan, the wonderful blacksmith, made for me. There is a furnace in each of their stomachs; and they breathe such hot fire out of their mouths and nostrils, that nobody has hitherto gone nigh them without being instantly burned to a small, black cinder. What do you think of this, my brave Jason?"

"I must encounter the peril," answered Jason, composedly, "since it stands in the way of my purpose."

"After taming the fiery bulls," continued King Æetes, who was determined to scare Jason if possible, "you must yoke them to a plow, and must plow the sacred earth in the grove of Mars, and sow some of the same dragon's teeth from which Cadmus raised a crop of armed men. They are an unruly set of reprobates, those sons of the dragon's teeth; and unless you treat them suitably, they will fall upon you sword in hand. You and your nine and forty Argonauts, my bold Jason, are hardly numerous or strong enough to fight with such a host as will spring up."

"My master Chiron," replied Jason, "taught me, long ago, the story of Cadmus. Perhaps I can manage the quarrelsome sons of the dragon's teeth as well as Cadmus did."

"I wish the dragon had him," muttered King Æetes to himself, "and the four-footed pedant, his schoolmaster, into the bargain. Why, what a foolhardy, self-conceited coxcomb he is! We'll see what my fire-breathing bulls will do for him. Well, Prince Jason," he continued, aloud, and as complaisantly as he could, "make yourself comfortable for today, and tomorrow morning, since you insist upon it, you shall try your skill at the plow."

While the king talked with Jason, a beautiful young woman was standing behind the throne. She fixed her eyes earnestly upon the youthful stranger, and listened attentively to every word that was spoken; and when Jason withdrew from the king's presence, this young woman followed him out of the room.

"I am the king's daughter," she said to him, "and my name is Medea. I know a great deal of which other young princesses are ignorant, and can do many things which they would be afraid so much as to dream of. If you will trust to me, I can instruct you how to tame the fiery bulls, and sow the dragon's teeth, and get the Golden Fleece."

"Indeed, beautiful princess," answered Jason, "if you will do me this service, I promise to be grateful to you my whole life long."

Gazing at Medea, he beheld a wonderful intelligence in her face. She was one of those persons whose eyes are full of mystery; so that, while looking into them, you seem to see a very great way, as into a deep well, yet can never be certain whether you see into the farthest depths, or whether there be not something else hidden at the bottom. If Jason had been capable of fearing anything, he would have been afraid of making this young princess his enemy; for, beautiful as she now looked, she might, the very next instant, become as terrible as the dragon that kept watch over the Golden Fleece.

"Princess," he exclaimed, "you seem indeed very wise and very powerful. But how can you help me to do the things of which you speak? Are you an enchantress?"

"Yes, Prince Jason," answered Medea, with a smile, "you have hit upon the truth. I am an enchantress. Circe, my father's sister, taught me to be one, and I could tell you, if I pleased, who was the old woman with the peacock, the pomegranate, and the cuckoo staff, whom you carried over the river; and, likewise, who it is that speaks through the lips of the oaken image, that stands in the prow of your galley. I am acquainted with some of your secrets, you perceive. It is well for you that I am favorably inclined; for, otherwise, you would hardly escape being snapped, up by the dragon."

"I should not so much care for the dragon," replied Jason, "if I only knew how to manage the brazen-footed and fiery-lunged bulls."

"If you are as brave as I think you, and as you have need to be," said Medea, "your own bold heart will teach you that there is but one way of dealing with a mad bull. What it is I leave you to find out in the moment of peril. As for the fiery breath of these animals, I have a charmed ointment here, which will prevent you from being burned up, and cure you if you chance to be a little scorched."

So she put a golden box into his hand, and directed him how to apply the perfumed unguent which it contained, and where to meet her at midnight.

"Only be brave," added she, "and before daybreak the brazen bulls shall be tamed."

The young man assured her that his heart would not fail him. He then rejoined his comrades, and told them what had passed between the princess and himself, and warned them to be in readiness in case there might be need of their help.

At the appointed hour he met the beautiful Medea on the marble steps of the king's palace. She gave him a basket, in which were the dragon's teeth, just as they had been pulled out of the monster's jaws by Cadmus, long ago. Medea then led Jason down the palace steps, and through the silent streets of the city, and into the royal pasture ground, where the two brazen-footed bulls were kept. It was a starry night, with a bright gleam along the eastern edge of the sky, where the moon was soon going to show herself. After entering the pasture, the princess paused and looked around.

"There they are," said she, "reposing themselves and chewing their fiery cuds in that farthest corner of the field. It will be excellent sport, I assure you, when they catch a glimpse of your figure. My father and all his court delight in nothing so much as to see a stranger trying to yoke them, in order to come at the Golden Fleece. It makes a holiday in Colchis whenever such a thing happens. For my part, I enjoy it immensely. You cannot imagine in what a mere twinkling of an eye their hot breath shrivels a young man into a black cinder."

"Are you sure, beautiful Medea," asked Jason, "quite sure, that the unguent in the gold box will prove a remedy against those terrible burns?"

"If you doubt, if you are in the least afraid," said the princess, looking him in the face by the dim starlight, "you had better never have been born than go a step nigher to the bulls."

But Jason had set his heart steadfastly on getting the Golden Fleece; and I positively doubt whether he would have gone back without it, even had he been certain of finding himself turned into a red-hot cinder, or a handful of white ashes, the instant he made a step farther. He therefore let go Medea's hand, and walked boldly forward in the direction whither she had pointed. At some distance before him he perceived four streams of fiery vapor, regularly appearing, and again vanishing, after dimly lighting up the surrounding obscurity. These, you will understand, were caused by the breath of the brazen bulls, which was quietly stealing out of their four nostrils, as they lay chewing their cuds.

At the first two or three steps which Jason made, the four fiery streams appeared to gush out somewhat more plentifully; for the two brazen bulls had heard his foot tramp, and were lifting up their hot noses to snuff the air. He went a little farther, and by the way in which the red vapor now spouted forth, he judged that the creatures had got upon their feet. Now he could see glowing sparks, and vivid jets of flame. At the next step, each of the bulls made the pasture echo with a terrible roar, while the burning breath, which they thus belched forth, lit up the whole field with a momentary flash. One other stride did bold Jason make, and, suddenly, as a streak of lightning, on came these fiery animals, roaring like thunder, and sending out sheets of white flame, which so kindled up the scene that the young man could discern every object more distinctly than by daylight. Most distinctly of all he saw the two horrible creatures galloping right down upon him, their brazen hoofs rattling and ringing over the ground, and

their tails sticking up stiffly into the air, as has always been the fashion with angry bulls. Their breath scorched the herbage before them. So intensely hot it was, indeed, that it caught a dry tree, under which Jason was now standing, and set it all in a light blaze. But as for Jason himself, (thanks to Medea's enchanted ointment,) the white flame curled around his body, without injuring him a jot more than if he had been made of asbestos.

Greatly encouraged at finding himself not yet turned into a cinder, the young man awaited the attack of the bulls. Just as the brazen brutes fancied themselves sure of tossing him into the air, he caught one of them by the horn, and the other by his screwed-up tail, and held them in a gripe like that of an iron vice, one with his right hand, the other with his left. Well, he must have been wonderfully strong in his arms, to be sure. But the secret of the matter was, that the brazen bulls were enchanted creatures, and that Jason had broken the spell of their fiery fierceness by his bold way of handling them. And, ever since that time, it has been the favorite method of brave men, when danger assails them, to do what they call "taking the bull by the horns" and to grip him by the tail is pretty much the same thing—that is, to throw aside fear, and overcome the peril by despising it.

It was now easy to yoke the bulls, and to harness them to the plow, which had lain rusting on the ground for a great many years gone by; so long was it before anybody could be found capable of plowing that piece of land. Jason, I suppose, had been taught how to draw a furrow by the good old Chiron, who, perhaps, used to allow himself to be harnessed to the plow. At any rate, our hero succeeded perfectly well in breaking up the greensward; and, by the time that the moon was a quarter of her journey up the sky, the plowed field lay before him, a large tract of black earth, ready to be sown with the dragon's teeth. So Jason scattered them broadcast, and harrowed them into the soil with a brush-harrow, and took his stand on the edge of the field, anxious to see what would happen next.

"Must we wait long for harvest time?" he inquired of Medea, who was now standing by his side.

"Whether sooner or later, it will be sure to come," answered the princess. "A crop of armed men never fails to spring up, when the dragon's teeth have been sown."

The moon was now high aloft in the heavens, and threw its bright beams over the plowed field, where as yet there was nothing to be seen.

Any farmer, on viewing it, would have said that Jason must wait weeks before the green blades would peep from among the clods, and whole months before the yellow grain would be ripened for the sickle. But by and by, all over the field, there was something that glistened in the moonbeams, like sparkling drops of dew. These bright objects sprouted higher, and proved to be the steel heads of spears. Then there was a dazzling gleam from a vast number of polished brass helmets, beneath which, as they grew farther out of the soil, appeared the dark and bearded visages of warriors, struggling to free themselves from the imprisoning earth. The first look that they gave at the upper world was a glare of wrath and defiance. Next were seen their bright breastplates; in every right hand there was a sword or a spear, and on each left arm a shield; and when this strange crop of warriors had but half grown out of the earth, they struggled—such was their impatience of restraint—and, as it were, tore themselves up by the roots.

Wherever a dragon's tooth had fallen, there stood a man armed for battle. They made a clangor with their swords against their shields and eyed one another fiercely; for they had come into this beautiful world, and into the peaceful moonlight, full of rage and stormy passions, and ready to take the life of every human brother, in recompense of the boon of their own existence.

There have been many other armies in the world that seemed to possess the same fierce nature with the one which had now sprouted from the dragon's teeth; but these, in the moonlit field, were the more excusable, because they never had women for their mothers. And how it would have rejoiced any great captain, who was bent on conquering the world, like Alexander or Napoleon, to raise a crop of armed soldiers as easily as Jason did!

For a while, the warriors stood flourishing their weapons, clashing their swords against their shields, and boiling over with the red-hot thirst for battle. Then they began to shout; "Show us the enemy! Lead us to the charge! Death or victory! Come on, brave comrades! Conquer or die!" and a hundred other outcries, such as men always bellow forth on a battle field, and which these dragon people seemed to have at their tongues' ends. At last, the front rank caught sight of Jason, who, beholding the flash of so many weapons in the moonlight, had thought it best to draw his sword. In a moment all the sons of the dragon's teeth appeared to take Jason for an enemy; and crying with one voice, "Guard the Golden Fleece!" they ran at him with uplifted swords and protruded spears. Jason knew that it would be impossible to withstand this bloodthirsty battalion with his single arm, but determined, since there was nothing better to be done, to die as valiantly as if he himself had sprung from a dragon's tooth.

Medea, however, bade him snatch up a stone from the ground.

"Throw it among them quickly!" cried she. "It is the only way to save yourself."

The armed men were now so nigh that Jason could discern the fire flashing out of their enraged eyes, when he let fly the stone, and saw it strike the helmet of a tall warrior, who was rushing upon him with his blade aloft. The stone glanced from this man's helmet to the shield of his nearest comrade, and thence flew right into the angry face of another, hitting him smartly between the eyes. Each of the three who had been struck by the stone took it for granted that his next neighbor had given him a blow; and instead of running any farther towards Jason, they began a fight among themselves. The confusion spread through the host, so that it seemed scarcely a moment before they were all hacking, hewing, and stabbing at one another, lopping off arms, heads, and legs, and doing such memorable deeds that Jason was filled with immense admiration; although, at the same time, he could not help laughing to behold these mighty men punishing each other for an offense which he himself had committed. In an incredibly short space of time, (almost as short, indeed, as it had taken them to grow up,) all but one of the heroes of the dragon's teeth were stretched lifeless on the field. The last survivor, the bravest and strongest of the whole, had just force enough to wave his crimson sword over his head, and give a shout of exultation, crying, "Victory! Victory! Immortal fame!" when he himself fell down, and lay quietly among his slain brethren. And there was the end of the army that had sprouted from the dragon's teeth. That fierce and feverish fight was the only enjoyment which they had tasted on this beautiful earth.

"Let them sleep in the bed of honor," said the Princess Medea, with a sly smile at Jason. "The world will always have simpletons enough, just like them, fighting and dying for they know not what, and fancying that posterity will take the trouble to put laurel wreaths on their rusty and battered helmets. Could you help smiling, Prince Jason, to see the self-conceit of that last fellow, just as he tumbled down?"

"It made me very sad," answered Jason gravely. "And, to tell you the truth, princess, the Golden Fleece does not appear so well worth the winning, after what I have here beheld."

"You will think differently in the morning," said Medea. "True, the Golden Fleece may not be so valuable as you have thought it; but then there is nothing better in the world; and one must needs have an object, you know. Come! Your night's work has been well performed; and tomorrow you can inform King Æetes that the first part of your allotted task is fulfilled."

Agreeably to Medea's advice, Jason went betimes in the morning to the palace of King Æetes. Entering the presence chamber, he stood at the foot of the throne, and made a low obeisance.

"Your eyes look heavy, Prince Jason," observed the king; "you appear to have spent a sleepless night. I hope you have been considering the matter a little more wisely, and have concluded not to get yourself scorched to a cinder, in attempting to tame my brazen-lunged bulls."

"That is already accomplished, may it please your majesty," replied Jason. "The bulls have been tamed and yoked; the field has been plowed; the dragon's teeth have been sown broadcast, and harrowed into the soil; the crop of armed warriors have sprung up, and they have slain one another, to the last man. And now I solicit your majesty's permission to encounter the dragon, that I may take down the Golden Fleece from the tree, and depart, with my nine and forty comrades."

King Æetes scowled, and looked very angry and excessively disturbed; for he knew that, in accordance with his kingly promise, he ought now to permit Jason to win the fleece, if his courage and skill should enable him to do so. But, since the young man had met with such good luck in the matter of the brazen bulls and the dragon's teeth, the king feared that he would be equally successful in slaying the dragon. And therefore, though he would gladly have seen Jason snapped up at a mouthful, he was resolved (and it was a very wrong thing of this wicked potentate) not to run any further risk of losing his beloved fleece.

"You never would have succeeded in this business, young man," said he, "if my undutiful daughter Medea had not helped you with her enchantments. Had you acted fairly, you would have been, at this instant, a black cinder, or a handful of white ashes. I forbid you, on pain of death, to make any more attempts to get the Golden Fleece. To speak my mind plainly, you shall never set eyes on so much as one of its glistening locks."

Jason left the king's presence in great sorrow and anger. He could think of nothing better to be done than to summon together his forty-nine brave Argonauts, march at once to the grove of Mars, slay the dragon, take possession of the Golden Fleece, get on board the *Argo*, and spread all sail for Iolchos. The success of this scheme depended, it is true, on the doubtful point whether all the fifty heroes might not be snapped up, at so many mouthfuls, by the dragon.

But, as Jason was hastening down the palace steps, the Princess Medea called after him, and beckoned him to return. Her black eyes shone upon him with such a keen intelligence, that he felt as if there were a serpent peeping out of them; and, although she had done him so much service only the night before, he was by no means very certain that she would not do him an equally great mischief before sunset. These enchantresses, you must know, are never to be depended upon.

"What says King Æetes, my royal and upright father?" inquired Medea, slightly smiling. "Will he give you the Golden Fleece, without any further risk or trouble?"

"On the contrary," answered Jason, "he is very angry with me for taming the brazen bulls and sowing the dragon's teeth. And he forbids me to make any more attempts, and positively refuses to give up the Golden Fleece, whether I slay the dragon or no."

"Yes, Jason," said the princess, "and I can tell you more. Unless you set sail from Colchis before tomorrow's sunrise, the king means to burn your fifty oared galley, and put yourself and your forty-nine brave comrades to the sword. But be of good courage. The Golden Fleece you shall have, if it lies within the power of my enchantments to get it for you. Wait for me here an hour before midnight."

At the appointed hour, you might again have seen Prince Jason and the Princess Medea, side by side, stealing through the streets of Colchis, on their way to the sacred grove, in the center of which the Golden Fleece was suspended to a tree. While they were crossing the pasture ground, the brazen bulls came towards Jason, lowing, nodding their heads, and thrusting forth their snouts, which, as other cattle do, they, loved to have rubbed and caressed by a friendly hand. Their fierce nature was thoroughly tamed; and, with their fierceness, the two furnaces in their stomachs had likewise been extinguished, insomuch that they probably enjoyed far more comfort in grazing and chewing their cuds than ever before. Indeed, it had heretofore been a great inconvenience to these poor animals, that, whenever they wished to eat a mouthful of grass, the fire out of their nostrils had shriveled it up, before they could manage to crop it. How they contrived to keep themselves alive is more than I can imagine. But now, instead of emitting jets of flame and streams of sulfurous vapor, they breathed the very sweetest of cow breath.

After kindly patting the bulls, Jason followed Medea's guidance into the Grove of Mars, where the great oak trees, that had been growing for centuries, threw so thick a shade that the moonbeams struggled vainly to find their way through it. Only here and there a glimmer fell upon the leaf-strewn earth, or now and then a breeze stirred the boughs aside, and gave Jason a glimpse of the sky, lest, in that deep obscurity, he might forget that there was one, overhead. At length, when they had gone farther and farther into the heart of the duskiness, Medea squeezed Jason's hand.

"Look yonder," she whispered. "Do you see it?"

Gleaming among the venerable oaks, there was a radiance, not like the moonbeams, but rather resembling the golden glory of the setting sun. It proceeded from an object, which appeared to be suspended at about a man's height from the ground, a little farther within the wood.

Left: Medea and Jason see the golden fleece shining in the distance, guarded by a fearsome dragon. Illustration by Virginia Frances Sterrett.

"What is it?" asked Jason.

"Have you come so far to seek it," exclaimed Medea, "and do you not recognize the meed of all your toils and perils, when it glitters before your eyes? It is the Golden Fleece."

Jason went onward a few steps farther, and then stopped to gaze. Oh, how beautiful it looked, shining with a marvelous light of its own, that inestimable prize, which so many heroes had longed to behold, but had perished in the quest of it, either by the perils of their voyage, or by the fiery breath of the brazen-lunged bulls.

"How gloriously it shines!" cried Jason, in a rapture. "It has surely been dipped in the richest gold of sunset. Let me hasten onward, and take it to my bosom."

"Stay," said Medea, holding him back. "Have you forgotten what guards it?"

To say the truth, in the joy of beholding the object of his desires, the terrible dragon had quite slipped out of Jason's memory. Soon, however, something came to pass, that reminded him what perils were still to be encountered. An antelope, that probably mistook the yellow radiance for sunrise, came bounding fleetly through the grove. He was rushing straight towards the Golden Fleece, when suddenly there was a frightful hiss, and the immense head and half the scaly body of the dragon was thrust forth, (for he was twisted round the trunk of the tree on which the fleece hung,) and seizing the poor antelope, swallowed him with one snap of his jaws.

After this feat, the dragon seemed sensible that some other living creature was within reach, on which he felt inclined to finish his meal. In various directions he kept poking his ugly snout among the trees, stretching out his neck a terrible long way, now here, now there, and now close to the spot where Jason and the Princess were hiding behind an oak. Upon my word, as the head came waving and undulating through the air, and reaching almost within arm's length of Prince Jason, it was a very hideous and uncomfortable sight. The gape of his enormous jaws was nearly as wide as the gateway of the king's palace.

"Well, Jason," whispered Medea, (for she was ill-natured, as all enchantresses are, and wanted to make the bold youth tremble,) "what do you think now of your prospect of winning the Golden Fleece?"

Jason answered only by drawing his sword, and making a step forward.

"Stay, foolish youth," said Medea, grasping his arm. "Do not you see you are lost, without me as your good angel? In this gold box I have a magic potion, which will do the dragon's business far more effectively than your sword."

The dragon had probably heard the voices; for swift as lightning, his black head and forked tongue came hissing among the trees again, darting full forty feet at a stretch. As it approached, Medea tossed the contents of the gold box right down the monster's wide-open throat. Immediately, with an outrageous hiss and a tremendous wriggle, flinging his tail up to the tip-top of the tallest tree, and shattering all its branches as it crashed heavily down again, the dragon fell at full length upon the ground, and lay quite motionless.

"It is only a sleeping potion," said the enchantress to Prince Jason. "One always finds a use for these mischievous creatures, sooner or later; so I did not wish to kill him outright. Quick! Snatch the prize, and let us begone. You have won the Golden Fleece."

Jason caught the fleece from the tree, and hurried through the grove, the deep shadows of which were illuminated as he passed by the golden glory of the precious object that he bore along. A little way before him, he beheld the old woman whom he had helped over the stream, with her peacock beside her. She clapped her hands for joy, and beckoning him to make haste, disappeared among the duskiness of the trees.

Espying the two winged sons of the North Wind, (who were disporting themselves in the moonlight, a few hundred feet aloft,) Jason bade them tell the rest of the Argonauts to embark as speedily as possible. But Lynceus, with his sharp eyes, had already caught a glimpse of him, bringing the Golden Fleece, although several stone walls, a hill, and the black shadows of the grove of Mars, intervened between. By his advice, the heroes had seated themselves on the benches of the galley, with their oars held perpendicularly, ready to let fall into the water.

As Jason drew near, he heard the Talking Image calling to him with more than ordinary eagerness, in its grave, sweet voice:

"Make haste, Prince Jason! For your life, make haste!"

With one bound, he leaped aboard. At sight of the glorious radiance of the Golden Fleece, the nine and forty heroes gave a mighty shout, and Orpheus, striking his harp, sang a song of triumph, to the cadence of which the galley flew over the water, homeward bound, as if careering along with wings!

PICTURE CREDITS